BURNING DESIRE

Other Books by

Ryan D Gebhart

The Jewel of Life

Splendor of Dawn

Hidden Within

Fading Lights

*Shadow of the Lost:
A Novel in the Jewel of Life Series*

Burning Desire

Part Four
of
The Jewel of Life

Ryan D Gebhart

Hardcover ISBN 978-1-7326355-9-3

Paperback ISBN 979-8-9853738-0-6

Distributed by Ingram Publisher Services

Printed in the United States of America

Cover design by Fiona Jayde Media

For Regis,

a true guide and friend,

and for his persistent encouraging grin.

Table of Contents

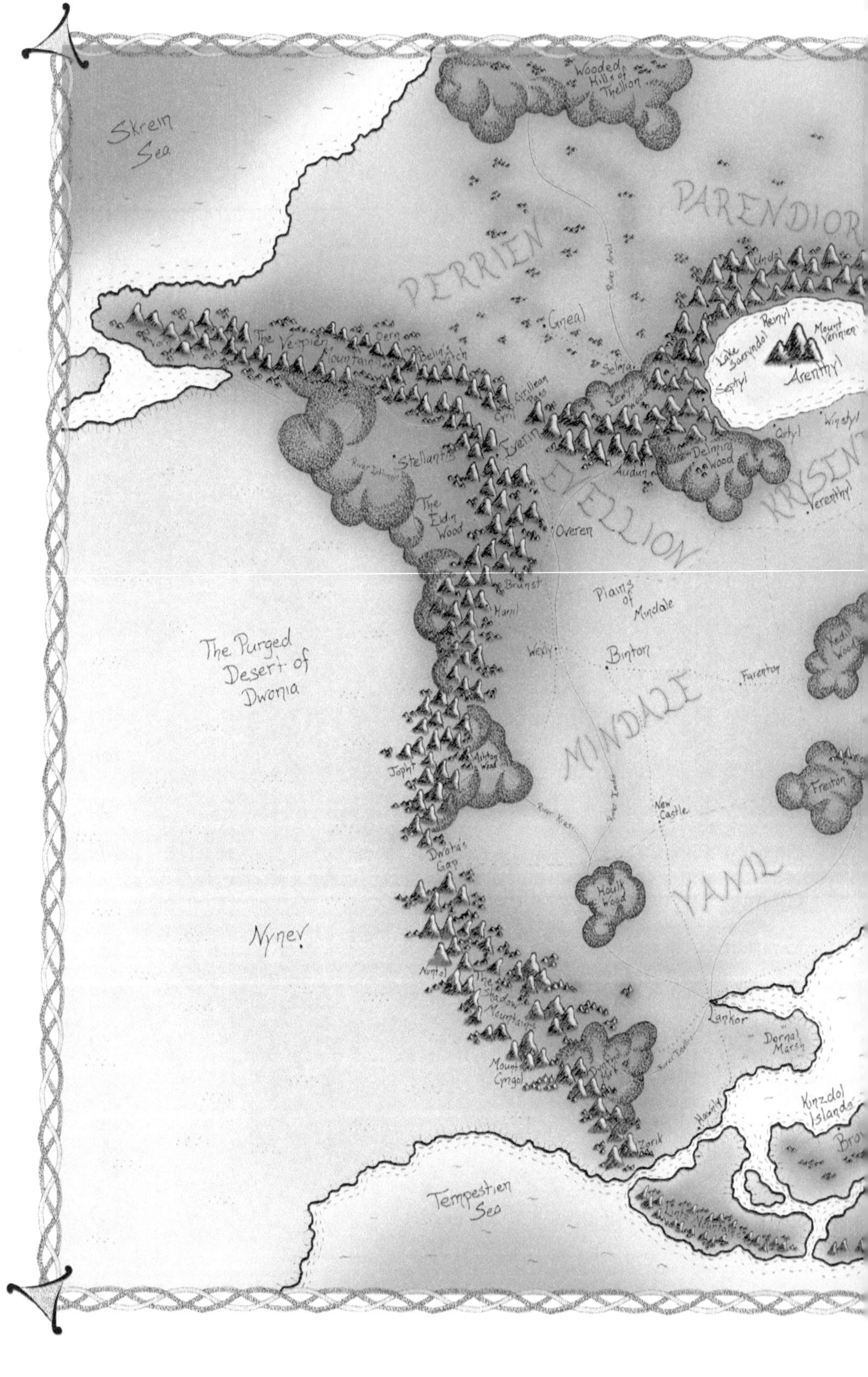

Skrein
Sea
PERRIEN
PARENDIOR
Wooded
Hills of
Thellion
Undol
Gneal
Reinyl
Lake
Saeryndol
Mount
Verinien
The Verrien
Mountain
Vorn
Oern
Belin's
Arch
Cyrillion
Pass
Cyril
Selma
Septyl
Arenthyl
Everin
Ootyl
Winstyl
River Delinnis
Stellanis
Delmira
Wood
KRYSENT
Audun
The Edin
Wood
EVELLION
Overen
Verenthyl
The Purged
Desert of
Dwonia
Brunst
Hanil
Plains
of
Mindale
Wexly
Binton
Farenton
Kedil
Wood
MINDAXE
Jopht
Ashton
Wood
River Krest
River Teala
New
Castle
Frenton
Dwota's
Gap
Houlk
Wood
YAWL
Nyner
Nuntol
The
Shadow
Mountains
Lankor
Dornal
Marsh
Mount
Cyrgol
Dunmore
Murk
Kinzdol
Islands
Zorik
Hanrlyl
Bron
Tempestien
Sea

The Unarian Sea
River Bethyl
orleia.
The Loudien Mountain
Glyol
Ceurenyl
Erithel
Lucillia
The Illumined Wood
Mount Saecrien
Kweil Aitch
ndyl
Roselan
SORENTHIL
Myrium
Ruins of Quellion
Peran
Daerinth
Plains of Orithil
River Nord
GESTORIA
River Myrien
RSIZ
Dead Wood
Hendil
Briel
Eddle Port
River Rafen
TIEL
Hardings Crossing
Nairin
Josque
N
W E
S
Irynien Bay
Ajien
Jamare
Jahro Islands
Daggers Point
Suderi
Jadien
Map of the Continent
EKLEAN
Inscribed in Ink
by the Hand of
RDG

End of a Pilgrimage

Toryn Vicalen could barely see through the thickening fog beyond the barrier. It had become more of nuisance with every passing day over the last year and was now making it difficult to properly perform her duties as a guard for the city of Lucillia. It wasn't the densest incorporeal mist she had ever seen in her short twenty years—she had traveled to Ceurenyl after all and had seen the fabled Shroud blanketing the fallen kingdom of Krysenthiel.

She had only gone to Ceurenyl to appease her father. In her opinion, the journey to Ceurenyl had been dreadful and the city itself had left much to be desired. Her father had hoped that Gwilnor Academy might accept her as a pupil with the Septyl knights, which would spare her the life of servitude that was his. Toryn, however, had immediately known that it would not be a good fit for her. She had no respect for the ei'ana she had met there, who were, in her opinion, nothing more than privileged nobles who could wield.

After they had visited Gwilnor, she had insisted that they get as close to the Shroud as possible. Being able to see the Shroud in person was the only reason she had agreed to the journey. He had refused at first, eventually reluctantly agreeing. She vividly remembered her mind being pulled into the Shroud when they had been near, and her father had had to shake her to pull her out of the resulting trance.

There was something about the Shroud that had called to her.

She imagined it did the same to every Luminari elf. How could it not? It covered the entirety of their lost kingdom. Although that was supposing that the people of Lucillia truly were elves. The debate over whether the inhabitants of Lucillia were elves or not had only grown more heated in recent years, intensifying when the Protection of the Wood had risen, cutting them off from the rest of Eklean. In Toryn's opinion, that had been a cowardly act. Toryn had many opinions.

While the Shroud's diseased appearance inspired fear, the unnatural fog that blanketed Lucillia didn't appear menacing to Toryn. As she peered out into the fog surrounding Lucillia, her hands rose to touch her pointed ears. It was not intentional, but she had found herself doing it more often, especially when she heard others argue about their shared heredity. Part of her wanted to believe that they were the descendants of the Luminari that had once ruled Krysenthiel, and by extension, the entirety of Eklean.

But no. If there had been any elven blood in them, it had dried up and left them with only pointed ears, the rest more human now than anything else. As one of the arguments leading to shouts on the Lucillian streets at any hour of the day maintained, they were nothing more than the offspring of elven and human slaves who had intermarried to such an extent over two hundred years during Emperor Erynor's last reign that their immortality was now bred out of them. Sure, they might have a drop of elven blood still, but they were no longer true elves. How could they be if they lived only a short mortal life?

A small part of her did hope though. Perhaps a renowned historian would prove that they really were elves, and that the myth about the Jewel of Life was true. She doubted it, but she dreamt about it, nonetheless. As her father always told her, wishing for something never hurt anyone.

She again wondered what the Lorenthiens had been like. Were they any better than the Narielles?

Every noble she had ever met was the same. Her father had spent his entire life as an attendant to Lord Toral Narielle. The Narielle aryl had given her father tiny quarters in their manor, enough space for the two of them, but not much else. Still, those quarters were nicer than anything her father could reasonably afford on his meager wages. She had always wished that her father had refused the offer to live in the Narielle's manor. The entire family was nothing more than a bunch of pretentious busybodies. She hated having to cross their paths daily. They wore nothing but the finest silks, while she was dressed in rough-spun wool, the style of which had long gone out of fashion. She had some cotton garments, but not many. Certainly not enough to meet the standards of the genteel Narielles and even what she did own, they considered as lacking style.

It was widely known that Toral's eldest son Trethien was betrothed to Princess Ellendren Roendryn, heir to the Lucillian throne. They would marry one day and Trethien would go from lord to king, something the Narielle's repeatedly mentioned. The thought made Toryn's skin crawl. She hated Trethien almost as much as she hated his mother.

Almost.

No one in House Narielle made her feel so despised as Lady Silvia Narielle. *All the better that that wretched school said no*, Toryn told herself as she looked out into the fog. If they had accepted her, not only would she have had to spend time with nobles while she trained, but she would have to see Trethien every day. She crossed her arms just at the thought. *Fool probably thinks he's an elf too.*

If she had been accepted, she would never have gotten her current position. It had taken her father nearly a year to convince the city guard that she should serve in their ranks. In her opinion, protecting Lucillia was a much more desirable occupation than sitting in a classroom with spoiled nobles training to become a knight.

Her post at the Lucillian watchtowers had begun only a month before the Protection of the Wood had gone up. In that single month, she had toured the various turrets along the city walls, learned how to signal the guard below if there was approaching trouble, and had even been on duty when that boy had flown over the walls on a blue dragon the day before her job duties had become utterly useless.

As her shift neared its end, she continued to stand proud and alert in her woven wooden turret, looking across the green plains that vanished into the fog. The grass beyond the barrier would have faded to a summer brown by now.

She didn't expect to see anything unusual today. The Protection of the Wood stopped anyone from coming within a league of Lucillia's walls. Still, she took her duties seriously—more seriously than anyone else, she had noticed. She often arrived for her shift early only to find the sentries stationed before her fast asleep. She was too young and too low-ranked to do anything about her comrades, but she made certain that she did not make the same mistake.

There was a ritual of sorts for the transition between shifts, but that had been abandoned shortly after the Protection of the Wood had gone up. She missed the ritual and the pomp that had given her post meaning back then. The barrier had taken away any sense of significance to a sentry's post. Her replacement, no more than five years her senior, climbed the ladder to find her standing at attention.

"See anything scary today?" he teased.

"Only just now." Toryn smirked at him.

Jaek had held the shift after hers for over a year now, and not once had he said anything meaningful before the exchange, always joking about something menacing coming through the barrier. His smile bothered her. She could never tell if he was mocking her or if he simply liked to smile. He was also one of those who were convinced that they were elves. *Moron.*

Still, his company was better than that of the nobles Toryn lived with.

"Any plans tonight?" he asked.

"No."

"A pretty girl like you doesn't have a date?"

Irritated with his comment and tempted to slap him, she brought her hand to her own face instead, cognizant of her windblown hair. "Don't joke," she heard herself say.

"Never said I was. Tell you what, that barrier has been up for about three years now, and I doubt it'll be coming down anytime soon. How about we sneak down and go to a tavern and grab a bite to eat?"

She quickly turned on him and crossed her arms. "Are you out of your mind?"

"It's not like we'd be the first to skip an hour or two of watch duty. I've seen some sentries skip their entire shift."

"I'll have no part of it."

"It's not like you're skipping *your* shift."

"We have a good job here; I'm not losing mine so you can fill your gut!" She crossed her arms and glared at him. If there was one thing she was grateful about living with nobles, it was that they could reprove anyone, even a king, with a glare. She'd learned to use one effectively too.

"I didn't mean to offend you or anything." Jaek muttered a bit and looked to his feet, abashed. "It's just, the way our shifts stand, we'll never be able to get dinner, you know, together."

Taken aback by the remark, Toryn found herself at a loss for words. A few thoughts went through her mind but none solidified into actual words.

Her eyes must have said a few things though, for Jaek blushed and started to babble apologies.

Toryn planted herself on the only seat, crossing her legs in the process. "You're not leaving your post."

A sheepish grin came to Jaek's face when she sat and he relaxed somewhat as they began to talk. Jaek learned that she despised nobles, while she learned that he emulated them. He had also conducted extensive research regarding their elven ancestry, while she took pleasure in discounting every bit of it. She looked occasionally over her shoulder toward the fog in the distance.

A couple of hours passed and their conversation slowed to the occasional comment. The sun had long since set and she began to question why she had not left yet. Was he even keeping watch?

Toryn stretched, a preemptive move toward standing to leave when a flicker in the sky above caught her attention. It wasn't vibrant, and she doubted a dozen people in the city would have noticed it. She rubbed her eyes, as though that would sharpen her vision. Perhaps she was seeing things. Not a moment later, a second shimmer pierced the sky. It arched toward the first, not unlike lightning.

"What are you looking at?" Jaek asked, his eyes fixed on Toryn rather than on the sky.

She pointed as a third flicker streaked across the sky. "What do you think that is?"

He stared for a couple of minutes, noticing more streaks. "Can't say, but as you pointed out, I can't leave my post. But you should make sure the captain of the guard is aware." His voice faltered and then he straightened, standing more alertly than he'd been a moment before. It looked like he was finally taking his duty seriously and for the first time, Toryn found him attractive.

She waved goodbye before climbing down the ladder wondering just what it was she had seen. In all her training, she had never been told what to do if she saw flickering lights in the barrier. Was that natural? Would anyone know what it meant?

It was probably nothing of consequence. She tended to overreact to the slightest of dangers. Not that she was sensitive or anything. In her opinion, she was cautious.

She walked along the woven wooden wall toward her commander's post, a small alcove set in the wall. She wasn't entirely surprised to find it empty. More proof that with the Protection of the Wood in place, the city's watch had declined to a lackadaisical vigilance. There were some, like herself, still completely devoted to their duties, yet the commander's absence concerned her. The city guard had a hierarchy of command, but she had never learned who oversaw the commanders.

She could spend the better part of an entire week searching from post to post for the proper authority, but in her opinion, that was a waste of time. She left the alcove, where her commander should have been stationed, and headed for the city proper, to the knights at the palace.

She knew they would never abandon their vigilance.

The streets were mostly empty. The sinuous buildings wrought from the very trees surrounded her, spaced far enough apart to create a street. Beautiful bridges and spires rose above, featuring intricate carvings inlaid into the buildings. Thick vines and branches curved about the larger trunks, filling the space between with walls for privacy, leaving holes for windows and doors.

Lucillia had seven districts, the outer three divided from the inner four by a woven wooden wall, the same as the outer wall where she and the other sentries were stationed. A third wall of the same sort protected the palace grounds. The inner and outer walls bowed out from the Illumined Wood in a gentle curve, radiating from the perfectly circular wall encompassing the royal palace. Toryn's station was toward the center of the outer wall, but not at the gate, which meant that she had to walk through the merchant district, the largest part of the city. Their shops were closed tight, and only a few buildings were lit from inside. On either side of the merchant district, were ei'ceuril to the north and soldiers to the south.

She had no intention of walking through either of those districts. Even though she was considered part of the Lucillian military now, she had no more love for soldiers than for nobles. She kept to the central avenue as it curved up the hill toward the gate to the inner wall.

"It's closing in on us…" shrieked a deranged man in rags, appearing suddenly out of an alley. "It rots from within! We can't escape it… Anaweh has abandoned us."

Toryn stepped back from the man. He looked dirty and she did not want him touching her clean tunic. He disappeared just as quickly down another alley. *What was that about?* she thought, watching the man fade into the shadows.

She reached the inner gate with no further disturbance, only to find another vacant post, the gate standing wide open for anyone to pass through, even that crazed man. She wanted to yell at someone responsible. Just because the Protection of the Wood was up did not mean they could abandon their defenses. No one inside was prevented from passing through the inner and outer districts—this wasn't Gneal after all—but that didn't mean the gates should be abandoned either.

None of the commanders would admit it, but it was quite likely that there were servants of Shadow disguised among the inhabitants of Lucillia. Toryn didn't see any difference between them and someone openly allied with Erynor. The enemy could have agents inside Lucillia without anyone being the wiser. This was a time for increased vigilance, not a loosening of security protocols.

She marched on through the central district where the nobles and other wealthy families lived, and because of her father's position with the Narielle's, where she too lived. Before long, she reached the sealed gate to the royal palace grounds. Two knights stood guard, armed with a sword and shield. Archers stood on the battlements, barely discernable in the dark. *At least someone is taking their posts seriously*, she thought.

The tall knights stared at her. It was late, the sun had set hours ago and there was no reason for someone to be walking about the city alone.

"I need to speak with someone."

"Do you?" the knight on the left replied. "And what does this concern?"

Her eyes narrowed at him. She wanted to kick him in the shins but didn't think that would end well. She looked up at the sky for the streaks of light she had seen crisscrossing above. They were dim, but visible if anyone looked up.

The knights followed her gaze above. The one to the right moved his lips to say something, perhaps something mocking, but whatever he was about to say never left his mouth.

"How long has this been happening?" the knight asked.

"I only noticed it this evening, after the sun fell. I'm a sentry on the outer wall," Toryn said, her shoulders squaring off.

"Siv," the knight called to the other side of the gate. The wooden doors creaked open enough for another knight to walk through. "Take this sentry to the Lord Knight. He'll want to hear what she has to say."

Siv bowed formally, before gesturing Toryn through the opening into the palace grounds. She followed Siv past the neatly manicured lawn, up a low hill with pristine trees, not a single leaf out of place, to the palace itself. The wood of the palace appeared shinier, as though it was different than the rest of the city, but she knew it was the same. The circular wall was much more evident from inside the palace walls, as it curved around the grounds and into the forest. Even with the fog, the naked wood glistened in the night.

The path split into three, the center one headed for the main entry, but they veered left. There were no stars visible above, the streaks she'd seen hardly visible because of the flickering lamps that illuminated the palace grounds with wielded light.

They came up to an archway leading into the palace. There was no door, only an opening. Siv led Toryn along a slender corridor with several doors on either side, but he took her to the door at the far end and knocked.

"Yes," came a voice from within.

Siv opened the door. A muscular man sat behind a desk, a small goblet near his hand, next to a half-full platter.

Like everyone else, the Lord Knight had pointed ears and the silver-rimmed, vibrant green eyes common to every Lucillian. His hair was a brilliant silvery blond, mixed with golden brown. "Yes?" he repeated, looking at Siv.

"My Lord, this sentry has something to report," Siv said, pointing at Toryn.

"Very well, that will be all, Siv," the Lord Knight replied, looking at Toryn as he gestured toward a wooden chair in front of his desk. "Please, have a seat."

Toryn looked at him uneasily. Most lords were pretentious and treated her as though she were scum, yet this one was being courteous. Perhaps his upbringing as a knight had beaten out the pretentiousness common to most nobles. She hoped Trethien would get the same sort of beating.

She sat, finding that the room was rather small so that she was terribly close to him.

"No need to worry yourself. I am Byron Roendryn, Lord Knight of Lucillia."

"I'm Toryn Vicalen," she stammered, staring at his unfinished meal; she was speaking to a royal, a descendant of Lucillia herself. She should have known from the vibrancy of his eyes and his unique hair color. Only the royals had a hint of silvery blond mixed with the more common golden brown. "I'm a sentry on the outer wall."

"I see. Now, why do you wish to speak to me?"

Toryn told him about the streaks of light that she had seen in the sky, and how she had tried to report it to her own or any other commander but had decided to come to the palace guards when she had discovered their vacant posts.

Byron listened attentively, obviously disturbed by the absent commanders, but more concerned about the glimmering streaks she described seeing in the sky.

"Do you have any idea as to what they are?" Byron's brow was wrinkled in worry.

She shook her head.

He paused before speaking. "The Protection of the Wood is failing. With its loss, it will leave us exposed. We elves are in danger."

Great, another one who believes we're elves, she thought, not realizing that her facial expression revealed her thoughts.

"Ah," Byron said, "You believe the elves all died out."

"All I know is that elves are immortal. We are not."

"That's a discussion for later, I'm afraid. You will do best to keep that opinion to yourself when you address the king." Since Toryn hadn't realized that what she'd seen was important enough for her to deliver the news in person to the king, she swallowed heavily even as her stomach knotted.

Byron stood and gestured at her to follow him out of his office and then through a set of heavy doors into a shifting corridor where the floor was a grass carpet and vines thick with leaves formed the walls.

After walking through what felt like half the palace, Byron stopped before an archway covered with vines and flowers. Silver and gold petals covered the floor of the chamber beyond. At the far end of the room were two thrones, although only one was occupied. Toryn had never met King Harnyl Roendryn before, but she had overheard the Narielles comment on his failing health since his wife's sacrifice. They could not wait for their son to marry the princess so that the two of them could assume the Lucillian aryldom.

Toryn followed Byron into the room and up to the thrones, pausing a few feet away. She curtsied to her aging king and realized that she had no idea how to address him, so she just looked at him, waiting until Byron or the king spoke. Harnyl slouched on his throne, too weak to support himself upright, then he made an effort to straighten, wavering slightly before steadying himself.

"Your Majesty," Byron bowed and glared sideways at Toryn to do the same. "This is Toryn Vicalen, a sentry on the outer wall; she is one of the few who still observes the obligations of the position. She has some disturbing news."

Harnyl nodded to Toryn, as though granting her permission to speak.

"There are streaks in the sky, Your Majesty" she said, forgetting all the details she had told Byron. "It looks like they're streaking across the

Protection of the Wood."

"Troubling news indeed. I thought we had more time before the barrier thinned," King Harnyl said, his voice surprisingly steady. "I cannot say how long she will be able to keep us safe. Vernal gave herself to protect her people, the people inside Lucillia's walls. I worry for those beyond the barrier."

"Can nothing be done?" Byron asked, his eyes focused on the failing king.

"An aryl cannot be a single person—it is too great a burden. My daughter must wed and take the throne with her husband."

"Should I notify House Narielle?"

"If these were different days, yes. But, before she passed, Vernal had come to believe that Ellendren's heart no longer belonged to the young Narielle lord, if it ever did. If I cannot tell her myself, Byron, you must find a way to inform my daughter that she is no longer bound to that betrothal."

King Harnyl breathed heavily, then turned to Toryn. "My dear, is it true, that you are one of our few sentries who have refused to abandon their post, despite the Protection of the Wood seemingly making it no longer necessary?"

Toryn nodded.

"Then, from this day forth, you shall be known as Lady of the Watch. May your vigilance remain steadfast and continue to protect the Luminari."

Stunned, stifling a gasp, Toryn went to a knee when King Harnyl Roendryn struggled to his feet and placed his hands on her shoulders.

As she gazed up at the king, a single leaf fell from the woven dome above and fluttered to the ground between them. It was unlike the other silver and gold leaves—it was a normal green.

Harnyl bent to retrieve the ordinary leaf. He examined it, twirling it by the stem.

"It seems the Protection of the Wood is not all that will fade from this world. Our pilgrimage in Lucillia is coming to an end."

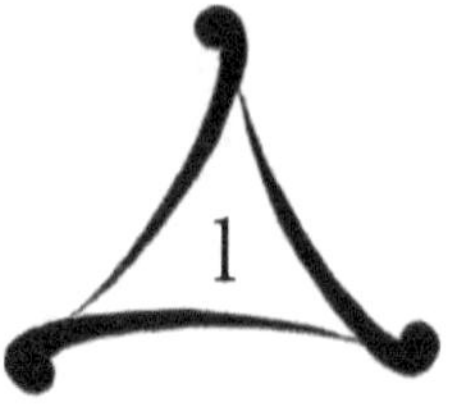

SEPARATED

Black dots flashed wildly in Devlyn's eyes so that he couldn't see clearly. It felt like he should see the world differently. Something was lacking. He drank in the humid air, gasping for breath as though it was the first he had ever breathed. He was lying down, not on a bed, but on a hard floor. At the edge of his eyes, he could make out horizontal wooden planks that formed the walls of the room, but the flooring under his hands was a black, porous stone, slick with moisture. Every bone in his body felt broken. What had happened? Where was he?

As his mind searched for answers, he noticed a hole in the roof. The hole was quite large and whatever had damaged the structure had done so with incredible force. He tried to turn his head to get a better view of the room, but a sharp pain tore through his body and he decided he'd better not. Despite the humid air, he was freezing. An icy chill dug into his bones.

Did I fall? he thought, looking at the damaged roof again.

Devlyn tried to gather himself to stand, but a wave of dizziness and nausea took over, and he fell into darkness once again, dots still swimming before his eyes.

Sometime later, he opened his eyes to look at the damaged roof once again but was surprised to see that it was now an undamaged, flat ceiling. Again, he tried to get up but he fell back onto a thin pillow.

Someone moved me.

A threadbare blanket lay over most of his body, only his head and chest uncovered. He tried to rub the sleep from his eyes, but his arms were heavy and uncooperative. He'd barely managed to lift one hand off the bed before exhaustion hit and his arm slumped to his side. Eyes closed, he struggled to maintain consciousness. His body told him he had been unconscious for a long while.

Memories tried to surface, none of them clear. He remembered swimming, and almost drowning, and someone else almost drowning with him—someone named Wyn. A familiar face with pointed ears came to the front of his mind—his cousin's face. He next remembered flying up away from the water.

That's silly, humans can't fly.

Tired of lying on the thin mattress, he struggled past his exhaustion and pushed himself forward to sit up. He swung his legs, slowly, over the edge. His body screamed in revolt, but he had managed to sit up, trembling from the pain. Devlyn slouched forward and tried to think. He remembered running away from someone. But, no, he had not run, he had flown away and there had been two people flying after him.

"Great, now I can't even tell the difference between dreams and reality."

He imagined a redheaded girl named Abbie laughing at him.

He tried to stand, pushing himself up and managing it with great difficulty and despite incredible pain, his body screaming at him. He patted himself and discovered that he was naked. He looked down and saw large, bulbous welts all over his shoulders, chest, arms, and legs. A large bandage wrapped his entire midsection, just beneath his chest.

He carefully patted around, looking for the wound, but there didn't seem to be one, other than the welts, on his front. He tried to check the bandage across his back, but just moving his arm back to do so brought white-hot pain to the center of his back and the pain was so bad, he lost his breath and hunched over, gasping for air, sucking in as much as he could without causing the pain to flare even more, and found himself once again sitting on the bed.

He remembered falling and crashing against something. Something had made him fall. Eyes closed again, he thought back, trying to recall who had forced him from the sky, but he could not place their faces.

Someone threw something at me from behind.

Breathing shallowly to not bring on the pain in his back, he forced himself to his feet once more. The enormous effort nearly crippled him. He managed a look around the dark room lit only by a small, flickering candle, but there didn't seem to be anything useful as an indicator of where he might be. He was in a simple, windowless room with a single door. The walls were wooden, as was the floor, and the furniture had a rough quality about it. He had to steady himself as he managed a step away from the bed, clutching the top of a rickety chair, determined to remain standing. He took a moment to regain his balance before trying a second step.

Someone had found him in the building he had crashed through, and that someone, whoever it was, had not only moved him to this room, but had bandaged him up.

He wondered if his attackers assumed he was dead. Surely, they would have investigated the area, looking for evidence of his body. A sudden fear flashed through his mind: *what if I'm their prisoner?* An image of a confining and too familiar cage surfaced in his panicked thoughts, followed by memories of a man with wings darker than the darkest nights. That man in the sky had a shadowy presence oozing from him, no light touching him as he sat on a great, winged beast.

Another unsteady step found him reaching for the same chair again, knocking it over. With a desperate attempt to balance himself, Devlyn reached out to the wall and managed to remain standing on his two shaky legs.

Settling himself after his almost-topple, he took a deep breath just as he heard footsteps on the opposite side of the door. He took a quick look around for a weapon; anything would do, so long as he could defend himself. A thought of breaking the chair and using its legs crossed his mind, immediately followed by another thought that he could barely stand let alone break a chair apart, and before he could step toward the overturned chair, the door opened. He reached for the chair anyways, and white-hot pain seared through his bones so that he crumpled to the floor, screaming at the pain.

Even with the incredible pain, he saw a raggedly dressed boy come into the room just before his head struck something and the black dots and the darkness returned.

———

Devlyn woke to find himself lying on the thin mattress again. He felt the new bruises covering the older ones, and he prayed he had not broken any bones. He looked around the room—the same one—to see that the chair was upright once more and occupied by an elderly woman.

"Never expected an elf to choose the floor over a bed," the woman said. There was a slight drawl to her voice, an accent that he couldn't identify.

He reached up to touch his pointed ears. Something about being called an elf resonated in him.

"Let me help you." The woman stood and stepped the short distance to the bed.

"Where am I?" Devlyn asked, appreciating the mystery woman's help to sit up. He winced at the contact of the pillow she propped behind his back.

She was surprisingly strong for someone of her age and height. The woman wore a pink dress of unimpressive silk, embroidered with a large green tree that stretched from the hem of the dress to her chest. Her feet were covered, but her arms were bare. A curious necklace hung from her neck and Devlyn lost himself in the onyx color of its large gemstone.

"Dangerous question for someone who fell from the sky." The woman walked to the door. "Stay here. I'll bring some tea." She was out the door before Devlyn could ask again.

So, I did fall.

Stretching further back through the foggy memory that ended with him plummeting from the sky, a girl riding a winged unicorn popped into his mind. He concentrated on her face and her beautiful silver-ringed emerald eyes stared back at him, her flawless face framed in silver and gold hair. She mattered to him. No, it was more than that. He cared about her and she had been doing something extremely dangerous.

Elle! In a flash, his memories returned.

Aren and the Deurghol striking him with their devastating tenebrys lightning. Ellendren rescuing her sister and getting them away, with Viren keeping them safe. Alethea carrying an unconscious Wyn away from harm on her griffin.

Everything came back. He remembered being unable to wield. Something had prevented him from wielding kien and tapping into the erendinth, rendering him powerless against Aren and the Deurghol who wielded tenebrys with ease.

Holding onto his restored memories, panic overcame him. *ALIEL,* Devlyn screamed through their connection. There was no response, and he waited a moment before searching telepathically for the phoenix. The only time they had been cut off from each other was when he had been locked in that cage by Queen Alesei of Tiel and the Tenebrae ei'ana.

He had been bonded with Aliel in their Phaedryn form. They were trying to deal with Aren and the Deurghol but without access to the erendinth, they had been struck down. His panicked breath quickened at the thought of Aren and the Deurghol capturing Aliel. Would they do the same thing to him as Erynor had done with the other phoenix? Food for his beastly dragon so they might never be reborn outside of his fiery belly? Driven by fear, he forced himself to sit upright again.

"Forcing yourself won't make you heal any faster." The woman had returned without Devlyn hearing her come into the room. "This won't do anything for your physical ailments, but I've always found tea to make the healing process a bit more endurable." She handed the hot cup to him, and he looked back at her as he held it.

"My name is Enna. And this is an orphanage in Lankor's southern peninsula."

"I thought Lankor was a floating city; how can it be a peninsula?" he asked without thinking, finding it fitting that he would end up in an orphanage.

"It certainly floats, but it floats off the marshes surrounding Lankor Bay, and the three rivers define the city's layout. You were up there in the sky; didn't you bother to look down?" Enna stared at him, unblinking.

Her gaze made him uncomfortable and he wanted to leave, but given his current condition, he knew that was not going to happen any time soon. Instead, he took a sip of the tea, only to burn the roof of his mouth.

"You won't be able to stay here once you're healed up. I hope you know that," Enna said without elaborating.

Unsure how to reply, Devlyn felt his bruised torso, careful not to brush against his back. Since he could only walk a few steps before falling, finding his way out of the city on his own seemed doubtful.

Enna held him in her gaze as she sipped her own tea.

"Did you see where they took the phoenix?" Devlyn asked, holding his breath, relieved to have finally asked the question.

"There was no bird of light accompanying you. One moment you had golden wings giving off a brilliant light, the next, I saw you falling from that great height into an indoor market. I was cleaning the building before it opened when you punched a hole through the roof; made a mess of the place, you did."

Aliel, where are you? Devlyn implored in their special form of communication where words and images were not necessary. But there was no answer, only silence in return.

"Why did you bring me here?"

"You were injured—badly. If I had not applied my ointments, you would still be in the fever dream. I was surprised you woke when you did, only three weeks after that fall of yours. I expected you would be out for at least two months." Enna eyed him as she took another sip of her tea. "It's the second week of Reventh, if that was your next question."

Devlyn gawked at the old woman. Three whole weeks had passed! Ellendren and the others could not have stayed near Lankor; they were too exposed here. Viren might have delayed a while and snuck into the city in search of Devlyn, but he needed to protect Ellendren and her sister, Kaela. He hoped they had managed to flee the chaos.

Brushing his hands through his untidy hair, Devlyn calmed his thoughts. Enna seemed to be looking at the mix of color in his hair— mostly brown with wisps of black, blond, and red.

"How bad is my back?"

"Are you sure you want to know?"

Devlyn nodded, even though he was somewhat uncertain as to whether he wanted the truth of the matter. Enna stood, gesturing him to sit forward. "Might as well; your dressings need changing anyway, and a new application of my ointment won't hurt."

She lifted the end of the bandage around his midsection and began to unwrap it. It went about his torso five times before he felt it pull at the scabs. He winced at the piercing pain, feeling it lance through his back and into his heart.

With the dressings undone, Enna grabbed two small mirrors and handed one to Devlyn as she held the second behind him.

Lifting the small mirror in his hand, he shakily positioned it until he saw the mess of torn and decaying flesh in the center of his back. It looked as though he had just been struck and the angry wound at the center of his back refused to heal. Seeing the damage only made it feel worse, and he was shocked that his spine wasn't visible, the wound seemed so deep.

Enna lowered her mirror, and with it, Devlyn's view of it.

Admittedly, he was relieved he no longer had to look at the wreckage that was his back. He doubted a wound like that would ever fully heal. Lost in his own depressed thoughts about how he would spend the rest of his days in a bed, unable to return to his feet or to his friends, Devlyn found it hard to breathe.

It felt as though someone had plunged him into an icy ocean. His body tensed, and his breathing quickened in shallow breaths as he tried to suck in more air as though that would help with the pain that he now realized originated on his back. The icy piercing pain endured, and it was only once he started adjusting to the agony that he realized Enna's hand was rubbing something gently onto his back.

His eyes were clenched shut, refusing to open. "What is that?" he asked through gritted teeth.

"My ointment." Enna continued to rub her salve into his wound. "There are many balms in Lankor. Every woman claims she concocts the best, but only mine *is* the best. You'll see. Your back is already ten times better than when I first saw it."

Devlyn doubted that. How it could be ten times worse than it already was seemed impossible. Ellendren and her gift for healing came to the front of his mind, and he was sure that he would have felt no pain if she were the one seeing to curing him. He winced again, still unable to open his eyes.

"Has anyone been looking for me?" he asked.

"Nonstop. I can't walk into the streets without being questioned. The city guards are asking everyone they pass about you. Even the Sons of Yanil have come out of the Yanilean's Keep to patrol the streets. Of course, they keep describing you as you were, still alight with those gold wings. I've never been sympathetic to our allegiance with the Erynien Empire, but if we're against one such as you—I fear we're on the wrong side of this war, and history is never apologetic."

"Can that change?" Devlyn gritted his teeth. The salve might be healing his back, but it did little to numb the pain.

"Anything is possible. Whether or not it's likely is a different question."

Enna removed her palm from Devlyn's back, but the icy agony endured. "Now that you're finally conscious, I need you to roll onto your stomach, and sleep in that position. The wound will heal better if it can breathe. You'll be more comfortable without any pressure on it."

Devlyn did as asked, and rolled onto his front, careful not to lose the sheets from around his waist. It might be better for his back, but the bruises on his front exploded in pain as he turned over.

"Those are only from the fall," Enna said comfortingly. "The wound on your back is much more serious than a few broken ribs," she added, as though a broken rib was nothing more than a minor scratch. "The jewel you carried when you fell from the sky is in the top drawer of the wardrobe. I couldn't believe how tightly you were gripping the thing when I found you. I had to pry your fingers back before I could get it loose. Curious bauble for someone falling from the sky smelling like seaweed and saltwater."

His head was turned away from the door when he heard it open and close, presumably taking Enna away. His body was still complaining about the broken ribs and the searing pain of his back, so Devlyn gave in to his darkening vision, too tired to check on the lucilliae.

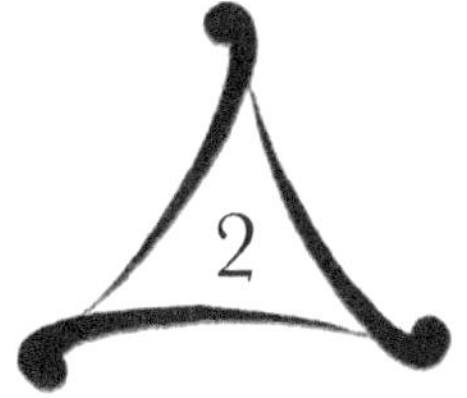

LEARNING TO WALK

Devlyn sat alone on a screened roof-top balcony, concealed from anyone passing by below while enjoying the fresher outdoor air. Early that evening, Bieto and Pico, two of the young residents of the orphanage where he was staying, had helped him manage his wrecked body up a flight of stairs and to a chair. Reventh had come and gone, and Kyrenth, the first month of autumn, was at its peak. The full moon hung at her zenith high above Lankor. Devlyn was accustomed to autumn being much cooler, but Lankor did not coincide with his memories of growing up in the cold lands and early winters of Parendior. Even after the sun had set, the air was still quite warm and humid here, a breeze from the bay being the only respite.

Stepping outside during the day was too dangerous, even when he was hidden behind the wooden latticework screen. Someone looking out from other nearby buildings might recognize him in the sunlight. The sun had to drop below the horizon before the orphans would help him up to the balcony for fresh air.

Devlyn quieted his mind as he gazed into the starry sky and opened himself, hoping to connect with any of his friends, either inside the city limits or beyond them. Aliel's absence dug into him.

Enna claimed there had been no phoenix nearby when she had found Devlyn naked and unconscious in the market. After the tenebrys lightning had struck him on that awful day, his golden wings had vanished and he had fallen from the sky, crashing down through the market's roof where Enna had been cleaning at the time. But there had not been any phoenix to be seen. Where had Aliel gone? Where could Aliel be that not only could they not communicate, they also could not bond?

Devlyn felt that quiet place within his heart, and just as it had every other time he'd tried to connect with Aliel, the wound on his back opened again, shooting intense, icy pain through his entire being, forcing him to withdraw from that quiet place. It was the same with every attempt he made.

Enna had yelled at him to stop straining his body, that if she caught him doing it again, she would box his ears.

The throbbing ache passed, and he returned his focus to the sky, remembering the sword the Deurghol had brandished. If only Devlyn had had a weapon of his own, he might have been able to defend himself, rather than run away from Aren and the Deurghol. He had had difficulty wrapping his mind around the fact that they could wield while he could not.

Devlyn had since learned that it was the floating rock that Lankor was built on that prevented him from wielding. It was the same material as the box that Alesei and the Tenebrae ei'ana had locked him in. Whatever that stone was, it negated the erendinth; only tenebrys could be wielded here in Lankor. That was what had allowed Aren and the Deurghol to throw their bolts of tenebrys at him and why he was unable to defend himself.

Eyes closed, Devlyn heard Bieto and Pico return.

"Are you ready for bed?" Pico asked.

Devlyn opened his eyes. He was tired but did not want to return to the windowless room, knowing that he would not be able to breathe fresh air—if the muggy air in Lankor could be identified as fresh—again until the following evening. Even with the sun long set, it still felt like he was drinking in the air rather than breathing it in. Unwillingly, he pushed himself onto his feet, using the armrests for support.

"Mama Enna says you shouldn't do that yet," Bieto said. He was kind and he sounded concerned. "She said we have to help."

Devlyn smiled weakly as the boys moved from behind him to either side of him. The tops of their heads only came to his chest. They were only five years younger than Devlyn, but neither had had a growth spurt yet. Still, they were both strong enough to help support him throughout the orphanage.

"Make sure I don't fall?" He moved one hand to the back of the chair for support before daring to move his feet away from it.

The boys shared a curious look as they waited.

Devlyn took a step away from the chair, testing his balance. His legs had grown weak after the past two months stuck in a bed, and, when he'd taken on Aren and the Deurghol, he had not yet fully recovered from the three months where he'd been locked in Queen Alesei's box.

His leg muscles quivered from his own weight. Taking a second wobbly step, his calves tightened and cramped. The two younger boys stayed close, arms extended, their proximity a wellspring of support in case he tumbled over.

Devlyn was under the impression that they expected him to fall. Sensing their doubt, he tried all the harder to remain on his own two legs. The screened balcony he walked across was not large, but the distance between the balcony and his small windowless room was. They even had to descend a flight of stairs to reach his bedroom.

Reaching the staircase took twice as long as before, but Devlyn was proud that he managed it on his own. Now, looking down the steps, he turned to Bieto and Pico.

They quickly put his arms around their necks and shoulders to support him.

There was no way he was going to make it down that flight of stairs unscathed if he tried it without the younger boys helping him. Devlyn's pride ached at needing assistance, but that was preferable to tumbling down the stairs. He had enough injuries that still hadn't fully healed and he didn't need to add any more. Fortunately, the wound in his back, thanks to Enna's poultice, had been healing at a startling rate. It was only when he tried to reach out to Aliel and bond with the phoenix that it reopened.

Every step reminded him of the tenderness of his back and he still woke in the night from the discomfort, yet he no longer gasped at the unbearable level of pain. Most of his bruising had healed and his ribs didn't ache as badly as they had when he first awoke after his fall.

Enna applied her ointment every night and every morning. Devlyn constantly wondered about her ingredients, thinking that Ellendren would pay a small fortune to learn exactly what the concoction contained.

With difficulty, Bieto and Pico brought Devlyn down the stair.

Once they were off the stair, Devlyn balanced himself once more, and with an unsteady step, returned to the small windowless bedchamber.

Enna awaited inside to apply her poultice.

"You're walking now." A hint of a smile crept to her face.

"Yeah," Devlyn said. "But no stairs yet."

"An achievement, nonetheless," Enna said. "You should be proud of yourself. My ointment has never healed anyone as fast as it has you. And your injury was the worst I've ever attempted to heal. The blood flowing through your veins must truly run gold as the legends say."

A shallow laugh escaped Devlyn. "I think you can vouch that it's not."

"Indeed—it's red when it spills out, just like everyone else's," she said, before gesturing Devlyn toward the bed to sit. She carefully helped him remove his shirt, which continued to be a painful ordeal as scabs that had melded into the fabric were pulled away from his tender flesh. She no longer wrapped his torso with bandages, claiming that he had healed enough to be fine without them. The chilly ointment seeped into his wound. "Still, you heal exceptionally quickly. It would be faster if you didn't keep forcing that wound open. It won't be long now."

"For what?" Devlyn asked.

"Soon you will be able to walk without worrying myself or those boys. You'll have to leave once you're healed," she added as she walked out the room, closing the door behind her.

The room darkened with the door closed, and Devlyn had little option but to drift to sleep. He lay down on his stomach and closed his eyes.

———

A dark and stormy sky loomed above hiding the sun behind it.

No longer lying on his stomach in the windowless room, Devlyn looked around and saw a black pit not two paces in front of his feet. The pit was much larger than Devlyn remembered.

"They're growing and the storm above surges all the stronger." Eagan Wintyr stared up at the menacing storm clouds above. "I know you do not consider this place a priority, but that which influences the Dream will not be bound here."

"I do care about Somnaeniel," Devlyn said.

"Your absence says otherwise."

"I haven't exactly had the time," he growled.

"Be that as it may—the Evil One's influence is growing stronger here. It won't be long until he claims this realm for his own."

"How is that even possible?"

"His prison weakens day by day." Eagan's eyes focused on a point on the horizon. "We cannot draw near it because of the Shroud, but if we do not intervene soon, much more will be lost."

Devlyn followed Eagan's gaze, although it was impossible to tell if they looked north or south. Devlyn didn't know where in Somnaeniel Eagan had brought him, and any directional aid from the sky was hidden by the menacing storm.

"How much longer do you intend to remain in Lankor? Your people require you."

"Once I'm healed, I guess." Devlyn had no idea how he was going to secretly slip out of the city when the time came. "What do you mean, *my* people?"

"Exactly as it sounds. And you have every power to leave. Do not dawdle—the Protection of the Wood is failing, and Lucillia will soon be vulnerable with no aryl to lead them."

"That's not possible."

"The barrier is deteriorating from within. Servants of Shadow and worse are behind its swift decay. It will not last much longer."

"Can anything be done to strengthen it?" If the Protection of the Wood was truly failing, his ability to leave Lankor seemed a minor concern in comparison.

"That time has passed. As foretold by Lucillia, the Luminari pilgrimage is ending, and with it, their city returns to the Illumined Wood. If you do not desire your people to wander the wilderness without a home, you must return to them."

"How am I expected to return while I'm still healing? I can't wield while in this wretched city, and to top it off, I don't know what happened to Aliel. I have no idea where he disappeared to or why I can't reach out to him." Devlyn heard the panic in his voice, speaking his fears and anxiety for the first time since he had woken in the windowless room, battered and broken, and without Aliel. He gasped for air, swallowing deep breaths, the pressure weighing on him as he had never allowed before.

A desire to flee overcame him. He wanted to get away. Away from Eagan, the World-in-Between, Erynor, the people he was supposed to lead—people he did not even know. He could stay hidden away here at the orphanage. Even though Enna had already told him that wasn't an option, perhaps he could change her mind.

Amid that panic, Ellendren appeared, her gentle smile and kind eyes filling his vision.

His heart slowed, and his breathing steadied.

"Learn to temper yourself."

Devlyn heard him but did not respond. All that mattered was Ellendren.

"She makes for Lucillia, to her people. She is aware of what is happening to the Protection of the Wood."

Devlyn woke the following morning in a stupor. His interaction with Eagan had left him unsettled and with the need to fully heal at the forefront of his mind. As jarring as their conversation had been, the Druid of Kweil Aitch was right. Devlyn had to get to Lucillia.

As he lay in bed, Aliel returned to his thoughts. If he could not discover a way to reconnect with the phoenix, leaving Lankor was pointless. What good was he as a Phaedryn if he couldn't bond with Aliel? He doubted he would make it to Yanil's border before shadow elves stopped him in his tracks, and without the phoenix, they would easily subdue him and cart him off to Broid. He wouldn't get past the city gates before someone recognized him.

If he did manage to find a way out of the city, he didn't have an iron angot to his name. All his possessions, save the blue lucilliae, were stowed away at Gwilnor. He didn't even have his own clothing with him now. He had stripped down to his small clothes before splashing into Lankor Bay to retrieve the lucilliae that night, and they had disintegrated once he'd bonded with Aliel before trying to take on Aren and the Deurghol.

Rolling carefully from his stomach to his side, Devlyn eased himself toward the edge of the bed before pushing himself upright. The task was painful, but he was determined. Back bent over his knees, with his feet planted on the ground, he took a moment to catch his breath.

With a final grunt, he stood on his own two feet. He wavered back and forth, resolutely maintaining his balance without the aid of any furniture. One unsteady step after the other, he made his slow way to the wardrobe. When he opened the uppermost drawer, a shimmering blue light spilled out into the room, casting a splendid array of color, reminding him of water, although not the murky bay he had plucked it from.

Grasping the lucilliae, he felt a sense of justice coursing through him. He could not say what had impelled him to retrieve it from its hiding place, but with the jewel in his hand, he felt compelled to do what was right. It was an odd feeling. Devlyn had never been inclined to act unlawfully, but with the additional insight, he wanted to go above and beyond, to right wrongs. The feeling lingered as he returned the lucilliae to its hiding place in the cupboard drawer.

Most important right now, though, was returning to Lucillia. The recurring thought refused to abandon him, even as he heard children playing outside his room. Hobbling out into the corridor, Devlyn came across dozens of small children running around. They were a rambunctious group, and Devlyn hoped they would calm down soon.

"Mama Enna! Mama Enna! He's awake and walking!" yelled a young boy Devlyn had not yet met. Enna appeared on the landing at the far end of the corridor, holding a bottle of her ointment.

"You do not look healed enough to leave yet." She appraised him and Devlyn couldn't seem to avoid wobbling or appearing frail. "Back in your room, please, and let me apply my ointment."

Denying this woman was impossible. Devlyn knew he would not get far, but neither could he lie in bed all day—again. Not only did he have to regain his strength, he also had to leave. But recuperating had to come first. He was just as likely to topple over one of Lankor's bridges and into the marshes as he was getting caught by a shadow elf.

Back inside his room, Devlyn sat once again on his bed. Enna followed him in and closed the door. She sat next to him and began rubbing the ointment into his wound.

The pain was not as severe, but neither did the icy sensation tickle. Devlyn no longer gasped when she applied it. *At least that's healing.*

"Have you wondered why I took you in?" Enna returned the vial to her pocket and sat on the chair beside bed and looked him in the eyes. "If it was discovered that I helped you, not only would my boys be tossed onto the street, but I would be killed."

He had not considered it.

"Enna—you can't put yourself in danger because of me," he said, uncertain whether he meant it.

"Nonsense. I know what you're up against and the fools in the Yanilean's Keep still think they are only aligned to the Erynien Empire, as does every other soldier and citizen of Yanil, all of them oblivious to Erynor's true role in the Wrath of Nauto."

"What do you mean?" Devlyn asked in a whisper, curious about what Enna knew, but also frightened. How much could an orphanage matron know of the evils facing the world just now? He knew that Erynor had caused the destruction of the original city of Lankor and had fooled those lucky to survive into thinking that he had been their savior.

"I would never allow his name to cross my lips and neither should you." She paused for a moment to look away from Devlyn to the closed door. "If that does not tell you what I know, nothing will."

Devlyn gawped at Enna.

She still wouldn't meet his eyes. "Erynor is more than he appears."

"How do you mean?" he asked.

"Don't you find it odd, that unlike the other Cyndinari, he endures without having to become a shadow elf?" She absentmindedly twisted the onyx jewel on her necklace.

"I only saw him once." Devlyn thought back to that terrifying night in Ceurenyl. "I was more concerned with getting as far away from him as possible at the time, and like the Deurghol, he had a shadowy presence surrounding him."

"Riding that beast of a dragon, yes?"

"The one that swallowed all the phoenix during the Ceurendol War?"

"Ythinor. The very same. That is no pet to our dear emperor. That dragon is his brother."

Devlyn's eyes popped open, too startled to comprehend what Enna had just said. "How is that even possible?"

"Tenethyl, oh Tenethyl, where dragon and maiden sleep…" Enna sang, but stopped herself from continuing. "Do you know of Tenethyl?"

Devlyn wracked his mind for any reference to the unfamiliar word. "It sounds elven. Was it on one of the Skylands?"

"Elven? No, no. It came to be long before the Skylands were gifted to the elves. During the Elder Days, before the Great Blessing and before the various races were established, there were three forms of anacordel, the two remaining Children, the elder ones who had grown from the Children and multiplied, and the dragons. Though truly, the dragons were more akin to the anadel in those days, and perhaps still are. But some were mesmerized by the elder ones who had built Tenethyl, a city unlike any other, a city of jeweled spires somewhere beyond the valley's borders—beyond the irythil's protection. These dragons took on a smaller, more similar form to us and mated with some of those people. Their descendants became known as the draelyn. And by today's standards, we would call them half-elf and half-dragon, or dragon elves according to some."

"Are you saying that Erynor is a draelyn from those ancient days?"

"Not from days as ancient as Tenethyl, for none there would mate with the dragon that sired Erynor. The once-splendid Tenethyl was destroyed before the Great Blessing by Ythinor's ilk and worse. Its people vanished. Even among the Cyndinari, few would consent to allow Erynor's father to draw near. But one did and she was no ordinary Cyndinari. Erynel Meriden, Erynor's mother, was one of the Sha'ghol." Devlyn's expression made it clear that he had no idea as to what or who the Sha'ghol were. "Do you know nothing?" Her voice was sharper now, almost insulted.

"I'm sorry, I've never heard of them. My magisters at Gwilnor never mentioned them."

"Fools. Pretending that something doesn't exist doesn't make it disappear." Enna took a deep breath and seemed to calm herself. "The Sha'ghol were among the first to communicate with the Evil One and the first to wield tenebrys since the forsaken anadel was sealed away. None of us know if the fool woman thought she could survive giving birth to the child of a dragon, but as every other woman who had mated with a dragon did, she perished. At least the children of the other dragon flights were free of the Evil One's touch. How Erynor's father and the others of the Dark Flight managed to elude imprisonment after the Great Blessing is beyond me."

"How do you know all this?" Devlyn asked, uncomfortable with how much the elderly orphanage matron knew.

Enna smiled, a secretive look in her eyes indicating she would not tell as she fingered the onyx gem hanging from her necklace. "Time to lie down again. The sooner you heal completely, the better. You cannot stay here."

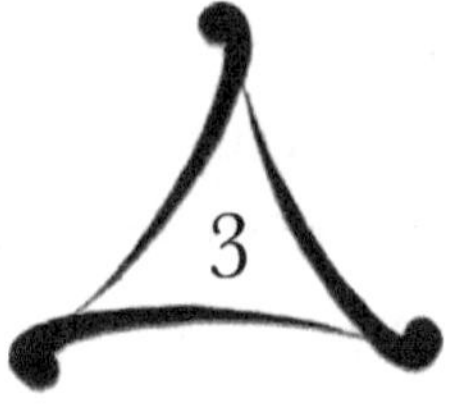

DAGGERS

A wave crashed against the jagged coastline, saltwater splaying up the cliffside before misting away. Some of the mist reached up and sprinkled Ellendren's face. Sudern was unlike any city she had ever visited. Its history was marred by treachery between its citizens to such a degree, it was said that children were given their first daggers before they could walk. The only time they collectively came together was when the Tieli pressed against their borders, trying to reclaim the city-state that had once flown the orange serpent of Tiel over their gates and castles.

Ellendren, Kaela, Viren, Alethea, and Wyn had been the duke's guests for almost two months now. It had taken a month to sail from Lankor to here and they had all known that they had only two choices when they decided to come to Sudern. Either attempt to blend in, something incredibly difficult given their griffins and alicorn, or reveal themselves for who they were. Ellendren and Kaela were Lucillian princesses and had rightly assumed that the duke would hastily usher them and their accomplices into his protection.

Immediately after they'd disembarked from Captain Terrance's boat at the docks, not yet inside the Mercantile Palazzo, Ellendren and her companions had been encouraged to purchase proper belt knives. Pointed ears or not, Sudernese only judged someone by the knife they wore. And for someone of Ellendren and Kaela's standing, they had to wear knives with jeweled hilts, otherwise Duke Farneis might never have invited the elven princesses into his palazzo.

The Mercantile Palazzo rested on a bluff looking over the ocean while the rest of the city swooped down from its height and toward the extensive docks. Ellendren felt her jeweled dagger at her side, a gift the duke had insisted on. Apparently, the ones she and Kaela had purchased were not fitting of their stations. She had already been appalled at the price she had paid for the one she had obtained at the docks and couldn't fathom how expensive the one she now wore was. It was much slenderer than the one she had purchased and it was polished to such a sheen that most mirrors didn't reflect her appearance as well.

As she looked over the cliffside from one of the palazzo's gardens, her eyes searched westward and into the setting sun. Far to the west was Devlyn. They had abandoned him in Lankor. Something had happened to him, something bad, and they had left him to fend for himself. She knew that they could not go into Lankor and hope to find him. Disguising themselves would be impossible and despite the Judges of Yanil's reassurance that they would look out for him, she worried. The judges were as invested in his wellbeing as any Luminari. They had been searching for him since their original capital had been destroyed by Nauto's Wrath seventeen centuries ago. And after finally finding the elf with the golden eyes that they had been seeking, they had no desire to lose him again so quickly.

She had tried to enter his dreams to communicate with him, but they were twisted and treacherous. It felt like a cyclone had claimed his mind and Alethea had insisted that Ellendren refrain from venturing into his dreams again. It was simply too dangerous.

"You're thinking of him again." Kaela spoke up from just behind her. Ellendren had not heard her approach. "You need to stop blaming yourself."

"I only blame myself for doing nothing at present."

"You've always felt that way, you realize that, yes? Never being able to do enough."

"That's simply not true. I'm quite capable of knowing my limitations."

"Among which is never being able to save the entire world from all of its misery." Kaela smiled. Ellendren had wanted to yell at her sister a moment before, but just couldn't do it. They had been apart for so long that it was impossible, even if Ellendren immediately recalled every peccadillo her sister had ever done to infuriate her. "I don't mean to be critical. Devlyn will be fine. He's a Lorenthien after all, and a Phaedryn. If Alethea isn't worried about him, neither should you be."

"I know he'll be fine, but I can't help but wonder what happened to him. None of us know why he fell from the sky and wasn't able to escape. We only know that he was in incredible pain and we couldn't do anything to help. We still can't do anything to help."

"You might be unable to help him in Lankor, but a whole kingdom needs you now."

"You feel it too?" Ellendren asked, her thoughts of Devlyn diminishing slightly as she shifted to the impending trouble to the north.

"I do. I felt the enchantment when our parents enacted it. I felt a remarkable connection to it, as though I was tethered to it. It reminded me of what it was like to gaze upon the violet lucilliae kept in the palace, but so much more like our mother."

"What do you think is happening to it, Kaela? What do you think is happening to her?"

"I'm afraid to speculate, but it feels like a sickness has fallen over it. It's weakening, as though it's tired. As for our mother, I can't say. I don't think there's any coming back after the Protection of the Wood is lifted. And even if there was a way, we'll be lucky if we make it back to Lucillia before it fails. We've stayed in Sudern too long."

"I think the same." Ellendren gazed west once more toward the setting sun, the sky awash in deep reds and oranges as the reddening globe of the sun dipped lower toward the ocean's horizon, coloring the waters.

Kaela extended her hand to Ellendren, encouraging her to follow her back into the palazzo. Despite the heavy appearance of the Mercantile Palazzo, the interwoven lacework and diagonal checkered stonework patterns provided a deceiving lightness to the overall mass of the building. Ellendren followed Kaela past the ground level arcade, through a vaulted corridor and into a large colonnaded courtyard at the apparent center of the building. Ellendren had grown fond of that cortile. Cecille, one of the duke's daughters, had insisted on teaching Ellendren and Kaela how to properly use their jeweled daggers. They had spent an hour every morning practicing in this courtyard. Cecille had not only taught them how to defend themselves with their daggers, something Kaela appeared all too natural at, but also how to carry their daggers while in public. Ellendren was quite proud of her progress but had no intention of defending herself with a dagger. She'd have to be cut off from the erendinth to even consider doing so.

Horses neighed in the nearby stables. Her alicorn and the three griffins had settled in with the flightless creatures, although she knew Laureniel was ready to return to the sky again. And if Ellendren was being honest with herself, so was she. It was time to return to Lucillia. Aside from the Luminari attending Gwilnor Academy and populating Ceurenyl, she had been away from her people for too long. Far too long for someone who would be their future aryl, and possibly the Exalted Aryl of Krysenthiel.

Leaving the sounds of the stable and other support rooms on the ground level behind, Ellendren and Kaela went up the marble stair adjacent to the courtyard. The duke hosted his guests and visitors on this level, as well as officiated any state business. Before either could determine where they ought to go, the duke caught them as they reached the top of the stairway.

"Duke Farneis, what an unexpected pleasure," Kaela said in a cheery tone. Both princesses curtsied to the heavyset duke, who bowed in return.

"You've been here two months, princess; formalities really aren't necessary," the duke smiled in return.

"Well, if you insist that we call you Paolo, you'll have to start using our given names as well," Ellendren replied, having picked up a few of the finer details of her sister's political finesse over the past months. She truly was impressed at how Kaela not only managed to get whatever she wanted, something that had infuriated Ellendren when they were children, but she also had a natural disposition toward immediately gaining someone's favor. Ellendren had thought those charms useless as recently as a year ago but seeing her sister in action had swayed her impression. In the past months, Kaela had not only guaranteed Sudern's support in the intensifying conflict with the Erynien Empire, she had also managed to politely decline the duke's marriage proposal to his eldest son, all the while garnering more support and shared interests between their two countries. If placed in that position, Ellendren doubted she would have been half as successful; she might have even caused a rift given her unshakable tendencies. She preferred to use that description instead of what Kaela called her: a stubborn, hard-headed perfectionist.

"Ah, do you ask for the impossible often, princess?" Paolo grinned. "If the rumors are correct, and if Erynor finds himself on the losing side of this war, I might have the need to call you suzerain."

"And what type of rumors have filtered into Sudern?" Ellendren asked.

"That a certain elven house did not entirely perish at the hands of Erynor all those years ago and that you and the young heir have been quite friendly with each other."

"I see; and how did such a rumor reach Sudern?"

"From my nephew, of course. I knew better than to inquire whether you might be interested in my son's hand in marriage."

"And who is this infamous nephew of yours?"

"Andrea Farneis, of course. But you'll know him as Andrew." The duke winked.

"Andrea? Convenient that he never mentioned his family name either," Ellendren said. Her mind whirled at the implications of Andrew being related to the Sudernese leader. How many others at Gwilnor were similarly related to prominent Eklean families, disguising their relations to go all but unseen? Septyl was a political foundation in Eklean, one that theoretically transcended nationalities. Ei'ana commonly acted as advisors to Eklean's monarchs, living openly in every city of Eklean. Garnering any sort of influence among the Ei'ana of Septyl was a worthy endeavor.

"My nephew is quite clever, isn't he? From what I've learned, he's not only a Septyl knight, he is also a trusted friend of the Phaedryn, a Lorenthien no less."

"Of course, you know that is not public knowledge yet, yes?"

"My house and court are quite aware. I trust that knowledge won't remain secret long though. The people need someone to restore their hope—someone to follow in these dark times."

"Keeping that quiet will grow more difficult with each passing day." Kaela reinserted herself into the conversation, smiling at both Paolo and Ellendren. "Shall we reconvene with the others? We need to discuss travel arrangements back to Lucillia."

"You want to leave us already? You've only just arrived."

"Almost two months have come and gone, dear Paolo, as you yourself just said." Kaela spared the duke a slight flirtatious smile.

"Two moons are too short for a visit from Vernal and Harnyl's daughters. But I understand the need to return to your own people. I believe the company you came with are in the library. They've had my poor librarians pulling every reference to Lankor from their shelves." Paolo was already moving before he finished speaking, a clear intent to escort them to Alethea, Wyn, and Viren.

The brightly lit main floor of the palazzo had mosaic tiles running beneath their feet the entire length of the main corridor. Sculptures and paintings lined either side, interrupted only by a well-placed door or window. Few of the doors were closed, and happy chatter filtered from the various rooms they passed before Ellendren recognized Viren's voice. And sure enough, Paolo had them turn into the next room. Despite the evening hour, the library remained bright and the three other elves stood around a central marble table. Aside from candles, wielded globes of light hung in the air. Ellendren chuckled at Paolo's amazed expression.

Drawing closer to the table, Ellendren saw that they were studying a large, scaled map of what had to be Lankor. Ellendren took pride in her ability to recognize most cities simply by looking at maps and Lankor's very distinct shape was an easy one to identify. This map, however, was folded over and identifying the city from just that given segment was quite difficult. She recognized that the broad empty lines set between the buildings where streets should have been drawn, were canals. Ellendren didn't know of any other Eklean city that incorporated waterways into their urban fabric. A river slicing through the city was one thing, but Lankor floated on top of the water. Building streets over the bay and marsh would have been a wasteful expense.

"Ei'lythel Ellendren, Ei'lythel Kaela." Alethea smiled as she acknowledged them enter. "And Duke Farneis, your librarians have been overwhelmingly kind to us."

"I'm pleased to hear it. They can be quite protective of their charges."

"We've assured them we'd treat your records with care," Wyn said, a slight hint of impatient irritation in his voice.

"I never doubted it." Paolo scanned the map. "Has my collection proven helpful?"

"Well, we've yet to find a secret passage, or even a sewer, into Lankor," Viren said.

"No wonder that bay of theirs was so disgusting," Wyn said, rubbing his arms as though he wanted to bathe again.

"My apologies, but I've never had the desire to discover an alternate passage into Lankor. Truly, I try to visit the city as little as possible.

All that is keeping their Yanilean from seizing me and shipping me off to Broid is our fragile trade agreement. It drives Queen Alesei and her clerks insane. I can't recall the last time we used the Tieli harbor to trade up the River Meyien. With the Tieli navy still in shambles, perhaps I should reinvestigate that trade route." Paolo examined the map again. "Forgive my intrusion, but the princesses had given me the impression that your next destination was Lucillia. I've been meaning to ask all day, why the interest in Lankor?"

"For all of us but Wyn, Lucillia is our next destination." Alethea looked from the duke to the two princesses. "Have you felt the Protection of the Wood weakening?"

"We have," Kaela said. Her positive facade wavered, possibly only enough for Ellendren to notice, but Alethea missed little. Kaela was just as worried about their home as Ellendren was. What would it mean for their people if their defenses fell? Would they flee into the Illumined Wood for safety?

"I've felt it too. It won't stand much longer." Alethea's brow creased.

"Do you know what's wrong with it?" Ellendren asked.

"I suspect servants of Shadow are behind it but I won't know for certain until I examine it in person. I'm hesitant to draw near it in Somnaeniel—I trust that realm less and less every day."

Viren looked from Kaela to Ellendren. For a moment, she'd thought he had been staring at her sister. *Is that why Kaela had outright refused Paolo's marriage proposal to his eldest son?*

"Have you come to accept our course of action?" Viren asked.

Leaving aside interesting thoughts about budding relationships, Ellendren grimaced. Admittedly, she was still torn and she knew that Viren liked their plan as little as she did. "I don't see any other way. Kaela and I need to be with the Luminari. And the longer that Devlyn is not also with us, the more difficult it will be for the entire kingdom to accept him." Ellendren turned to Wyn. "Are you recovered enough to make the journey on your own?" Wyn had taken a while to recover from his near-drowning in Lankor Bay—he had slept three days straight when he'd first been rescued, and he'd kept to himself much of the journey to Sudern.

"Eolwn will keep me plenty safe and Alethea believes that Devlyn is somewhere in this area." Wyn gestured to the map.

"Have you been able to reach out to him?" Ellendren asked, unable to visit his dreams herself.

"He's alive and healing, but something is terribly wrong. I haven't been able to communicate with him. He feels twisted in knots," Alethea said.

"What of Aliel?"

"I cannot sense the phoenix."

Ellendren's heart plummeted. She assumed the worst about poor Aliel, terrified that that dragon had consumed the phoenix, the beast's fiery belly preventing his rebirth.

"Don't fret just yet," Viren said. "We won't know any of the details until we find Devlyn. And Wyn is quite capable of bringing him back to us."

Wyn grinned at the acknowledgment from the Guardian knight, knowing full well that it tore Viren apart that he was not going to retrieve Devlyn himself. While he had sworn to protect Devlyn, it had been agreed that a Guardian knight's presence in Lucillia would help reassure the elves there.

"Well, if you must leave us soon, would you accept my invitation to a farewell banquet tomorrow evening? Surely, you'll need a full day to make your arrangements before departing. I'm sure my daughter would also like to squeeze in another training session. We can't have you leaving our fair city without being skilled with those daggers. I couldn't bear the embarrassment if one of the other Sudernese families found that you could not effectively use our gifted daggers."

"That would be lovely," Kaela answered before the others could reject the offer. Wyn was the only one who looked like he might prefer to leave this very hour and fly straight to Lankor.

SHA'GHOL

A third month had passed, and today, Devlyn sat across from Enna in her small sitting room. He now walked with relative ease from his room in the orphanage to the stairs and hoped that he would no longer need assistance from Bieto and Pico to negotiate the stairs to the balcony. His wound was nearly healed and his strength was returning with every passing day. Enna had asked for his company in her own room, and he had managed the journey from his room to hers without help. Enna had already examined his injuries; her ointment was still icy against his back. She had suggested that the wound was indeed healing well and he might not need the ointment much longer.

The plastered walls of Enna's room were free of any decorations but there was a floral couch sitting on top of a burgundy rug, with two rickety chairs facing the couch. The room did have a small window looking over a canal. Glancing around the room once again, Devlyn couldn't find any evidence to suggest that this room belonged to the sweet and good-natured Enna. From what he had learned of the elderly woman, she had been fostering orphan boys in her home for decades. Surely, she would have kept some memorabilia of the children who had been here during her many years of service.

Enna sat leisurely, content to sit in the silence.

Uncomfortable with the prolonged silence, Devlyn realized that he knew little about Enna, other than that she was old, ran an orphanage, and had saved his life. "So, how long have you been taking in orphans off the street?"

Enna smiled at the awkwardly worded question. "You're digging for something, aren't you?"

"I'm sorry," Devlyn replied, suddenly embarrassed.

"I have no qualms in revealing my identity to you, Devlyn. Don't take it as an insult, but you are powerless at present, capable of standing, but not much beyond that," Enna said.

"I don't understand. Who are you?" Devlyn asked the elderly woman, now very confused.

"Odd. I had presumed that I had given you enough hints over the past months. I suppose it's easier to show than explain." Enna stood and as she moved, her appearance shifted, as though a covering over her entire body faded away. "My name is not Enna, but it was the most tolerable name I could think of at the time."

Once her appearance solidified, Devlyn sat looking, mouth agape, at a stunningly beautiful woman. Cinnamon hair fell in voluminous loops around her bronzed face and silver eyes looked back into his own. She brushed her hair back and that was when Devlyn noticed the pointed ears. "You're Cyndinari." Alarmed, he shifted uneasily in his chair.

"Darling, that is the least of who I am."

"Who are you and why are you showing me this?"

"Do you think my finding you was an accident? That a frail old woman not only found you, but had the strength to move you from where you fell to hide you away here?"

"How *did* you move me?" He had never thought to ask before, although he might blame it on his groggy state when he first awoke in the windowless room.

"I'm flattered, but I did not move you. Clovis and Raelinth had the honors. They didn't become my attendants because they were lacking in anything. Although truly, given your state at the time, I likely would have only required one of them to carry you back here. I had so hoped that

Jaerol and his past lover would have been among my attendants. You do know Jaerol Solaris, yes? I do hope he is doing better. My heart shattered when I watched what he had to do at the Grand Tourney. What happened there is part of the reason I now live in hiding."

Devlyn's mind swirled. With every new statement the woman made, a dozen new questions sprouted. *How had Jaerol known this woman, and more importantly, how did she know that we are friends?* he thought.

"I apologize. Your thoughts are exceptionally loud. Still, I did gaze into that head of yours when you were unconscious. You see, you are a Lorenthien and I trust you as little as you should trust me." She crossed her legs, looking to the table beside her, as though wishing there were a drink or a bowl of fruit awaiting there. "My name is Yloran, and I'm one of the Sha'ghol. No need to tense, I have as much love for Erynor and the Evil One as you do, but that doesn't mean I was going to trust a Lorenthien before getting to know him. And yes, that involved examining your memories."

Despite himself, Devlyn pushed himself back against the chair and ignored the resulting flash of pain from his much-improved back. He couldn't help feeling offended about the breach of privacy and for a fleeting moment, he worried over what she had gleaned from him. "Does that mean you can wield tenebrys and have met Ra…" Before he could speak half the name, Yloran leapt up from her seat, toppling the side table in the process.

"*Fool,*" she shrieked. "Never speak his name." Yloran examined the room and hesitantly returned to her seat, ignoring the overturned table. "I have betrayed him and the other Sha'ghol. If they learn of my whereabouts, I won't live a day without experiencing excruciating pain."

"So, the name really calls him forth?" Devlyn asked, alarmed by Yloran's response. He had seen Eagan react similarly in Somnaeniel but didn't think the rules applied to Teraeniel as well.

"He cannot. Not yet. But others who are listening can, particularly if they are seeking you. Or in this case, seeking me." Yloran looked expectantly, almost impatiently at the door. Devlyn nearly asked if she was waiting for someone when the door creaked open. A handsome elf with rippling muscles entered, making Devlyn very cognizant of his own weakened physique.

"Hello, Devlyn. It's nice to see you're feeling better. By the looks of you, I won't have to help you up and down the stairs again." The Cyndinari beamed a jovial smile, then offered the glass he was carrying to Yloran before leaving.

"My enchantment was connected to all of them—my attendants, that is," Yloran supplied, partially answering Devlyn's questioning expression.

"The orphans? Was that Pico or Bieto?" Devlyn asked, staring openmouthed at the door.

"Bieto. His real name is Raelinth and he despises the name, Bieto. I said it accidentally once in front of a neighbor. Calling him by his elven name would have been disastrous, undoubtedly leading to more questions and unwanted attention than I cared for. He understood, of course, but that doesn't mean he's forgiven me for that slip either." Yloran took a sip from her glass. "Pico's real name is Clovis. They've felt responsible for you ever since they carried you back here."

Devlyn tried to collect his thoughts. It felt as though his grip on reality had come completely undone. Seeing a frail elderly woman transform into one of the most beautiful elves he had ever seen and learning that an orphanage of nearly thirty boys who were in fact grown men serving Yloran's every desire destabilized him. Instead of trying to filter through everything, he started with the simplest. "Why trust me now? I'm still a Lorenthien."

"Yes, and you have the same traits your ancestors possessed, none of which I find appealing. To answer your question though, it became evident that you weren't going to go screaming out the door and blow my cover. I wasn't exaggerating when I said that you couldn't stay here. Your presence will draw Erynor's attention and I would very much like to avoid that worm and his lackeys."

"If you're trying to stay hidden, why save me at all? Why reveal yourself now? I could have left without knowing anything about you."

"I'll admit, your ignorance of the Sha'ghol made revealing myself easier. If you knew who we are, you would not be acting so calmly. Truly, I thought for a moment that you were trying to manipulate me, but no. Your mind revealed just how little you actually know."

Devlyn squirmed uneasily, irritation bubbling to the surface at the insult.

"No offense intended, darling. And before we get too far off topic, I'm telling you what I know because it has become abundantly clear that you have no idea what you are fighting against and that you are distracting yourself with Erynor."

"Erynor has been keeping us rather preoccupied. He's always been one step ahead of us, sieging unprepared cities, assassinating the Ceurtriarch, and infiltrating Gwilnor."

"Darling, Erynor is a pawn. He has always been a pawn and the longer it takes you to realize that, the worse your position will be."

"I don't understand."

"Erynor's war was never about Ceurendol. Its loss was a happy accident for the one I once called Master, but it is only a trifle to him—a dusty bauble to be forgotten on a mantel and nothing more. Life will be miserable if the so-called Lucillian Alliance loses to the Erynien Empire. But there will at least be life to be had. The Evil One isn't interested in slaves or claiming Teraeniel as his own dominion. Do not be mistaken— if he is freed, that will happen. If your Lucillian Alliance can barely hold its ground against Erynor, we are doomed. Much worse is coming if my former master is freed from the Void. And after he has his fun, proving his point to the other anadel and Anaweh, everything will be lost—swallowed by the Void."

Devlyn couldn't fathom how things could possibly get worse. It was true, the Lucillian Alliance was crumbling. They'd had some victories, but Erynor had only just started releasing the Deurghol back into the world. Devlyn couldn't stand against a single one of them or Aren. Fighting Aren and a single Deathless had resulted in his near death. If not for Yloran, he now would either be dead or Erynor's prisoner.

"I don't mean to frighten you, darling, but you *do* need to be frightened—you need to know what you are really fighting against, and more importantly, fighting for."

Devlyn was about to ask another question when Yloran hushed him, her body tensing. "Leave. Quick."

Confused, Devlyn nevertheless tried to stand. His body was still incredibly feeble, but he could stand and walk on his own, only very slowly. Yloran spared him a frantic look. "It's too late. Listen to me carefully; you haven't learned to guard your mind, so do not think of anything that you do not want an enemy to learn. Instead, think of the ocean during a violent storm. Fill your mind with the crashing waves and the chaotic current. Think…" Yloran couldn't finish what she intended to say next.

The door opened and a Cyndinari came in. He was just as handsome and strong looking as Raelinth, but there was an air to this elf that the other did not have, and that made Devlyn feel uneasy.

"Yloran Eth Gnashar," drawled the man.

"Jaris Iln Desaris."

"A Luminari pet now? A weak and troubled one by the looks of him. Perhaps you and Erynor are more similar than I had assumed." Jaris went over to peer out the window. "I prefer your mansion in Broid by the way. The aesthetic here doesn't agree with your palate. From what I've heard, the Deurghol are looking for a Luminari in this city."

"I never took you for an elf who cared for what might be of interest to the Deurghol."

"You're not wrong in that assessment and I hold as much disdain for Erynor as you do, but really, Yloran, you're being childish. Come back to the Citadel where you belong and await our Master's next assignment. Bring your pets if you must. I doubt they'll last long, given their disposition."

"You know as well as I do, Jaris, what our Master intends for us."

"We've had this conversation before. Our Master's desires will see us as lords of this land. A shame that Erynor was promised the dragons and elves to reign over. But I suppose he is a draelyn. Fair is fair. Erynel did give her life for that."

"And how long do you imagine that idyllic fantasy will last? You and I both know his true aim."

"I know what you think you saw, and really, you're fortunate that I was the only one paying close attention tonight. You would not still be conscious if one of the others heard this boy's near slip. It was just enough to glean a brief glimpse of your panicked expression. I take it you're training him, rearing him to take the place of one of your aging, oh what do you call those men, attendants?"

"We were fools, Jaris. We never should have ventured to Mount Cyngol—those dwarves knew enough to stay well away all those millennia ago. Both those schtams are now his slaves, thanks to our meddling."

"Do I hear remorse? It has an awful stench, especially coming from the likes of you, Yloran. Perhaps Oduin is right about you being lost to us."

"Child, come here," Yloran commanded. Devlyn had been observing the entire exchange, careful to maintain a stormy sea in his mind's eye. Still, being called child was humiliating.

"So, you are hiding the Phaedryn that Erynor is looking for."

Devlyn swallowed as he shuffled over to Yloran, his back toward the other Sha'ghol. He thought he had been so careful with his mental defenses. Yloran's eyes flicked. She had maintained a calm demeanor in front of Jaris, but Devlyn saw something quiver in her eyes.

"What game are you playing at?" Jaris demanded.

"I once loved you, Jaris," she said, grabbing Devlyn and pulling him close. Her words caught Jaris off guard and unprepared for the torrent of power that ripped away the floorboards beneath him, catching him in the explosion that shot past Yloran and Devlyn, leaving them unharmed. Devlyn thought he caught the briefest look of betrayal in the Sha'ghol's eyes before he was overwhelmed.

The thrum of energy faded, its residue electrifying the air in the now ruined room. A wide hole punched through the room's ceiling toward the dark sky, directly above a similar sized hole in the floor. Devlyn had fought against enough shadow elves and worse to know that that was the most powerful outburst of tenebrys that he had ever seen. Aren and the Deurghol were weak playthings compared to Yloran's power in creating that explosion. Although, perhaps, Aren and the Deurghol were holding back their true potential when it came to Devlyn. Erynor was more interested in having him taken alive.

"I did love him." Yloran whispered, the room eerily quiet and still in the wake of the violent blast. "He had had the same glimpse into our Master's mind that I did. He interpreted it differently. He believed that what we had seen would be the fate of this world if our Master lost. That if we helped him, not only would we be rewarded as lords of Teraeniel in his name, but that we would avoid that cataclysm. None of this was told to us, but rather, it is how we had interpreted it for ourselves."

"What did you see?" Devlyn asked in a near whisper, still shocked by the blast but wanting to understand.

"We saw nothing. Only Darkness and it was not due to blindness. In the place of creation—of existence—there was only the Void."

Devlyn could barely think straight. "What…How…?" He didn't know what to say or even how to ask it.

"Did you think I surrounded myself with men who could not protect me? That I was only interested in their appearance?" Yloran smiled, coming back to herself. "Each of my attendants is a kien wielder—all are remarkably strong in their respective talents. As I said earlier, they are lacking in nothing. A shame that we won't be able to stay here any longer. The other Sha'ghol will be aware of what has happened to Jaris. He'll be back of course, but he'll have to walk blindly through the Void first." After a slight pause, Yloran went on. "I will expect proper accommodations the next time we meet. I did save your life twice now."

Devlyn stared at the holes in the floor and ceiling, barely registering what Yloran was saying.

"A friend of yours should arrive shortly to take you away."

5

WINDSWEPT

While Devlyn's back had been healing, Vespenth had grasped Lankor in a cold burst. The late summer and early fall weather were but memories as the heart of Yanil prepared for an uncommonly cold winter.

Accustomed to winter making its early presence known, Devlyn wrapped his arms about his torso, attempting to preserve the warmth still in his body. He hadn't expected to feel cold here. Cor'lera and Ceurenyl endured prolonged wintery weather and short summery weather, but those places were far to the north. Resigned to not being able to leave Lankor as soon as he would have liked, Devlyn had looked forward to enjoying the warm breezes off Lankor Bay as his body healed. But it seemed that a warm cloak wrapped about his torso was the only warmth he would enjoy for the coming months. Despite the best cloaks, none warmed his nose.

Devlyn walked with relative ease from his room in Enna's orphanage—no, after last night, this was Yloran's residence—toward the stairs to the balcony. With his wound nearly healed, Bieto and Pico were not needed for this evening's assistance to the balcony. Devlyn had to remind himself that they were not children, but adults, and that their names were Raelinth and Clovis. The events surrounding Jaris' spectacular disappearance had left Devlyn in a daze. He still didn't truly understand what the Sha'ghol were, only that they could wield tenebrys, and were evidently extremely powerful. Devlyn had found it difficult to sleep after the explosion. Yloran had not renewed her enchantment, and instead of an elderly woman and orphan boys filling the space, a single, very attractive woman and dozens of handsome men in their prime went about the residence, which still appeared somewhat dilapidated beyond the newly formed gaping holes in Yloran's room.

Reaching the rickety staircase, Devlyn appraised it carefully. He patted his pocket to remind himself that he had the lucilliae. Since learning the night before that he was surrounded by Cyndinari, he felt the need to carry the blue jewel on his person again. Taking a cautious step on the first tread, a swell of determination encouraged him to continue. Each step was slow and calculated but resulted in a twinge of pride with his renewed independence.

Unintentionally, Devlyn tried to share his triumph with Aliel, but there was no answer. The stark reminder of the phoenix's absence brought with it a heavy depression. Reaching the top stair, Devlyn allowed the pain in his legs to subside before continuing onto the balcony. The sore muscles eased and several steps later, his legs almost buckling twice, Devlyn stood on the balcony.

The balcony offered little in the way of a view of Lankor, especially since he had to stay behind the lattice and it was dark. There was only the constant sound of water lapping in the canals against the floating black stone and the smell of the sea to remind Devlyn that he was still in Lankor.

Peering into the sky speckled with constellations he had never learned the names of, he thought of what soon lay ahead of him. Eagan had not drawn him back into Somnaeniel since that night not so long ago, but his sense of urgency had left an impression.

Devlyn could not believe that the Protection of the Wood was failing. Ellendren's mother, Queen Vernal Roendryn, had supposedly sacrificed her life to protect her people. The notion that such a profound gift had only lasted three years was difficult to imagine.

Why would someone willingly die to ensure only three years of security?

Vernal's face and her kind and generous manner surfaced in his mind. The first and only time he'd met her, there had been no doubt that she was Ellendren's mother. Lucillia's queen should not have died. If he had known and understood the consequences, he might have tried to convince her to use a different plan of action.

Through his ponderings, Devlyn gazed at the stars above. It felt as though they reached out to him—called to him, beckoning him upward. If ever he returned to Gwilnor as a student—a prospect that was looking less and less likely with every passing day—he intended to study the constellations and the secrets they held in the night sky. The Eldinari understood their place in the sky, perhaps better than anyone still living, and could provide some instruction.

Gaze set on the stars, Devlyn felt his heart drop as he watched some of the stars disappearing and rematerializing. He blinked and rubbed his eyes, but the momentary disappearances stretched along an indiscriminate arc.

Even with his limited knowledge of the stars, he knew they never disappeared in such a fashion. The fluid motion made Devlyn think of a flying sentry. The city watch was on guard for someone matching his description, but they would never have the liberty of searching from the sky above. Even if they were given such a privilege, the Yanileans rejected anything unnatural, at least anything atypical of their own perspective.

Devlyn desperately wanted to wield kien, to press into the erendinth and strike the beast above, attacking it before it had the opportunity to harm him, or even Yloran and her attendants. They had saved his life twice now. The nearly healed wound on his back reminded him of what the blot in the sky was capable of.

He could not wield while he was in Lankor. The black stone separating him from a watery plunge severed that connection, although the black stone did nothing to prevent anyone from wielding tenebrys, as had been demonstrated by Yloran and her attendants against Jaris.

Keeping his eyes fixed on the being above, Devlyn realized that the creature was approaching the balcony. It had a large wingspan, but Devlyn saw no evidence of the leathery and sinuous wings proper to dragons.

These wings were feathered.

Quieting his mind, Devlyn tentatively reached out to whoever rode the winged creature. Devlyn felt the other's consciousness, hoping that he would recognize it, but also intending to disguise his location if needed.

Devlyn!

Wyn's thoughts poured into Devlyn, the friendly reminder that he was not alone in the world making him gasp in relief.

The griffin, Eolwn, circled above with Wyn hugging his neck. In a rush of feathered wings, Devlyn's face was washed in the abrupt breeze caused by Eolwn flapping his wings as they descended further.

The balcony was not large, certainly not big enough for a griffin to land comfortably. Backing as far against the wall as possible, Devlyn brushed against the griffin's feathery eagle-like features, its lion-like hind crammed against the far side, his tail stuck through the wooden screen to dangle above the street below. Devlyn hoped that no one would notice in the darkness of both the balcony and the night sky.

Sliding down Eolwn's side, Wyn rushed to Devlyn and wrapped his arms around him in a strong embrace before pushing back to look into Devlyn's eyes. "Are you all right? We've been worried sick about you." His relief was evident in his silver eyes which shone brightly in his dark face and nearly invisible black hair.

"I'm fine—well, I am now," he said with a wide smile for his friend and cousin.

Wyn brought Devlyn in for a second squeeze as footsteps scuttled across the opened doorway where Raelinth and Clovis poked their heads out.

Despite the lack of light, Wyn immediately recognized the elves as Cyndinari. "It's fine," Devlyn said, stepping between Wyn and the

Cyndinari.

"You're aware of who they are, yes?"

"Yes, I am, and they saved my life—twice. Well, Yloran and they did."

"Yloran?" Wyn gasped. "There's only one Yloran—Yloran Eth Gnashar."

Before Devlyn could explain, Yloran herself followed Raelinth and Clovis onto the now very cramped balcony. Just as Devlyn had been the night before, Wyn was struck by her appearance.

"Welcome to Lankor, Child of Eldinare—I trust you understand that you cannot remain, nor can I extend any hospitality."

"I know what you are." Wyn gripped a dagger.

"As does Devlyn, even if he doesn't truly understand what that means."

Wyn spared a brief glance at Devlyn but kept his focus on the three Cyndinari. "Devlyn, they serve…"

"Do *not* speak the name," Yloran interrupted. "We've already had one unpleasant visitor and it was only because of his infatuation with me that we were able to destroy him, even if it is temporary."

"How can I trust you?" Wyn demanded.

"Simple. You shouldn't. I'm a Sha'ghol whose goals are no longer aligned with my Master. You should take Devlyn away from here and quickly. If it wasn't for Devlyn being in my care, I would not have risked staying another night myself after we destroyed Jaris last night. And truly, I almost didn't. The thought of one of Erynor's slaves finding Devlyn was too much to bear. However, I am now at risk of another Sha'ghol investigating what happened to Jaris, since very few can kill a Sha'ghol. Do know that you won't find us in Lankor after tonight. Now, you must go."

Still clutching his dagger, Wyn bowed his head to Yloran and remounted Eolwn.

"Is there anything I can do for you?" Devlyn asked, wanting to hug the woman who had saved and healed him.

"Only what you're destined to. If you manage that, I'll want for nothing and might even be free of my Master."

Devlyn gave in to his impulse and hugged Yloran. She returned the embrace, and despite her impassive tone, her hug was warm and loving. Wyn watched the embrace skeptically from Eolwn's back as he waited for Devlyn to join him.

Devlyn grinned at Raelinth and Clovis as he moved stiffly to grab Wyn's hand and joined the Eldinari on the griffin. Without warning, Eolwn leapt into the sky.

It only took several powerful flaps of his wings before the griffin was above Lankor. The city sprawled beneath them as two large floating peninsulas. Lamps from windows shone onto the canals, and sparkled, illuminating the buildings in the still waters.

Devlyn clutched the lucilliae against his chest as the griffin took them higher over Lankor. It didn't feel secure in his pocket as he flew on the griffin and he grimaced at the thought of dropping it into the bay where it had lain buried and forgotten for seventeen centuries. He had never intended to be here more than a day, but events had caused him to be in Lankor an additional four months in hiding while he recuperated from the injuries received at the hands of Aren and the Deathless.

Lankor diminished behind them as Eolwn took Devlyn and Wyn from the city, and as it became an indistinguishable blot on the murky water, Devlyn pressed into aerys. The air felt as he remembered and wielding kien for the first time in four months felt like drinking water after spending an eon in a desert.

Relief flooded through Devlyn as he wielded the erendinth, confirming that it was only the buoyant black stone Lankor was built on that had kept him from wielding and not something more serious. At least that was one thing he didn't have to worry about.

Despite the overwhelming relief that he could still interact with the erendinth, he still had to find Aliel. He sought that quiet light as it lay dormant in the hidden place in his heart, waiting for him to stir it once again.

That central node of his spirit resonated with him more intimately than any part of his physical body, wholly himself, yet wholly other, defining who he was. When Devlyn entered that place nestled inside his being, he was always greeted by Aliel's presence. This was the place where their beings met and mingled. Nothing could prevent him from reaching Aliel.

But the moment Devlyn tapped that place to bond with Aliel, the wound on his back opened again, and for the first time since Aren and the Deathless had knocked him from the sky, he screamed. He had not meant to shriek, but the piercing pain wrenched the sound from inside.

A shocked Wyn looked back in distress as Devlyn grasped Wyn tighter so that he wouldn't fall off the griffin.

"We can't stop now, we're still too close to Lankor," Wyn called back. "Can you hang on until it's safer to land?"

A slow tear rolled down Devlyn's cheek as he nodded at Wyn. Gritting his teeth, Devlyn bore the agony exploding across his back. It was too early in the night to halt their flight. They were only an hour outside the city, and soldiers were likely stationed along the outskirts of the Yanilean capital. There was even a chance that shadow elves were somewhere beneath them. Those vile creatures had likely heard Devlyn scream, if any of them were close enough. That would lead to a whole other series of problems.

He had been so hopeful that he could reach Aliel. He felt his back ooze with fresh blood from his reopened wound—the wound he had thought healed. Taking a deep measured breath, Devlyn tried to regain a sense of composure.

Two weeks had passed since he had last attempted to reach Aliel. Two weeks of his wound closing as Yloran applied ointment to quicken the healing process, which would have to begin again.

Eolwn flew on, presumably at a safe elevation. Aren and the Deurghol flying his dragon were still a concern, but fortunately, only the stars filled the sky tonight. Devlyn did not think regular shadow elves were granted the use of the Erynien Empire's limited stock of dragons and were unlikely to be participating in the search. If they had been, their chances of being discovered would have risen exponentially. *How many dragons does the Erynien Empire have?*

Not allowing himself to dwell on that question, he focused his bleary eyes on the dark horizon in the distance, ignoring his wound as best he could. Even as he thought it, he couldn't help but wonder what Yloran had meant when she had said the Ceurendol War was a distraction. *A distraction from what?*

The sun had only just begun to rise when Wyn brought Eolwn toward the ground to land.

Devlyn had no idea where they were exactly, only that they were still within Yanil's borders. It would take longer than a single night's flight to escape the large southern country.

Eolwn settled down, pawing at the dirt after landing and allowing the two elves to dismount. Devlyn might have just mastered using stairs again, but he was still more likely to topple off the griffin than replicate Wyn's feline agility and Wyn helped Devlyn down from the griffin's back.

"You'll have to remove your shirt so I can take a look at that," Wyn said once their feet were planted safely on the ground.

Devlyn removed his cloak then carefully peeled his shirt off, wincing as the now-dried blood on the shirt tore at his damaged skin. His stomach turned at the size of the blot on the back of his shirt, and he imagined the wound reflected its enormity.

Devlyn couldn't avoid gasping when Wyn gently moved his fingers along his wounded skin. He was wielding, trying to heal Devlyn, making a circular motion with his hands, not only along the wound, but across his entire back, along his arms, again through his back, then down his legs, and ending in his heels.

Arms outstretched, Devlyn felt Wyn's fingers spiral across his body, creating sinuous designs, that he would have thought beautiful if he wasn't in such pain. Wyn didn't speak, just wielded, finally removing his hands. Devlyn eased at the absence of touch on the wound.

"I've never seen such a thing," Wyn said, scratching his head. Devlyn turned to face him. "It's as though everything is all tangled on the inside—your insides."

"How do you mean?"

"You know when you take a length of string and stick it in your pocket, only to find it later that same day all knotted and twisted up on itself?" Devlyn nodded. "It's like that, but it's not string, it's you—all of you—your spirit, soul, and body that is. I don't know how you're still able to function."

"That's a bold statement." Devlyn tried to chuckle, but that hurt his back even more. "Are you able to set it straight?"

"I can't, and neither can anyone else. I think that only you can untangle it. Others might be able to guide you through it, but it's an internal spiritual matter. Have you tried reaching out to Aliel? He might be able to get you through it."

A pang struck Devlyn. He looked away toward the rising sun cresting the eastern horizon. "I've tried…" he said, breaking off, not wanting to admit that he could not reach Aliel—that he hadn't felt Aliel's presence since that fateful night four months ago.

"We'll figure it out."

"Yloran saw me fall. She said there was no phoenix when I was struck. One moment I had wings and when I was struck by the bolt of tenebrys, they vanished." Devlyn choked on his words, allowing the despair to take hold. It had threatened to consume him since he first opened his eyes in that marketplace after falling from the sky.

Wyn must have recognized the agony, for he pulled Devlyn into his arms to hug him, taking care to avoid the wound.

A tear rolled down Devlyn's cheek at the closeness—at the care and concern his cousin had for him. He felt miserable and wanted nothing more than to wallow in his pitifulness.

LORENTHIEN RETURNS

As the sky lightened with the approaching dawn, Wyn helped Devlyn dismount from Eolwn. Jumping down on his own was still beyond his ability, even though it had been two weeks now since he'd tried to connect with Aliel and had reopened his wound. The pain was once again manageable, but the wound itself still caused him trouble, although it had scabbed over. When he'd explained to Wyn that it had been his attempt to bond with Aliel that had caused his nearly healed wound to burst open, Wyn had suggested that Devlyn restrain from doing that, especially while airborne, until they could talk to someone about how to resolve the twisted nature of his insides. It was while airborne that he felt most inclined to bond with the phoenix, but he could see the sense of not trying unless he was on firm ground. He was also concerned about ruining another shirt now since Wyn had brought Devlyn's lierathnil with him.

After four months in Lankor, Devlyn found it difficult to comprehend the distance Eolwn had taken them in a short two weeks. At the end of their first seven days in flight, they had reached Yanil's border and entered Tiel, north of the river connecting the two kingdoms.

Mountains stretched skyward to the east, and Devlyn could make out the streams flowing from them and meeting to form the River Reifen. The river valley they had landed in was known as Briel, a remnant of a once-vibrant kingdom that had once claimed nearly half of the lands of Tiel but was now reduced to the small river valley it defended against Tiel from within its borders.

The little that Devlyn knew about Briel was that both kingdom and capital shared the same name. The city of Briel was not the kingdom's only city, but it served as the sole entry point across their borders. The entire kingdom was bordered by the rivers forming the River Reifen, while its eastern border was a mountain range with the corrupted Dead Wood lying on its eastern slopes. The only bridges that crossed the two rivers were in the capital, one crossing north into Sorenthil, the other south into Tiel.

They had flown the entire way from Lankor along the River Reifen. Flying along the river's path had provided several comfortable camping spots for resting during the day and an ample supply of water for drinking and washing. Wyn seemed to have packed enough rations for their trip, although they still foraged around each camp site but typically only found berries of some sort so it was good that Wyn had packed rations.

Wyn had insisted that they fly only when the sun was down to avoid anyone noticing their passage, the direction they were taking, and particularly where they landed.

There was nothing wrong with traveling at night, but it had left Devlyn unbalanced. Traveling when he normally was asleep and sleeping, or rather, trying to sleep when he was typically about his day, was terribly disorienting. He looked forward to reaching Lucillia, especially since Ellendren would already be there, and was relieved that it would take only a couple more weeks. Wyn had described their group's course of action after the events of that fateful day in Lankor, their lengthy voyage sailing away in Captain Terrance's boat and eventually reaching Sudern where they'd spent two months. When Wyn had returned to Lankor after those two months, Alethea, Ellendren, Kaela, and Viren had all left Duke Farneis to journey to Lucillia. Wyn had also spoken of their worries about the state of the Protection of the Wood, and how they hoped to be able to solve the problem, and if that wasn't possible, protect the Luminari.

Wyn saw to Eolwn's needs as Devlyn refilled their water sacks from the nearby stream. Since they were now inside Briel's borders and didn't have to worry about the threat of the Yanileans or Tieli seeing their campfire, they would cook a hot meal before resting, perhaps a stew with some of the preserved vegetables in Wyn's food sack.

Exhausted after the flight, Devlyn wanted to unroll his pack and sleep the morning away. His eyelids felt heavy as he carried the water back to their camp. He was tempted to go without eating and lie down on the soft grass and just sleep. As he enjoyed the quiet sounds of the early morning, he heard something that did not belong—hoofbeats, and from several horses. Wyn was also aware of the approaching riders and had moved back to stand nearer to Eolwn. Devlyn just stood in place, hanging on to the sack of water.

A stern-looking young woman on horseback appeared through the trees surrounding the clearing. She was making no attempt to be quiet or to approach secretly, but simply rode up to Wyn and Devlyn, standing beside Eolwn. Where were the rest of the horses they'd heard?

"Are you aware that you have entered Briel?" the young woman asked, not looking at either of them but staring at Eolwn as though she was trying to determine what the griffin was. "And what *is* that creature?"

"Yes, we know we are in Briel, and this is Eolwn, my griffin." Wyn patted Eolwn as though there was no reason to be surprised at the creature.

"Then I need to see your papers. Only those preapproved by His Majesty are granted passage into Briel." She held her hand out, even as she continued to stare at the griffin. She was also struggling to steady her horse which was stepping nervously at the nearness of the strange animal.

Eolwn's talons ripped at the grass beneath his feet and the woman's nervousness increased although she had no way of knowing that it was normal behavior for a griffin when he felt protective.

"We have no such documentation, as we are simply traveling north to Lucillia," Devlyn said, moving to stand beside Wyn.

"Then under order of His Majesty, King Irvienne Haert, I will escort you to Briel, where you will await trial for unlawfully entering Briel."

"Ma'am, we do not have time for that; we have to get to Lucillia." Devlyn had never heard of a country closing their borders, let alone arresting anyone who crossed them without permission.

"It's Lieutenant Genevie and you will follow me or you'll meet the edge of my sword." Genevie's hand was now resting on the pommel of her sword. It seemed that the sound of her raised voice was a signal, since twenty, armed cavalry had come into the clearing, leaving little space for anyone to move around.

From the corner of his eye, Devlyn glanced at Wyn before pressing into the erendinth. They had no time to deal with petty laws over traveling restrictions. When he pressed into terys and aerys, the ground trembled beneath their feet and the air stormed about everyone in the clearing, spooking the horses and making the knights struggle to calm their mounts.

"Shadow elves! Subdue them at once!" a furious Lieutenant Genevie yelled at her fellow knights, her sword now freed from its sheath and pointing at Devlyn and Wyn. "Only a shadow elf would dare risk wielding kien."

Amid the growing chaos, Eolwn bent his front legs, his talons tearing at the grass, intent on protecting Wyn and Devlyn.

Wyn placed a hand on the griffin's beak, calming him instantly. "We are not shadow elves—they are our enemy just as much as they are yours. My name is Wyn Lierafen, I'm an Eldinari from the Eldin Wood. And this is…"

"Devlyn, a Luminari from Cor'lera. The ei'ana are working to restore the Balance of kien and kiara. Kien wielders are learning to wield with control once more at Gwilnor Academy. Septyl is becoming whole again—Balance is returning." As he spoke, Devlyn let go of the erendinth, allowing the ground and air to still.

Genevie narrowed her gaze, breathing heavily as she seemed to assess whether they were telling the truth.

Her men paused their attempts to seize Wyn and Devlyn, which had been quite ineffectual given their mounts' unease and looked to her expectantly. Devlyn could tell that they understood that they had no defense against two kien wielders.

"Suppose I believe you," Genevie said, returning her sword to its sheath while still trying to calm her horse who seemed to want to move away from the griffin. "Why have we not received notification from Ceurenyl?"

"Perhaps your king has," Devlyn offered.

Genevie tensed. "Then you will not object to accompanying us to settle this manner. Since you claim you're not shadow elves, you should have no issue with following your *allies* to the city to address the king." She turned her horse and trotted away from the clearing, assuming that Wyn and Devlyn would meekly follow her without further protest.

Devlyn glanced at Wyn who looked particularly untroubled by the whole encounter. "Should we go with her?" Devlyn asked. Genevie didn't have to deliver the implied threat of *or else*, but the collective tension from the gathered cavalry made it clear that Devlyn and Wyn would be coming to the city, one way or another. None of them seemed eager to attempt to subdue two wielders and a griffin but they all gripped their sword pommels, ready to unsheathe them if needed. Their horses pawed at the ground as their riders repeatedly sized the griffin up, debating what it would take to defeat it if they had to.

"She did claim we were allies." Wyn didn't appear concerned about Eolwn's safety. "What harm could it be to meet another monarch, especially one that isn't trying to pawn you off to the Erynien emperor?"

Annoyed at the delay, and wishing he could just lie down and sleep, Devlyn shrugged at Wyn, who helped Devlyn onto Eolwn, while Wyn walked beside the griffin. Genevie didn't turn around to see if they had agreed to follow, but neither did she move off too far ahead.

The rising sun offered a better view of the landscape once they were out of the clearing. It wasn't much less than an hour into the escort to Briel before Devlyn saw a city rise behind the knoll they had just crested, its buildings painted in reds and oranges in the morning light.

Devlyn was surprised at how close their chosen camping spot had been to the city. No wonder Genevie was so agitated with them. "Why didn't you take us further away from the city?" Devlyn leaned toward Wyn to whisper. "Eolwn could have easily flown further away from their capital." Wyn smirked, making Devlyn wonder if coming to Briel and getting an audience with King Irvienne Haert had been intentional. It had the workings of Velaria written all over it. Why didn't Wyn just tell him if that had been the intent? "Were you planning this all along?"

Wyn didn't answer. A large gate guarded by what seemed to be at least twenty soldiers rose before them as they neared Briel. Twin flags featuring a heron in flight on a yellow and black checkered field, one on each gatepost, billowed in the wind.

Genevie marched them through the gate, every guard watching openmouthed as the griffin passed them. They also seemed rather surprised at seeing that one of the two elves had darker skin than they had seen before.

As they were led through Briel, Devlyn was relieved to see cheerful faces again, a sight very much lacking in Lankor, not that he had spent any time outside Yloran's home. Just as the guards at the gate had done, the townsfolk gasped at the sight of two elves and a griffin walking through their streets. The city grew louder as more people realized what was happening and more people rushed outside to catch sight of them. The Brieli reminded him of Cor'lerans, both cut off from the larger part of Eklean, Cor'lera by geography, Briel by the necessity of defending herself against Tieli aggression.

Devlyn's back started to bother him again and his stomach rumbled. He was exhausted, hungry, and desperately wanted to sleep after flying all night. *Does she intend to march us through the entire city?*

Wyn showed no evidence of exhaustion—he never did.

Old stone walls opened before the group. There was no gate separating the city from the Brieli castle. The stones of the castle, as well as the rest of the city, had originated in the riverbed hundreds, if not thousands, of years ago. Devlyn knew that Briel was not a young kingdom. The Brieli stretched back to the time of Thellion, and from the looks of this castle, it did too.

Genevie marched through the bailey and looked behind her at Devlyn and Wyn. She hadn't once looked back at them through the entire walk, confident that her knights would make sure they had followed. She spoke briefly with a castle guard near an entry before he dashed into the castle.

"Are you comfortable leaving your mount with our stable hands?" Genevie asked.

"Eolwn hates stables. He thinks they're too confining." Wyn helped Devlyn down from the griffin's back, patting Eolwn before the griffin plopped on the ground and closed his eyes to rest, unthreatened by the Brieli filling the bailey. The Brieli seemed to feel quite differently about the situation though, maintaining a wide berth between themselves and Eolwn even as they stared.

"Very well, follow me." Devlyn and Wyn followed her into the castle and up three flights of a central stair, where it opened onto a wide corridor. At the end of the corridor where large wooden doors stood, a finely dressed man and the same castle guard they had first seen speaking briefly with Genevie now waited for them.

"I am Etienne Jiethel, the Grand Chamberlain for His Majesty, King Irvienne Haert of Briel." Upon his chest was the crest of Briel, the same as the flag, and hanging from his waist, where knights would wear a sword, hung elegant golden keys. "I will be presenting you to the court and to the king himself today. Now, might I have your names to introduce you to His Majesty's court?"

Devlyn hesitated for a moment, considering how much he should reveal about himself. Exhaustion and hunger dictated his decision, which he hoped he wouldn't regret later. He couldn't hide behind the Telvin name any longer, or even the Feolyn name for that matter—Eagan was right, people needed to know who he was. They introduced themselves and on hearing Devlyn's name, Etienne quickly excused himself. He left them with Genevie as he walked hurriedly down an adjacent corridor, disappearing as it turned. Devlyn's heart was beating rapidly as they awaited Etienne's return. Had he made a mistake in revealing his name? With only Wyn as his escort when he spoke his true name, it might have been wiser to wait until he was surrounded by a retinue of Luminari elves.

As he fretted over it, Etienne returned, catching his breath as he took his place in front of the doors. "The king and his court will see you now," he said and the doors behind him opened.

Etienne turned and led them into the large but crowded room where dozens of finely dressed men and women stood about speaking quietly in small groups. Genevie did not accompany them as only nobles and dignitaries were permitted in the Brieli court.

Looking out over their heads to the far wall, Devlyn could see large windows, looking west over the River Reifen.

"Ei'ethil Wyn, Child of Eldinare, of House Lierafen." The chamberlain called out in a loud voice.

Wyn stepped forward and inclined his head, as was the custom of the Eldinari elves.

"Ei'ethil Devlyn, Child of Luminare, of the Exalted House Lorenthien, heir to the Crystal Throne of Krysenthiel," Etienne announced next.

Devlyn stepped forward, noticing that the quiet murmur that had hovered over the assembly now rose, with gasps and surprised chatter punctuated by some rude shoving that provided a view of the person who claimed to be a Lorenthien.

Etienne closed the doors behind him and Devlyn scanned the room, wondering whether there were any other elves present.

Various nobles approached Devlyn as the chamberlain led him and Wyn through the space, introducing themselves and their titles without end. They weren't so rude as to impede their passage toward the king, but they rushed to ensure that the Lorenthien heir knew them, fully expecting that he was seeking to ascend the Crystal Throne and wanting to claim a level of acquaintance.

Eventually, there were no more nobles pressing in, and Devlyn saw a short man, a bit round in the midsection, with dark brown hair and droopy skin beneath his eyes, standing before the large west facing windows. He was more richly dressed than the other nobles and wore a heavy gold chain with the crest of Briel around his neck. He stood with his hands clasped loosely behind his back. The Grand Chamberlain stopped before him.

"Your Majesty, I present Ei'ethil Devlyn Lorenthien and Ei'ethil Wyn Lierafen."

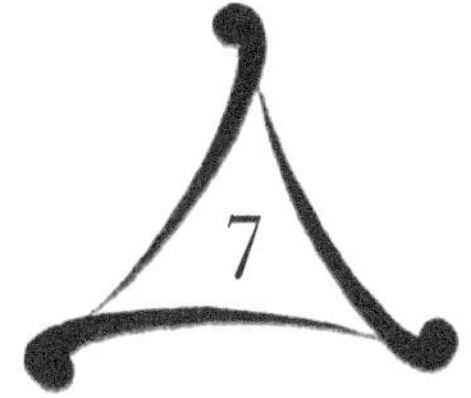

A King's Welcome

King Irvienne stayed silent for a moment, as though weighing whether he believed Devlyn's claim. Everyone knew that Erynor had killed every member of House Lorenthien during his last reign. Only fools would try to claim they belonged to that extinct house, or else they considered the person they told as the fool. "Thank you, Etienne." The chamberlain bowed and stepped away.

Devlyn closed the distance to the king and bowed slightly. "It's a pleasure to meet you, Your Majesty." Wyn echoed the bow but did not address the king.

"The pleasure is all mine, Ei'ethil. But please, Irvienne is more than sufficient." The king seemed to warm up to Devlyn and Wyn easily enough.

Devlyn smiled and nodded, relieved to do away with formalities.

"Please, would you both accompany me to the balcony? It offers the best view Briel has to offer, even if it does look beyond our current borders." Turning away, Irvienne led them through an open door and onto an expansive balcony.

Devlyn caught his breath at the sight of the rivers joining beneath the castle to continue their westward journey before eventually emptying into the Erynien Bay. Irvienne gave them a few moments to appreciate the view, then led them to a table where an assortment of cheeses and grapes had been set out. He helped himself to a chunk of cheese and indicated to Devlyn and Wyn that they should help themselves. Devlyn gladly grabbed a stem of grapes as his stomach had rumbled more than once on the walk from the clearing.

"I heard from my chamberlain that Lieutenant Genevie gave you a difficult time. You must forgive my lieutenant; she had no way of knowing who you are. She means well, and if we lived in more secure times, she might have been gentler."

"She was just upholding Brieli law," Devlyn said, wanting to ease Irvienne's concern.

"Thank you for your understanding." Irvienne took another mouthful of cheese and chewed it as he considered them both. "If you don't mind my asking, what brings you through Briel?"

"We had matters to see to in Lankor—Princess Kaela Roendryn as the Yanilean's *guest* among them." Devlyn avoided mentioning the lucilliae. He still didn't know who could be trusted with the knowledge that not only was he gathering them, but he currently had one on his person. Irvienne didn't seem untrustworthy, but the consequences of others learning what he carried were too risky, especially someone he had just met—even if that person seemed kind and was an ally. For all that he knew, Irvienne could very well be a servant of Shadow in Erynor's pocket, like so many other monarchs. He didn't think that was likely, but after the Tenebrae ei'ana had sneaked into Gwilnor and abducted him, Devlyn didn't know who he could trust. And while at the moment, he could wield just fine, he doubted he had the strength to fight a shadow elf.

"Have they sunken so low?" Irvienne practically spat and covered his mouth with a handkerchief. "Eklean will be torn asunder if Erynor continues with his conquest. I know his eyes are set on Briel and we've done everything we can to halt his advance, despite Queen Alesei constantly pressing against our borders. I'm sure you already know, but the corruption of the Briel Wood happened during his last reign, turning it into the Dead Wood. Nothing but wraiths and sickness in those cursed trees now."

"My people still weep for the Briel Wood. We felt many of its miervae passing. On behalf of the Eldinari, please accept our condolences." Wyn dipped his head.

"Thank you. I can't say that it's of much use now. Every Brieli child knows what Erynor did though. You won't find any Erynien sympathizers in Briel. If there is anything I might do to assist in this war, you have only to ask."

"Thank you." Devlyn thought back on his time in the Illumined Wood and the miervae that had almost become a wraith because of Aren. If the entire forest hadn't come together, the Illumined Wood could have very likely turned into another Dead Wood. "That time might come sooner than later."

"Is that so? Do you intend to reenergize what's left of the Lucillian Alliance? I'm sure you don't need me telling you this, but the Erynien Empire won't stand by and watch. And they certainly won't allow the power and influence they've already gained to slip through their fingers."

Devlyn considered telling Irvienne more. He couldn't say why, but he liked Irvienne; the king seemed honest and good-natured. It also helped that he despised the Erynien Empire. Wyn gave Devlyn a mental jog, urging him to share more with the king. "I don't know when, but I plan to destroy the Shroud covering Krysenthiel. And I know Erynor will not wait idly by as I do so. The Luminari will need every advantage to take back our home."

"If what was written about Krysenthiel is half as true as they claim, I pledge my entire kingdom in support of its return. And to think, the very reason for the strife beginning all those years ago lies in Arenthyl. I shudder at the thought of what it would mean for Eklean if Ceurendol was unveiled." Irvienne walked to the balustrade overlooking the river. "Ceurendol wasn't the only thing that was lost because of the Erynien Empire. While our resources are currently much diminished, the Brieli remember serving on the Guardian Senate. In respect of that noble council, we have continued to uphold that tradition and if you were to reinstate it, the Brieli senators would return to their seats."

Devlyn knew there were significant gaps in his education covering Eklean's history, particularly where Krysenthiel was involved. The Guardian Senate was among that long list of historical bodies that he knew nothing about. None of his magisters at Gwilnor had mentioned it and neither had Viren, a Guardian knight, ever spoken of the Guardian Senate.

"Thank you, Your Majesty. Your support and encouragement are greatly appreciated." Devlyn assumed that was the correct thing to say in this instance. He wished Ellendren were here—she would have known the correct response. "What role did Briel have on the Guardian Senate?"

"Our individual responsibilities are long forgotten. I'm sure records exist regarding which councils the Brieli senators were part of and I'm sure they had their role in upholding the august body that brought peace to all Eklean and beyond. Before your ancestors established the Eklean Senate, which later transitioned into the Guardian Senate to bring all Teraeniel together, Eklean only knew fighting, disease, and death. The last time Eklean had enjoyed peace was before Thellion's civil war divided the continent—and that was nearly six thousand years ago! It's a wonder we still idolize that kingdom." Irvienne turned away from the balustrade. "You might find garnering support for restoring the senate difficult."

Raising an eyebrow, Devlyn saw a hint of concern and doubt cross the Brieli king's features. Devlyn feared that after all his talk of support, Irvienne was going to withdraw it. "And why is that?" It was only after he spoke that he realized he sounded sterner than he'd intended.

"Nothing to worry about from Briel." Irvienne offered an encouraging smile and open palms. "But there are reports coming in of unsettling arrivals along Eklean's coasts."

"How so?" Devlyn crossed his arms.

"They call themselves the Daer and claim they are from another continent. They have not attempted to settle on Eklean soil, but the boats they travel in are a threatening presence, especially the deep blood red sails they raise."

"Where's this news coming from?" Devlyn asked, hoping for an opportunity to strike an alliance.

"We received a bird from Eddle Port. The message expressed concern at the sight of the Daer ships drawing near their harbor."

"Are the Daer only near Eddle Port?" Wyn asked.

"I've heard reports of some Daer ships along Tiel's coast as well, but I haven't received news of others as we're rather isolated here in Briel."

Without any warning, a yawn overcame Devlyn. He covered his mouth and he felt his ears turn red, embarrassed that he had yawned in front of a king. "I'm sorry, we've been traveling at night and we haven't slept today." It didn't matter how tired he was, Ellendren would hang him by his toes if she ever found out that he'd yawned in front of a king.

"Truly? I would have never known. I've taken up enough your time as it is. Please, stay here in the castle and rest as long as you need. Unfortunately, you will have to pass through the court again to get to the guest wing, and the nobles will make it difficult to get through without being accosted. I'm afraid it may be a while yet before you rest."

"Thank you, Irvienne. That's incredibly hospitable of you." Devlyn and Wyn bowed to the Brieli king, whose return bow was just as heartfelt if a little less deep, and they left his company.

Irvienne had spoken truthfully. Once back in the court, they were met by the chamberlain, but despite Etienne's best efforts, they were repeatedly stopped as various Brieli nobles introduced themselves. Devlyn's exhaustion was deep and he was finding it more and more difficult to be polite. When they finally neared the exit to the audience hall, a woman with smoky red hair crossed their path. Her pointed ears identified her as an elf, but her eyes were unlike any Devlyn had ever seen. They were crimson, as though fire burned behind them.

The woman said something, clearly a greeting of some sort, in an unrecognizable language, and left. "Was that Aelish?" Devlyn asked Wyn.

"Perhaps a forgotten version, but that sounded older than even High Aelish. But I don't know how that's possible." Wyn looked just as confused as Devlyn felt.

While Devlyn wanted to find out who this red-eyed elf was, he was far too tired to investigate now. Instead, he gladly allowed the chamberlain to lead him and Wyn to the castle's guest wing. Wyn said something about seeing to Eolwn as Devlyn opened the door to the room he'd been assigned and immediately found his bed.

<hr>

Devlyn slept through the rest of the day and all night, waking the following morning to a crisp chill. A large open window looked east over the city, and a soft golden sun was beginning to show itself, sending gentle rays over the room's furnishings. He pushed back the covers and made his way over to the window. As he took in the incredible room the Brieli king had let him stay in, he saw that someone had not only brought in his pack, but also a bowl of fruit and a small loaf of bread. He went to the washstand and dunked his head into the washbowl to remove the sleep from his eyes.

He dressed quickly in his blue lierathnil then ate two apples and the bread. When he opened the door, he found Wyn already awake, and waiting for Devlyn in the corridor.

"Are you ready?" Wyn asked.

"We're not waiting for nightfall?"

"Yanil and Tiel are behind us now, and once we cross Briel's northern border, we'll be in Sorenthil, so no need. We'll have to be careful to avoid Daerinth though—it appears they've aligned themselves with Erynor."

"Does Daerinth have any connection to the Daer sailing the

coasts?" Devlyn asked.

"I couldn't say. If they do, it's a very old connection, indeed. Daer-inth and its ruling princes have been around since the time of Thellion." Wyn paused, seeming to think about something. "The name does seem to suggest that the city hails from the same continent that the Daer call their home, Daereneth."

Devlyn followed Wyn through the castle to one of Briel's gardens. It was part of the castle's grounds, but there were no walls enclosing it, so that anyone from the city could enjoy the lush, shaded walkways.

Along the edge of the garden lay Eolwn, his large eagle-like head resting on his front talons. The instant he saw Wyn, the massive creature stood, rising to his full height, his head arching above his four mighty legs.

"He didn't like the bailey and refused to step foot in the stables," Wyn said, before leaping on. He planted himself firmly on Eolwn's back, then the griffin lowered his front legs. Wyn extended his hand to assist Devlyn and as soon as he was mounted, Eolwn pushed his hind legs against the ground, extended his wings in a broad sweep and carried them above Briel.

Trumpets sounded from below.

Devlyn waved with a single hand, his other wrapped tightly around Wyn's waist. Long shadows etched across the land below, as the sun slowly brightened the autumn day.

As the days went by, the landscape below shifted. The green valleys along the rivers, lightened the further north they flew, as though the grass was hibernating beneath frost. The chilled air grew colder, and by the third day, Devlyn and Wyn pulled heavy cloaks from their packs. The fifth day, the landscape was speckled with white. It was only the twenty-fourth of Vespenth, winter was officially still over a month away, but already there was snow on the ground.

A week and a half passed before the boughs of the Illumined Wood came into view. The immense trees created their own barrier to a country wholly other than the rest of Eklean. Within the wooded border was an enclave, with Lucillia nestled in it. The city was named after the woman who had given birth to Ellendren's ancestor, Roendryn and his twin, Devlyn's ancestor, Feolyn, who had unknowingly married a Lorenthien.

Devlyn had only visited Lucillia, the capital city of the Luminari, once before. That visit had been all too brief as he had been quickly ushered out of the city and into the Illumined Wood to begin his novitiate. Now, he returned, not as an ei'ceuril novice, but as a Phaedryn and a Lorenthien, a Luminari house that all Eklean had adored, but believed had become extinct at the hands of Erynor.

As they approached, Devlyn saw that Lucillia was changing. The city intricately spun from the very trees was no longer as seamless as he remembered. While still noticeably a city, it looked like the Illumined Wood was reclaiming it. An unkempt wildness was taking hold. Most noticeable though, once they were past the fog, was that he was able to see the city—that should not be possible.

The Protection of the Wood shimmered, the shield visible as sunlight glistened against it, but there were holes in it. Wyn directed Eolwn toward one of the larger gaps into Lucillia and then toward the palace. The streets below quickly filled with people calling out greetings to the riders on the griffin flying over them.

As they neared the palace, the single dome still rose above the rest of the complex, with curved courtyards defining its overall geometry. Only a few knights stood guard in the plaza leading to the palace, but the gates behind them were shut. Devlyn wondered if Wyn intended fly over those gates and directly to the palace proper. Eklean had to get used to the ineffectiveness of strong gates now that flying mounts had been reintroduced. Even though Wyn could have easily flown over those gates, he landed in the empty plaza, raising a reaction from the knights.

Two of the three knights gripped their ceremonial spears, not in a threatening way, but as though they were nervous. "Calm down, we've been expecting these two," the other knight said as he bowed crisply and elbowed the other two to do the same. "Welcome to Lucillia, Ei'ethil. I must admit, I prefer you arriving on a griffin and stopping here than on a dragon and flying directly toward the palace gates. You gave us all a right fright when you were here last. We thought Erynor had returned to finish the job he'd started fourteen hundred years ago and burn our city to the ground, starting with Lucillia's direct descendants."

"Well, I had just flown from Ceurenyl after Erynor attacked the city. I had honestly thought that that was precisely what he had intended," Devlyn said as Wyn helped him down from Eolwn.

"If it hadn't been for your warning and the aryl raising the Protection of the Wood, he probably would have," the knight said. Before the knights were able to open the gate to the palace grounds, Devlyn caught a shimmer of gold and silver hair in the distance. He knew there were dozens, if not hundreds of Roendryns in Lucillia, but only one made him feel weightless, as though there was nothing wrong in the world. Time seemed to freeze and he didn't even realize the gates were opening as he watched Ellendren draw near. He was sure that he only imagined she was nearly running toward him.

Everything that had happened since he had been abducted from Gwilnor by the Tenebrae—every pain and setback—seemed to melt away. Even the pain of Aliel's noticeable absence dimmed a little at seeing Ellendren for the first time in nearly five months. He didn't realize that he had started moving toward her. And then they pulled each other into a tight embrace.

"I've missed you, Elle." Devlyn didn't notice that her embrace rubbed against the wound, the pent-up emotion that was now oozing out of him as he held onto her taking some of the sting away.

"You're here now." They both pulled back, yet still held on to each other's hands looking into each other's eyes. Devlyn lost himself in her eyes and without a thought, he leaned toward her as she did the same and their lips touched. The kiss deepened, and if it wasn't for an uncomfortable cough from Wyn, Devlyn would not have ever wanted it to end.

"Where is Aliel?" Ellendren asked as she pulled back, her cheeks a rosy hue.

Everything from the past five months rushed back, and with it, that hole in his heart where he often found Aliel gaped.

"I don't know." He felt his eyes tear up.

"Oh, Devlyn."

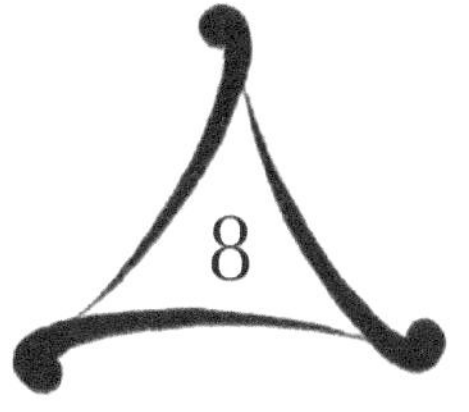

Burnt Out

Things have definitely taken a turn for the worse around here, Jaerol thought as he thumbed through the newly approved tome assigned for use by the students of Kai's politics class. Kai was one of the few magisters who had not been relieved from her teaching responsibilities following the events involving the rogue kien wielders. It was obvious to Jaerol that she hated the new assigned reading just as much as her students did. But she never commented on Hannah's recent decisions, aware it would be foolish of her to do so when the chancellor chose to refer to the event as an unfortunate, yet all too predictable, accident because kien wielders were being taught how to wield. She had grumbled that it was too late to reverse the decision made by the Seven Chairs and young Ceurtriarch, but necessary changes would be carried out at Gwilnor to ensure the safety of her students. To no one's surprise, Fyreh and Myrah had been the first magisters asked to step down from their teaching responsibilities. Rumors hinted that Hannah had even encouraged them to return to the Eldin Wood where they belonged.

But as far as anyone knew, the Glaeda twins had continued to reside in the castle, although no one was quite sure just where they were. And while their dismissal was unsurprising, Hannah's decision to excuse old Ethyl from her history class had been the most unexpected sacking. After decades of teaching the same class, Ethyl had outright refused to change her syllabus based on a new chancellor's whims. She too, had also been given the option to leave the castle. She hadn't. This was her home—all she knew of the current world was Gwilnor Academy. Jaerol had caught her strolling dazedly past her old classroom to sneak a peek at the skeletal magister who had replaced her. And as for theoreticals, the class had simply been disbanded altogether without any replacement magister. Gwilnor was an odd place without Therril bobbing and humming along through the halls.

Jaerol blinked at the pages of the horrible book he was required to study. Already forgetting what he had just read, Jaerol turned back several pages. Whether Hannah intended to or not, she had successfully devised a reading list worse than the one he'd had at the Imperium. At least the Imperium hadn't discouraged its students from wielding. What was the point of attending Gwilnor Academy if he couldn't continue learning to wield?

His eyes glossed over again. The students were expected to write a report on the unintelligible book that sat in front of him and he couldn't even remember who had written it. He chanced a look at Liam who seemed just as interested in his own copy of the book as Jaerol was, but Liam was terrible at disguising it. After spending an entire decade in a jail cell, he didn't have the patience or willingness to pretend or disguise his feelings. That was something which Jaerol was all too happy to accommodate—especially since they were sharing a room again, where they were able to speak openly in the privacy of their quarters.

Unfortunately, though, all the newer kien wielders had also been bunked together. While Jaerol and Liam benefited from the switch, the kien wielders who had only recently come to Gwilnor to study did not since other than the continuing debacle that was Yvonne's art of wielding class, the untrained kien wielders' only exposure to learning how to wield had been from their more experienced roommates. Even though they had been blamed for causing the destruction a few months past, the truth was that they were all capable of controlling the erendinth without causing harm to themselves or others and certainly not to the castle.

Jaerol had made the mistake of informing Hannah that he had recognized the men who had attacked Gwilnor—none of them were students. They were all wielders who had escaped the temple on the same day Ealyndol had been assassinated. Hannah had been quick to ask if he had access to the school's enrollment records. He was still serving his months' worth of detention after that and had dish duty three times a day. His fingers had never been so wrinkly.

"Eyes down on your reading material, Master Solaris," Saendre said from the back of the classroom. She had been assigned to assist Kai's politics lessons. Jaerol knew little about Saendre, only that she was still a student but had chosen the Albiens after her novitiate. She wore her Albien pin and white robes as proudly as the most pompous of ei'ceuril.

"I can handle it, thank you, Saendre," Kai said grimly. Every magister had been assigned a teaching assistant and while Kai had maintained a certain level of autonomy in her classroom, refusing the chancellor's directive that teaching assistants would henceforth be assigned to all magisters was not a good idea if she wanted to keep her teaching position. Even so, that didn't mean she treated Saendre politely. All the magisters' assistants reported directly back to Hannah. In fact, they tended to revolve around the chancellor as though she was their center of gravity.

Other than Kai and Saendre, the rest of the classroom was filled with the residents of the eighth floor of the boys' dormitory. Every other class was the same, the boys separated from the girls for all the classes. The only time that Jaerol saw any female students was at mealtimes and that was strictly supervised. Exits were meticulously guarded and students were scrutinized if they headed off in a direction other than their dormitory after dinner. Jaerol and Liam still attended Yvonne's art of wielding class but Yvonne was the only woman in sight there. Worse, Razcul had remained her assistant. Unlike before, every student now had to attend Yvonne's class, even if they had never showed the faintest inclination toward wielding. Luckily for them, wielding certainly wasn't a requirement in that class, since Yvonne's teaching methods suppressed and discouraged any type of wielding. Hannah had apparently made it her mission to ensure that the next generation of wielders never saw Balance returned.

The Arenthylean bells finally tolled and Jaerol was free to grab lunch. Before he could stand though, Kai called him forward. Jaerol looked over his shoulder to see Liam leave and noted that the ever-nosy Saendre watched curiously, eager to know what his punishment might be so she could report it back to Hannah.

"Eyes down," Kai said, shocking Jaerol at the severity of her voice. She wasn't necessarily a warm woman but she had never been unkind or harsh to him before. "I have certain expectations during my class." Jaerol glanced up, wondering if he should make eye contact to apologize. "I said eyes down." She slammed her hand on the desk.

His eyes flashed down to where she had slapped her desk. One of her fingers was making funny gestures on the desktop. It started at one point and looped about as she moved it to the right.

"Pay attention when I'm telling you something," she said, just as sternly.

Jaerol's eyes widened when he realized that she was trying to tell him something without Saendre realizing it. Focused anew on her finger, he spelled out what she wrote. *East Tower—Ten—Eighteen.*

"Do you understand?" Kai asked. Jaerol had tuned out her voice as he tried to decipher her desktop invisible writing while she continued lecturing him about the importance of completing his reading material. He heard that last part though and nodded. "Good, now go back to your tower, to whatever floor you live on, and make sure you are never late for your lessons."

"I promise," he said, and hurried out the door to find Liam.

"Watch, he'll likely be tardy from here on out just to spite us," he overheard Saendre comment sarcastically.

"Don't you have a lunch to get to?" Kai asked.

Jaerol smiled as he hurried away, their conversation fading. The corridors were eerily quiet since useless chatter when walking from one room to another was now punishable. The sound did pick up as he neared the dining hall. Silencing students while they ate simply wasn't feasible. Instead of passing through the base of the North Tower and grabbing something to eat, Jaerol made his way up the tower's stair hall. Even though it was time for lunch, he knew he would find Liam in their shared room. After Gwilnor had been attacked—when the Seven Chairs and a great many others had disappeared that night and since—they had agreed that if either of them was held back in class for any reason, they would meet in their room after.

East Tower—Ten—Eighteen, Jaerol repeated silently as he went up the stairs. He had to make it seem that he wasn't in a rush; he couldn't afford to be seen acting suspiciously. Fortunately, he hadn't passed anyone who knew that he had to wash the dishes after lunch. *Those dishes could wait—it's not like they could get any dirtier*, he thought.

Jaerol pushed his way through the door and quickly closed it behind him. Luckily, only Liam was in their room, and he blurted out, "East Tower—Ten—Eighteen."

"Sorry?" Liam said, confused.

"East Tower—Ten—Eighteen. Does it mean anything to you? Kai wrote it with her finger on her desk for only me to see while Saendre watched like a hawk from the back."

"More like a vulture. Did she give you any other hint? The East Tower is easy enough to interpret but the numbers not so much. Are you sure they're in the right order?"

"I think so. The ten definitely came after the tower, and the eighteen after the ten."

"So, that could be…the tenth floor and the eighteenth door. Or the other way around. The tenth door on the eighteenth floor."

"Does the East Tower even have eighteen floors?"

"Who's to say after that fire those rogue kien wielders started?" Liam pushed his fingers through his hair. "Did she give you any more hints? Those numbers really could mean anything."

"She did say something before I left, something about returning to my tower, on my floor, and to not be late."

"She said it that simply?" Liam asked, grinning. "In front of Saendre?"

It clicked as Jaerol noted Liam's knowing expression.

———

That night, Jaerol and Liam crept out of their room, then down the stairs to the main level of the North Tower, where they had to quickly change direction to avoid the patrolling ei'ana, and silently dashed into the dining hall. It was empty but it wouldn't stay that way for long, so Jaerol took Liam down a servant's stair to the kitchens below.

If they were caught outside of their dormitory three hours after curfew, they would be punished with detention for at least a month. Jaerol's hands were already raw from his current punishment, and they would never heal if the detention was extended. Still, he had grown quite familiar with the kitchens, which at first, seemed like a maze with various rooms and no clear central corridor. But after getting lost when he'd first started working there and ending up in one of the storage rooms, he had made a point of learning the logic to the room placement. More importantly, he had learned how to get out of the kitchens while remaining on the same level. If not for the grand space above them, the kitchens would have seemed just as appropriate for a dining hall. Beautiful stone vaults supported the space above. The only difference was that the kitchens were much more divided and the piers seemed twice as thick as the impressive columns above that stretched from the floor to the steep vaulted ceiling, vining past a clerestory level.

At this time of night, their only obstacle through the kitchens was one of the chefs who had fallen asleep there, snoring as he lay on his back on a pallet. They crept quietly past him and in no time, they were back on the main level. They still had to be careful since they now were in a more public area and the patrolling ei'ana could appear at any point.

Jaerol and Liam knew that Gwilnor had an abundance of secret passageways, but they only knew the one that connected the castle to the temple. They simply hadn't lived in the castle long enough to stumble across any of the others. Instead, Jaerol prayed that Anaweh might keep them hidden or better yet, put whoever was on guard duty to sleep.

Now, they just had to get through and past the Knight's Courtyard where Jaerol could see a light bobbing—one of the sentries. None of the Septyl knights had been entrusted with guard duty. Hannah knew their loyalties were not to her or the Tenebrae occupying the castle. The sentry who approached was clearly an ei'ana with her wielded globe of light hovering above her palm. Liam and Jaerol ducked below the windowsill as the light came nearer. It was too risky to try to see if he recognized her. Whoever this was, she was about to cut them off from the quickest route down the corridor and past the door to the East Tower. That didn't guarantee their safety but at least they wouldn't have to take another detour.

Jaerol managed a glimpse ahead toward the opening where the ei'ana was headed; it was still in the shadows. Sweat beaded his brow and he knew Liam was just as nervous. Before he could think it all the way through, he yanked Liam's wrist and pulled him toward the opening. All they had to do was get across it before the ei'ana brought her light close enough to see them.

Jaerol was tempted to get a better look at the ei'ana. He kept his eyes closed instead, partly hoping that if he couldn't see her, she wouldn't see them. Liam's fingers dug into Jaerol's wrist as they hurried across, keeping as light and quiet on their feet as possible.

They reached the double door on the far side of the corridor and Jaerol thought they might be safe. The budding elation vanished as he tried to push the door open. It rattled in place and refused to budge.

"Who's there?" the ei'ana called.

Liam pulled at the other door, and blessedly, it opened. They slipped inside the East Tower just as the ei'ana called out again, and before the door closed behind them, they heard another voice reply. They rushed down the corridor and to the stair hall as they heard the door they had just come through open. Two sets of feet hurried in.

Instead of sprinting up the stairs, Liam pulled Jaerol beneath the nearest stair landing and down into a crouch as close to the bottom of the stairs as they could fit. Holding their breaths and too scared to breathe, they heard their pursuers enter the stair hall.

"Do you see them?" Jaerol recognized this irritated voice. Razcul kept up his Eldinari disguise but Jaerol—and the missing Seven Chairs of Septyl—knew who he truly was. There was no doubting who pulled the strings at Gwilnor with Razcul walking freely about. Jaerol hadn't expected the ghosts of his past to resurface and had been appalled when he'd recognized Yvonne's new assistant as Razcul, his old classmate at the Imperium.

"I already told you, I heard something. I didn't see anything."

"So why are you wasting my time?"

"I apologize—I didn't intend to."

"Think twice before you do next time." A slap echoed through the stair hall, followed by the receding sound of one set of footsteps. A few seconds passed before the second set drew away.

Jaerol and Liam waited, breathing as shallowly as possible without passing out. They likely were alone but there was no way to tell without coming out of their hiding spot. The glass-like Arenthylean bells started to chime the eighteenth hour, all but inaudible to anyone who had already fallen asleep. Jaerol weighed the risk of creeping out from under the stair and possibly confronting the ei'ana or Razcul. Either one of them could have returned. However, if they didn't reach the tenth floor in time, there was no telling what they would miss out on. The second bell chimed as Jaerol peeked past the stairs. The stair hall was empty.

"Come on," he whispered as the third glass-like bell pinged. They took the stairs two at a time, quietly racing up. The bells were still chiming when they reached the tenth landing but Jaerol had been too focused on counting off the floors that he didn't know how many more times the bells would chime. They went through the only door on the tenth-floor landing and paused at the sight of the destruction in the corridor beyond.

There was no doubt that this had been one of the floors most severely damaged in the fire. A swell of pride bloomed inside Jaerol. If not for his quick thinking, the damage here could have been significantly worse, with a staggering loss of life if the residents here hadn't been warned by Jaerol's creation of an explosion in the courtyard, alerting them in time to escape the fire.

Still confused as to why Kai would have sent them here, Jaerol looked around the wreckage. Perhaps he had mixed up the numbers or even read them wrong. He started to second guess himself as he followed Liam who was peeking inside the various rooms that had been private apartments for the Vyoletryns.

Then he noticed that at the far end of the corridor, flickering light cast shadows onto the floor in front of a doorway. Who could possibly be hiding in the burnt-out shell of the East Tower's tenth floor? Surely this wasn't where the missing Chairs and ei'ana had gone? He suddenly wondered whether Kai had purposely sent him into danger. What if she too belonged to the Tenebrae School?

He grabbed Liam's hand, motioned to him to stay quiet, and peered around the doorframe into the room.

"Hello there, Jaerol, Liam." Fyreh smiled back at them in the most unthreatening manner possible. Whatever fears had been building up immediately dissipated and they stepped into the room.

Fyreh wasn't alone. Three dozen students, a mix of kien and kiara wielders, surrounded him and Myrah—they'd all been participants in his unofficial elthion league. Those games had long ago been suspended by Hannah—both the official and the unofficial games. By the looks of the large room, whoever had once lived here had to have been quite the respected ei'ana. Most notable in its current state was that there wasn't a single cot or blanket. This wasn't a place to hide from the Tenebrae. No one was sleeping here.

"Care to resume your lessons in wielding?" Myrah asked with a smile.

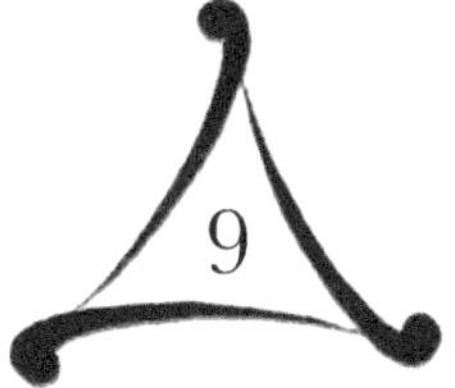

UNWELCOMED REALITY

The Orenth sky above Lucillia was awash in bitter clouds, clouds that threatened to blanket everything below in snow and ice. Cold winters were familiar to Devlyn, and there was certainly nothing abnormal about late fall turning cold, but something about this weather had put him on edge. It felt unnatural and wrong as the temperature dropped more every day. Those ever-present clouds clung to the thin remnant of the Protection of the Wood in a dense fog, making it impossible to see past the city walls. The clouds reminded him of the ones he'd seen in the World-in-Between, but it was impossible for anything in the Dream that was Somnaeniel to take effect in Teraeniel. Somnaeniel was an entirely separate realm, unconnected, wholly other than Teraeniel.

The Lucillian palace was a welcome respite after Lankor. The grassy floor and soft wooden arches, woven from the very trees of the Illumined Wood, lightened his heart. Despite the crisp weather, he remained comfortable inside his room, even though none of the windows in the city had any glass to keep the elements out. During his first visit to Lucillia, he had wrongly assumed that the mild temperature prevented the necessity of glass panes. Instead, a wield of some sort lay over the open windows, maintaining a comfortable atmosphere inside the palace. He assumed the same wield had been extended to the other buildings of Lucillia. If it was already this cold during Orenth, the coming winter months were sure to be harsh.

A soft knock came at the door, followed by a boy poking his head around the door. It was the same boy that had tended to him the first time he had visited Lucillia, but he was now a teenager. "Are you ready, Ei'ethil?" he asked, before coming fully into the room.

It was not the same title he had used for Devlyn three years ago. In the short time since he and Wyn had arrived in the city, he had learned that the old elven titles had been adopted by much of the Lucillian court. Alethea and Viren were likely responsible for the change, given that neither of them addressed elven nobility as lords or ladies, as had become the custom over the years in Lucillia. The last time Devlyn had visited the palace, he had been recognized as the heir of Feolyn, Roendryn's twin brother and son of Lucillia. Today, while Devlyn was still of the noble lineage that had liberated the Luminari and brought about the downfall of the Erynien Empire twelve hundred years ago, it was now known to a wider circle that he also descended from another line, a line nobler than any elven house to have walked Teraeniel.

"I am, thank you, Lyren." Taking a deep breath, Devlyn mentally prepared for the reaction to come when his identity would be proclaimed today to the entirety of the Luminari elves. Despondent over his continuing inability to reach Aliel, he once again searched that place within. The only response was the familiar sharp pain that meant the scab had once again opened and he felt the seeping blood begin to soak his shirt.

The experience was becoming second nature. Whenever he tried to reestablish their bond, he was met with agony, which occasionally was severe enough to incapacitate him. He was becoming somewhat used to it by now, but it was increasingly becoming an inconvenience, especially since it always meant that he had to change his shirt.

"Actually, can you grab another shirt for me? My wound opened again."

Lyren pulled a clean shirt from the wardrobe while Devlyn peeled his current one off and sat on the bed. He pressed into aquaeys, thankful that he could still wield, and swished water across his back to clean the wound. Lyren helped him with his shirt, then waited patiently while Devlyn grabbed the outer garment of his lierathnil, the dark blue robe with gold scroll work. He would have worn the entire ensemble, but with the wound regularly re-opening, he refrained from wearing the lierathnil shirt.

Lyren led Devlyn through the palace, which was as he remembered, although he also thought that parts seemed rougher—wilder—than what his memory recalled. He imagined that this was how the palace had appeared during its final months of construction, wrought by magical means, but retaining much of the natural elements of the flora it was made from. The wooden arches and pillars, the intertwining vines were all still whimsical and stunning, but the palace, and the entire city was noticeably waning.

They did not go to the throne room where Devlyn had first met the Aryl of Lucillia. If his memory was correct, this corridor led to the main entry hall. Granted, the only time he had walked through that grand entry was after he had flown to Lucillia on the back of Yelaris as Erynor and his shadow elves attacked Ceurenyl. His mind had been so frantic at that moment that he was surprised that he recognized this part of the palace at all.

A few knights stood at the front of the large entryway, each wearing armor and a sword at the hip. Devlyn knew they would prove little resistance if a shadow elf marched through the entry, but they would do everything in their power to thwart them. When Devlyn approached, two of the knights opened the large double doors, flooding the vestibule with a wash of light.

Lyren gestured at Devlyn, indicating that he was to walk through the doors, then took a step back. Devlyn had to do this part on his own.

Stepping forward, he could see out of the palace to the plaza where more elves than he had ever imagined existed were waiting for him. The sight overwhelmed him. Growing up alienated and alone in Cor'lera, where elves hoped to minimize their pointed ears and height by slouching, the sight was one he was unprepared for.

A trumpet sounded an eloquent high-pitched tune that cascaded like a river, beautiful and fierce, hopeful and tragic, ending just as King Harnyl Roendryn rose to greet Devlyn, embracing him, bringing forgotten memories of being hugged by his own father as a small child. The comfort nearly brought a tear to his eye, for the touch of a father was lost in the past until brought into his memory. Trying to hide the unexpected emotion, Devlyn smiled at the older elf. He looked about, and was relieved to see that Ellendren stood nearby, as did her sister Kaela. Royal cousins filled the steps in front of the palace while aryls from other elven houses lined the front of the plaza.

At Devlyn's side, Harnyl began to speak in a powerful voice, resonating with emotion that drew in the gathered elves. "As our pilgrimage in Lucillia fades, our home returning to the trees who so graciously gave of themselves to shelter us in our time of greatest need, so does Roendryn's faithful service pass, to be returned to the noblest of our houses, a house long believed extinguished at Erynor's hand.

"This house has sacrificed much for us Luminari and for all races. They birthed Teraeniel's first wielders. They united us while we still inhabited the Skyland of Luminare above, despite our differing views. They influenced Septyl and the founding of Gwilnor Academy so that our arts and wisdom might be shared with every people, regardless of their origin. When the Darkness fell on Luminare, they ushered us to safety in these lands below, founding what became Krysenthiel, where we spent thousands of peaceful years.

"We dreamt of sharing our Life immortal with all and succeeded with pouring ourselves into Ceurendol, only for it to be cast beneath a Shroud of death and darkness, not only severing us from our Life immortal, but preventing us from sharing it and banishing us from our homeland.

"For two hundred seventy-two years, we were enslaved before Lucillia gave birth to Roendryn and Feolyn. Neither Feolyn nor his wife

Gwendolyn knew of her illustrious lineage. Their children lived away from us in Cor'lera, passing on that noble line down quietly through the ages.

"As our laws dictate, I present to all Teraeniel the heir of Feolyn and Gwendolyn, who was the heir of the last Exalted Aryl of Krysenthiel, High King and High Queen of Eklean, Ei'denai Faerndryn and Ei'terel Ithendryl Lorenthien.

"Ei'ethil Devlyn Lorenthien."

The entire gathering applauded and the trumpets began anew. Devlyn smiled and waved, feeling awkward and out of place as the multitudes cheered. He knew all this was because he was a Lorenthien, but having others applaud his existence, not because of anything he had done, but because he was born of a certain family, was difficult to reconcile. From his perspective, he was no one special. He was collecting the lucilliae, but that had to remain a secret, even though Erynor was now aware of it. As far as anyone knew, he had done nothing spectacular to deserve any acknowledgement. The only remarkable thing that might deserve such recognition was his bond with Aliel, and the phoenix was not even present.

Trying to mask his insecurities to the people expecting him to be their next king, Devlyn continued to wave and smile.

Following the presentation, Harnyl hosted a banquet for the Lucillian court led by House Roendryn, his last official duty before it formally transitioned to the Krysenthien court led by House Lorenthien. Little would change among the aryls and the Luminari elves, only that a Lorenthien would be the Exalted Aryl again after the Roendryns abdicated their position as monarchs. King Harnyl sat at the high table reserved for the aryl and the aryl's family at one of the two aryl's seats; the other, Vernal's, remained empty. Ellendren sat next to her mother's empty seat, and Devlyn sat next to Ellendren. The seats were spaced so that despite sitting next to each other, two additional chairs could have been comfortably placed between them.

Per custom, Devlyn could not become the Exalted Aryl of Krysen-thiel outside her borders, let alone the more pressing law that applied, that an aryl was composed of ei'denai and ei'terel; Devlyn had to marry before he could sit upon the Crystal Throne as aryl, a fact that every elf enjoying Harnyl's banquet knew.

His interest in Ellendren was known to them all, but that did not prevent the various ei'terels from presenting their daughters to Devlyn. Some were near his own age, but others were decades older, and one was so young she could barely speak, making him uncomfortable that her mother was trying to arrange a marriage when her daughter was so young. Devlyn greeted them all politely, sidestepping their advances as he murmured courteous words.

Ellendren sat holding her chin high. Before beginning her studies at Gwilnor Academy, she had grown up here in the Lucillian palace and she knew everyone who approached Devlyn. Once a noble had spoken with Devlyn, they moved down the high table and spoke twice as long with Ellendren. They all asked about Aaron becoming the new Ceurtri-arch and sought details regarding Ealyndol's passing.

Devlyn caught himself staring at Ellendren whenever he had the opportunity. The endless line of nobles required constant attention, but during the brief pauses between them, he would glance sideways to find Ellendren speaking pleasantly and confidently with the noble he had just spoken to. This was a side of Ellendren that Devlyn had never seen be-fore. She was in her element here at the Lucillian court. She even calmed the worried nobles who asked about their children still at Gwilnor. They hadn't received any word from Ceurenyl about the state of Gwilnor, but Devlyn feared the rumors that Gwilnor Academy had fallen into the hands of the Tenebrae School were true. It wasn't all that difficult to imagine after he had been abducted while he slept in the castle.

Just thinking of Gwilnor being occupied by the Tenebrae was enough to ruin the evening. Surely Velaria and the other Chairs of Septyl wouldn't allow that to happen. When no more nobles presented themselves, Devlyn got up and closed the short distance between himself and Ellendren. Having been offered over a dozen marriage proposals while sitting next to the girl that made him feel special had been incredibly uncomfortable. If only those nobles knew that Ellendren had already claimed his heart. Apparently, none of them had seen the kiss they had shared in front of the palace when he had arrived, nor the others that had followed. Or perhaps they had and chose to deny any meaning to their display of affection, hoping to entice him with their own daughters.

"Hi, Elle."

She smiled, turning to look up at him. "Are you enjoying your first Luminari banquet?"

"The food's certainly tasty, but it's a lot of people all at once. Most of my dishes were cold by the time I had a chance to take a bite."

"I felt that way once, although it was a long time ago and I was much shyer at the time. You learn to sneak in bites between each guest."

"How long will this go on?"

"The banquet?"

"Every noble in Lucillia offering their daughters in marriage to me."

"Until you sit upon the Crystal Throne as ei'denai with your wife's hand in yours, as the Exalted Aryl of Krysenthiel." Ellendren smirked as she said it. Had she overheard the endless marriage proposals?

Managing a weak smile, Devlyn tried to exhibit a sense of confidence, and he melted in her returned warm smile. He was suddenly taken by a desire to bend his knee to propose. At only sixteen years old, the thought was ridiculous; he wasn't even of marrying age yet. He was about to return to his seat when another elven couple walked up to them.

"Ah, sweet Ellendren," the woman said. "We have received word from our son. Surely, there's a way we can patch things together. Youthful decisions can never be trusted to longevity. Especially considering the uncertainty of your own house."

"Thank you for your concern, Ei'terel Silvia, but I do not believe there was any hope of permanency with that betrothal."

"Emotions expressed at an age so young and tender should be tested and tried true," said the man accompanying Silvia. "Surely, Trethien will apologize for whatever he did to affront you. You must think to your future. Now that Lucillia begins to fade, there is no reason the Roendryn aryldom need fade with it."

Devlyn's feeling that he should recognize the man solidified the moment Trethien's name was mentioned. Trethien's parents even shared his arrogant smile. Devlyn was impressed at Ellendren's ability to conceal her fury at their response to her broken betrothal with Trethien Narielle. Hoping to sidetrack the difficult conversation, Devlyn stuck his hand past her chair by way of introduction, and Ellendren seized the opportunity to change the conversation.

"Devlyn, this is Ei'denai Toral and Ei'terel Silvia Narielle. They're Trethien's parents, and the Aryl of Winstyl."

"Pleased to meet you at last. Our son has mentioned you in his letters, before anyone knew of your true heritage, of course," Toral said, looking down his nose at Devlyn's extended hand. "Is that how the elves of Cor'lera greet people?"

Withdrawing his hand, Devlyn placed it over his right breast and inclined his head.

"Ah, so you're not entirely unfamiliar with our culture," Silvia said.

Neither Silvia nor Toral made any movement toward the appropriate formal greeting of respect in return.

"Tell us, where is this phoenix we've heard so much about?" Toral asked.

It had taken Devlyn the same amount of time to dislike the Aryl of Winstyl as it had taken him to dislike their son. He had no intention of telling them anything, not even Aliel's name. "Our time in Lankor was quite strenuous, and he's unable to make an appearance."

The banquet hall quieted, and suddenly the loud and boisterous gathering focused on the high table and its conversation regarding the phoenix.

"I was under the impression that Phaedryns were inseparable from their phoenix," Silvia said, her eyes staring into Devlyn's. "Has something gone wrong?"

"The records indicate that there has never been an Exalted Aryl of Krysenthiel who was not a Phaedryn. I wonder, if we manage to return to our ancestral home, will we find records of the necessity of that connection for the Exalted Aryl?" Toral added.

Growing more frustrated, Devlyn wanted nothing more than to tell off Trethien's parents, but he felt a smooth hand rest on his, gentling his fury.

"Such would, of course, be welcome," Ellendren said, her voice calm. "The more we learn of Krysenthiel before our arrival, the better."

"Indeed. And what makes you so confident that we'll be able to return?" Silvia asked.

"Devlyn has already managed to pierce the Shroud, with the phoenix's aid. Devlyn's golden eye color can attest to his bond with the phoenix. Our return to Krysenthiel is imminent and the care of Winstyl returned to your noble house."

The Narielles looked at one another. "I would never question the young Lorenthien's claim. Let us hope that whatever has happened to cause the phoenix's absence is remedied, for all our sakes," Toral said, loud enough that everyone at the now nearly silent banquet might overhear. Turning on his heel, his wife in hand, they left the high table.

The elves in the banquet hall began to murmur, hesitantly at first, but the previous volume eventually returned, and Devlyn stood stunned next to Ellendren. "You actually agreed to become part of that family?" Devlyn asked, at a loss for anything else to say.

"Actually, Trethien would have become a Roendryn," Ellendren said, her tone dangerous. "The lower-standing elf joins their spouse's house. It's the reason you are a Lorenthien and not a Feolyn. An elf's sex matters little in where they stand socially."

"Sorry," he responded, recognizing her tone.

"You should be," she said, her voice gentler. "Wealth and power have odd effects on us all."

"You are nothing like them." Devlyn tried to make the point that the Narielles having wealth and power was no excuse, since Ellendren's family was wealthier and more powerful.

"I'm not excusing their behavior." Taking his hand in her own, she began to lead him away from the table. "Would you like to quell some of those advances?"

Unsure as to what she meant, he smiled when he heard the music in the background. "What are you suggesting?"

Ellendren only smiled her sweet smile in response and Devlyn felt as though he was about to float away.

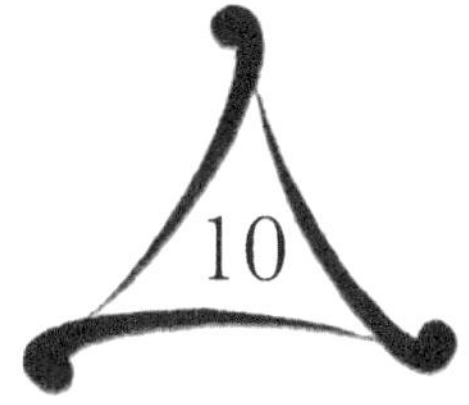

Titanic Reports

Alex sat at a finely carved dark wooden desk and wished he could be anywhere but there. The oversized desk was large enough for him to lie on without any of his limbs spilling over the edges. However, that would first require removing the mountain of reports littering the surface. Even so, this large, cluttered desk wasn't any normal desk either. Before the Perrien Council ousted Perrien's monarchy, this desk had been used by the Dennion kings. As a direct descendant of that royal line, he now sat at the very same desk, his fingers to his brow as so many others had done before him.

A bright sun washed into his office through the windows of Gneal's ancient castle. The sun would undoubtedly give way to grey clouds later in the afternoon. But just now, it was a nice relief after the snows that had already blanketed the city and probably the entirety of the northern countries of Perrien and Parendior. His scouts had reported snow as far south as Selma. They knew to avoid the Cyrillean Pass, but the pass and the valley separating the Laudien and Vespien Mountains was also likely buried beneath an early and heavy snowfall with snow drifts taller than horses.

A comfortable fire warmed his office and kept the chill out. It was not a large fire, especially when compared to the size of the hearth it burned in. Alex had examined the elegant granite fireplace surround several times, and still could not find a single seam. The entire thing was made from one large chunk of granite. Just thinking of how the thing had been moved made Alex's back sore. Lost in the flickering flames, he was tempted to brush the mountains of reports into the hearth, and not for the first time that morning. He'd even be satisfied with half the pile going up in flames.

Alex had taken on the responsibilities of a council composed of multiple councilors, each performing a share of the work. As a single monarch, Alex had to comb through all the reports on his own. Surely there were aides to assist with this sort of thing?

One missive lay on what had been the only bare surface at the center of the desk. Alex had read over the parchment no less than ten times. The contents of the message were difficult to believe, but how could he doubt something written in the hand of Queen Lara of Evellion? Before opening the message, he had run a finger over the unbroken wax seal, feeling the impression of an eagle, the royal seal of Evellion, authenticating the author.

The queen's message implored the recently restored Kingdom of Thellion for help. She asked that the provinces of Perrien and Parendior rein in their renegade army in the Cyrillean Pass, the army led by the king's own uncle, General Lex Telvin, and defend Evellion from the encroaching giants discovered in the mountains.

Alex recalled Tye journeying through Dwota's Gap to warn the Lucillian Alliance of giants making their way east, but that had been two years ago. He held the parchment, still not quite believing the words scrawled across the page in the queen's fluid script. He knew better than to doubt her words, but the idea of an army of giants managing to stay unnoticed for two years was difficult to swallow.

Even if the giants did remain hidden in the Vespien Mountains, surely at least one recluse hermit would have noticed them. Although, being recluse hermits, they probably would not have told anyone. And the queen did not speak of a single giant, but an army of them, marching toward Everin. Alex couldn't believe that not a single person had identified the giants until now—Eklean's population was not insignificant.

Unfortunately, the message failed to mention whether the giants traveled in the company of a shadow elf. It also didn't state how many giants marched for Everin. Granted, if any scouts had drawn close enough to the band of giants to count them, they likely would not have escaped with their lives, especially if a shadow elf were among the number. Soon to be besieged on two fronts, the Evellion queen sought the aid of her nearest potential ally, even if that ally's only notable act had been ousting the Perrien Council while their army sieged Everin.

The death of King Amry this past year was still difficult to believe. Lex's army had not breached the city, and they still had managed to assassinate the Evellion king. Despite the Evellions remaining strong, the shock must have crippled them. Alex knew Amry and Lara had two or three children, but he had never learned their names or their ages. Lara and Amry were by no means old, and their eldest child could not surpass his own age, and that only if they had begun having children when they first married.

Surely, one of them is a boy and the heir. The laws of Thellish succession, which Evellion still held true to, dictated that the eldest son was the heir.

A marble plinth stood in the center of the room, an intricate crown of white gold, silver, and the largest diamonds Alex had ever seen resting on it. Aewen had ensured that the crown of Thellion had been returned to its rightful bearer. Alex could only bear the weight of it for an hour, and even that was too long. Fortunately, he only had to don the crown during official state business. Lost in his thoughts as he gazed at the crown, Alex barely heard a knock at the door.

The knock came a second time, but instead of waiting for a reply, Aen just came in.

"Were you staring at it again?" he asked.

Alex had forbidden him from using a title when they were alone. He had grown tired of everyone addressing him as 'Your Majesty,' especially behind closed doors.

Aen carried a stack of parchment under his arm.

"More reports?" Alex ignored Aen's question even as he dreaded the answer to his own.

"Yes. And official letters." Aen heaved the stack onto Alex's desk, handing one directly to Alex. "You'll like this one though; it's a complaint from Crifton. He wants his old quarters returned to him."

Taking the parchment in hand, Alex skimmed its contents. Alex had wanted to toss the deposed councilors into the deepest and darkest cells beneath the castle, but they were still important dignitaries, and despite losing their councilor positions, they had been given accommodations in the palace as appropriate to their former stations. Most of the councilors had retained their own apartments although under house arrest. Linus Crifton, however, had occupied the royal apartments, and had been given much more modest accommodations, which he instantly refused as below him. The reaction had brought a pleasant grin to Alex.

This latest was another complaint. "He just won't give up."

"You should toss him in the dungeons—I don't think they have stationery down there." Aen frowned.

Aen was right and tossing Crifton into the dungeons would relieve a significant amount of the mountain of parchment on his desk. Alex still had not decided on a final judgment for the deposed councilors. Horrendous crimes had been committed under their directives, their supposed care for their own people clearly revealed as non-existent in that very first walk through New Gneal.

Unfortunately, exile was not an option, for they would take Perrien's secrets south to Broid and hand deliver them to Emperor Erynor if they had not already sold them to the Erynien Empire along with their dignity.

"When's my next meeting?

"We should probably leave now; they'll be waiting for us."

"Very well."

Taking Queen Lara's letter, Alex left his office with Aen on his heels. Three of his knights tucked in behind them to escort him through the castle. It still seemed strange to Alex, five months since taking Gneal, that he had gone from owning nothing except what he wore on his back and what his family extended to him, to possessing more worldly wealth than any person in Cor'lera could fathom, except perhaps his mother. He was the reinstated King of Thellion.

Alex had earlier shared the contents of Queen Lara's missive, although no one else had seen the actual parchment. Now, a few generals, Arlyn, Prince Sanjin, several ei'ana, and for a reason he could not fathom, Abbie Wintyr waited for Alex in the war room. Maps of Evellion and Perrien and detailed maps of mountain passes leading to Everin and the tunnels through her surrounding mountains were strewn across the table in the center of the room. The tunnels had been blocked for three years now, and there was no way that he was going to have an army scale the side of a mountain.

As he drew near the table, a resounding, "Your Majesty" echoed through the room. Alex was still surprised to hear it, having to remember that the title was addressed to him, and not someone walking in behind him.

"Are we certain the message is not a forgery?" Karl asked. The son of Gneal was now a general, appointed by Alex the moment he'd been named king.

"To what end would someone write a forgery?" Oliver asked.

"To draw us out of Gneal so they can retake the city." Karl planted his arms on the tabletop. "What better way to make us leave the city than go to provide assistance to an ally."

"Might I see the actual message?" Reia said, although she wasn't asking permission.

Alex handed over the letter as though it was a homework assignment.

Reia studied the message, her eyes lingering on the broken wax seal. "If this is a forgery, it's the finest I've ever seen. Remember, Lara is not only the Queen of Evellion, but also an Azurelle ei'ana; few can forge our correspondences." She handed it to Sara, who took a quick look then handed it to Arlyn.

"But giants…" Arlyn said, trailing off. The room grew quiet. Fighting a giant was beyond their combined experience.

"I cannot speak about giants, but I would presume their fighting style is similar to that of the ogres," Prince Sanjin answered. "We will have to take them by surprise and wipe them out quickly. The moment they learn of our presence, they will attack and will destroy whatever barricade is in their path, which, let me assure you, they *will* obliterate."

"How are we to stop them, especially up in the mountains?" Karl glared across the table. "We can't lead a cavalry charge up a mountain, let alone get our horses there to begin with."

"Perhaps we could find a way to stop them in their tracks," Sara said, her attention on the map.

"What are you proposing?" Arlyn asked.

"The Vespien Mountains have never been known as hospitable, especially the crags surrounding Everin. The people who built that city, Elothkar's refugees, all those years ago, sought a place where they could rebuild safely. I know we're talking about giants, but there has to be some way to stop them before they reach Everin. I'm not suggesting building another wall, but what if we amplified a crevice that is already in their path, making their passage all but impossible?"

Alex absently scratched his chin, considering Sara's idea. "Will your counsels permit you to wield such chasms?"

"As long as we are not directly inflicting damage on anyone that is not causing us harm."

"If you think the dwarves will allow us to trench into their mountains, you have another think coming," Reia said.

"Why wouldn't the dwarves want us to stop the giants?" Alex asked.

"Tera's Treaty. Legend says that when humans began to climb the mountains and settle on them, the dwarves tried to fight them off, but before war could unfold, the enthiel, Tera, intervened in the affairs of dwarf and human. Everything below belongs to the dwarves, and everything above to the humans," Sara said.

"To delve into the surface is to break that treaty and breaking a treaty with the dwarves will bring unwanted conflict," Reia said.

"Can we get the dwarves to help?" Alex asked. The room fell quiet. Unable to make eye contact, Alex noticed how everyone was suddenly enthralled with the maps on the table. "What am I not being told?"

"The dwarven schtams have done everything imaginable to remain isolated from this war," Reia said. "Even with a besieged Everin, rather than assist their closest human ally, they have sealed their tunnels into the city and have severed any contact."

"How do we get their attention?"

"Oern Schtam has always maintained the best relations with humans. If the King of Thellion appears in Belin's Watch, they would be hard pressed to reject him."

"That might work. How soon can we leave for Belin's Watch?" Karl asked.

"Are we decided already?" Alex asked, disturbed at how quickly they had agreed on the course of action.

Before Karl or anyone else could respond, a messenger came in. Alex didn't recognize him but took note of the worried expression on the man's face. The messenger made a quick bow to Alex before placing a rolled-up parchment in his hand. Alex recalled that the practice was that the messenger would have memorized the message in case it was destroyed. The man needed to learn to control his expression though, because it was clear that the message brought news of a serious problem.

And having the message brought directly to him was odd, as protocol insisted that all messages and reports were to be delivered to his office. A hint of irritation arose, partly due to the messenger's apparent inexperience, but also because this message had no wax seal, instantly degrading its importance.

> *To His Majesty, Alexander of House Vaerin,*
>
> *Twelve foreign ships with red sails have docked along the Skrein coast, nine leagues north of the Vespien Mountains. They have begun building a settlement using forced labor. The slaves appear native to Perrien, farmers and villagers from along the coast.*
>
> *Scout Rodney*

The room waited in silence as Alex read the message, his mouth gaping. Arlyn stood closest to his left, and a stunned Alex handed the parchment to the ei'ceuril. He moved to the table to examine a Perrien map, following the routes toward the Skrein Sea. The northern sea was rumored to freeze over in the winter months, making maritime travel impossible.

The maps on the table did not show where the Skrein Sea emptied out. He did not know if it was surrounded by land, or if it connected to another ocean. That corner of Eklean was largely forgotten.

The message worked its way around the room, surprising everyone except Prince Sanjin. "So, they desire to stretch their greedy paws even more outward."

"You know these ships with the red sails?" Reia asked, seeming to accuse the Charrenese prince of something.

"You told me once you were not completely ignorant about those lands." Sanjin pinned Reia with his dark eyes. His right hand disappeared into his loose jacket and retrieved a red gem. Reia and Sara gawked at the dimly glowing crystal.

"Is that one of your arcane gems?" Arlyn asked.

"A lesser one. The red gems have the smallest amount of power. They're mostly used for relaying information, as they are capable of holding and transferring thousands of images and messages," Sanjin answered and the red light expanded outward to display a beautiful city of slender towers and sprawling domes.

Alex blinked at the image of two land masses near one another, separated by a narrow body of water. The city was situated in the center of the sea, not floating on the water, but at least two hundred feet above the water's surface. There were no chains from above to hold the city aloft, nor pillars from below.

"Karithel," Prince Sanjin said, looking upon his home. "The Kilnae Del monitor the arcane gems set in those slender pillar-like towers, ensuring the city maintains a constant and steady elevation. But that is not what I wanted to show you."

The lighted city shrank in size as the two land masses on either side grew.

Alex was unfamiliar with either, but they eventually formed two continents.

"The northern continent is Ogren, the southern is Daereneth, home of the Daer Empire. They've built their *free* empire by oppressing others, enslaving their neighbors and carting them off in chains. The Daer tend to focus their efforts on Ogren and Ja'Horan, but it appears they are seeking to expand their influence on Eklean now."

"There's only one course of action," Karl started. "We'll have to push them off our coasts and retrieve our citizens; their actions are an act of war and we'll have to respond appropriately."

"And abandon Queen Lara's request?" Oliver asked.

"We can't ignore a foreign invasion, particularly one that enslaves our own in the process," Karl said.

"So, it's agreed, Thellion cannot do both," Sara said.

"Perhaps it would be worthwhile for me to investigate, until we devise a course of action for Evellion." The image from Sanjin's arcane gem disappeared. "I won't drive them off your land, as doing so would be the spark they need to declare war on my father. But I can find out what they are doing here and what they want."

"That would be helpful," Reia commented, appraising Sanjin as though she still didn't completely trust him. "We should also send a message to Lucillia. The Luminari elves—Devlyn in particular—could help us sway the dwarves to join our cause and defend Everin."

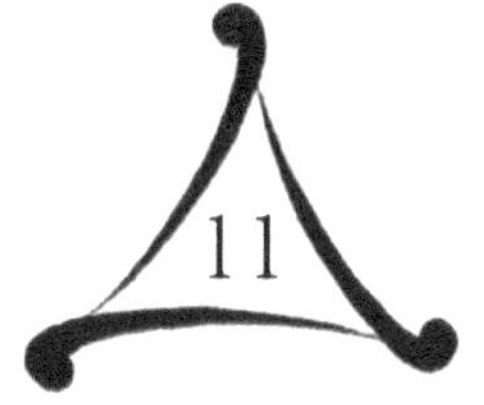

Deteriorating

The intricate vines sprouting silver and gold flowers that formed the dome of the Lucillian throne room were different from the last time Devlyn had gazed up in wonder. Half the petals had shifted to green, and the vines themselves grew wilder, more naturally, as though they no longer were magically cultivated. Devlyn felt as though he stood in a forest now, more than in a throne room as before.

He was not alone. Dozens of nobles filled the space and although King Harnyl Roendryn sat on his throne, his body was slumped and he appeared much older without Vernal sitting next to him. Devlyn was amazed that he had been able to deliver the speech to introduce Devlyn as a Lorenthien to the Luminari elves. Whatever strength he had preserved to be able to deliver that speech and then sit through the banquet had been spent, and Devlyn didn't think he would ever stand on his own again. Harnyl was fading as quickly as the Protection of the Wood was and Lucillia with them both.

Devlyn had arrived in Lucillia only two weeks ago, and even during that short time he had noticed a difference in the buildings. The city woven from trees of the Illumined Wood was rapidly returning to its origins. Many of the elves feared that a building or bridge would abruptly return to the forest while occupied by an unlucky elf or two. Devlyn, distressed at the increasing speed of the changes, had suggested a gathering of the nobles and aryls to discuss leaving Lucillia for Krysenthiel. As

Harnyl had stated before he introduced Devlyn to the Luminari as their future Exalted Aryl, their pilgrimage in Lucillia was coming to an end.

They had agreed, some of them somewhat reluctantly, and now the last of the nobles had finally arrived for the discussion. Only the aryls were permitted to speak, but the final decision rested with the aryl of the Luminari. As there currently was no such aryl in that capacity, the decision became more of a diplomatic endeavor since the other aryls gained more authority in the absence of an Exalted Aryl. Even though Harnyl still sat on the Lucillian throne, he was no longer a Roendryn aryl, because his wife had died. Since Devlyn had met the various aryls at the banquet, he had an idea as to some of the points that would be made during the discussion. Most of the elven nobility were kind and looked forward to the return of a Lorenthien sitting on the Crystal Throne, but others, such as the Narielles, doubted they would ever return to Arenthyl, and the talk around that meant that the gathering would be a lengthy one.

"Under what pretense do you believe we can do what no other has been able to do in fourteen hundred years?" Ei'denai Iridil Taerinior asked.

"I have already managed to pierce the Shroud once, proving that it is possible to disperse it," Devlyn answered, trying to keep his temper under control. Ellendren had warned him of the dire consequences if the Luminari aryls noticed any weakness or fault in him. Patience and understanding were of the utmost importance right now.

"You pierced it? And how large was this hole you created? A league? Perhaps two? Does it reach the skies?" Silvia clicked her tongue.

"Roughly the size of a large tree canopy, but it does go all the way up." Devlyn replied, aware that every noble in the room had already known that. It was a repeat of a discussion that had already occurred.

"You want us to leave our lands, our homes, based on an action that provided no more than a few paces of cleared space," Ei'denai Ciraenth Ginielle said.

"For fourteen hundred years, we believed the Shroud was immutable—that myth has been shattered. We now know that we can rid it from our world and we will, together," Ellendren said. Neither she nor Devlyn had express authority to speak, but the unusual circumstances surrounding their status prevented anyone from silencing them.

"My dear, you are loved and respected by us all, but how can we so willingly abandon our only defensible position for the open plains between here and Krysenthiel? Assuming we reach the Shroud safely, and that's a large assumption, we'll be vulnerable until we are able to remove the Shroud. And there is no proof that we will do so. We might very well be walking into an open slaughter." From the nods that accompanied the words of Ei'denai Kyiel Lauriel, a kindly older elf, many others agreed.

"Might as well put our shackles on ourselves and walk straight to Broid," Toral said.

Devlyn watched Harnyl look up from his slumped posture, as though he wanted to say something, but did not have the strength.

"We are just as exposed if we stay here," Ei'denai Therrin Reyndien said. "The entire east wall of my palace has returned to the Illumined Wood. How long before the outer walls protecting Lucillia do the same?"

"Actually, they have already started to fade," a young elf not much older than Devlyn said.

"You do not have the authority to speak in this chamber," snapped Silvia.

"As Lady of the Watch and as regards Lucillia's defenses, Toryn has every right, Ei'terel," the Lord Knight said. "Please continue, Toryn." Devlyn had only met Byron once but had learned that he was Vernal's brother and therefore Ellendren's uncle. Silvia sneered and looked to her husband for support.

"A northeastern section of the outer wall has thinned considerably," Toryn said. "Judging by the rate of the thinning, the wall will be compromised within the week. It's only a matter of time before the rest of the wall catches up with it. We're expecting that there will be dozens of similar breaches in the outer wall by the end of Estlenth, if not sooner. In addition to those concerns, the Protection of the Wood is nearly gone. Anyone who wishes can go through any of the large holes in it. Those holes are growing larger by the day."

"Why have we not had prior notice of this?" Ei'terel Enoria Taerinior asked.

"Among other reasons, that is one purpose for this gathering. The wall's return to the Illumined Wood was just discovered a few days ago. Its rapid deterioration is one of the reasons why we called this meeting and did not wait for our scheduled meeting," Byron said. "If we decide to remain here, we will have nothing above our heads at night but the forest canopy, and nothing to protect us from the Erynien Empire but our swords and bows, the same defenses we will have if we journey to the Shroud."

"We at least have a future if we travel to the Shroud," Ei'terel Binoral Clarion said.

"As the prophecy dictated, our time here was but a pilgrimage," added Ei'terel Valerie Aerquin, garnering more support for traveling west.

"Do we know why the Protection of the Wood is failing and taking our home with it?" Kyiel asked.

"The Protection of the Wood is a gift of the Illumined Wood, but the forest does not sustain it," Alethea said, eyes closed. "Servants of Shadow would have found it difficult to pierce the protective barrier from the outside."

"Are you implying that there are servants of Shadow inside Lucillia?" Silvia asked.

"I'm not suggesting it; I'm informing you that a branch of the Luminari have turned to the Evil One. His lies and sickness are eating away at the Protection of the Wood and quickening its demise. This city will not survive its collapse."

The throne room was stunned into silence at Alethea's pronouncement, shortly followed by cries of denial and oaths to Anaweh. The conversation eventually returned to leaving Lucillia.

"I will not agree to leave this place until I have proof that Devlyn is in fact a Phaedryn, something which has yet to be demonstrated to any of us," Toral said.

"It is not a party trick, Toral," Valerie remonstrated. "Besides, look at his eyes. Only the Phaedryn have ever been recorded to possess golden eyes. And on top of that, our own Ellendren and Kaela Roendryn have both vouched for him. What further evidence do we need? It's not like the Roendryns would willingly hand over their right to rule."

Devlyn's pulse quickened. Not only was he unable to reach out to Aliel, but their connection also had regressed to such a degree that he couldn't even locate the phoenix. For all he knew, Aliel could be in this World-Below, the World-in-Between, or the World-Beyond. He felt empty without Aliel. He could not even enter that quiet place within his heart without the wound on his back splitting open.

"What happened? How were you a Phaedryn one day, and not even able to show us the phoenix the next?" Enoria said, ignoring Valerie.

Her words felt like a sword through his heart.

"The strength of the Luminari never dwelt in the Phaedryn," said Viren, speaking for the first time. "The phoenix came to us based on the strength and virtue we already possessed, most evident in Kien and Kiara."

"And who are you to speak among our number?" Silvia asked, jerking upright at Viren's words. Devlyn's heart froze at the insult.

"You really have grown young," said Alethea, musing more to herself than remonstrating those present. Silvia heard the comment though, and stared daggers at the ancient Eldinari. Devlyn could see that she struggled not to speak out against someone as distinguished as Alethea, once an ei'terel and aryl among the Eldinari. The Luminari aryls could barely fathom her age and the wisdom that came with it.

"My name is Viren Dekenurel. I'm a Guardian knight, and along with ninety-nine others, I was sworn by Ei'terel Ithendryl Lorenthien herself to forsake my kin as they were slaughtered and enslaved by the Erynien Empire over fourteen hundred years ago to protect the last phoenix egg." Viren spoke calmly despite the insult.

Silvia melted into her chair. Everyone knew who the Guardian knights were—the once sworn protectors of not only the Luminari, but all Teraeniel when the Guardian Senate had existed. They answered only to the senators who represented every nation around the globe, with the Lorenthien aryl as prefect of the senate. The aryls and lesser nobles whispered excitedly among themselves. The existence of the Guardian knights was a boon none believed possible. Their prowess was long believed extinct, dying out with the Lorenthiens.

But Silvia refused to give up "As Luminari aryls, we have the right to know why you won't or can't give us a demonstration."

Devlyn's blood boiled, and he struggled to reply politely. "When I was struck by a bolt of tenebrys wielded by Aren and a Deurghol, something happened," Devlyn admitted without explaining that he feared Aliel's loss might be permanent. Ellendren placed a hand on his arm in comfort. He had not even said it to her, the reality too painful for him to voice. Only Wyn knew the whole of it. Keeping his emotions in check, he managed to stop several tears from rolling down his cheeks. He could not allow the Luminari aryls to see their future Exalted Aryl so weak. The confession quieted the room.

"With your permission, Ei'ethil Lorenthien," Viren said using a formality Devlyn rarely associated with the Guardian knight. "I would return to the Guardian knights' keep and have the remaining knights prepare for the arrival of the Luminari elves on the outskirts of Krysenthiel. We no longer number a hundred, but short of a Deurghol and an entire army, there are enough of us to fend off any that dare test us."

Thankful for the change of topic, Devlyn looked to the Luminari aryls. "This decision does not belong to me alone," he said, finding strength and resolve.

"How many Guardian knights still walk Teraeniel?" Iridil asked.

"Eighty-nine."

"And you are certain they can defend us?" Ei'terel Zara Reyndien asked.

"They would supplement the strength already here, and possibly train those who desire to join our numbers."

"Then, are we agreed?" Ei'denai Naesiv Aerquin asked.

"Under a single condition," Silvia said. "That the Lorenthien heir assures us that he will do everything in his power to reestablish his connection with the phoenix."

"Ei'terel Narielle," Devlyn said as respectfully as he could, "that vow was made the moment I could not bond with Aliel."

Silva grunted and the aryls dispersed, leaving the Lucillian throne room in noisy chatter as it emptied. Many questioned whether the Aren that Devlyn had mentioned was the same Aren Lorenthien that had vanished on Aldinare when the elves had fled the Darkness that was consuming their Skylands.

Viren had left Lucillia on a griffin immediately following the meeting's conclusion, leaving Devlyn without his sworn protector once again. Devlyn sincerely hoped that it would not be another five months before he saw the Guardian knight again.

After the meeting, Devlyn had gone to the palace's library. Walking through the aisles, he searched the bookshelves seeking any information that could give him an advantage. Although the library was part of the palace complex, it was available to any of Lucillia's citizens, at least during visiting hours. The library had its own entrance, separate from the royal residences. The librarians had already begun removing and packing the tomes from their shelves, carefully organizing them into crates. Whether or not the Luminari agreed to leave Lucillia, the library was fading and the books were in jeopardy if left on the shelves.

Devlyn was not entirely certain what he was looking for, but after his failed battle against the Deurghol and Aren, he hoped to find something about the verathn. Stories of the fabled weapons of power were passed down through the ages, stories re-enacted by small children playing with sticks, pretending they were Guardian knights with their legendary verathn. Viren had never mentioned who created the verathn, nor how he had obtained his. Swords like Viren's had not been seen since Krysenthiel had fallen. It was rumored that Erynor had gathered every verathn from the fallen knights and then corrupted them to his own designs.

Devlyn had considered going to the royal armory and asking for a proper sword, but then he decided to do what Ellendren would have done and looked for a book. The problem with this method was that he had no idea what he was looking for. He was about to leave the library to find Ellendren and ask her when he saw Alethea walking among the bookshelves.

"Never expected to see you here," he said, hoping for a chuckle from the ancient elf.

"It's not what these tomes contain, but the knowledge that is not here, that has been forgotten, that interests me." Devlyn didn't know how to respond. The library certainly looked impressive to him. "What half-truth are you hoping to discover here?"

"I was hoping to find something that could give me an advantage the next time I came across a Deurghol or Aren. The Deathless had a corrupted verathn, and I had no means of fighting him in Lankor since that black stone prevented me from wielding the erendinth. All I could do was flee."

"Perhaps you are searching in the wrong place."

"Do you know where I can get a verathn?" he asked, hopeful.

Alethea smiled, a small attempt to reassure Devlyn. "I was not referring to a location in Teraeniel. That which you require lies within—it has always been there, if out of balance." Devlyn was all too familiar with Alethea's philosophy, but there was no time for it, especially since he could not bond with Aliel. "There are rumors, but they are old." Alethea calling something old almost made Devlyn laugh. "Are you familiar with the Monastery of Kyrendal and the monks who live there along the slopes of Mount Saecrien?"

"I think they took in my sister, Leilyn, and cared for her after she fled Cor'lera."

"That sounds like them," Alethea said, still walking among the shelves so that Devlyn had to follow her if he wished to continue the conversation. "There's an unverified rumor, as I said it's old, that the one who first discovered how to create verathn dwells there. The same rumor claims the monastery was named after him." There was nothing abnormal about that. "It also claims that he knew Kien and Kiara." Devlyn froze in place even as Alethea continued to walk on.

"That would make him ancient," he said to her back. She turned to face him again.

"Indeed. If the rumor is true, even I would appear a youth standing next to him."

Devlyn vaguely remembered what his sister had told him of the Saecrien monks, how they had taken a vow of nonviolence, departed the world to live in solitude, and how their lives were not wrought into Ceurendol. Still, could this Kyrendal really have known Kien and Kiara, the legendary elves that first bonded with the phoenix and by extension, the first wielders?

"Do you think they'll help us?" he asked, avoiding his other questions.

"I cannot say, but I believe much will be revealed if we go there." Alethea put a hand on one of the books on the shelf next to her. "I have not walked among those trees for far too long now, and I have always wanted to visit that blessed mount."

Newly determined, Devlyn left Alethea in the library, and went to find Ellendren. Although the palace was largely a single level, that did not make finding anyone in the palace a simple task. He first checked the throne room, thinking she might be with her father, but it was empty, save the ever-changing petals. He knocked at the door to her quarters, but there was no answer.

It occurred to him that he might have to wait to tell her what he had decided, but Devlyn did not consider himself a patient elf, so he continued his search, which became more of a directionless stroll through the fading palace. He checked the various courtyards, overflowing with beautiful gardens, before finding his way to the circular chamber where Lucillia's statue stood on a plinth at the center of a small pond. The jewel of faith had rested in her outstretched palm for centuries, undisturbed, until Devlyn had taken it.

Ellendren sat at the edge of the pond, her legs soaking in the water, her gaze fixed on the statue of Lucillia.

"You look like her," Devlyn said, approaching and then sitting down beside her.

"You're too kind," she replied, her voice quiet.

"And you're beautiful," he said, blushing as the words left his lips.

She smiled, not at him, but toward the statue. "And you're a flirt."

"I need to go to Mount Saecrien, to the Monastery of Kyrendal."

"Do you? What of the Luminari?"

"They've managed without me before."

"They have, but they know you now, and even though you are not yet their Exalted Aryl, they already hold you to those standards. They will not look favorably on you abandoning them."

"I'm not abandoning anyone."

"You would abandon me, to remain with them while you go to the monks."

His tongue stuck to the roof of his mouth. Her accusation caught him off guard, but even as she spoke it, he felt the truth of it, the necessity of one of them staying with the Luminari. Her father was too weak to speak for his people, let alone guide them from Lucillia to Krysenthiel through the swiftly approaching winter months.

"I used to come to this place with my mother as a child. I remember looking up at the wooden statue of Lucillia, and praying for her blessing, that I might one day be as brave as she. Devlyn, I care for you and I will, of course, support you. I cannot see the future, but if we are to become the Exalted Aryl of Krysenthiel, our decisions must be made by us both."

"I never meant…"

Placing two fingers on his lips to quiet him, Ellendren looked into his golden eyes. "Do what you must. When you return, I fear there will not be a Lucillia to return to, nor will there be a people here waiting for you. We cannot stay here and wait for you to return."

Before Devlyn could respond, a royal attendant entered the chamber and bowed in apology for interrupting them.

"Ei'lythel," he addressed Ellendren.

"Yes?"

"His Majesty requires you. He is failing. Your presence would soothe his transition to Lumaeniel. Your sister is already with him."

"Thank you." A tear rolled down her cheek and she looked at the wooden statue of Lucillia once more.

"I'll come with you," Devlyn said, holding her hand.

They followed the knight through the palace and to the aryl's private quarters. Devlyn noted that here too, the royal apartment was returning to the forest.

Harnyl lay in a silk-covered bed, his face gaunt, his breathing strained, the rise and fall of his chest barely shifting the blankets.

Ellendren moved quickly to his side, next to Kaela whose face was wet with tears. Devlyn approached the bed, but hung back a bit, supporting Ellendren by his presence but not encroaching on the sisters' last moments with their father.

"Oh, Elle, he's going fast."

Harnyl's eyes fluttered open, straining to look at his daughters. "Where is…my…" He could not finish.

"Aaron's at the Temple of Ceur, father. He's the Ceurtriarch, don't you remember?" Ellendren said, tears rolling down her face.

"His mother…would be…so proud." Harnyl managed a smile for his daughters. "Don't…cry. I can…feel…Ana…weh's warmth. The Light…calls…me home."

His daughters stilled—hoping their father was still with them. A final breath escaped Harnyl Roendryn, and with it, his eyes closed and the room darkened.

Shocked silence replaced the sound of the fading breath, broken only by the sobs of his daughters.

Devlyn wrapped his arm around the elf who had claimed his heart for her own, his own heart aching at her pain. Knowing what it was to lose a parent, Devlyn's sorrow for Ellendren was deep. A forgotten memory swelled inside him, a toddler crying as he lay on top of his unresponsive father.

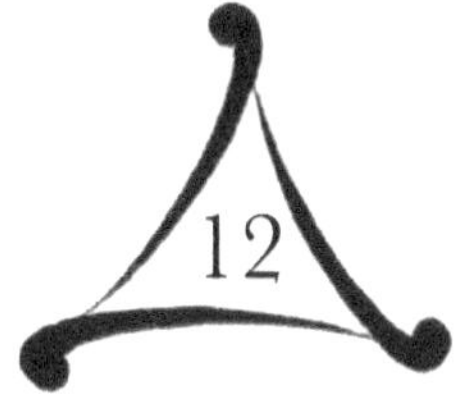

INTO THE WOOD

No hint of sun broke through the forbidding clouds above to honor Harnyl Roendryn as he was placed in the ground behind the royal palace, or rather, where the royal palace had once stood. As was customary for the elves, as soon as the last dirt was placed over the grave, a tree sprouted above his remains, identical to the one that stood over the remains of his wife, Vernal Roendryn. The bodies of the last Aryl of Lucillia rested beneath the ground of Teraeniel, while their spirits traveled to Lumaeniel, the World-Beyond.

Hundreds of other graves lay nearby, each with a tree rising above, creating a forested area. Older trees of earlier aryls had intertwined, weaving into a single canopy above.

Devlyn stood with his arm wrapped around a shaking Ellendren. Her parents had sacrificed their lives for their people. The Protection of the Wood had been tied to them both, its rising demanding Vernal's life, and with its fading, taking Harnyl.

Where the palace had stood but a week before, now only the towering trees of the Illumined Wood rose. The Pilgrim City of Light, Lucillia, was no more. Following the king's death, the entire city had wailed and groaned, much of it fading quickly into the trees it had once been. When Harnyl had been placed in the ground, whatever still held the city together had snapped. It had been a docile transition. But, even so, nothing of Lucillia remained, save the wooden statue of Lucillia herself, standing at the center of the gentle pool.

Strewn about the forest floor were the scattered belongings of the elves, their homes now gone. The Lucillians themselves were somewhat distraught as they struggled with ensuring that their possessions were protected, packing what they would take with them to Krysenthiel, many of them hopeful yet also cynical about their journey. The librarians were the most frantic as they had only managed to pack and categorize half of the library. Many books and scrolls lay unprotected on the forest floor as they rushed to encase what they could before any damage occurred. Although everyone had known that the city had been returning to the Illumined Wood, no one had expected that it would take place so quickly.

For Devlyn, none of that mattered at present. All he cared about was supporting Ellendren in whatever way she needed. He knew he had to undertake an important journey before he could join her on the caravan to Krysenthiel, but he could not bear leaving her so soon after her father's death.

Ellendren turned her head, her silky hair brushing across his cheek. "It's time, Devlyn."

He didn't respond and rubbed the small of her back instead.

"Go now but return as quickly as you can. I fear Erynor knows our intentions, so I don't know what we'll face as we cross Sorenthil."

Devlyn wrapped both arms around her, pulling her into a warm embrace, hoping his touch would protect her from the increasingly cold weather outside the forest, even if only for a brief while. He knew the journey would be difficult. Moving an entire population during the winter months promised nothing but trials. After all, Lucillia wasn't the only Luminari settlement. Dozens of villages, towns, and smaller cities were scattered up and down the Illumined Wood's edges.

He looked down at Ellendren just as she looked up at him, and without having intended it, their lips found each other's. Hers were warm and smooth, and he worried that his chapped lips would irritate her, so he pulled back sooner than he'd have liked. He could go on kissing her forever. Their lips parted, her arms loosened their hold around his waist and she stepped away.

Devlyn felt his heart catch in his throat, and he struggled to speak but his emotions were too strong, so he stood looking at her, trying to say something, anything.

"I'll see you when you return," she said, turning away to walk among the trees marking the final resting place of her forebears.

Devlyn wanted to call out to her to wait, that there was something important he wanted to tell her. But he had no idea what exactly that was.

Wyn and Alethea came up to him as he watched Ellendren walk away.

"You look like you've fallen in love," Wyn said, waving his hand in front of Devlyn's face.

"I think I have."

Alethea remained silent, just looking about her at the trees around them, Eolwn and Leithel at her side. The two griffins waited patiently to move on.

The last time Devlyn had left Lucillia, Ellendren's mother had died, although he hadn't understood at the time that raising the Protection of the Wood meant that she would pass on. Now that he was leaving again, it pained him that her father had also gone. Turning from what was once Lucillia, he began to walk further into the Illumined Wood, Wyn and Alethea behind him, mounting their griffins.

Stretching an arm to Devlyn, Wyn pulled him onto Eolwn's back, and the pair of griffins flew up toward the canopy of the Illumined Wood.

Flying from dawn to dusk became their daily routine. Alethea insisted that they stop briefly at certain points without explaining why it was necessary.

The Illumined Wood was as Devlyn remembered it. Trees taller than any he had ever seen stretched into the sky, rivaling the towers of

Gwilnor. The green leaves with secretive hints of silver and gold, only visible from the corner of his eye, glinted as he passed. Birds soared through the trees with them for a time, before the griffins' swifter pace left them behind.

Devlyn had no idea where Mount Saecrien and the Monastery of Kyrendal were, but Alethea led them with purpose through the trees. She kept the griffins far below the canopy, but high enough above the ground that Devlyn felt uncomfortable not bonded to Aliel.

Eight days later, Alethea changed their direction, then flew on for a short while and landed in a small clearing. The sun was still visible through the multitude of leaves shading their heads, making Devlyn wonder why they were stopping so early. There was plenty of sunlight left to continue traveling.

Alethea dismounted and signaled that Wyn and Devlyn do likewise. She took a few steps to the nearest tree and placed one palm on the trunk.

It had been quite some time since Devlyn had seen the ancient elf tap her inner sense. He wondered what or who she might be communicating with—was it the trees, the monks, or perhaps even the centaurs? Tempted to join her and discover who or what she sought, Devlyn was distracted by the sound of footsteps on the leafy ground.

"Alethea Lenwyn, Child of Eldinare, the Illumined Wood welcomes you, as do the Saecrien monks." An elderly elf stepped out into the clearing.

"Kyrendal, you honor us by greeting us yourself," Alethea replied.

Age had touched Kyrendal differently than it had embraced Alethea. Neither had a trace of their original hair color, both now a wintry white with silver strands gleaming in the rays of the sun that managed to pierce the forest canopy. But where Alethea stood upright with her shoulders back, every bit the noble elf that she was, Kyrendal was slightly hunched over, and required a cane for support. Wrinkles etched his entire face and the parts of his body that weren't covered by his deep blue, almost black robes.

Turning away from Alethea toward Wyn, Kyrendal looked deep into his eyes. The encounter was brief but resulted in Wyn placing his hand over his heart to bow deeply, well past the angle of Kyrendal's stooped posture.

Devlyn felt Kyrendal before their eyes met. His heart and mind felt the elf's presence, a presence more ancient than Alethea, one that probed and plucked every part of him. Nothing of who he was remained private as Kyrendal unraveled his most intimate secrets. Devlyn felt affronted at the invasion until he sensed Kyrendal's being in exchange.

His rebellious mind quelled the moment he felt and understood the elf's identity. "It's true," Devlyn said, his words failing him.

A quick smile came to Kyrendal's face, his wrinkles multiplying with the movement.

"The truth within rumors surprises you?" Kyrendal asked. It was not an accusation, but something about it bore the same weight. He turned to Alethea. "You have taught him much, and it pains you that you cannot teach him everything he needs. Take consolation in knowing he is alive and thrives because of your influence." Kyrendal turned away from them and walked back through the trees in the direction he'd come.

There was no invitation to follow, but the three did so, while the griffins leapt up and soared out of sight. Devlyn watched them disappear into the leafy canopy.

Kyrendal walked surprisingly quickly for someone needing a cane, and they kept a moderate pace for nearly an hour before a simple portal rose before them. It was nothing more than an oversized wooden post and lintel not connected to a structure but standing along an invisible path. Ivy lined the ground here just as it did everywhere else in the Illumined Wood.

Kyrendal did not veer but continued along the path and Devlyn felt the ground begin to shift. The incline became more severe, and through the gaps in the trees and foliage he saw a wall of stone. He knew there were mountains in the Illumined Wood, but he had never imagined that he would reach them without ever noticing his surroundings change. The trees hid the top of the mountains, and they continued to grow sturdily from the stone and up the slopes.

He could hear cascading water in the distance, and after Kyrendal led them around a steep cliff, a clearing opened with the sun's rays falling on a slender waterfall, causing a rainbow of colors to brighten the surrounding stone. The water emptied into a pond that must have led to an underground river, for the pond remained the same size despite the waterfall.

They followed Kyrendal along the pond's edge and Devlyn was surprised when they went behind the watery curtain and into a tunnel. The tunnel was not long, and even from the entrance behind the waterfall, Devlyn could see the other end where sunlight flooded in.

The tunnel opened into a large valley surrounded by towering peaks on every side. Although Devlyn knew they were still in the Illumined Wood, here the trees were sparse among the grass, wildflowers, and fields bathed in the sunlight.

At the far end of the valley, a mountain rose twice the height of the others that formed the valley. Its peak disappeared in the clouds enshrouding its upper reaches, making it even more mysterious. It had to be the tallest he had ever seen.

"Welcome to Mount Saecrien, source of the river which flows from the heavens," Kyrendal said, gesturing at the impressive mountain.

Looking about the valley, Devlyn noticed many elves at work, tilling the land and caring for the crops. None of the valley's residents appeared young, and children were notably absent. Devlyn was easily the youngest present.

"There are monks here who have had children in the past, but now live a life of solitude," Kyrendal said, knowing Devlyn's thoughts better than Devlyn wished. "We are no longer Luminari, or ei'ana, or ei'ceuril as we once were when we came to this mountain, we became something entirely different. We no longer belong to this World-Below, we simply inhabit it until Anaweh calls us home. Here, we monks belong more to Lumaeniel than we do to Teraeniel."

"Is that why you're still alive? Why you didn't participate in the forming of the Jewel of Life?" Devlyn asked.

"It is—a number of us came here before Ceurendol was even conceived of by our brothers and sisters. Others came after Ceurendol was wrought and they have made their great transition into Anaweh's Light."

"Why did you come here?" Devlyn asked, walking beside Kyrendal at a slower pace than the one the elderly elf had set on their walk here. Alethea and Wyn followed behind, Wyn carefully paying attention as Kyrendal spoke. "Why did you leave everyone?"

"That is not the question on your heart."

The ancient elf was right. The question Devlyn desired an answer to was on the tip of his tongue, yet he feared to ask it.

"I cannot answer if you do not ask," Kyrendal said, his voice filled with compassion and understanding.

"Why have you never returned to your people? They were slaughtered or enslaved. You could've helped." Devlyn hadn't meant to sound accusatory and quickly apologized for his tone.

Not bothered by the question or Devlyn's tone, Kyrendal continued his slow walk through the valley, his cane lending support as he spoke. "I made a vow long ago to make reparations for my sins. I did not come here for solitude, and although we live in solitude, it is not for the sake of solitude. When I was young, and first learned to wield, I wanted nothing more than to become a Phaedryn, like my parents.

"In my pride, I wanted to display my abilities and strive to advance them, stretching for the stars. However, I was limited since a phoenix did not choose to bond with me. My parents claimed they were never ashamed that their son did not become a Phaedryn, but the shame was my own and fueled my eagerness to prove myself.

"I sought other avenues. They were neither dark nor sinister, but they were bent on power. After centuries of study and meditation, I learned to create the verathn. There was no need for verathn for we lived in peace on the Skyland of Luminare. The necessity of weapons was a callous avenue of study."

"They came in handy after the elves had to leave the Skylands though, right?"

"We did not need them, but we used them nonetheless," Alethea spoke up from behind Kyrendal, her words revealing just how old she was.

"Indeed." Kyrendal remained quiet for a time, stopping to look toward Mount Saecrien. "I continued to craft my verathn; from the sprouts of the Tree of Life, they were wrought. I sung my creations of death into existence. At one time, they only injured those who threatened the peace. Our kin never dealt a mortal blow, but there came a time at the height of Krysenthiel's power that someone used them to kill. I felt that killing blow as though I had dealt it and received it myself.

"It was only the beginning but I felt within my heart of hearts that thousands would soon die because of my part in bringing the verathn about. So terrible was the weight of regret, that I, and those who shared in my craft, fled Arenthyl, traveling as far east as we could go. With every day, I felt the slaughter of more and more. The torturous pain tore at me. I fell to my knees along the coast of the Unarian Sea, imploring Anaweh to take me, even knowing that I did not deserve to enter that blessed realm beyond.

"It was then that a girl approached me. She brought me and the others to this valley, asking us to tend it for her. The girl's identity was known to us, just as we knew her brother, and we told her we were unworthy to serve one such as she. In response, she said we were not serving her, but serving Anaweh as we cultivated a life of peace."

Overwhelmed by the information Kyrendal had shared, Devlyn

found himself lost for words as he digested everything the Saecrien monk told him.

"I know you seek a verathn, but my vow is immutable," Kyrendal said.

"But what of Erynor, the Deurghol, and the shadow elves? They're spreading darkness over all Eklean, killing and consuming spirits to elongate their own lives. If we don't fight them, everything will be lost," Devlyn said, more passionately than he'd intended.

"If by the sword you defend yourself; by the sword shall you live and die."

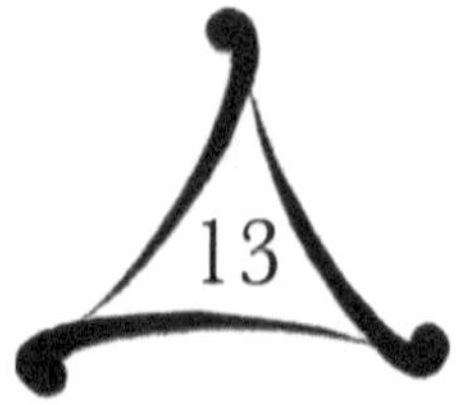

TURNING TOWARD

The road that joined what had been Lucillia with Erithel in Sorenthil was packed with a stream of wooden wagons that rolled along at a pace so slow that Ellendren's patience was sorely tried. She longed to let Laureniel fly, if only to be away from the dust and noise, but instead rode the alicorn beside Kaela and Byron who were astride horses. Keeping the alicorn on the ground and to the slow pace of the caravan was in recognition of her role among the Luminari from not just Lucillia but also the Luminari from the smaller settlements and villages along the edge of the Illumined Wood.

Both of her parents had passed and Ellendren was next in line to the Lucillian throne. However, that throne and kingdom no longer existed. If not for the resurgence of House Lorenthien, Ellendren would have followed the path her mother had taken and would have brought someone into House Roendryn as her husband, and together they would have become the next Aryl of Lucillia. Devlyn had changed everything. She had never expected that she would be the one to join a different house—she had never expected to come across a house more distinguished than her own. But Devlyn was a Lorenthien and the rightful heir to the Crystal Throne of Krysenthiel. While she was confident that she would be the next Exalted Aryl of Krysenthiel with him, an official betrothal had yet to be announced. She knew she could not act as the heir of the Lucillian throne anymore nor as the presumptive Exalted Aryl. Instead,

Ellendren had to be seen and loved by everyone. She had to be a leader-ship figure without an official title, at least until the betrothal. When the time came, the Luminari would eagerly place her on the Crystal Throne as the Exalted Aryl. So Ellendren rode on the ground with the rest of the Luminari.

Most of the elves could only walk along, ride on horseback, sit in carriages pulled by horses, or in wagons pulled by oxen. But Ellendren, accustomed to flying among the clouds and crossing the length of the continent in a fraction of the time normal horses could travel was grow-ing weary of the slow, steady pace. With vague thoughts on whether Lu-cillia's road network would wither with the rest of their faded kingdom, she also chafed at the necessity of protection due to her position. She stayed near her sister, but her uncle escorted her as well. She was con-vinced that others protecting her was a poor use of their resources. Sure-ly, they were needed elsewhere. She was training to become an ei'ana, so she was hardly defenseless.

Her ability with the erendinth outmatched most others', other than shadow elves, and Byron and his knights would provide little resistance to shadow elves, if any were to turn up. In addition to her own prowess as a wielder, Laureniel could easily get Ellendren away.

But Laureniel was part of the reason for the slow pace of the Luminari, who were fascinated at the sight of a winged unicorn and insisted on gawking, slowing the pace further. Seeing a unicorn would have been fantastical enough, but Laureniel was one of the few alicorns that had been spared the destructive fate of Aldinare. Ellendren was all too aware of the elves' recent skepticism, since many Luminari believed that the true elves had all died out, and that their pointy ears were simply reminders of their long-gone ancestors. So not only were unicorns ac-cepted as mythical creatures, but a unicorn with wings was a fabrication for children's fairy tales. Ellendren could only hope that seeing an alicorn would be enough to shake them back into the reality of who they truly were and what existed.

She could have ridden in the royal carriage—she was still a Roendryn—but Ellendren preferred not to spend her time inside it. While it was certainly luxurious, she preferred the fresh air and she also thought being seen was beneficial for the Luminari. And the pace of travel would be no faster. It had only been a week since Ellendren had led the Luminari elves away from the wooded remains of Lucillia. This exodus from Lucillia and the other Luminari settlements would be a treacherous one. The journey didn't just involve transporting the entire Luminari population away from the Illumined Wood, it meant a military campaign to protect their people, remove the Shroud, and reclaim Krysenthiel and their lost cities, if they still stood. The elves had filled their wagons to the brim with their belongings and prized possessions. This wasn't a simple move to a new city—which was not yet even accessible—but the elves had to bring their livelihoods and memories with them. Blacksmiths and tailors and librarians could not simply pack their belongings in a small knapsack for a minimalist journey.

In addition to carrying their worldly possessions, the monetary wealth of the elves was also accompanying them. Fortunately, the Goblin Guild managed most of Lucillia's finances and were overseeing the transport of the royal coffers and financial accounts of the Luminari as they moved toward their lost kingdom. The goblins had hired their own mercenary unit as an additional security measure. While they were clearly concerned about transporting an entire civilization's wealth, they were not overly concerned by the prospect of shadow elves. The goblins of the Kinzdol Islands maintained a meager alliance with the Erynien Empire, and even Erynor wasn't foolish enough to attack his own allies, especially when those same allies also managed his empire's wealth.

Even with the Goblin Guild's assistance, most of the elves had filled their purses with as many coins as possible. If bandits dared to attack the Luminari elves, they could potentially become very wealthy bandits although they'd have to be a large bandit company, since there was a military force of several thousand strong accompanying the elves on the move.

Ellendren was jolted out of her musings when she heard loud shouts coming from behind. A beautiful carriage had pulled out of its place in the caravan, and had carved a path past the slow wagons, the driver shooing wayward children and walkers out of the way to draw up beside Ellendren. She immediately recognized the large, gilded crest of House Narielle and groaned. *Why would anyone wish to draw attention to themselves when traveling?* Ellendren thought. Did they want a to attract the specific attention of bandits?

A linen drapery covering one of the carriage's windows was pushed aside and Silvia Narielle waved for Ellendren's attention, smiling insincerely. "Oh, Ellendren, dear, you must accompany us; you have to be dreadfully exhausted from riding in this wintery chill."

More than ever, Ellendren wanted to nudge Laureniel into the air and away from Silvia. Only a week after Devlyn, Alethea, and Wyn had gone, appalling rumors about him had reached her ears. The worst had claimed that he and Velaria, a Cyndinari who had infiltrated Septyl, had fabricated the entire story about his ability to wield with control, his Lorenthien background, and his link to a phoenix to become a Phaedryn. Even more outlandish, the rumors claimed that it was only through sinister means wrought by the Erynien Empire and not because he was an elya or a Phaedryn that he could wield the erendinth with control. The rumors also insinuated that documentation existed, certifying that the last Lorenthiens had indeed perished as slaves at Erynor's hands, making it impossible for Devlyn to belong to that exalted lineage, let alone be the legitimate heir as the youngest of the youngest child.

Investigating the source of the rumors would have been a waste of time. Not only were they already too widespread to put a stop to them, but the likely fabricator sat comfortably in her gilded carriage next to Ellendren.

She forced herself to smile, an ability she had mastered as a young girl when interacting with House Narielle. Decorum demanded that Ellendren accept Silvia's offer—to refuse was equivalent to slapping an aryl in public. Despite how much Ellendren wanted to do just that, she said instead, "You are too kind, Ei'terel."

"Please, call me Silvia. I'm still getting accustomed to these new, or rather, old titles. And just because you are no longer a princess, does not mean our relationship need change."

Furious at the woman sitting in the carriage, Ellendren almost embraced the erendinth and wielded ignys to set the carriage aflame. But years of politics and private instructions from her mother had taught her how to interact with people like Silvia, even though the training did not make it easy to stomach the vile woman. Kaela, ever the polished diplomat, leaned over to place a soothing hand on her arm.

"Thank you, Silvia," Ellendren said.

Reluctantly dismounting from Laureniel, Ellendren climbed into the Narielle carriage.

Expensive silks lined the interior, the cushions were plump and comfortable, but the air was suffocating, and not just because Silvia and her two daughters sat inside. The fresh wintry air outside the carriage had been kept out by the heavy drapes. Silvia did not even permit natural light into her carriage.

"Oh, my dear, your beautiful eyes have changed. Your house had some of the most wondrous emerald in their eyes," Silvia said.

"None of us expected that the green color would fade with the city." The further the caravan had ridden away from where Lucillia had been, the more the Luminari's eyes had turned fully silver. Ellendren noticed it most in Kaela and Byron—the green in their eyes had been just as bright as her own, but their eyes were now entirely silver too. What sort of connection to the Illumined Wood did they really have and was it entirely gone now with their home?

"What an interesting curiosity. I must admit, I already miss the green hue. I'll have to completely rework my wardrobe. What good is a green gown if it can't bring out the color in my eyes anymore?" Silvia turned one of her daughters' head to look at her eyes.

"I'm sure the tailors will be thrilled." Ellendren could tell that Silvia was calculating the cost of adjusting her family's entire wardrobe.

"I'm sure they will be. Now, eye color aside, we must speak of these nasty rumors circulating throughout the caravan," Silvia said as her daughters nodded in agreement. "I have always been a firm believer that every rumor begins with a thimble of truth. Now, what this truth is, I cannot begin to surmise, but we cannot dismiss what others are saying and believing. After all, we know little of this so-called Lorenthien. Correspondence with Cor'lera ceased centuries ago, and from what I've heard, it's not an admirable village, with the exception of their ice wine. I've never tasted a Cor'leran Blue that I haven't enjoyed."

"I appreciate your concern," Ellendren said, keeping her tone in check.

"That is a relief, because I've even heard that this pretender who is trying to undermine our government has a romantic interest in you to further legitimize his claim."

Both daughters nodded their heads. Their mother had trained them well—never speak while she spoke but always silently agree.

"Your family has served the Luminari admirably for twelve hundred years. Surely, you can see how encouraging his advances would only tarnish your house. We do not want you falling below your station. Now, my husband and I are prepared to honor the arrangement between our Trethien and your noble self, made by us and your parents, the late Aryl of Lucillia. The very thought of you not becoming an aryl keeps me awake at night. I can't name a single elf who has received better training for the position than your noble self. You were training to be our next queen after all."

Fuming inside, Ellendren took a deep, and she hoped unnoticeable, breath. The stifling air inside the carriage was suddenly more than she could bear. "As to the source of these rumors, slandering the future Exalted Aryl of Krysenthiel seems rather foolish to me. I can't imagine what would happen to someone insinuating that Devlyn is other than who he says. Can you imagine the repercussions for whoever was the source of the rumors?"

Silvia gasped faintly, frowned, then bravely went on. "Surely, you can understand and respect why they surfaced? Our home is gone and based on insufficient rationale, we travel for the Shroud, with no assurance that it can be removed. It has stood for fourteen hundred years without so much as a single diminishment."

"It has been pierced—Ei'ethil Devlyn Lorenthien has pierced it. And that was before he became a full Phaedryn." Ellendren held Silvia's gaze, careful to keep her tone one of respect while she struggled to find a comfortable pose on the plush cushions.

"And what do you expect we will find if the Shroud is removed? A poisonous mist has lain over Krysenthiel and her cities for fourteen hundred years, Ellendren. Wrought by the elves or not, no manner of construction can endure without proper maintenance over such an extended period. If we do reclaim Krysenthiel, we will have nothing to return to; our long-abandoned cities will be in ruin. Surely, the fear that permeates this caravan is understandable. We could have far more easily rebuilt our cities and towns along the Illumined Wood."

Silvia's words needled into Ellendren. She hated to admit it, but Ellendren herself had considered the same point. No one knew what remained of Krysenthiel. Did any of its cities still stand? Or had they all been reduced to rubble? How could they protect the entire Luminari population without defensible fortifications?

"We'll have to be prepared for whichever eventuality. I've heard no reports to suggest that any of the Krysenthien cities would have decayed. And if they truly are wrought from lumaryl, well, I can't imagine that the stone has deteriorated at all. It was the very substance of our Skyland of Luminare after all. Alethea claims that it's incorruptible."

"Yes, we all know the myths about the Skylands. But they are just that—myths. Their validity is just as likely as us still being full elves."

Silvia smiled.

Despite all her training, Ellendren grimaced. Was Silvia trying to get under her skin? It pained her, but she could not afford insulting Silvia. Ellendren needed the support of the Luminari aryls—all of them— to maintain any semblance of authority. Most of all, she had to keep the Luminari united on this journey to Krysenthiel. If even a single aryl splintered away, they would be that much weaker when Erynor came for them. Even though the Luminari had had every advantage during the Ceurendol War, Erynor had still bested them. Legend said that not a single Krysenthien city had fallen, but because of the Shroud, they were also lost, and the Luminari had been taken into slavery.

It wouldn't take much for the Narielle aryl to sow unrest among the other aryls. Silvia had already lain the foundation. Ellendren only wished that she had a better understanding of the ei'terel's motives. Did she hope to manipulate the current vacuum of power and insert herself and her husband into a stronger position? Having their son marry the once-crowned princess of Lucillia would certainly garner the support of the other aryls seeking continuity. The Roendryns might have abdicated their position among the Luminari to transition to the return of the Lorenthiens, but that did not mean that Roendryns would have simply disappeared. She had more royal cousins than she could count. Some had accepted her father's decision, one that he had clearly agreed on with her mother before her passing, but many other Roendryns were furious about the abdication. While they might not have been in line for the throne, their family name had always given them privilege and prestige.

That latter group of Roendryns worried Ellendren, especially with Silvia's attempts to rekindle the broken betrothal between Trethien and her. Ellendren would have preferred to make her affection toward Devlyn more public but doing so would have also been politically difficult. Simply by being free of any engagement, Devlyn had attracted the notice and support of the Luminari aryls who hoped to pair him with their daughters. The repercussions of agreeing to Silvia's request and then later breaking it would be disastrous. But as Ellendren considered the implications, she realized that perhaps she didn't have to do anything. She had watched Kaela circumvent dozens of proposals, without ever outright rejecting a single advance.

Pondering her options in what was becoming a long silence, she was relieved when a knock came at the carriage door. Silvia cracked the door just enough for Ellendren to recognize one her uncle's runners. He wasn't a knight himself, or a soldier for that matter, but he would be extremely quick and light on his feet.

"Ei'lythel, a Sorenth messenger has arrived from Myrium."

"If you'll excuse me, Silvia." Ellendren bowed out of the carriage, happy for any excuse to get away from Silvia and her daughters. She quickly followed the runner through the column, their pace faster than the caravan's. She could neither see the front nor the rear of it, but it was impressive to see the entire Luminari population on the march. She realized that she had never seen the entire population at once—had anyone ever seen the entirety of their kingdom at once before? Granted this wasn't everyone, since more groups joined every day, all of their villages either vanished or changed. Only Lucillia had been completely woven from the Illumined Wood, but nearly every village had at a minimum one wall woven from that sacred forest, a wall which would have returned to the Illumined Wood. Byron had seen to it that a runner had gone to every Luminari settlement, informing them of what had happened and inviting them to join the caravan.

She wondered how many of these villagers would have preferred to stay along the Illumined Wood.

Up ahead, she could see Byron and Ei'denai Naesiv Aerquin speaking with a messenger in a light blue uniform emblazoned with the Sorenth blue dolphin. The messenger had a stern expression.

"Ei'lythel," Byron said, "this messenger is from Queen Myranda."

"Her Majesty, Queen Myranda of the Royal House Lariviere, Sovereign of the Sorenth, and her court request your immediate presence," the messenger said, his accent noticeably Sorenth.

"And to what do I owe the pleasure of such a summons?" Ellendren asked, shocked at the severity of the messenger's tone. She had been friends with Myranda while they had been at Gwilnor together and Ellendren had even come to the Sorenth's aid when Tieli and Torsillian forces had held Myrium under siege. Her response shocked the messenger, who had evidently expected her to immediately agree to accompany him.

"Truly, you jest," the messenger balked.

"Mind who you are speaking to, sir," Byron growled.

"I speak on behalf of my queen." The messenger wore that entitlement like a shield. "Your entire population is occupying Sorenth territory, trampling through our borders, practically forming a new road through our countryside. You have not requested permission from the Sorenth crown."

Ellendren understood the messenger's anger now. In the chaos that had followed her father's death and the disappearance of Lucillia, she had forgotten to reach out to Myranda and explain the Luminari's plight. "I understand. I will draft up a letter for Myranda at once."

"That is not acceptable. You have been summoned before Her Majesty. I am to return with you."

"As you can see, the Luminari are in an extremely delicate situation at present. I cannot abandon them." Silvia would turn this news to her own advantage if Ellendren went off to Myrium. It would be another layer to add to the Roendryn's misgovernment of the Luminari elves.

"I have my orders," the messenger repeated himself.

"You must understand," Naesiv interjected. "Our home is no more. Lucillia has returned to the forest, as have most other Luminari cities and villages."

"I have my orders." The messenger repeated his previous words, but his expression clearly said that he was sure they thought he was naïve.

"Allow the ei'lythel to draft her letter and have the Sorenth search the Illumined Wood where Lucillia once stood. All they will find will be a statue of the woman the city was named after," Naesiv said.

"And allow you to continue to tramp through our lands? Eventually settling inside our borders?"

"We have no intent to settle within Sorenth borders," Ellendren said, glaring at the messenger. "We make for Krysenthiel where we intend to remove the Shroud."

The messenger gaped unbelievingly, taking a step back, positive that they were lying. He finally swallowed, pulled his shoulders back and said, "I will take your letter back to Myrium. It is not for me to weigh the authenticity of your words, but for the queen and her court. Know this—they will not be pleased that you refused the summons."

"In good faith, I will bring the letter myself to Myrium and present it before Queen Myranda," Naesiv offered.

"Are you certain, Naesiv?" Ellendren asked.

"It will be nice to sleep in a bed again. My wife and I are not as young as we once were and this journey has been quite hard on us. A warm bed will be most welcomed on our diplomatic mission."

"Thank you, Naesiv."

"I suppose we should halt the day's march and have the tents erected," Byron said.

"Do not be ridiculous, we still have an additional six hours of traveling. We should not waste the good weather while we still have it. I will simply draft my letter for Myranda in my carriage. Just give me a few moments."

Song Within

Devlyn woke in the dark, well before the first hour of the day and sunrise still some time off. As always, whatever enchantment lay over the Illumined Wood meant that he slept comfortably in its temperate climate, even though beyond the forest, the cold winds of Estlenth promised an icy winter. But he had slept better than he had in days, perhaps because here, he might find an answer to his quest for weapons that would put him on equal ground with Aren and the Deurghol.

The Monastery of Kyrendal was far from what he had expected. Growing up in an abbey school and then living with the ei'ceuril again in the Temple of Ceur, Devlyn had anticipated a grand building filled with pious monks surrounded by devout artworks. While there was no lack of reverent monks, their seclusion permitted little patronage of any form of art and the monastery itself was not a single large building. Instead, the mountain slopes offered modest caves, like a series of beehives, that were well-suited to providing shelter to the monks.

Most of the monks had journeyed to Mount Saecrien with Kyrendal four thousand years ago. But there were others who had stumbled into this area of the Illumined Wood and chose to remain within the sacred forest. Ei'ana and ei'ceuril novices and supposedly senile elderly people from Cor'lera who were thought lost, never to return, now lived here.

The caves of the first monks were still occupied, since they had not lost their immortality, and as they awaited Anaweh's call to pass to the World-Beyond, they observed the younger monks, the ones who had traveled into the Illumined Wood over the years and had come to live among their community for a time, eventually leave this World-Below for the World-Beyond. Some of the younger monks only survived for a year in the Monastery of Kyrendal, while others spent decades along the slopes of Mount Saecrien and the other mountains that enclosed the valley.

Devlyn had heard that his maternal grandfather had been among that number of newer monks. He had not gone senile as Abbot Entiel had informed him, but had been drawn to the valley by Anaweh, the Creating Light, to live out the rest of his days there.

The rhythm of the monastery was still a mystery to Devlyn. They had arrived two weeks ago and without intending to seclude himself when all along he'd intended to pursue acquiring a verathn, Devlyn had spent most of the time isolated in meditation, attempting to commune with Anaweh as best he could, but it did not come naturally. Alethea and Wyn had also secluded themselves to meditate and Devlyn doubted they had difficulty remaining still with only their thoughts for company. How the monks here managed to spend their entire day in silent contemplation was beyond him. He often saw monks tending the fields, but he had yet to figure out their schedule. Some days the fields were filled with monks, other days there were only a handful.

At first, Devlyn had thought the weekdays were divided, such that on Gwynthaen they would rest, Thenaen they would work, and so on, but neither of the two Thenaens he'd passed at the monastery was the same. The first Thenaen, the valley was abuzz with workers. The following Thenaen, Devlyn was hard pressed to find a single monk in the fields. He didn't think it had been a feast day, but why else would they not be working?

Perhaps if they were to stay longer, he would better understand the inner workings of the monastery. But remaining for an extended period was simply not an option. The entire population of the Luminari was now traversing through Sorenthil and while there was certainly no threat from the Sorenth, no one had ever ascertained whether all the shadow elves had been destroyed or at least forced out of Sorenthil after the unsuccessful siege of Myrium. Devlyn worried that the large caravan would draw shadow elves out in the open.

Dozens of ei'ana traveled with the Luminari, but unless they carried a verathn, their chances of defeating a shadow elf were slim. Devlyn was unaware of any policies enacted by the Seven Chairs of Septyl regarding the few verathn still in their possession, but doubted the rare weapons were entrusted to those who ventured beyond the walls of Gwilnor.

A gentle breeze found its way into the cave Devlyn was staying in. He sat with only his thoughts and fears in the dim moonlight, awaiting the sunrise. At Gwilnor, he had learned that the rising sun was special to the Luminari. It was certainly a beautiful sight, but he never understood why. The relationship was somehow connected to one of the enthiel, Auriel, the anadel that guided the Luminari. Still, that didn't make the correlation any clearer to him.

His musings on the Luminari and the sun faded when a gentle breeze tickled at him, calling out to him, as though it wanted to draw him out of the cave. It was still too early to run into anyone, so he pulled a simple robe over his almost naked self and walked barefoot on the soft grass, damp with morning dew. It seemed as though the breeze was encouraging him to take a specific direction. It felt a bit moody, as though it could change from light and pleasant to hard and thunderous in an instant. That brought Brother Bernard, the librarian at Cor'lera's abbey school, to mind at the thought of the wind having a personality.

"Take me where you will, brother wind, as a leaf upon your current," Devlyn said softly. He had often heard Brother Bernard say something similar. He called everything brother or sister, whether they were alive and capable of moving or not.

The breeze grew stronger, no longer a breeze, and almost lifted him from his feet as it guided him across the valley. He had wanted to watch the sun break through the night's hold, but in the near-dawn, he was pulled into a tunnel on the far side of the valley. It was difficult to tell which mountain he had gone into, but he suspected it was the largest, Mount Saecrien.

The violent pull of the wind brought goosebumps to his arms and his heart started to beat faster. He was no longer in control of his movements and struggling against the wind only caused it to strengthen, making Devlyn's attempts even more futile.

The only other tunnel he knew of in the valley was the one behind the waterfall, the one they'd come through into the valley. That tunnel was much shorter than this one, and as he was pulled further in, it grew narrower, only wide enough for a single person and only a head taller than himself. He was not yet fully grown, so could not imagine what it was like for an elf as tall as Kyrendal had once been before age had brought a stoop to his spine. He likely would have bumped his head on the rough ceiling.

Reaching out to feel the stone walls, he was shocked to discover that they were as smooth as glass. Curious now, and no longer interested in uselessly struggling against the breeze, he allowed the wind to resume its now gentle pull.

Once he surrendered to the breeze, he began to hear the sound it made as it swept along the glassy walls. He had never heard that sound before, but oddly, he recognized it. It was reminiscent of the song ever on his heart, yet distinctly different, as though it was written and sung by the same musician but performed at a different time.

The melody soothed him, his muscles relaxing as the song filled him.

Time was forgotten as he was swept deeper into the tunnel, unable to judge whether several minutes or several hours had passed. The tunnel opened at last into a cavern with a lake as clear as the stars themselves and a euphoria washed over him. His heart leapt as he looked at the still water.

He had never seen water so pure. Not even melted ice and snow produced water as pristine as this. Amazed, Devlyn allowed his heart complete control as it sung the most joyous song he had ever known.

A part of him wanted to dive in those depths, to bathe in the purity which lay before him. He was confidently aware that no outer filth or inner darkness could ever taint it, not even the depression layering his own heart.

"I brought your sister here once before," a girlish voice said.

Turning to see who was speaking to him, Devlyn recognized the girl he had met during his novitiate. Calling her a girl sounded foolish to Devlyn. This was one of the Children. "You brought me here? Did you wield aerys to pull me from my room?" he asked, sounding more accusatory than he'd intended.

"We do not wield, my brother and I, and neither did those who were once as we are," said the Child. "We interact differently with the erendinth—wielders have confined the erendinth to only seven aspects."

"There's more?" Devlyn grew more confused.

She laughed. "Has no one told you? They will, but don't let the limited grasp of wielders restrict you. Can you hear the song?"

"Yes—it's beautiful," he said, not yet ready to switch topics since he had so many questions.

"Just as beautiful as the one singing within you. You should not hide it within yourself; its beauty will restore more than you can imagine." The phoenix came to mind.

"Will it bring Aliel back?" Devlyn pleaded, desperate. The song faded slightly.

"It's possible, but it will bring so much more if you allow it to permeate your entire being, allow that which is within to shine forth for all to see." The girl dipped her toe in the water and swirled it. "When you return to these waters, you'll hear the song more clearly; you will know what to do then."

"When will I come back?"

"That depends on how long you'll need to unknot yourself and balance your entire being. Someone is coming to take you away from here—you'll know when it's time to return."

"Who?"

She didn't answer, but dove into the water and disappeared, leaving Devlyn alone on the edge of the lake. He tried to follow her movement in the water, but she swam as though she was part of the lake. Devlyn considered reaching out to Aliel to try and reestablish their bond—he hovered on the precipice of that quiet place inside his heart but decided to heed the Child's words and not go further. Instead, he turned to leave the cave. The gentle song diminished as the lake fell further behind, and faded entirely when he stepped outside the tunnel and into the valley.

Out in the valley, Devlyn recognized Wyn, Alethea, and Kyrendal among the other monks, all gazing upward and to the south.

Looking over his shoulder, he saw Aren hovering, his body devoid of light, tendrils of a shadowy presence seething from him. Was Aren who the Child meant he was to go with? Devlyn felt his stomach clench at the notion—surely, she didn't mean Aren.

Still unable to bond with Aliel, Devlyn felt a growing sense of dread. He would not allow what had happened six months before to happen again. There was no Deathless to augment Aren's own tenebrys lightning, and Devlyn would do everything he could to prevent Aren from harming the monastery. Prepared to press into the erendinth, Devlyn was surprised to hear Kyrendal speak.

"You have no power here, nephew. Leave this place."

"I do not know you, monk," Aren said. "My business is not with you but with the boy."

"You, as you are, and your business are not welcome in this forest. Already, you have caused harm beyond repair. Leave this place, nephew, before you are unmade."

Snarling from his height, Aren threw a bolt of tenebrys at the monk, a bolt easily dissolved in a bright light cast by Kyrendal, and visibly shocking Aren. Beyond a doubt, Kyrendal wielded lumenys. He wasn't using his cane for support but rather used it to swat away the lightning. Clearly, Kyrendal still had his verathn.

After launching several more bolts of tenebrys toward the valley with each of them dissolving in the same fashion, Aren did not speak, but left them, returning south from where he had come. Devlyn watched Aren disappear, relieved that he had been untouched by tenebrys.

"Come with me," Kyrendal said, walking toward a nearby cave, leaning slightly on his cane but otherwise no different than he'd been before.

Devlyn followed. The cave was small and unadorned, much like the one Devlyn slept in, nothing to denote Kyrendal's station among the monks.

Kyrendal sat on a large cushion and crossed his legs, then waved Devlyn toward another cushion. "He came because he felt that which he wrought upon you—as long as your wound remains, he will find you. He knows of this place only because of that beacon."

"Will he come back?" Devlyn asked, terrified that Aren might destroy this valley.

"He cannot," Kyrendal said, confident.

Uncertain whether he should apologize for drawing Aren to the valley and the monastery, Devlyn couldn't think of what he should say, so remained silent.

"Do not let such thoughts burden you, Devlyn Lorenthien."

It was all too easy to forget that Kyrendal was a Luminari from ancient days where thoughts were not private. It wasn't an intrusion of privacy, but despite Alethea's teachings, Devlyn still couldn't gentle his thoughts enough to prevent other elves from hearing them so clearly.

"You called him nephew."

"Because he is, even if he does not remember our relationship. My sister was his wife's grandmother. As the youngest of our siblings, she became the Aryl of Mar'anathyl with her husband. But that is not what I wanted to speak of."

For a moment, neither spoke and Devlyn glanced at Kyrendal's cane.

"Ah, you've figured it out." Kyrendal smiled. "It was once in the form of a staff, but I snapped it when I came here. When you first arrived, I spoke about my vow and my philosophy toward weapons. While my vow prevents me from revisiting my abandoned trade, after hearing your song from Mount Saecrien, there is something I can do."

"Will you teach me how to make my own verathn? Will I be able to make one like the swords the Guardian knights have?" Devlyn jumped to conclusions in his excitement.

"A sword's inherent nature is to draw blood," Kyrendal said, his tone revealing his displeasure at Devlyn's enthusiastic outburst, reminding Devlyn just how much younger he was. Kyrendal tapped his fingers against his knees.

"How can I fight someone with a sword without one for myself?"

"You assume that the threat of death is only answerable by another threat of death. The violent cycle has all but destroyed Teraeniel. A staff, while it too can strike a mortal blow, will best serve as an instrument of peace. It will defend you against any sword, but its inherent nature is other than death." Devlyn considered what holding and fighting with a staff would be like. "As a verathn, it will possess all the amplifying abilities you could ever desire while wielding the erendinth, while also deflecting the most powerful swords. It was the preferred verathn among the Vyoletryns. They too believed justice was best served without violence."

"Will you create two?"

"You know of someone as deserving?"

"I do."

"Would she vow to use it for the purpose of defense and justice?"

Surprised that Kyrendal knew Devlyn referred to Ellendren, he was nevertheless confident. "Yes—better than myself, admittedly."

Kyrendal smiled at the confession. "You care for her."

"Very much so," Devlyn said, embarrassed that his feelings for Ellendren bled though, without him even mentioning her name.

"You forget, I will not be revisiting my abandoned craft."

"Then how?"

"Do you know of the draelyn?"

"Dragon elves?"

Kyrendal smiled and looked past Devlyn toward the cave opening.

TENETHYL

Looking over his shoulder, Devlyn turned to see what Kyrendal was looking at. The curious looking elf he'd met in Briel, the one with the red hair and eyes, stood in the opening.

"Ah, you are most welcome here, Prya." Kyrendal did not stand but waved Prya toward another cushion. "Devlyn, may I introduce you to Prya, daughter of Olfra, descendant of Cythol of the Red Flight. Prya, this is Devlyn Lorenthien."

"Thank you, Kyrendal. And we despise the colloquial term dragon elf, elf-boy. You can refer to us as draelyn."

Remembering that Yloran had told Devlyn that Erynor also was a draelyn, Devlyn leaned back, trying to increase the distance between himself and the draelyn, suddenly uncomfortable with Prya's red eyes.

"You really ought to calm your thoughts if you don't want others to know them," Kyrendal said. "And you should know that the larger draelyn population are just as aligned with Erynor as are the Luminari."

"That is quite the understatement. Unlike your past aryls, our leaders refused Erynor's request to come into our city. Our gates stayed closed and our city remained hidden from him, and from his father and brother." Prya crossed her arms at the apparent insult.

"We never knew that he was a draelyn. I only learned that after coming to this valley when draelyn and dragon alike visited. We certainly never expected that Erynor had been fathered by a dragon of the Dark

Flight aligned to the Evil One," Kyrendal said.

"My people still don't understand how you missed the stench surrounding him. We didn't need to meet his cursed dragon family to identify him as such."

"An error all of Teraeniel is still paying for."

Prya glanced back toward the cave opening, as though she was about to leave. "Well, are you ready?" she asked, turning to Devlyn.

"Ready for what?"

"I thought you told him?" she asked Kyrendal.

"I only alluded to it, so perhaps he does not know what I meant."

"The Child did say someone would be taking me away from here; when I saw Aren, I was afraid she meant him."

"Well, I'd rather not waste the daylight any more than necessary, so let's get flying."

"Fly to where?" Devlyn looked back and forth between the two, all too aware of his inability to bond with Aliel and fly on his own.

"Tenethyl, of course. Where else do you imagine Kyrendal learned to make verathn? The centaurs?"

Kyrendal chuckled. "Alethea and Wyn will be here when you return."

"Won't they want to come as well?" He had no idea where or what Tenethyl was or whether he should trust a draelyn.

"Alethea has expressed an interest remaining here with Wyn to commune with the anadel. Mount Saecrien eases the required focus to connect with them." Kyrendal remained sitting on his cushion as Prya turned for the cave opening. She was leaving whether or not Devlyn was ready.

"I guess I'll see you when I get back." Devlyn followed Prya out of the cave, pausing just beyond the opening when he came face to face with a massive, red-scaled dragon. The dragon's sinuous neck snaked down, bringing its head a handspan from Devlyn's own. Devlyn gasped, his heart racing.

"Liara likes you," Prya said.

Devlyn stared at the large red dragon. "How did Liara hide in Briel?"

"And here I was thinking that you didn't recognize me. The blue dragons you know haven't told you?"

"What would they have told me? That they can turn invisible and hide in plain sight?"

"Interesting. Perhaps the Blue Flight is more reserved than I gave them credit for."

"What does that mean?"

"That the Blue Flight are the only dragons to have revealed themselves again, and they are somewhat protective of themselves." Prya climbed onto the red dragon's back, situating herself at the base of Liara's neck. She extended a hand to Devlyn and pulled him up so he could sit behind her. "Perhaps you'll find out in due course. Now, hold on tightly. We've wasted enough time as it is."

Liara didn't wait for an answer and sprang into the air, the force of her movement making Devlyn's stomach drop. Liara had only flapped her wings twice and already they were high above the monastery. The dragon's great wingspan reflected a red tint on the valley below. To think, not even an hour ago, Aren had darkened the valley with bolts of tenebrys and his own dark wings. Everything had happened so quickly that morning, from the moment he had been pulled into the mountain cavern with the lake, to Aren appearing in the sky, to Prya and Liara arriving and taking him away from the monastery. If he had known how that morning was to unfold, he would've dressed in his lierathnil instead of the simple linen robe that he now wore. The blue lucilliae was tucked away in his lierathnil's hidden pocket, and as long as Aren didn't show up again, it should be secure in the cave he had slept in over the past two weeks.

Liara flew up and over the mountains surrounding the monastery and once they were past the mountain range, he saw a great body of water glimmering below in the morning sun. He felt a pull to follow that rising sun eastward. *What is it?* he thought, wishing he could ask Aliel.

Only silence answered. Knowing better than to reach out to Aliel while in flight, he let the question slip from his mind. Whatever it was, it called strongly and he really wanted to accept the call. As far as he could see, there was only water. If he ever managed to rekindle his bond with Aliel, perhaps they could fly in that direction one day. How long could they fly without taking a break? Flying over an endless ocean didn't seem like the best place to test their limits.

Liara turned north, flying along the mountain range. The snowy mountain peaks rose and fell, some stretching higher into the clouds until at last, they dipped toward another body of water. It was difficult to say from his perspective, but it looked like the shimmering bay, surrounded on three sides by mountains, was connected to the larger ocean to the east.

They flew in the center of the bay and directly west, where the bay narrowed the further inland it went and before long, Devlyn could hear and see a great waterfall. Mist filled his vision the closer they drew to the large waterfall cascading from a great height. Devlyn thought he saw something glimmer at the top of that waterfall, and when he peered at it, he saw that the water divided in two around whatever was sparkling, but the watery mist kept him from seeing exactly what it was.

It wasn't until they drew closer to the waterfall that Devlyn realized that it was a jeweled spire, surrounded by other spires and an entire city sprawling around it hidden in the mist. The entire city sat on an island at the edge of the waterfall and Devlyn couldn't see a single bridge connecting the city to the mainland on either side of the broad river. Drawing still closer to the city, he gazed upon the largest jewel he had ever seen nestled into the architecture of the tallest of the jeweled spires. Colored jewels of every sort lined its curved and sinuous walls. It looked more like a sculpture than a building and as Devlyn looked away from the central tower, he noticed that the entire city had that level of detail and ornamentation and appeared sculpted from the finest marble and set with jewels.

Liara dove toward a large platform extending past and over the waterfall and Devlyn noticed that that platform was far from empty. Dozens of finely dressed people lined the far side, leaving plenty of room for landing dragons. Preparing to do so, the red dragon fluttered her wings, sending the clothes and hair of those gathered billowing, then alit lightly, with no noticeable bump. Devlyn and Prya dismounted, and were quickly surrounded by dozens of others.

Prya looked around at those gathered and then at Devlyn, raising an eyebrow. "Who are you exactly to have these fine ones welcome you to Tenethyl?" she asked under her breath.

"Who are they?" he whispered back. Some of the people gathered were incredibly tall, muscular and with well-proportioned bodies.

"The Ealyn, the seven rulers of Tenethyl, as well as Galithinol the Gold and some of the other dragons from the Elder Days."

"The only dragon I see is Liara," said Devlyn, turning to look at the red dragon. He could only gape when her shimmering red scales faded and her massive wings and body shrank as she transformed into a beautiful but large woman. She looked much like Prya with crimson hair and ruby eyes, but taller and stronger and very naked.

"Don't gawk, youngling. Surely you haven't forgotten everything," Liara said, accepting a red robe from a much shorter woman.

As Devlyn took in his surroundings, he realized that every person had pointed ears, but they all had different colored eyes, and only the shapeshifted dragons' ears were proportionally much longer than the typical pointed ears of elves. According to Prya, they were waiting for him, and he decided that all he wanted now was answers.

"Tenethyl welcomes you Devlyn Lorenthien," said a normal sized woman with hair that seemed spun of gold. He was surprised to see that she, like him, had golden eyes. "I am Vivien, descendant of Galithinol the Gold, and Ealyn of the Gold House." Vivien inclined her head as though to acknowledge the person named Galithinol beside her, and Devlyn understood that he was a dragon. His eyes were also gold and his thick hair resembled Vivien's.

"He reminds me of Thien." Galithinol shifted his weight, his full-length black robes trimmed in gold billowing in the slight wind.

"Who?" Devlyn asked, looking from Galithinol to Vivien, and realized that he was being rude, not having acknowledged the two who had spoken to him, so quickly gave a little bow that he hoped would suffice.

"My brother. Presumably now with Anaweh in Lumaeniel. After Tenethyl fell to the Evil One, he met Loren in the Valley of Saeryndol, and from that moment, he would never be separated from her."

Devlyn frowned. Tenethyl looked very much whole and intact to him as he looked from one incredible jeweled spire to the next.

"Don't bother," Prya interrupted, inclining her head politely. "He knows precious little of the Elder Days. He didn't even recognize Tenethyl's name when I mentioned it."

"We knew much would be forgotten, but never imagined that it would be to this extent," Galithinol rumbled. "Perhaps we have cloistered ourselves for too long. That the Fall of Tenethyl is forgotten does not bode well for the state of the world."

Again, Devlyn glanced at the intact jeweled spires.

"Now is not the time to sing of the past," Vivien answered Devlyn's inquiring gaze. "You came here for a weapon because Kyrendal's oath prevents him from doing it himself."

"Yes."

"Many of us here remember the destruction of before and which has returned. Unlike Kyrendal, while we have remained away from Teraeniel's conflicts, we have not become pacifists. We are sired from dragons and will fight tooth and nail to protect our home and those we love. But what you seek is not given out lightly."

"Only one other was given the knowledge to create verathn, and while Kyrendal did not share his knowledge, the fruit of his work has been corrupted. It was an abuse of that knowledge," the man in white said.

"Ealyn Allister is quite right. We cannot give you the same knowledge that was given to Kyrendal. It is not a matter of trust in you. It is that the potential harm could be devastating. Therefore, you must undergo trials." Vivien folded her hands in front her. "Ealyn Daela, please describe the trials to Devlyn."

A lovely woman dressed in various shades of purple stepped forth. "Many have taken these trials. They are designed for and by the draelyn. Over the millennia, hundreds have come to Tenethyl to seek what you seek and hundreds more will come after you. But of all the attempts made by those from outside Tenethyl, only Kyrendal has passed our trials."

"What happened to the others?" Devlyn asked, afraid of the answer.

"They perished." Daela replied simply. Her amethyst eyes flashed. "Tell us, Devlyn, have you mastered jienzu?"

Devlyn frowned at the unfamiliar word.

"I'm thinking he is too young to begin learning jienzu," said a sapphire-eyed draelyn.

"I believe you are right, Niron," Daela said.

"If he is too young to learn jienzu, does that not mean he is too young for the trials?" asked a woman with emerald eyes and mossy green hair.

Devlyn took mild offense at being disparaged this way. While he was only sixteen years old, he felt that his accomplishments so far deserved more credit than these draelyn were giving him. Granted, he was deliberately ignoring his past failures and defeats, which quite possibly outnumbered his victories.

"I suppose the decision belongs to Devlyn. Who are we to refuse the trials if one is willing?" Vivien gazed into Devlyn's eyes as she spoke.

"We do not have the time to train him to be successful, Vivien. You know the consequences of failure. Once he begins, the trials cannot be stopped," Daela said.

"Do you have confidence in yourself, Devlyn?" Vivien asked, her gaze steady.

"I do," he said, assurance welling in his chest. He still had no idea what these trials entailed, and that was a bit of a concern, but he needed a weapon to defend himself. Wielding was simply insufficient, especially when he was cut off from the erendinth. Who knew how often that would happen? Devlyn suppressed the reminder that he still could not bond with Aliel or even sense his presence.

"I thought so." Vivien smiled. "Please continue, Daela."

"I inquired about your training in jienzu because the trials are based on jienzu. Now, the trials do not require you to perform the various forms, but their principles would be invaluable for your success." Daela stepped forward, away from the formation of the still gathered draelyn. "As I'm sure you're aware, anacordel are composed of body, soul, and spirit. It is those three components, distinct but unified, that led to the development of jienzu. Jienzu aims to bring Balance. The trials are a test of Balance, that is your balance between yourself, other creatures, the erendinth, the Creating Light, and the larger world.

"Devlyn, the world has been out of Balance since the Evil One's rebellion. Anaweh never intended for Teraeniel to be a place of chaos. There is a reason why only one person born beyond our city has passed the trials."

"You've frightened him quite enough, Daela," Vivien said.

"He should know the consequences."

"And I believe he does."

"Very well, the trials will begin tomorrow. Since you are a Luminari, we'll give you the advantage of starting at dawn. We're aware that that time of the day is special to you. May Auriel and the other anadel of the morning sun guide you."

"I have a request, Daela. He is young. Allow us a week to teach him some of the forms," Vivien said.

"Very well," she replied, after a pause. "Learn the basics. Balance must return to Teraeniel."

With that, Vivien and Galithinol stepped forward as the other draelyn and dragons dispersed. "Walk with us, Devlyn. There is much we should discuss before your trials begin," Vivien said.

He followed Vivien and Galithinol from the platform on the city's edge. After having spent a not-insignificant amount of time going no further than the platform, Devlyn was excited to see the rest of Tenethyl. From what he had seen when flying into the city, it was most impressive. He didn't think that even Arenthyl could outshine it.

Vivien walked through the jeweled archway lined with sculptures of what seemed like living draelyn. The naked sculptures appeared to have been created with the figures in mid-dance, their movement frozen in time. Devlyn found it difficult to walk past the sculptures, too mesmerized by them.

"Dragons of every flight were drawn to the beauty of Tenethyl. So captivated were we, that we even fell in love with the inhabitants. Unfortunately, it took us too long to realize the harm our mating would cause the mothers of the draelyn, and even longer to acknowledge it." Galithinol paused briefly in front of one of the statues, as though he knew the woman frozen in mid-dance.

"No one knew the consequences back then, and we are all richer for who we are now. And my grandmother loved you." Vivien took her grandfather's hand in her own.

"And I her."

"What happened to the female dragons who mated with men?" Devlyn asked.

"I imagine they would have crushed their mate in the process." Galithinol chuckled. "You see, female dragons will not mate in their smaller forms." Galithinol moved on and into a broad street. Devlyn barely kept his jaw from dropping at the sight. Lacy bridges arched above among jeweled spires thrusting skyward. The architecture was unlike anything Devlyn had ever seen before. The fluid structures felt alive, and like the statues, looked as though they too were about to dance. The city reminded him of the elven architecture he had seen, but there was also something quite different about it.

They continued through the wondrous streets of Tenethyl until they reached a golden spire, speckled with jewels like the others.

"Welcome to the gold spire. Unlike the other houses here in Tenethyl, Galithinol was the only dragon of the Gold Flight to sire a child, and because of that, the Gold House is relatively small and it is confined to a single spire. Each dragon who sired a child gave birth to a new house."

"How were there only seven ealyn then?" Devlyn asked.

"You have a quick mind," Galithinol said. Devlyn blushed. He had little other than Luminari politics on his mind of late.

"While there are dozens of smaller houses that belong to the Sapphire House, they've chosen one of their number to be their ealyn."

"So, that means that each of those blue spires that I saw when flying here, are all their own house?"

"Correct." Vivien strode up the elegant flowing staircase to the entry portal. The great gate was open and Devlyn followed her, somewhat curious as to why this elite among the draelyn had taken an interest in him.

Inside the spire, dozens of golden-eyed draelyn of all ages greeted Devlyn. Vivien smiled at her family, which from the numbers of draelyn here, was still growing. "I thought you said your house was the smallest?" Devlyn asked, trying to count the gathered draelyn.

"Galithinol sired our house in the Elder Days, before the Great Blessing when the only anacordel roaming Teraeniel were dragon and those we now call the elder ones."

This time, Devlyn couldn't stop his jaw from dropping.

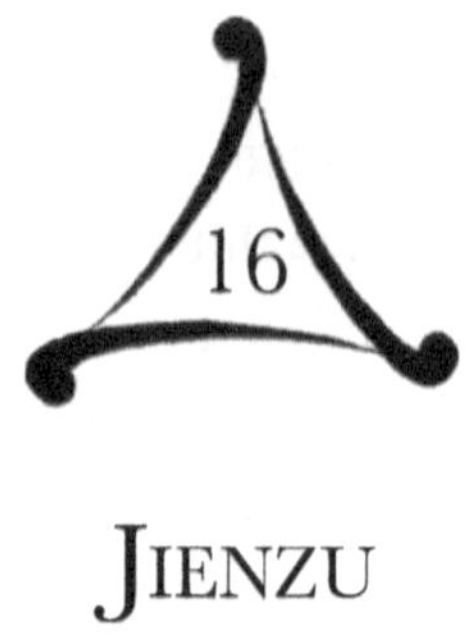

16

JIENZU

Every morning after Devlyn had arrived in Tenethyl, a quiet bell had woken him. It rang before the sun rose, and every day, Devlyn was asked to dress quickly and follow Ciaren to a balcony where Vivien and Galithinol had spent the past week training him in jienzu. They had told him that they would have preferred to take an entire year just to introduce him to the forms, but Daela had only given them a week. And even a week felt too long to be away from Ellendren and the Luminari elves as they traveled to Krysenthiel. The longer he was away from them, the more peril they could be in.

Every one of those days of training had begun with an hour of meditation with Vivien, both sitting on the floor with their legs crossed, until the sun rose. They had just ended today's meditation, and Vivien stood, inviting Devlyn to do the same as she patted her garments. She was clad in the loose silks intended for flexible movement, rather than the glittering gown she typically wore. "As we have been doing, I would like you to replicate my movements. They might come naturally to you, as I suspect Viren has already begun instructing you in the basics."

She extended her arms to either side and held them there. She had led him through various forms over the past week, and each day they had become more difficult. The first breath was always easy, but by the time he reached twenty breaths, some part of his body, the part the form had focused on, throbbed. He didn't consider himself in bad shape, even after having to regain his muscle mass twice in a single year. He had barely regained his strength after being locked in that cage before he'd had to fight Aren and the Deurghol only to fall from the sky and lie bedridden for months. He tried to convince himself that he was back to his previous strength but if he was, it was inadequate for what Vivien had him doing now. Although, he did recognize these forms. Viren had led him through a series of stretches before and after some of their practice sessions, but Devlyn had assumed they were just for the sake of stretching his muscles, and not specific forms of something called jienzu.

"My suspicions over the past few days are now confirmed," Vivien said, holding the form and indicating that Devlyn should take it up as well.

"What were you suspicious about?" He mimicked her pose.

"When you came to us, I was startled to learn that you had never heard of jienzu. I would not have believed it possible for one not practicing the forms to achieve communion with a phoenix, who is, as I'm sure you know by now, one of the lorendil."

"What does jienzu have to do with my bond with Aliel?" Devlyn felt a pang in his heart at the reminder of his wound and his broken bond with Aliel.

"Everything. An unbalanced anacordel could never achieve such a bond. And as our brief meditation has shown, you are no novice in these forms."

Brief?

Yes, brief. Vivien's voice echoed in his mind.

Devlyn blushed. He kept forgetting that his thoughts were not confined to himself.

"The draelyn greet every morning with a similar meditation. An hour is typically the minimum." Vivien offered a warm smile. "While Alethea and Viren might not have explicitly trained you in jienzu, I believe that they were likely preparing you for its formal study. The Guardian knights are not unknown to us here, nor are their customs. Tell me,

Devlyn, did you ever see Viren practice his morning forms? I'm sure Alethea and Wyn would have accompanied him as well."

Devlyn considered, and all he could recall was waking up earlier than usual one day and seeing them doing some odd stretches. The other elves didn't seem to need as much sleep as Devlyn did, and he only ever saw them a few times as they were finishing up. There didn't seem to be anything special about it.

"As Daela mentioned when you arrived, jienzu is intended to bring balance within us. We are no longer as Anaweh created us. The Creating Light has blessed our changes over the eras, even as we became different races, wholly other than what we first were. And while the draelyn and elves remain closest to that original intent, we are still different, and truly the elves are nearest to the elder ones. Because of the Evil One's past and current influence, maintaining Balance is something we must struggle to achieve. Chaos is all too willing to claim this realm."

"If the Evil One hadn't fallen, would the different races have come to be?" Devlyn asked.

"From the very beginning, many of us rebelled. Without knowing what time and aging were, we wanted them both. Only two remained as Children. Whether that rebellion came from the Evil One or from our own free hearts, it's impossible to know. I've always suspected it was a combination of the two. It did not take much for those who came before to be swayed."

Devlyn considered her words as Vivien shifted into a new pose, and he followed, glad to lower his arms but already anticipating that his legs would be sore in no time. As for what Vivien had said, he knew that he was far from perfect, and he didn't think that anyone had forced that imperfection on him. Rather, he saw it as something that guided him, trying to do better—to be better. "So, if we're just unbalanced, how do we correct that?"

"The anadel are the purest of Anaweh's creatures, composed of spirit and soul. The beasts are simplest, composed of body and soul. As anacordel, we are the most complex of creation, for we have spirit, body, and soul. What the anadel and cordel do by nature, whether through fault of ours or the Evil One's meddling, we must work to achieve what they do as naturally as breathing."

As she spoke, Devlyn realized that he had begun to sweat. A basin of water sat nearby, and he glanced over at it, his legs aching. It felt as though his tendons were about to tear from their attachment points. Vivien ended the pose, and Devlyn exhaled a sigh of relief. He had no idea how much time had passed, but his limbs were crying out. He took a step toward the basin, looking around it for a cup or a ladle, and finding neither, groaned. His not so private thoughts caught him again, but rather than begrudge them yet again, he grinned as a globule of water rose from the basin.

"I understand that you are young, but I do hope you don't expect me to deliver the water for you," Vivien said.

"Sorry, I have never drunk water that way before. I've always used a cup," he said, blushing again. He drank the globule in a single gulp, then wielded aquaeys to bring a second larger globule out of the basin. Unfortunately, he brought more than he should have and half of it splashed over his face, soaking his sweaty chest in the process.

Vivien laughed as Devlyn frowned. He didn't need to have his thoughts overheard to embarrass himself, he was quite capable of doing that openly on a regular basis.

"I have a question about jienzu," he said.

"I'm listening."

"What exactly is it? Is it the forms that we just practiced, or is the meditation part of it?"

"Yes and no." Vivien wielded a globule of water for herself, easily drinking it without splashing any of it. She also appeared to be in much better shape than Devlyn since she didn't seem the least bit exhausted from the exercise nor was she sweating. "Jienzu is a means to balance oneself. There are thousands of forms and techniques to do so. Kyrendal developed his own forms and shared them with the Luminari, and the practice spread beyond the elves. But we draelyn devote our entire lives to Balance. Some require more focus on a specific part of their being, while others on another part. The basic forms encompass all three aspects of an anacordel. As they progress, they learn what they specifically need, and often that is not a constant. Our needs change over the years, and so we must adapt to what we need."

"I don't understand. The way you've described it makes it sound less like an exercise and more of a means to an end."

"It is a way of life. In our unbalanced world, we must strive to achieve Balance."

"I think I understand."

"The first grasp at understanding feels like the entirety, when in reality it is only a thimbleful." It wasn't a rebuke, and she said it kindly enough that Devlyn didn't take offense.

Instead of questioning the point, he looked out across Tenethyl, the multitude of spires glittering in the now late afternoon sun. He tried to understand the logic behind the towers. While there was only one gold spire, there were a few more onyx and amethyst ones, and there were many more emerald, ruby, sapphire, and opal spires. The gold spire was not the furthest east of the spires, but it did rise tall enough for Devlyn to gaze east across the cityscape, over the waterfall's mist, and out the bay. He knew that the Unarian Ocean stretched beyond that bay. The magisters at Gwilnor had spoken of that ocean reverently, as though it possessed a spiritual quality, akin to the Illumined Wood.

"Perhaps I can explain. Your thoughts are quite loud; truly, I'm not trying to intrude on them."

"You're not the first to comment on that," Devlyn said. "I understand that each spire is connected to a specific dragon flight, but what dictates the varied proportions?"

"For every dragon that sired a draelyn, a spire was built. While the original city was founded by children of Anaweh, now referred to as the elder ones, this city was built well after and was solely inhabited by draelyn. It's not that those without dragon blood didn't come with us, but at that point, we had intermarried to such an extent that the two groups became one. So, our design intent shifted from the original city."

"It's really beautiful."

"Thank you. Thien thought so too when he came to visit."

Before he could question who Thien was, Vivien turned away from the balustrade, her demeanor urging Devlyn to do the same. He followed her into the spire and came across Ciaren as they stepped on the grand stair. Music drifted from somewhere deep inside the spire, as did some delicious smells. Devlyn nearly allowed his nose and ears to draw him to the source but the younger draelyn noticed and winced.

"Surely you want to bathe first, yes?" the child asked, looking between Devlyn and Vivien.

"I'm sure he would appreciate that. Will you escort him to the bath hall, Ciaren? It would be a shame if Devlyn came to our spire without seeing it." Vivien left them and went further into the spire.

"Well, follow me." Ciaren walked off, leaving Devlyn to follow and instead of taking the grand stair up, they went down another stair and past the main level and further below. *How deep do the foundations of this spire go?* Devlyn wondered. He didn't know what was so special about the bath hall, since the tub in his room had been more than sufficient to clean himself so far.

"Thanks for helping me out this past week."

"You're welcome. It's not like I could say no to Vivien though."

"I suppose not." Devlyn laughed.

"Are you nervous about your trials tomorrow? I wasn't born yet when the last person tried to take the trials, but I think he was pronounced dead in less than an hour."

Devlyn nearly swallowed his tongue at that, coughing as his only response, due to his shock. Vivien had failed to mention that. Finally, they reached a low vaulted room where a large pool in the center steamed in shapeless whorls. Ciaren looked from Devlyn to the water expectantly as Devlyn dawdled by the side waiting for Ciaren to leave before undressing.

"I'd heard a rumor that mortals were uncomfortable with others seeing them naked. I honestly discounted it and thought my older brothers were making fun of me. I never expected that it also applied to elves."

Alethea flashed through his mind. He had lost track of how many times she had instructed him to accept all of who he was and be comfortable with nudity.

"I've already bathed today, but I can hop in as well if it'll make you more comfortable."

"That's quite all right," Devlyn said, thinking, *turning around would make me comfortable.* Devlyn discarded his clothes, ignoring Ciaren who was at least a century old and still only a child. The water felt amazing. Devlyn splashed around, using the soapy cloth Ciaren pointed out to remove the grime.

"Have you decided what type of verathn you will choose?" Ciaren asked. "Assuming you pass the trials."

"I have a choice?"

"Can't imagine why you wouldn't. I like the sword ones."

"They do seem the most useful when fighting against a Deurghol. I wasn't able to defend myself the last time I fought one of them." He remembered narrowly avoiding the corrupted verathn's blade, and then being struck by tenebrys. His hand reached for the center of his back where he had been struck. Despite it being mostly healed, he winced. He sunk beneath the warm water, hoping to ease his emotions.

Pulling himself out of the pool, he found a towel and a change of clothes waiting for him. The garments fitted him as perfectly as his lierathnil did. He felt bad that he didn't have any coins to pay his hosts for their hospitality and the clothing they provided.

Ciaren took Devlyn back up the winding stair to the spire's main level and into the crowded great hall. Tables laden with food lined the space and merry songs filled Devlyn's ears. He'd assumed the feast would only include the members of the Gold House, but on second glance, draelyn and dragons with all sorts of different colored hair, eyes, and skin tones crowded the space. Shocked by the sight of so many different people, Devlyn eventually noticed a large young man with bright sapphire hair and matching eyes staring at him. Before Devlyn made it halfway across the room, the blue-haired young man rushed over to Devlyn to grab him in a tight hug and lifted him off the ground.

Confused by the display of emotion, Devlyn pulled back in the stranger's embrace.

"You don't recognize me, do you?" he laughed, clearly intimately familiar with Devlyn and loosening his hold somewhat. "I don't think the Gold House would appreciate me taking on my true form in their banquet hall since I'd probably knock over several tables in the process."

Devlyn blinked, suddenly recognizing the person in front of him. This was not one of the draelyn, but a dragon. "Rusyl?"

Devlyn returned the hug, then held him at arms' length to look at him, as though he didn't quite trust what he was seeing.

"I wouldn't have survived that blast from Aren if I had been in this form, that's for certain." Rusyl smiled easily, clearly fully healed after being struck by tenebrys while defending Myrium over a year ago. Devlyn caught Rusyl up on everything that had happened after the Battle of Myrium. Even though it had only been a year ago, it felt as though it had been a decade since that battle.

They chatted cheerfully throughout the evening.

"I see you've reacquainted yourself with young Rusyl," Galithinol commented when he approached with Vivien.

"It's getting late. You should probably retire for the evening. You'll need your strength for the trials," Vivien said.

She was right and Devlyn knew it. He said goodnight to Rusyl and the others before retiring to the rooms he had been given for their stay.

DRILLED

Jaerol was by no means a master at jienzu but he'd made it his mission to spar with as many students as possible to subtly restore Balance. He could only spar with the male students at Gwilnor, since Hannah now had the school divided by gender. He had shared his thoughts about instructing Gwilnor's students in jienzu with Fyreh and Myrah and the former magisters had immediately been cautious about it. It wasn't so much that they didn't want Balance returned or that the students were too young but rather that they were sure that the Tenebrae ei'ana would see right through the scheme.

Jaerol had reassured Fyreh and Myrah that they wouldn't. The only reason he had come to a deeper understanding of jienzu was because of Elayne, a Guardian knight who had been living in secret in the lowest levels of the Temple of Ceur and had taught jienzu to Jaerol, Liam, and their bunk mates Stephen and Renaud. Jaerol had also told Fyreh and Myrah what he had learned of jienzu at the Imperium. They had stared back dubiously, unwilling to believe that anyone who knew of the old forms could forget its true purpose, let alone limit it to sword techniques. In Aelish, jienzu meant balance!

Despite the chill in the air and the packed snow beneath his feet, sweat beaded down Jaerol's back as he whipped his sword up against Talen, the kien wielder he had once shared a room with. Jaerol might not be able to teach Talen how to wield anymore but he could at least instruct him in jienzu and let the forms be his teacher. Talen was the third person Jaerol had dueled with today and other than Fyreh and Myrah's nocturnal lessons, it was the most productive he'd felt in months. Jaerol couldn't believe that he had avoided the Knight's Courtyard for so long. It was a miracle he wasn't as clumsy with a sword as he would have expected after several months without adequate training. He'd wrongly assumed that student wielders were barred from dueling with the knights and their pupils but no one had stopped him when he had grabbed a practice sword and first dueled with Liam just this morning.

His session with Liam was followed by one with Andrew, one of Devlyn's classmates who had been with him in Sorenthil. Andrew had watched his match with Liam and had insisted on dueling Jaerol after that, and several other knights and their pupils requested a turn as well. Andrew clearly had more years of experience with a sword than Liam did and it appeared that he had also learned something from his time with Viren, both abroad and here at the castle.

While Jaerol faced Andrew, Liam had dueled another one of Devlyn's classmates. Trethien Narielle was incredibly skilled with a sword but had never been trained in jienzu, so he was at a disadvantage with Liam. Jaerol was surprised when Trethien accepted defeat with grace. From what Devlyn had told him and Liam about Trethien, he was nothing more than a spoiled and pompous brat. Jaerol assumed that they simply didn't get along because they both had their eyes set on Ellendren; Trethien had once been betrothed to her after all.

More knights and pupils had wanted to spar with them, but Jaerol and Liam had a mission to teach jienzu to other wielders to help bring Balance back, so he had kindly declined and now dueled with Talen. He had to be careful with Talen and make sure he didn't lose himself in the forms. Talen didn't have any experience with a sword. If he had stayed at the temple for another year as a lay votary, he would have likely either joined the ei'ceuril or the temple knights. Not because he felt called to do either but because life as a lay votary was dreadfully boring.

Focused on Talen, Jaerol noted that his eyes had changed. He had only noticed the change a couple weeks ago, but it seemed that the green hue had completely vanished from every Luminari elf's eyes. Eye color didn't just change—unless of course that person was Devlyn and also a Phaedryn.

As Jaerol sidestepped around Talen, someone cackled from the arcade surrounding the courtyard. "Did your uncle teach you to move like that? Or did you learn how to dance like that from your oh-so-precious Kiron? Or perhaps your lethien taught you some new tricks." Razcul taunted as he sauntered into the courtyard and pushed Talen aside and stared at Liam. "Miss dueling, do you? Want a real challenge? This is a miserable excuse of a setting though. It's not even warm enough to duel as we're meant to. You miss the sun shining on your bare back, don't you? Or is it the scenery you miss? Don't think I never caught you staring at me while I was on the training field. I can see it in your eyes, Jaerol. You belong here just as much as I do." Razcul came close enough for Jaerol to smell his rotten breath.

"What do you want…Danyol." Jaerol had once made the mistake of calling Razcul by his real name and had ended up unconscious and woke a day later with a dreadful headache. Granted, it had been an accident but that mattered little to a shadow elf with a short temper.

"An innocent duel with an old classmate," he whispered, close enough for only Jaerol to hear. "Or would you rather visit me in the South Tower for a cup of tea? I'm on the sixth floor in one of the south-facing apartments. Hannah was kind enough to give me the largest of those."

"I'll settle for a duel," Jaerol said, although he felt anything but fine about it. "Practice swords are in the shed."

"Those are for children," he sneered as he went to the sword rack instead. "Surely you don't still prefer to play with toys."

Jaerol followed him to the sword rack and caught a worried look from Liam. He tried to give an encouraging smile back at him, but not even he believed its sincerity as he picked out a sword that looked decent. It was a far cry from the quality of sword that he preferred but it would have to do. It wasn't as though the shadow elf had a better selection to choose from.

"Ramiel's hell, these are awful—are these really what the Septyl knights are using?"

"We receive our own blades after we're knighted," Andrew said, keeping his anger from flaring. "These are only practice swords. Most of them are older than any of us here."

"Ah, a Septyl knight in the flesh. Where's your pretty armor? Do you think it can save you from the scary shadow elves? What color did you add to it?" Razcul looked hungrily at Andrew, as though he wanted to consume his soul here and now, uncaring whether the castle's residents found out his true nature.

"I'm with the Azurelles." Andrew stuck his chest out some, clearly proud of the School he had chosen.

"What are you waiting for, Danyol?" Jaerol intervened, having seen that look on Razcul before and wanting to distract him before there was no turning back. "Having second thoughts?"

Razcul cackled. "I've been waiting a long time for this. I understand why you were paired with Kiron at the Grand Tourney but I so wanted to go against you that day." Of all those in the courtyard, only Liam would have had any idea what Razcul was talking about. To them, Razcul—Danyol—was an Eldinari. They had no way of knowing that he was a Cyndinari like Jaerol and that the two of them had been classmates at the Imperium together. Jaerol wondered if any of them had suspected that the so-called Danyol wasn't who he said he was. He hoped so, if only so they might avoid him.

Jaerol stepped in position and raised his sword.

"Have you forgotten etiquette? Bow." Razcul stared, daring Jaerol to do otherwise. It was customary for equals to bow to each other. But Razcul did not see Jaerol as his equal and expected Jaerol to bow first as his inferior. It pained him to do it but the repercussions would be far worse if he refused. He didn't like having to bow to Razcul first, but it was only his pride that would hurt.

Razcul launched at him in a flurry of quick powerful blows after that, forcing Jaerol into a defensive stance. Razcul had grown stronger since the last time they had dueled as students—and he'd been nearly unbeatable there—but then, so had Jaerol. Learning jienzu from a Guardian knight herself, and not the poor imitation that the Cyndinari had taught him, had given him the advantage. He now had muscles on parts of his body that he never knew existed before. As Jaerol parried the attacks, he began to see Razcul's technique.

Their swords clanged against each other again but didn't part this time, turning into a battle of strength as they pushed against each other. Jaerol put all his strength into his upper body to keep Razcul's sword from cutting into him.

"You've learned a few tricks, haven't you, Jaerol?" Their bodies were practically touching as they strained against each other. Jaerol remembered what Razcul looked like beneath his Eldinari disguise. His repulsive body was corrupting from the inside out, refusing to accept his unnatural means of prolonging his life. His ashen grey skin was blistered and scabbing.

If Razcul hadn't stolen the souls of others, he would have been an attractive elf. Jaerol remembered watching him in the practice yard when they were younger. It was impossible to avoid staring at the gorgeous specimen that had been Razcul back then, especially since the Cyndinari grappled without clothing in the bright sun. Kiron had jokingly told him as he stared one sunny afternoon that Razcul was out of his league. Kiron knew whose heart Jaerol's had belonged to. But Kiron was gone now and Razcul wasn't the same pretty elf that he had once been, even if his soul had always been rotting from the inside out, even before he'd become a shadow elf.

With a final thrust, Jaerol pushed Razcul's sword back, causing the shadow elf to stumble back clumsily. Jaerol exhaled a sigh of relief but that feeling did not last when he saw the dangerous look Razcul shot at him.

Razcul threw his sword down and rushed toward Jaerol at a dizzying speed, zigzagging across the space between them. He had the ferocious look of a tiger ready to leap on its prey.

Jaerol lifted his sword but wasn't fast enough as Razcul came at him from the side, grabbed his sword away while tackling him to the ground in the same maneuver. Jaerol thudded onto his back, his head slapping against the packed snow. Dazed, Jaerol automatically lifted his forearms to guard his face as Razcul pummeled into him.

Bruises and welts were the least of Jaerol's concerns right now. This wasn't a shadow elf who merely wanted to hurt him—a blood lust had come over Razcul. These punches were meant to maim and perhaps even kill.

His body screamed in agony as he moaned under the assault. Wasn't anyone going to stop this? One of the knights? An ei'ana? Liam?

But no, they were all too terrified to stop it. They might not know that Danyol was a false name but they did know enough to not get in his way. Even Liam knew there was nothing he could do—interrupting Razcul would only make it worse. Jaerol would be lucky enough to escape with only injuries—he knew they'd be severe but at least he'd still breathe. If Liam interfered, Razcul would surely take Jaerol's soul and likely Liam's too for good measure. He might even do it with witnesses filling the courtyard.

"Why, Danyol," Hannah said cheerily as though nothing was amiss. Another blow landed on Jaerol's face, causing his ears to ring.

"Chancellor," Razcul said as he leaned back onto Jaerol's thighs and keeping his eyes on Jaerol lying flat on the ground in a bloodied mess.

"Is that Jaerol beneath you? Really, I am only guessing based on the red hair."

"He wanted a few dueling and sparring lessons—lessons I was only too happy to oblige."

"Boys will be boys," Hannah said with a high-pitched laugh. "Well, climb off him and come along with me. We have matters to discuss. It's about these rumors flooding through the castle about unsafe and unsanctioned lessons in wielding. They cannot be permitted to continue." Hannah peered around the courtyard, seeming to look each kien wielder there in the eyes. "I will not allow someone—anyone—regardless of their station to risk the safety of my students. Now come along, Danyol."

Jaerol started to push himself up as soon as Razcul began to stand, but Razcul shoved him down again before he was fully off Jaerol. The feral glint in his eyes seemed to promise his intent to steal Jaerol's soul the moment he was permitted to. Truly, if Hannah hadn't called for Razcul, Jaerol didn't think he would still be breathing.

"What did you do to make him so angry?" Fyreh asked as he wielded a simple healing into Jaerol's very damaged face. While Fyreh could have easily mended Jaerol good as new, he had to restrain himself and leave the more visible wounds largely intact. Razcul would know if Jaerol had been healed and wouldn't hesitate to reinjure Jaerol for breaking the rules.

Wielding was now outlawed at Gwilnor. So instead of completely healing Jaerol, Fyreh soothed the visible wounds and eradicated all the invisible ones. The ringing in his ears had finally stopped and it no longer felt like his face was broken. It was still sore but at least he didn't have to worry about any fractured bones.

"I bested him in a duel. I forgot how rudimentary the jienzu forms I had learned at the Imperium were—the sword forms that Razcul still uses."

"Forgive me for saying this, and it is by no means a reflection on you, but when all the Cyndinari lust for is power and brute strength, it leaves them terribly unbalanced. Your success today, however brief, is a testament to that. Still, it was foolish to beat Razcul at his own game. You might have escaped with only a bruised eye, not the mess that you're currently in."

"I know. It did feel good to beat him though."

Fyreh laughed. "Well, I think you're in as good a shape as I dare heal you for now. Go join Fiona and practice wielding together."

Jaerol thanked Fyreh and went to join Fiona where she was practicing with two others while Jaerol was being healed.

Fyreh had repeatedly grumbled about the inability of most of them to touch their inner senses, saying that they might as well be blind. The only advantage to that was that the Tenebrae ei'ana running Gwilnor were just as ignorant to that innermost sense and couldn't make any use of it either. If they had been able to, Jaerol and Liam would have been easily discovered the first night they had sneaked into the East Tower and hid under the stair.

To replace the ability to reach that innermost sense, Myrah had them learn a wield that was the next best thing. It was by no means a substitute for growing their self-awareness and tapping their inner beings but it would at least help them better avoid being caught when sneaking around the castle at night.

This wield simultaneously manipulated the four elemental erendinth and, when done correctly, could fool someone looking straight at them into thinking that they were not there. But they had to perform a second wield for it be effective. While the first wield made them invisible to a particular observer, the other made the wielding all but indiscernible. Naturally, the second wield was only necessary when trying to hide from another wielder. If someone couldn't sense the erendinth being wielded, there was no reason to try to hide their wielding. However, in a castle filled to the brim with wielders, the second wield was pivotal.

Fyreh and Myrah had spent the past several weeks teaching them the latter with great success. Every student had managed to hide their wielding and could easily do so now. After spending months in Yvonne's ineffectual classes, the Eldinari twins' teaching methods were a breath of fresh air. It was nice to learn something useful again, although he couldn't discount learning to sleep with his eyes open as a useless skill. While Fyreh and Myrah had only taught them how to conceal their wielding for the sake of the other wield, Jaerol immediately saw the advantages of wielding in plain sight without anyone else being the wiser.

Fiona attempted the invisibility wield first. Jaerol focused on her, watching carefully to not miss anything. If they made one mistake in front of a Tenebrae ei'ana or a shadow elf in disguise, they wouldn't have a second chance. Granted, if they performed the wield correctly, no one would see them disappear in front of their eyes. The wield would have to be in place well before they were seen.

It felt as though Jaerol's eyes went out of focus when Fiona vanished right in front of him. She didn't flicker or shimmer. One moment she was there and the next she was gone. Jaerol blinked. It felt like his eyes were playing tricks on him or he was delirious from exhaustion.

"Did it work?" she asked, still invisible to Jaerol, although only to Jaerol.

"Yeah—it was weird. I didn't even notice you disappear." Jaerol looked about in case she moved from her original position. However, as Myrah had told them, moving made maintaining the illusion more difficult, so Fiona couldn't move if she wanted to remain invisible to Jaerol. The wield didn't make her invisible but rather fooled the other person into believing that she wasn't there. It affected only the target's eyesight.

They switched off for the next hour and by the excited tone in the burnt-out room in the East Tower a little later, all the students had successfully accomplished both wields simultaneously. Fyreh and Myrah went from group to group, observing them and having the students they were unsure about use the wield on one of them. They wanted their students to be experts at these two wields before they left for the night. That was even more important now since Hannah was actively trying to find out where these lessons were being held and who led them.

Learning the two wields didn't come with a grade. No one was trying to achieve the foremost mark. Rather, the point was to stay safe.

THE TRIALS

Devlyn followed Vivien through a round portal that led to the place where his trials would start at dawn. They had traveled well below the central and tallest of the jeweled spires, the one that had the largest gem that Devlyn had ever seen floating above the peak. It was hard to tell, but it looked larger than the bedchamber that he had occupied this past week.

The walls of this subterranean level were thick and he could have stood in the middle of the portal with his arms stretched out and still not reach either side of the opening. While Devlyn knew that his trials had been scheduled to start at dawn because he had a special connection to the morning sun, that connection didn't seem particularly pertinent this far below the city. When was the last time the sun had reached this deep? Had it ever?

Gemstones sparkled where lighting fixtures might otherwise be, glimmering in the near-dark. As Devlyn followed Vivien through the chamber, he felt something he had not felt since he had visited Oma's cave in Belin's Watch. The deeper into the chamber, the more he felt the space pressing in on him. He paused and reached for Vivien. "This stone…" he breathed, unsure how to finish his thought. He had no idea what the stone in Oma's cave was and had no idea whether this was the same. It felt much the same.

"Is awake." Vivien pulled Devlyn along. "This is not the only location, but it is one of the few remaining. She stays awake for us. She remembers what even our ancient minds forget with each passing millennium."

Feeling the stone's pressure building around him as though it was trying to penetrate the outer layer of his mind, Devlyn grew unsteady and unsure whether this was the right thing to do or not. Daela had made it clear that he could die in these trials. If only Kyrendal hadn't made that stupid vow of his to stop crafting verathn, Devlyn wouldn't have to do this. Kyrendal could have at least stored a few extra verathn in that cave of his. Given how easily he had driven off Aren with the cane crafted from the one he had snapped, he had seemed more than capable of protecting any extra verathn.

"Your mind is still in chaos. Only Balance will see you through these trials, Devlyn." Vivien's voice comforted him. The interaction was odd; it felt almost motherly. His short stay at the gold spire had him feeling as though he was visiting distant family for the first time. They had all been excited to see him and eagerly welcomed him into their home, which in all respects was a palace, simply confined and shaped into a single spire. Truly, it was an experience that Devlyn had no comparison for. Despite the draelyn mostly being ancient—Vivien had been born before the Great Blessing—they were completely relatable. The younger ones did complain about having to talk to Devlyn in the Common Tongue though. They were much more fluent in High Aelish, considered the Aelish that Devlyn had learned as juvenile, and preferred to speak in Draelish, which they claimed was the closest linguistic branch to the Elder Tongue, and which they also spoke fluently. Kevn would have a field day learning the Elder Tongue.

Devlyn had quickly learned that all the children he had met were considerably older than he was. The draelyn who looked like teenagers were even older than Wyn. Wyn was of course an elf, and like all anacordel other than dragons, descended from the Children who had become the elder ones. However, the draelyn were descended from the elder ones and the dragons. Did their draconic ancestry alter how they aged?

The further Vivien took Devlyn into the chamber, the more the lighting dimmed. "Why is it getting darker?" Devlyn had no idea how close they were to the center of the chamber, or if it was even a cylindrical chamber. He had assumed so, given that it had to be part of the foundations of the round spire above. When Vivien didn't respond, Devlyn squinted, but the more he tried to focus his vision, the less he could see. Panicked, he spun around, reaching out for Aliel in the process.

No response. He was alone.

Thankfully, the agonizing knot in his stomach was absent; the solitude and fear were enough to deal with at present.

When his surroundings brightened, he realized that he no longer was in the chamber beneath Tenethyl's central spire. Had he walked all the way through and out into a clearing? He stood on a vast plain; the sun had already risen, yet a blight clung to the horizon. He moved toward it, hoping to get a better glimpse of what he was becoming more and more sure was a threat. The nearer he drew to it, the more he became convinced that it must be a mistake. Unless it was part of his trial?

It was only when he crouched low to the ground that he realized that he seemed to have changed his clothing. Focusing his gaze in the direction of Ramiel's expected arrival and the threatening blight, he could make out terrifying monsters and beasts, the likes of which he had never dreamt of before. They clung to the blight, or the blight clung to them, he couldn't tell, but the area around them withered as though it was diseased. All the grass and plants in the vicinity of the awful beasts had died. What was this?

Turning around to look back toward the city, his heart leapt. It wasn't the same Tenethyl that he had arrived in the week before, but oddly enough, it *was* Tenethyl. There was no other city that could compare to it. And something awful—Ramiel and his delegation—was coming. He crept toward the city and away from the blight and its monsters, waiting until he was further away from the approaching blight before standing to his full height and sprinting as fast he could back to the safety of the city walls. His mind slipped between reality and what he thought he knew—Tenethyl was in the Illumined Wood, on an island precipice at the top of a vast waterfall.

Even as he thought it, he laughed at the ridiculousness of such a location. If the city were on an island, he wouldn't be able to sprint there as he was doing now. It's not like he could fly. He might be a draelyn, but that didn't mean his grandfather was going to fly him over the river and walls. Dragons rarely permitted someone to ride on their back, family or not.

He shook his head. *But I'm not a draelyn. I'm an elf and a Phaedryn.* Neither of those words resonated as he picked up his pace toward the city. None of this made any sense. Was Ramiel manipulating his mind—unraveling his grasp on reality? He had to tell his father and grandfather what was happening to him. He had to tell the queen about the approaching horde!

Thien gasped, his breath short after his sprint across the Plains of Orithil. He had never ventured far from home and the glittering spires of Tenethyl had never been out of his sight. But today was different. He had seen Ramiel's delegation peeking over the horizon. They'd been told by Ramiel's herald to expect wonders from the irythil of umbrys, but what he had seen was unexpectedly grotesque. Rumors had spread throughout Tenethyl that umbrys was the antithesis of lumenys. As a child born to the Gold Flight, Thien knew otherwise. The erendinth existed in Balance, none opposed the others. Their unity had created Teraeniel.

Still, after seeing Ramiel's delegation of creatures wholly other than he had ever seen before, Thien thought otherwise. Perhaps the erendinth were polarized. If that was so, how had Teraeniel been created?

Thien paused briefly outside Tenethyl's gates. The defensive wall was a newer addition and people still complained about it. It had been terribly expensive. Hundreds of laborers had spent fifty years completing it. Thien had not been selected as a laborer, his family too important for that. His father, Lord Weilyn, son of Galithinol the Gold and head of his house, would never allow his only son to stoop to menial labor. There was nothing menial about this wall though. Thien marveled at its design and its intricate patterns of arcane gems that lined the walls in swooping patterns.

There had been much controversy about the wall. It had been requested by the dragons, who had gone to investigate troubling news that had come out of the west, news of great destruction, and the dragons had flown there to see it for themselves. When they returned, they had expressed their concern about what they had seen to Queen Kaelien and her advisors, many of whom were draelyn, and they had suggested building a wall around the entire city. A ludicrous idea.

Nothing in Teraeniel had ever been destroyed. The erendinth created, and that which was created continued in that creative process. Destruction and violence were not known to Teraeniel. And the news that there indeed had been violence and destruction was not accepted in Tenethyl. Queen Kaelien had demanded to see the supposed destruction for herself. Myrasha of the Purple Flight had reluctantly obliged the queen and permitted Kaelien to fly on her back, even while making it known that the dragons resented not being believed more than letting someone fly on their backs.

Upon her return, the queen had ordered the wall built. She would not speak of what she had seen, simply had given the order. Thien had pestered his father for details, but Weilyn had none to give.

The people of Tenethyl had finally agreed that if they were to have a wall surrounding the entire city, it had better be beautiful. The queen and her people would have nothing less. Tenethyl's splendor is what had brought the dragons to her in the first place.

Walking through the gate—another new addition to Tenethyl—Thien nodded to the guards. Long metallic tools that the dragons called swords hung from belts at their waists. Galithinol, the only gold dragon in Tenethyl and Thien's grandfather, had professed regret for their introduction to Anaweh's children. Violence had no part in the Creating Light's design. Even so, the dragons taught them how to use these weapons, fearful that their friends and descendants would perish if they could not defend themselves.

Thien quickened his pace. He was already late for the queen's council, but he had wanted to see Ramiel's delegation for himself. While the anadel were a common sight in Tenethyl, a visit from one of the seven irythil was not. Ramiel was the first irythil to visit Tenethyl. Even the enthiel rarely appeared, other than Feniel who frequented the city regularly. But she had been absent for several months and Thien knew that the queen longed for her guidance.

At the broad plaza that opened at the base of the Jeweled Spire, Thien yet again marveled at the delicate stonework twining upward. The sight helped calm the terror he'd felt at the sight of the approaching blight.

The stone was sleepy, but even it had stirred at the song of Anaweh's children. The further one went from the city, the more tired the stone became. Galithinol had described the nature of created things and how the stone, while alive, detested movement. It had done enough of that during Teraeniel's birth. The other elements had had it easy—they weren't solid.

A great crystal shimmered above the spire's peak, hovering over the royal complex. Thien gazed at the crystal, the pride of his people. Twelve people would have had to link hands to encompass the great jewel. Surrounding the Jeweled Spire were smaller spires competing against each other for height and beauty, but none rivaled the central spire. The outlying towers belonged to the great families and houses of Tenethyl. Thien lived in the gold spire, the smallest of the draelyn houses, with his family.

As the eldest child of his house, Thien had been invited to the queen's council to receive Ramiel's delegation, and he entered the throne room only a little late despite his short venture beyond the city wall. Queen Kaelien's throne room was crowded with her advisors, Thien's father Weilyn among them. Several dragons had shifted to their smaller forms—still larger than Anaweh's children. The throne room was extensive, but it was not big enough for several dragons in the larger form! Galithinol was nowhere to be seen. Thien wondered where his grandfather could be. Surely this was a gathering he would not want to miss.

Queen Kaelien sat on her jeweled throne, where a gem resembling the one above the spire was embedded into the crest of the throne, just above her head. Kaelien looked exhausted, as though preparations for Ramiel's visit had kept her much occupied. Ramiel's delegation would reach the city tomorrow and this chamber would take on a very different atmosphere.

Thien tamped the feelings of disquiet and fear that threatened to overwhelm him again and walked toward his father, easily locating him by his golden hair and eyes, especially among the other draelyn who had taken on the physical appearances of the dragon flights of their sires. A sea of ruby, azure, ebony, amethyst, emerald, and diamond hair and eyes swirled in the room. Not everyone in the room was a draelyn or dragon though, since half of the councilors had their origins solely in the Valley of Saeryndol. Queen Kaelien was among that number and her silver eyes saw everything. "This council is called into session," she said.

Voices hushed in a quick wave across the room and the queen's advisors moved to form a crescent around their queen. Thien stood directly behind his father, as did all the eldest children stand behind their parent, creating a two-rowed crescent.

"This very morning, I was approached by Uriel, Lord of the Stars," Kaelien said, her words followed by a wave of whispers along the outer ring of the court's attendants where Thien stood. While Uriel loved and cared for Anaweh's children, he cared most for those who had never left the Valley of Saeryndol. Even the lesser anadel of lumenys rarely ventured past the valley where the Children first woke. That Uriel had come to Tenethyl was surprising indeed.

"The irythil cautioned against inviting Ramiel's delegation into our city. Uriel has confirmed that Ramiel is responsible for the corruption and violence spreading across Teraeniel, Ramiel and his horde of beasts bent on destruction." Kaelien paused. She looked into Thien's eyes. "You've seen them, haven't you, Thien?"

Lord Weilyn looked to his son in shock. There hadn't been enough time to tell him why he was late before the queen had called her council into session. And Thien had not told his father what he had intended when he had left their spire for the city wall that morning.

"I have, Your Majesty." Thien became the center of attention as the council members of the first row shifted to allow him to face the queen with no others in between.

"Tell us what you saw."

Thien offered an apologetic look at Weilyn before speaking. "Creatures the size of dragons or bigger march toward our city. I've never seen anything like them before. I won't pretend to know Anaweh's mind, but these seem foreign to the Creating Light. They look—well, they are difficult to describe, but they seem twisted and corrupted, a danger to all of us here. They don't seem to have any resemblance to umbrys. They also look incredibly powerful, more powerful than the dragons, I think. When I first saw them on our plains, I was terrified."

"Terrified?" The queen did not seem surprised at this. "While I have not seen the creatures that you saw, I have seen the destruction they are capable of. I could not imagine at the time that an irythil would plot against Anaweh's children, but Uriel has confirmed it. Ramiel is behind Teraeniel's unrest. In fact, his crimes against creation have stripped him of his position among the irythil. He is banished and Remiel has replaced him as the irythil of umbrys."

"My queen," one of the advisors said, "what does Ramiel want with us?"

"Uriel could not say for certain, but the refugees who have started to trickle back into the Valley of Saeryndol seeking safety have made an unbelievable claim. They say that Ramiel offered the villages and cities two options: join him or perish." The exhaustion Thien had noted earlier was now explained. Kaelien must have been considering different options since Uriel's visit.

"We are too far from the Valley of Saeryndol to make it there safely," Weilyn said. Thien feared his father's next words. "And even if we decide to flee for the valley, could we really abandon Tenethyl?"

"So, our only option is to defend our city?" Kaelien asked.

"Is there no other way?" asked Gael, the queen's niece, daughter of the queen's elder sister, who had died giving birth to Gael. At the time, the connection between a mother's death and the birth of a draelyn was still unknown. Gael's mother had been queen before Kaelien. Gael's emerald eyes implored her aunt for another solution.

"Our options are limited. Weilyn is correct. We will never reach the valley safely. We ventured too far before building our fair city. If we make the attempt, we will surely die on the journey home. Irithel, enlist as many hands as you can—the fires in your forges will burn bright tonight and for as long as our city stands threatened."

"Yes, my queen." Irithel's eyes gleamed red, as though those fires had already started.

"Aeryth, I need you to learn as much of this enemy as you can—do not let them find you. Stay in your shadows." A series of instructions went out, mostly directed to the draelyn. They were capable of things others not born of dragons were not. Thien knew of lumenys' wonder, but he questioned how helpful it would be in defending the city from Ramiel and his minions.

In the hours following the queen's pronouncement, the city burned with life and determination. Every citizen wanted to contribute to Tenethyl's security. Hammers sung in Irithel's forge to meet the demand as people clamored for swords to defend the city.

Thien sat with his family in their spire's great hall. Weilyn had called a gathering and informed everyone of the queen's decision. Precious little was said after. Even Galithinol the Gold had few words for his descendants. The dragon's smaller form radiated a golden sheen, making it difficult to see the identifiable features that he had passed on to his son and descendants. The gold dragon still mourned for his late wife, Weilyn's mother. Thien knew that his grandfather had blamed himself for her death. Anaweh's children simply could not survive giving birth to a dragon's offspring.

Thien's mother, Raleniel, held her youngest daughter, Thien's sister, Vivien. The small girl did not understand what was happening but held her mother tightly.

"What options do we have? Weilyn, our walls cannot stand against these monsters. If they're as large as Thien claims, not even the dragons will be able to protect us," Raleniel said.

"I've already explained that we would never make it to the valley; we are too far to reach it safely. Ramiel arrives tomorrow. And based on what the refugees who made it back to the valley said, we will be given two choices."

"Galithinol, couldn't you at least carry our children to the valley for safety? Couldn't the dragons save our children?" Raleniel pleaded.

"We have considered it. Our fear is that if we attempt it, we will be brought down, killing anyone we carry. Ramiel has already corrupted some of our kind. He wants more of us. We will help defend Tenethyl, but we fear that it will be at great cost."

"There has to be a way. What of the subterranean rivers?"

"They are too dangerous to navigate," Weilyn replied.

"Can't the draelyn born of the Sapphire House control them? They have power over the waters, just as you and our children have power over the light. And there are more of them than there are of us. Surely their combined strength could save us."

"As a contingency, that could work. I will speak with Naithos; Thien, you'll accompany me," Galithinol said.

"In the meantime, we should prepare," Weilyn said. "I'll look to the house guard and find out what Queen Kaelien intends for our house." Weilyn left the room.

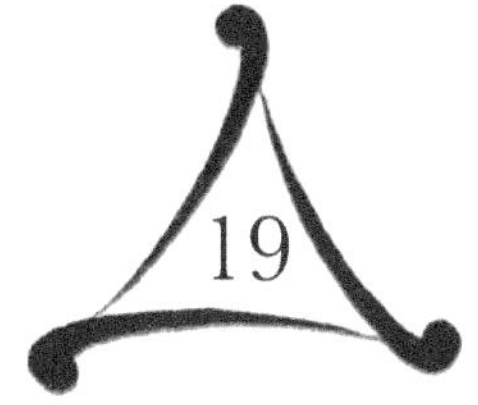

ANCIENT FOE

Thien had gone to Irithel's forge early, an hour before the sun crested over the Plains of Orithil, but the entire city seemed to have awoken before daybreak—if anyone had even managed to sleep the night before. The children of Tenethyl seemed to be the only ones capable of sleeping through the night; Thien had seen that his sister was one of those. He had tried to lie down to sleep but had instead spent several hours staring at the dark ceiling. Rather than waste the night away, he had trained, Galithinol instructing him in several forms that would prepare him for the sword that he now held.

He hadn't expected the weapon to be so heavy, but given that his power was over lumenys, he figured that he had better learn to use this sword. What harm could light do against a beast twice the size of the largest dragon Thien had ever seen?

On top of the outer wall, Thien now stood waiting with a dozen of his house guard. He had nearly protested during the queen's audience the night before when he had received his assignment for the coming battle. Queen Kaelien had ordered them to accompany the children and vulnerable out of the city by way of the subterranean rivers, a decision that had infuriated Thien. He wanted to stay and fight.

Their escort would not begin for another two hours, so, since nothing the queen had commanded prevented him and his house guard from helping now, they would patrol the outer wall until it was time to provide the escort out of the city. From the top of the wall, he could see that Ra-miel's delegation was much closer to the city now than when Thien had first seen it the preceding morning. As before, the grass and plants with-ered at their approach and Thien could now see the scar their march to Tenethyl left across the land.

Despite having seen it the previous day, a sudden swell of terror rose inside him at the thought of such destruction being the result of Ra-miel freed from his prison. Shaking his head, Thien grounded himself. Ramiel wasn't bound in any prison. Even if he should be, what sort of prison could contain the likes of Ramiel? Even if Anaweh had expelled him from the irythil, what sort of realistic punishment or penalty could the irythil enact against him? Whatever the other irythil planned for Ra-miel, Thien feared that it would come too late for Tenethyl.

He prayed for a miracle. Were any of the anadel listening? Was Anaweh even aware of what was happening? Could the Creating Light intervene and save Tenethyl? Like all the other anacordel, Thien knew that they had ventured far from Anaweh's original designs. As Thien saw it, only the two Children and the anacordel who had never left the Valley of Saeryndol remained true to his primal desires for his creations. Already the different communities across Teraeniel were changing. He half expected some of them to turn into fish or into trees, given their admiration of the oceans and the forests.

But the current sight filling his vision was something else entire-ly—not in his wildest nightmares could he imagine any of Anaweh's creations turning into these horrible creatures. Were these beings truly created by Anaweh, then corrupted under Ramiel's influence? Or had Ramiel gained the power to create in his own image? Thien didn't know how to classify the anadel anymore. Despite Ramiel's role in bringing umbrys to the creation of Teraeniel, he no longer was the irythil of that erendinth. What did that make him now? Thien recognized umbrys well enough to know that the encroaching horde was not manipulating shadows. This was something else—something wholly other and sinister.

Perhaps the rumors that had started to infiltrate Tenethyl were right; perhaps whatever Ramiel had become was the antithesis of lumenys. *Tenebrys.* He shivered at the word; it was one he had never heard before.

Gripping his sword, he was surprised to hear the first horns sounding. They were early. Ramiel's delegation had approached the city much sooner than anticipated. Focusing his eyes, he noticed figures standing erect near the front. A shadowed cloud clung to their forms, but that was not umbrys they were manipulating. The figures didn't appear to be anacordel, but even so, that uncertainty in the back of his mind recognized them. *Deurghol.* Another word he did not recognize floated in his mind and with it, a deadening fear. The Deurghol had not existed until the Shroud had been unleashed on Krysenthiel.

"My lord, are you all right?" Mara asked. "You've gone pale. Perhaps we should return to your family." Although he had known Mara all his life, she was a recent addition to the staff of the Gold House, one of the first to join the house's guard. Many of the wealthy residents of Tenethyl had decided to hire house guards when the outer wall had been built because the safety of their city was threated. The dragons had instructed them personally to protect Tenethyl and its people.

"I'll be fine, thank you, Mara." Even as he said it, he felt his mind unraveling. His sense of reality slipped from his grasp.

The shadowed creatures floated above the rest of their delegation, suspended in the air. "Submit," they chanted in unison, their shallow voices echoing in the night. "Tenethyl survives if you submit to Ramiel, Master of All."

Their voices pierced Thien's heart, nagging at him to surrender. He believed them. Tenethyl would fall whether they fought against these beings or not. It didn't matter if the collective dragon flights battled this assault. Not a single dragon defending Tenethyl could survive against the approaching beasts. To fight meant the city would be destroyed.

"Submit," the Deurghol repeated.

As he stared at them, he noticed that they were not the same as the one that had attacked him months ago. These were more ethereal—phantoms without a host. Is that what had happened to the Cyndinari that had brought about the Shroud? Had they been possessed by these anadel chained to Ramiel? With those thoughts, Thien shook his head—he had not been attacked months ago. Where did that come from? And what was the Shroud?

"My lord, I must insist that we return; you are not well." Mara reached for his elbow; the rest of his house guard already turning back, eager to leave.

From an open balcony on the Jeweled Spire, Queen Kaelien's voice thundered, "We will not submit to whatever you and your master have become." When he looked up toward the spire, the bottom of the balcony prevented Thien from seeing his queen, but his imagination filled in the gaps. It was a powerful response, one that might cause anyone coming before her to mistake her for an anadel sent from Anaweh.

"By your edict, your people will die."

From beside him, Mara tugged on his arm, no longer polite or gentle. "Lord Thien, we have to reach our post, we must go now." She hauled him out of his daze as he mumbled unrecognizable words to himself.

What was happening to him?

His fear bubbled over when one of the smaller beasts, its claws half the length of its forearms, flew over the wall, blocking their path to safety. The creature was scabbed, as if it had been tortured horrendously. Its eyes bulged, the centers a recognizable black, but the white edges were rimmed in vicious red veins.

It dawdled above them, shifting back and forth where it waited, as though curious about how they would react to it. Was it conscious?

Thien shook his troubled thoughts away to ask, "What are you?" The creature seemed to be in pain.

It tilted its head, recognition brimming in its eyes. Thien took a step forward, but the creature screeched and lunged at him, sharp claws slashing toward his chest. He raised his sword just in time to impale it. Thien saw light escape from its eyes as it slid into death, and shocked, he vomited. Thien had never killed another creature before and didn't know of anyone else who had either. And whatever that thing had been, it had been a living thing created by Anaweh. Thien didn't know if it had been an anacordel or simply a cordel, but it had been alive not a moment before and now it was dead.

For a moment, Thien wondered where this creature's soul would go. Would it wander Teraeniel for eternity—lost? Or would it travel to Somnaeniel or even Lumaeniel? His next thought was for himself. What would happen if he died here? What would happen to anyone who was killed? Other than the mothers of the first draelyn, no one in Tenethyl had ever died before. Questions about death were never asked, not even by the scholars and mystics. Why ask a question that didn't matter? But now, it did matter and Thien was terrified that he didn't have an answer.

Lumaeniel. The part of his mind that had been providing the un-recognizable names spoke again, and even as he accepted the word, he worried.

"What is happening to me?" he asked and then Mara was beside him again, eager to get him as far from the outer wall as possible. Still shaken, he allowed Mara to pull him down the stairs.

Chaos had ensued in the brief time Thien had been in a daze. Hundreds, if not thousands of those creatures had flown over Tenethyl's protective walls and were slashing at anyone they came across. Thien's heart wallowed in pain as he watched his people and the creatures die. This was wrong—so wrong. Why would Ramiel want to do this? Why did he want to corrupt and destroy Anaweh's wondrous creation?

Lost in his agonized thoughts as Mara pulled him along, the sound of a great bonging crash brought him to himself. Tenethyl's wall had been built taller than any of the attacking beasts, but it seemed that their intent was to bring it down. The attackers smashed against the thick wall that had been designed to protect the city from these very creatures. Despite the thickness of the wall—three times as wide as any of the horrific beasts—Thien still felt the ground shake under the unending assault.

He thought of his siblings, and hoped that the youngest, Vivien, was still asleep. None were old enough to fight yet, and there was only the house guard to protect them. Galithinol would be with a contingent of dragons, who should even now be striking the rearguard of the attackers. Thien uttered another prayer, this time for his grandfather's safety.

Several of the flying creatures surrounded Thien and his house guard. Like the first one Thien had come across, the creatures seemed to be looking at him hesitantly, as though they recognized something about him, or rather, something that they did not have. Something that they remembered as having once had but had been stripped of. This larger group reacted faster than the first one though, and they lunged in unison at Thien and his small group. Thien fought back tears as his sword plunged into one and then another, the rest dispatched by the house guard. The guilt pressing on him was only barely outweighed by the need to protect his city—his family. All he could focus on was the onslaught attacking him as he fought toward the gold spire, terrified that his family was in danger.

His fear increased the closer he drew to his home and still the beasts attacked. Reaching the plaza in front of the gold spire, his heart plummeted when he saw one of the larger creatures trying to force its way through the spire's entrance, which fortunately, appeared to be holding firm. But it wouldn't be enough to simply reach his family inside the spire, he had to get them to one of the entrances to the underground rivers.

Taking a deep breath, Thien steadied himself before rushing into the throng of beasts in the plaza. His sword flashed and the metal shone in the morning sun, its glint somewhat tarnished with red as he swung and stabbed through the enemy toward his home.

He eased back a bit when he noticed that the number of attacking creatures had diminished, but then he saw Mara, hunched over just a few paces behind him. He rushed to her side.

She turned away from him. "Go, protect your family. Get them out of here."

Thien reached for her, and felt her tunic moist and sticky, with fresh blood oozing from a hidden wound. "How long were you fighting like this?"

"Save them," she pleaded. "Get them out."

Thien tried to haul her up, but she cried out in pain and he let go when the blood seemed to flow faster from her side. As his own anguish welled inside of him, he reached for the primal instinct that had always dwelt within. He had only been able to make flashes of light, nothing useful, certainly nothing beneficial in a battle. But as he interacted with that part of him passed down from Galithinol the Gold, he felt lumenys explode from himself and into Mara. The soothing light flared bright, forcing the attacking creatures to scatter away from the gold spire, and poured into Mara's wound, knitting her insides anew. The ruptured organs and severed skin recreated themselves and her body became whole again.

She looked up at him, her mouth agape. "What have you done?"

This should not have been possible. Thien didn't know whether it was a forbidden power, but he hadn't simply made a flash of light, as he had for Mara as amusement when they were young. This was more. This was something completely different. This was useful. He knew he wasn't strong enough to save the city but, perhaps, he was strong enough to save as many people as possible.

He rushed to the gold spire's entrance, calling out to those hiding inside, and raced in the moment the door was opened to him and the house guard. Everyone who lived in the surrounding neighborhood had come here for safety, joining his family and others who lived in the spire. He recognized many of his neighbors and was greatly relieved to see his mother holding a quietly crying Vivien, tears rolling down her face.

More enemies had reached the gold spire by the time everyone inside was organized, although they seemed less intent in trying to get in-side the spire. The number of people in his care was larger than expect-ed—he was only supposed to be protecting his family and house, not an entire district of Tenethyl! Fortunately, everyone understood the urgency of their situation and only carried what they needed.

Thien led them out of the spire. The house guard and anyone who could carry a sword cleared the way forward through the streets. The more able-bodied in their group protected the rear of their column. Carving through the attacking beasts, Thien gulped when something much larger blocked their path. It must have recognized that the people of Tenethyl were fleeing and it roared at Thien and the larger number of people in his care.

The monstrous beast loomed ahead, standing on two stubby legs the width of mature tree trunks, raising one leg and stomping, then the other leg and stomping again, the stomping making the city tremble and the buildings quake. It repeated the stomps and Thien realized that it wasn't just trying to intimidate him and the others, no, it was trying to bring the surrounding buildings down, the pounding causing the build-ings to weaken and fall. Dust and pebbles fell from above, and with each of the beast's stomps, the debris grew, full stone blocks now falling.

Their time was limited. If Thien and the others didn't think of a course of action soon, not only would the surrounding buildings fall on top of them, but the underground rivers might very well be buried. Mara, now healed, stood beside him, ready to leap into the fight against the corrupted creature. Thien had no idea what it had once been, but it was no longer recognizable as something of the Creating Light. *A giant?* Again, the unfamiliar name made little sense to Thien. This beast was certainly large, but what was a giant?

Thien instructed the house guard to stay back and protect their group at all costs, and if something happened to him, to get them to an-other subterranean entrance. Then Thien and Mara charged the large beast, Thien suddenly wishing that he had something longer than his sword. This creature was much larger than him and he wanted to maintain as much distance as he could.

The beast didn't seem to be able to move quickly, so Thien managed to narrowly avoid the beast's outward thrust of its massive forearms to slash his sword across its side, while Mara attacked it from the other side. His first slash into the creature's hide had little effect, other than a responding yelp and some blood oozing from the wound, but Thien followed the slash with a hard jab that jammed his sword into the creature. Unfortunately, the creature now knew exactly where Thien was as he struggled to pull his sword from its side.

The beast grabbed Thien, crushing his midsection and tossing him against the side of the nearest building. Luckily, the toss had also pulled Thien's sword out, and his ribs aching, unable to draw a deep breath, his head spinning from the knock it had taken against the building, he tried to regain his footing.

Whatever this creature was, it now seemed intent to finish Thien off, ignoring Mara who, despite some hard thrusts, was unable to penetrate the creature's skin. It came clumsily over to Thien on all fours, its stubby back legs unable to support its entire weight for long, plodding forward on its bulbous fists as well.

Thien felt for that power again, that power that he had thought useless, and used it on himself, groaning as his body healed, the various bones recreating themselves, muscles and crushed tissue reforming. He had to time this right. He watched Mara position herself, realizing what she was about to do. Dancing from leg to leg, she launched herself from behind the hunched over beast, leaping onto its back, sword raised as the beast aimed one bulbous fist toward Thien. Just before Mara's sword connected with the creature's neck, Thien exploded lumenys and the creature screamed at the bright light and the pain of its slashed neck.

Mara was off the creature in seconds, before it rose tall on its hind legs, wobbling backward in manic confusion then crashing dead to the ground.

Turning to see where his family and neighbors were, Thien realized that the rest of the guard had fought off several smaller beasts. Everyone seemed somewhat dazed despite the continued danger that surrounded them. His mother still carried Vivien, no longer crying but petrified. Thien approached his family, limping and uncertain how much more abuse his body could take.

"Let's get everyone in the tunnels before something else finds us." He looked at his mother. "The guards can take all of you there. I have to find Father."

"No, Thien," his mother said, her voice authoritative. "You can barely stand. You were charged to protect us and see us to safety; this is not over yet. Your siblings will not make it to the Valley of Saeryndol without you."

"But Father…" Thien protested.

"Knew that he wouldn't survive the city's fall. Do not tarnish his sacrifice."

Thien's knees buckled. His father was still alive. He could do something to save him. He couldn't run away from the fight.

"He loves you, Thien, he loves us all, and that is why he is doing what he is doing." Raleniel's voice quivered, as she tried to mask her fear and her grief. "He needs you to protect us—he is already so proud of you."

# VERATHN

Devlyn awoke slowly in the chamber, the one that had been dark, only it wasn't dark now, since glittering gemstones covered all the walls. He was lying on the floor of the cavern, his mind still foggy, and he realized that, at some point, he had forgotten who he was. Somehow, he had become Thien, a draelyn fighting to save his people because Ramiel had attacked Tenethyl, a Tenethyl unlike the one Devlyn knew. How long ago had that happened?

As he lay there, gathering his self and his thoughts, Devlyn understood that this space had not been constructed as part of the jeweled central spire above, but rather was a natural cavern. Had the gemstones always been there? He shook his head to try to clear the mild confusion he was feeling. He had had no idea what to expect from the trials, but it certainly wasn't what he had just experienced.

His grasp of reality and identity had never been so challenged before. What was real and what was he to believe about what he'd experienced? He could still feel the cavern pressing against him and saw that he was the only person here. Hadn't Vivien walked with him in here? Was she meant to lead him in and then leave him to his trials or had she assumed that he would fail and die?

Wanting answers, he sat up, and located the round door he'd come through—it seemed to be the only door into the cavern. But he was sure there hadn't been a door before. Hadn't it been a simple circular portal, open to the cavern?

He moved to the door, but once he stood before it, realized there was no doorknob to open it. He tried to push it open but it wouldn't budge. "Hello?" he called, tapping on the door. "Anyone there?"

The door trembled, the wood stirring as if it was waking up. Devlyn felt its consciousness press against his—was this what Alethea had taught him, that the trees were alive, only sleepy? No mere tree had ever reached out to him before. There were no words, but Devlyn knew that it was shocked that Devlyn was alive as well. Clearly, it was not something the door was accustomed to. And Ciaren and others had said that few left the cavern alive after the trials. Thick roots curled away from the door. Devlyn hadn't noticed the swirled pattern until it started to move and the opening widened. Passing through the portal, Devlyn remembered to express his gratitude as the wood shifted and sealed the cavern away again.

On this side of the closed portal, only Galithinol in his smaller form waited for him, sitting in one of two padded chairs that Devlyn could not recall seeing when he'd walked through before.

"You were there," Devlyn began. Galithinol gestured toward the other chair, and Devlyn sat.

"Was I? And where did the trials take you? Or should I ask when?"

"The Fall of Tenethyl, only it wasn't this Tenethyl."

"Ah," rumbled the gold dragon. "And whose life did the trials make you live through? So few from that time still walk Teraeniel."

"Thien. You mentioned him, when I arrived here last week; well, I think it was last week. You said I reminded you of him."

"And that you do, and seeing that you survived the trials, you're more alike than I thought." Galithinol closed his eyes. "But no, you did not arrive a week ago. An entire week has passed since you went into that cavern."

"A week? Only two days passed in that vision."

"That was no vision. And yes, a week. Time acts oddly in that cavern, as I'm sure you're aware, as it also does in the Illumined Wood."

"What happened to Thien, his family, and Tenethyl?" Devlyn sat beside the gold dragon.

"His sister, Vivien, you already know. She's no longer the small child she was when Tenethyl fell and has grown into quite the respected leader of my house. My son, Thien's father, perished that day, as did so many others. He died protecting his queen in her final moments on Ter-aeniel. All my grandchildren escaped and reached the Valley of Saeryn-dol, and for that I am eternally grateful, and they all went on to have their own families. The Gold House, as you saw, has grown quite large over the millennia. After the Great Blessing, most of the draelyn sought to rebuild Tenethyl, but away from anyone who would burn it again, so we came here. I and the other dragons led our children and descendants to this place, blessed by the irythil, Theniel and Sariel.

"Not all of the draelyn came here though. Eight became leaders among the Aldinari and are viewed by some as gods. The draelyn try to correct that notion as best they can. I'm worried about their current state."

"Do you think they're still alive?" Devlyn couldn't stop himself from interrupting.

"I do. None of us can breach the Darkness covering the Skylands, but we know they are there. We can feel our descendants still breathing. I felt my grandchild fade and transition to Lumaeniel. Theseryn was always a brave and stubborn boy. But because of him, so many know of Anaweh's Light."

"The founder of the ei'ceuril?"

"And your relative—a very distant uncle."

"Pardon me? My relative? What do you mean?"

"When Thien reached the safety of the Valley of Saeryndol, he fell in love with a woman whose people never left the valley for they were blessed and loved by Auriel. Lereniel also favored them. After the Great Blessing and the flooding of Lake Saeryndol, the White Flight took them to what became known as Luminare. The woman that Thien fell in love with was named Loren. And the two of them founded Mar'anathyl, establishing the noblest of elven houses to look over this land."

"Thien and Loren…"

"Their children honored them when they eventually transitioned to Lumaeniel, beckoned by Anaweh's call. Their house would ever be named Lorenthien. Their love, and the love of those who followed in their footsteps, would change the world. It was a love which has been known to reappear in their descendants throughout the generations."

Devlyn's breath caught in his throat. He knew the Lorenthien line was old, ancient even, but he never expected that it stretched back to the Elder Days and that his oldest ancestor was a dragon of the Gold Flight, the very same one sitting beside him now. "Is that why I saw Thien's memories? Because he's my ancestor?"

"It's possible. We have no idea what the trials will present to those willing to undergo them. I'm afraid it's more than your common relation though. You saw a glimpse of what the Evil One is capable of. He's spent tens of thousands of years waiting to escape his prison. If he is freed, he will inflict much worse pain, violence, and destruction than what you saw through Thien's eyes. He has not been idle while in the prison of his choosing." Devlyn shivered. He couldn't imagine how there could be anything more terrifying than what he had already seen. "Tell me, Devlyn, what do you know of the Darkness—the Void?"

"The Void? I've only heard of the Darkness and that it consumed the Skylands and that tenebrys is somehow connected to it."

"They are one and the same. In the Elder Days when the Evil One forsook Anaweh, his power was in turn corrupted, turning from umbrys, the essence of shadow, into tenebrys, the essence of the Void. Before the creation of Teraeniel and Somnaeniel, there was Lumaeniel and the Void, all that which was not. The Void was all but destroyed when the other irythil followed the Evil One out of Lumaeniel and created two other realms, Teraeniel and Somnaeniel. However, the Evil One hid away some of the Void—it was pure and raw—and like Anaweh and Lumaeniel, it has always existed, so in the Evil One's understanding, the one who controlled the Void would become equal to the Creating Light.

"When the Evil One claimed the Void as his own, he set himself against Anaweh and asserted they were equals—opposing forces. He claimed that primordial essence and fused it with his own being, changing himself, corrupting himself into something different. Tenebrys was born in that corrupted fusion. The Evil One has ever sought to return the Void to its former breadth and width—encapsulating everything that is. If he could manage it, he would destroy Lumaeniel, or at least diminish it to the small pocket of existence that the Void is now."

Devlyn saw what Galithinol's words described, his mind forming the terrifying images.

"How can we stop that from happening?"

"His escape should not be possible. He is locked away in the Void and the only way he can escape, is if Verakryl, the Tree of Life, dies. If that happens, the Evil One will be the least of our concerns. Do not be fooled, Devlyn, for the Evil One knows that the Tree of Life on Teraeniel is Anaweh, just as he knows the breath in Somnaeniel is Anaweh, and the all-encompassing Creating Light of Lumaeniel is Anaweh."

Devlyn's head swam in the mystery, growing dizzy the more he thought of it. "Was Anaweh divided into those three?"

"Anaweh is wholly each three."

"But none are the same—they're not even in the same realms. How can Anaweh be three different things in three different realms?"

"I doubt Anaweh would appreciate being reduced to a thing." Galithinol chuckled and stood, inviting Devlyn to do the same. "Come now, the ealyn await. But perhaps we should stop by the gold spire and get you washed and fed first."

"Won't they be waiting?" Devlyn asked.

"They have waited a week, another couple of hours won't do them any harm."

Devlyn followed Galithinol out of the lower levels of the central Jeweled Spire and back to the gold spire. His mind still held by the events that had taken place tens of thousands of years ago, Devlyn grappled to reaffirm his place in the current time. Tenethyl had been rebuilt, draelyn and dragon alike thrived here, and it was in the securest location possible. Walking beside Galithinol, Devlyn did notice that this Tenethyl had not been built as a replica of the fallen city. It was certainly similar, and the untrained eye would have claimed that it was the same, but Devlyn had just walked those ancient streets. While ancient Tenethyl had been incredible, the draelyn had refined their style and abilities when they set about reconstructing their city. This city did not look as though blocks of stone had been used to build upward, but rather the stone itself seemed to have sprung to life to form every structure. The entire city danced together as a unified whole, each building and every portal, bridge, and column reacting to one another. Removing a single statue or bracket would unbalance the rest.

"Near the end of its creation, the dragons helped form Teraeniel. The anadel themselves instructed in beauty. And while the original Tenethyl was spectacular, its creators did not have us to contribute to its design, nor could those early ones interact with the erendinth. I believe the Luminari had a class of wielders wholly dedicated to architecture."

"If only some of them had survived." Devlyn heard himself speak with a negativity he had not intended.

"They might not have, but lumaryl will not turn to ruin under the Shroud. The architects might have passed to Lumaeniel with their secrets, but their accomplishments still stand. Not a stone will be out of place. And if you think that Kien and Kiara didn't find Tenethyl when they journeyed to learn from us, well you'd be sorely mistaken."

Devlyn was about to ask Galithinol what he meant when they reached the gold spire.

"A story for another time." The gold dragon smiled. They walked up the sweeping stair and entered the glittery spire. "I trust you know how to reach the bath hall?"

"Yes, thank you."

"I'll wait here for your return. Don't take long—the ealyn will have already gathered."

Without hesitation, Devlyn darted down the steps, tearing his shirt off before reaching the bath hall, and dove into the warm water the second he was in the bath hall. He washed himself off as quickly as he could, eager to meet with the ealyn. When he came out, he noticed immediately how much better he smelled. He dried himself off and dressed in a fresh set of clothes.

He walked back up the stairs to rejoin Galithinol who was surprised to see Devlyn return so quickly.

"Are you ready?" he asked, holding out a vaer.

Devlyn's mouth watered. He knew that Tenethyl was in the Illumined Wood, but he had never expected to see the purple fruit anywhere but on a tree. He finished the fruit quickly and they headed back to the Jeweled Spire. It wasn't the only recognizable spire in Tenethyl's cityscape, but it was certainly the tallest and proudest of them.

Devlyn tried to count all the spires but kept losing track of them when they rounded a bend in the street. The walk to the Jeweled Spire was not long, and once there, Devlyn found himself retracing some of the steps he had just taken in the opposite direction. But Galithinol abandoned that familiar path and instead of going down, they ascended the intricate curved staircase. The entire structure looked like water frozen in place as it wove downward in a fluid sweep.

At the top, they stood in a centrally placed entranceway of an impressive elliptical shaped gallery. A door stood at either end of the wide, open space, but neither was as impressive as the double-doored portal that stood directly across from the stair on the far side of the gallery. Gemstones of every color were woven into the sculpted stonework of the portal.

The doors opened on their own, welcoming Devlyn and Galithinol into a grand chamber, reminiscent of the Chamber of the Seven Chairs of Septyl. Here, the thrones were arranged in a semi-circular fan and none were placed on a high plinth to look down on the prospective student or supplicant. Instead, each was set on a dais just three steps high. Each throne was encrusted with small gems of a single color, and at the head of each was a massive gemstone of the same color, giving off a light of its own. Vivien sat on the golden-gemmed throne in the center of the thrones.

"You stand before the Ealyn of Tenethyl." Galithinol said, gesturing to the onyx gem-encrusted throne at the far side of the line. "Ealyn Torik of the Onyx House." Torik nodded. "Ealyn Daela of the Amethyst House. Ealyn Niron of the Sapphire House." Daela and Niron inclined their heads simultaneously. "Ealyn Vivien of the Gold House. Ealyn Allister of the Opal House."

"You are welcomed here, young Lorenthien," Allister said as Vivien smiled.

"Ealyn Helen of the Jade House. Ealyn Mellory of the Ruby House." Galithinol finished as Helen and Mellory smiled in welcome at Devlyn. The seven ealyn all looked intently at him, sizing him up from their thrones.

"We're pleased to see that you survived the trials, Devlyn." Vivien looked like a queen and he felt inclined to bend a knee in homage when she spoke but restrained himself.

"Thank you. I learned quite a bit from the experience."

"I'm sure that you have, and if you could stay with us longer, you would learn even more." She paused, then went on. "While you have survived the trials, you are still out of balance and your wound cripples you. You must make learning jienzu a priority. We draelyn spend centuries perfecting the forms, practicing our meditations daily. Jienzu is not a mere exercise, it is a way of life, Devlyn. And if you wish to bring Balance back to Teraeniel, you must find the Balance in yourself first. Remember the basics that we taught you and practice them."

"I will, Vivien."

She nodded in return, pleased with Devlyn's earnest commitment. "Now, it is time for you to stand before the ealyn. You have passed the trials and you may claim your prize. Are you prepared?"

Devlyn tried to suppress the childish excitement bubbling over. "Yes."

Though none of the ealyn's thrones were high above him, he still felt each of them looking down on him as a supplicant, judging his worthiness.

"Only one other from outside our city has succeeded in the trials," Niron said, shifting his weight on his sapphire throne. "Perhaps the trials are unfair in that only the descendants of Thien are capable of surviving them. If Aldinare was not still lost to us, I would have half a mind to invite the draelyn descendants among them to undergo the trials."

"You're just bitter that none of the favored ones of the Blue Flight have completed the trials," Allister said.

"We all remember Thien," Helen said from her emerald throne. "It should not surprise us that his descendants are the few who are capable of passing the trials. I do not think that them being favored by the White Flight has anything to do with their success in the trials, Allister. Kyrendal and Devlyn are not merely elves; dragon blood runs through their veins, just as it does through ours."

"Yes, from Galithinol the Gold, no less. But you are right, Helen, perhaps only a draelyn can pass the trials. And yes, Niron, I would very much welcome Princess Gael and the others back to us. I shudder at the thought of what has happened to them," Daela said.

"The princess made her choice," Torik said.

"That she has, Torik," Vivien said. "We have not convened to discuss our lost royal line, but rather to provide Devlyn his reward for his success in the trials." Even as Vivien spoke, thunderous roars echoed from outside the spire, loud enough to make Devlyn's heart skip a beat. He looked at the large windows behind the ealyn, stretching upward toward the domed ceiling. Dragons of every flight flew past the glass in sweeping arcs.

"Foretold has your name been." Daela spoke in an otherworldly voice, as though she had left her physical body and spoke from somewhere else. "Devlyn Lorenthien, child of Luminare and every Skyland, descendant of Galithinol the Gold, heir to the Crystal Throne, destined to be the Exalted Aryl of Krysenthiel, High King of Eklean, and Prelate of the Guardian Senate, what form do you desire your verathn to take? Consider wisely, for you are destined to bring Balance back to Teraeniel, and if you fail, all will be lost to the Darkness."

Devlyn felt a chill run through him. The dragons continued to roar outside the Jeweled Spire, and Daela's distant voice filled him with a sudden dread over the consequences of his actions, past, present, and future. Devlyn hadn't thought of Lucillia's prophecy for quite some time, but by the manner in which Daela spoke, the prophecy she referred to now was much older than Lucillia. Devlyn also remembered Kyrendal's words. If he chose a sword, he and the future of Teraeniel would live by the sword.

He glimpsed it briefly—what that future would look like as he gripped a sword, conquering all who threatened his reign. The Deurghol would fall to him, and Erynor would bend his knee before being decapitated for his crimes. Teraeniel would know peace, but it would be a peace instilled by fear, cultivated by the sword's edge.

"A staff," he said, past the lump growing in his throat. He had no idea how he could possibly fight a Deurghol, or worse, with only a staff. If Ramiel was freed, much worse beasts than the Deurghol would visit Teraeniel again. What good was a staff? "I choose a staff."

"A king you shall be, leading Teraeniel into Balance. A scepter shall you wield, as will the one you have named your equal in all things."

A flash of light blinked across the chamber and Devlyn could no longer tell if the dragons outside were still roaring or if a storm had started and lightning filled the sky with thunderous booms. The space stilled and the lighting returned to normal, except that Devlyn no longer stood in the ealyn's audience chamber, but in a walled garden filled with exotic flora. A large crystal tree rose from a clear pool of water and Galithinol stood between Devlyn and the tree that Devlyn knew was one of the verathel, a sprout of the Tree of Life.

Galithinol stepped aside and gestured for Devlyn to approach the tree. As he neared the pool at its trunk, Devlyn could see its sinuous roots illumine the watery depths. His gaze followed the roots upward as they transitioned to trunk and then to branches with an immaculate canopy bearing fruit that Devlyn had never seen before.

"You must ask the verathel what you seek," Galithinol said, now standing beside Devlyn.

Devlyn had only interacted with a verathel twice before. Both times, the trees had been silent yet he had felt the vast intelligence in them. They were not just trees, and not even the miervae were comparable to them. He knelt at the edge of the water and cupped his hands in supplication. "My name is Devlyn Lorenthien." He paused, unsure of how to frame his question. He considered telling the verathel of the trials that he had undergone as though the verathn were the deserved reward but decided to keep his request simple. "I seek two verathn to protect the realms against the Evil One and his servants."

Nothing happened and it seemed that the tree didn't hear Devlyn's request. As Devlyn began to wonder if he had to ask more or prove himself, the verathel's leaves shimmered and music seemed to fill the garden. A large, fist-sized seed fell into his still cupped hands. He could hear a melodious voice on the wind as it passed through the verathel's branches, and remarkably, Devlyn understood it. "For Ellendren of House Roendryn, I offer a verathn of dawn and dusk." Devlyn looked down at the seed that looked very unlike a scepter.

The leaves shimmered again and a second seed dropped into his palms. "For you, Devlyn of House Lorenthien, I offer a verathn of dawn, day, dusk, and night."

Devlyn beheld the two large seeds. Each gave off a golden green hue. "How do they become verathn?" The verathel remained silent and the still air kept the leaves frozen in place as the song in the garden faded.

"They require nourishment and will need to be tended on each of your people's high feasts," Galithinol answered. "For Ellendren's, that will be only on the equinox feasts. But for yours, Devlyn, your verathn must be tended on each equinox and each solstice, for you are an elf of every kin, as well as a draelyn, the one destined to bring Balance to Teraeniel."

Devlyn again looked at both seeds, confused about what he was supposed to do with them. But he bowed his head in thanks, grateful for the gifts the verathel had given him.

SEEDS

Devlyn held the jienzu form, breathing slowly and deeply against the screaming of previously unknown muscles in his abdomen. It seemed as though they refused to recognize that this wasn't the first time he'd stood in this form and should be used to being called on by now. Vivien was happy to guide him through the basic forms one last time before he returned to the Monastery of Kyrendal. Despite his short stay at Tenethyl, he had grown to love the draelyn city and felt incredibly comfortable here. The draelyn had welcomed him with open arms as though he were a long-lost family member, which, to an extent, he was. It was strikingly different from the reception he'd had during his brief stay in Lucillia where only some of the Luminari aryls had accepted him.

To keep his mind off his screaming muscles, he debated what it would be like to go back to the Luminari and Ellendren. He knew that with her well-honed political skills, Ellendren would hold her own against the aryls' influence. The same couldn't be said about his own diplomacy and tact, and it would have been much easier for Devlyn to stay in Tenethyl. The draelyn lived in a peaceful society, unfazed by the rest of the world's troubles and bickering. Although, that couldn't last if their fears about Ramiel trying to escape came to pass. Nothing would remain the same if that happened. Any sense of peace would be shattered and chaos would overtake Teraeniel.

Shifting to another jienzu form, his abdomen muscles eased and several other parts of his body took up the protest. Despite having practiced the forms with Vivien only during his short stay in Tenethyl, he could already feel the benefit. It would take quite a while for his body to show his progress, but he did feel it, and to his shock, he felt better about himself too. Perhaps the draelyn were right about jienzu and balance. He couldn't remember the last time he had felt so whole. To his surprise, he felt grounded, more positive, and sure of himself, even while confronting his doubts about the future and lost connection with Aliel.

Vivien eased out of the latest form and wielded a globule of water from the basin to drink. She had yet to show any discomfort while performing the jienzu forms. Devlyn was quite the opposite, panting and dripping with sweat as he too eased out of the form. He managed to wield a more appropriately sized globule for himself and none of it splashed in his face this time. He smiled, remembering how refreshing the cool water had felt when it had soaked him due to his clumsy wield when Vivien was first teaching him.

"I forget how quickly mortals grow. In the short time you have been with us, I have already seen a marked improvement. Our younglings take years to accomplish what you've managed. Perhaps it has nothing to do with being mortal, but rather the present urgency."

"Thank you. You've been a great teacher."

"Others have laid the groundwork." Vivien took another drink. "I'm afraid it is time for you to leave us."

"I feel the pull too. Events are happening in Eklean that need me. My people need me."

"All of Teraeniel needs you." Vivien brought Devlyn into an embrace; it was incredible that this woman was his distant aunt. She was family. "You are destined for much, Devlyn, more than anyone has the right to ask of you. But we need you; we all need you. And I am already so proud of you, as would be my brother, Thien, and his spouse, Loren."

"Thank you, Vivien. For everything."

"You are most welcome."

"Out of curiosity, how long will the seeds take to become ver-athn?" He looked to the seeds beside the water basin.

"They will take time to grow into a verathn. Like all seeds, they will need water."

He already knew that he would have to wait until the autumn equi-nox, but he still had no idea how to care for the seeds and Vivien was providing few details for how to do so.

"They're not as I imagined they would be. Kyrendal said that he sung verathn from verathel, sprouts of the Tree of Life. How is it that I've been given two seeds and not two verathn?"

"We taught Kyrendal one form of crafting verathn all those years ago, one which he could replicate. The process he knows is much longer as he sang the verathn from their sacred trees. The verathn would come whole and ready for use but required years of cultivation before they could be separated from their host. For you and Ellendren though, these will be different. The verathel here in Tenethyl is one of the oldest of shoots from Verakryl, and the tree offered the seeds to you. You will find no other verathn to match the ones that come from those seeds."

"Thank you."

"You are welcome, but remember, we are not the ones to thank. Anaweh is taking special care of you."

He offered a quick prayer of thanksgiving to Anaweh and tried to reach out to Aliel, only to be reminded that he couldn't. Devlyn looked up, crestfallen; he had hoped that everything he had gone through while in Tenethyl would've be enough to reconnect with Aliel. As he looked up into the sky and over the city, instead of seeing Aliel's golden light, he saw a blue dragon glistening in the sun. It wasn't long before Rusyl angled downward toward the balcony and transformed in a swift flash of color, his brilliant azure scales disappearing to become naked flesh. When the last of the scales faded, Devlyn noticed the discolored scar that ran down the side of his belly. Devlyn felt his own scar.

The blue dragon didn't seem the least bit bashful about being exposed in such a manner, not even when standing in front of Ealyn Vivien. Instead of blushing, as Devlyn was inclined to do, Rusyl made a formal bow to her as though nothing was out of place. "I've spoken with Caephenol and he's agreed to let me join Devlyn." Devlyn's eyes widened in shock. Rusyl was only supposed to fly him back to the Monastery of Kyrendal, then return to Tenethyl.

"It is not yet our time, Rusyl." Vivien's voice was now crisp and authoritative.

"Not for all the free dragons and draelyn, but it is time for me. I've already been part of the skirmish and my sister is still with them."

"Are you certain? Yelaris is quite a bit older than you. You know the dangers—you have already been hurt."

"I know and I am set on this path. I want to help my friends."

"I will not argue against the will of the Primus of the Blue Flight. If he has agreed, I will not object. Be safe—Teraeniel grows more dangerous with every passing day."

Rusyl transitioned out of his smaller form, once more a fully realized blue dragon. Devlyn bowed to Vivien and scooped up the seeds he'd placed under the nearby table while he had practiced jienzu with her.

Rusyl bent his front legs and Devlyn climbed up and onto his back. Once situated, Rusyl leapt off the balcony. They took a long circle around the city, rising with the spires then soaring around the Jeweled Spire. Devlyn finally had a good view of the size of the jewel suspended there. He had understood that it was massive but being this close to it destroyed his sense of scale. It was truly an awesome sight.

They left Tenethyl, the island city glittering behind them on the precipice of that waterfall. The bay below sparkled in the morning light under the rising sun.

Fortunately, Rusyl seemed to know exactly where the Monastery of Kyrendal lay hidden in the mountains, because while Devlyn had a sense of the way back, he was far from certain.

They soared over the lower mountain peaks and through their valleys whenever they dipped. Finally, Mount Saecrien filled his vision. He didn't think he had lost track of time, but they came to it much sooner than he had expected. Already he felt Alethea reaching out to him.

When he landed in the valley, Rusyl thumping down beside him, Kyrendal and some of the other monks came to greet them. Devlyn couldn't help taking a long look at the skies above, still troubled about Aren's appearance just before he'd left for Tenethyl. The last time Aren had been in the Illumined Wood, he had assaulted one of the miervae and driven her mad. Only the combined power of every living being in the forest had given Devlyn the strength to banish that sickness and free the miervae from her suffering by allowing her spirit to pass from Teraeniel.

Devlyn eased himself off of Rusyl's back, and a moment later, the dragon transformed to his smaller form. Rusyl still didn't seem to care that his smaller body stood exposed to all. Since he was still much larger than an elf, there was a great deal of naked body to see.

"I always suspected that you dragons could take a smaller form," Alethea said, drawing near the very naked Rusyl, taking in his deep azure hair and sapphire eyes. She appeared to examine every inch of his well-muscled body as though she were reading a book.

"A secret that we no longer feel the need to guard entirely."

One of the monks offered Rusyl a large robe. Rusyl took garment, which turned out to be too small. He tried to push his arms through the sleeves but that quickly proved impossible so he simply folded it once and wrapped it around his waist so his lower half was somewhat covered. Devlyn wondered if this counted as him being dressed, since his entire torso was still exposed.

"Did you achieve what you sought, Devlyn?" Kyrendal asked, abruptly ending the other conversation.

"I did, although you didn't mention I would have to undergo trials."

"Did you expect them to just hand over their secrets for free? I see they've given you two as you hoped. And where did they tell you to plant those seeds?"

"I was just told to keep them watered." Devlyn still didn't fully understand how the two seeds could grow into verathn.

"Clever of her. Do know, I will not permit them here if you chose swords. Violence has touched enough of this world; I won't let its tools taint this place too."

Without warning, the Child appeared. One moment she wasn't there and the next she was.

"Even if they were swords, Kyrendal, I would bring them into my waters. But surely you can sense that they are not. You've had a strong influence over his choice."

As she spoke, Rusyl prostrated himself before her. "Favored Child of Anaweh and Theniel."

"It's a pleasure to meet you, Rusyl. Please rise." She had the voice of a girl, yet the blue dragon was behaving as though she was a god herself. Rusyl stood to tower over the much smaller Child.

"Shall we see to the verathn?" Kyrendal shuffled away, bent over his cane. It was hard to tell, but he looked sad to see the seeds that would become verathn. "We should see that the seeds are prepared before Borephaen."

"We could fly there, to get there quicker." Devlyn jogged to catch up with Kyrendal, who moved surprisingly quickly for someone who used a cane.

"I'll never understand the impatience of the Phaedryn. My parents were the same, as was my sister and her children." Kyrendal did not turn to look at Devlyn and the others but walked with the Child at his side. "Not everything in this life is about the destination."

As he considered what Kyrendal said, Devlyn found himself at odds with it. He agreed that important things occurred during a journey but did not think it was fair to say the journey was just as important as the destination. Especially after his time caged in a box like a beast followed by all this time separated from Aliel.

Despite his disagreement, he kept those opinions to himself. He hoped his thoughts were private, although he was nowhere near mastering the ability to calm his mind despite Alethea's continuing instruction. He well knew that his inner musings were rarely quiet or private, something that had been proven more than once while he had been in Tenethyl. The more unsettled his mind was, the louder his thoughts were to anyone who could hear them. It wasn't considered an intrusion on his privacy when his thoughts were akin to someone shouting. The same was true for nearly every mortal in Eklean.

Devlyn somewhat regretted speaking about having to get there quicker. He had assumed they would have to travel somewhere far away to plant the seeds, and then worry about keeping them watered but instead they went into the cave near the base of Mount Saecrien. It suddenly clicked. The seeds he had been given weren't going just anywhere. They would be placed in a body of water, specifically, in the sacred waters held in Mount Saecrien. Devlyn knew little about the properties of that water, but somehow knew that it flowed from the World-Beyond.

A large group had accompanied them to the cave, but only Devlyn and the Child walked through the tunnel to the glimmering blue pool. The natural crystal rock of the cave sparkled a sapphire blue. Like the first time he had come here, he heard the song, only it felt louder this time and he felt it thrumming in his chest, as though it wanted to be released.

"You can hear the song better now." The Child grinned.

"I suppose I can." Still holding the seeds, Devlyn looked at the Child, uncertainly offering her the seeds with an awkward gesture.

She smiled but shook her head. "They are tied to you. You must place them in the water."

He had come to this mystical pool once before, but dare he place these seeds, seeds which would become weapons, there? Devlyn took a hesitant step forward.

"You must take them completely into the water and submerge yourself with them. You must take nothing but yourself and the seeds into the water," the Child said.

Devlyn understood and removed his shoes, carefully placed the seeds on them so he could disrobe then took them up again and stepped into the chilled water, ignoring the goosebumps that swept across his skin. The pool's floor slanted away from the bank quickly and Devlyn quickly found himself fully submerged. His hair floated weightlessly as he held out the two seeds in front of him. They were warm in his hands despite the cold water and shimmered as though each had a dull inner light. He released them, and they simply floated in front of him, as weightless as his hair. He watched the seeds for a moment, and his trepidation that they would sink to the bottom of the pool and be lost vanished as they just floated. He turned and swam back to the surface, not realizing that he had been holding his breath until he breached the surface and gulped in fresh air.

At the edge of the pool, the Child waited for him. He turned to look down and could see the seeds just where he had left them, glowing below the surface, green and golden light.

"Only one more thing remains." The girl looked into Devlyn's eyes as he swam toward her.

"What more needs to be done?" He asked, emerging from the water and turning back to the seeds.

"The song within you is getting louder. Your being is no longer as twisted as it once was when you first came here. Your wound remains but it is from a single knot now, and only because you let it remain."

"It hurts…" Devlyn didn't want to admit the level of pain his wound caused whenever he tried to reach that place inside his heart. Despite what the Child said, he couldn't heal himself and he had tried time and time and again to reach out to Aliel with no success.

"I expect that will continue. But the darkness you allow into your heart, the despair it's creating, has no place next to the song upon your heart. I cannot remove it; I can only give encouragement as you let the pain pass from you. If you let it, the wound will heal, as all wounds do."

"What if it does more damage? What if my bond with Aliel is irreparably broken?" He felt the fear rise. There were no tears, only panic.

"Only that which belongs will remain, if you allow it."

A nervous spasm coursed through his body, the horrible thought that the doubt and darkness were proper to him. What if Aliel had chosen wrongly? Panicked, he now wanted to leave the cave and the lake with the untarnished water. He felt so impure standing beside it, violated by the darkness claiming his heart. An image of Aren passed through his mind. What if he was becoming like him? Was this how Aren had become a Dark Phaedryn?

If he was going to turn into another Aren, he wanted nothing more than to hide himself from the rest of the world. He could run to the Purged Desert of Dwonia and no one would ever find him again. Ellendren would manage just fine without him. If she and the other elves figured out how to beat Erynor, she would lead the Luminari back into a golden age and the Roendryns could maintain their near monarchical role among the Luminari.

The Child looked at him, her eyes patient and kind, holding a compassion that Devlyn had rarely seen. He imagined his mother having eyes like that, looking at him like that, even after all these years. Would she be proud of who he was becoming?

Devlyn wanted the Child to say something—anything.

She remained silent, the only sound a calming whisper from the near still water. He looked into the depths of the lake, and his heart returned to its normal rate.

"You'll stay with me?" he asked, his eyes pleading as he waded into the water.

"Would you like to hold hands?"

Devlyn nodded and the Child stepped into the water and took his hand. Her hand was tiny in his own but it gave him strength he had not expected. Through the touch, he could feel who she was, ancient and among the first to awake on Teraeniel.

Quieting his mind and allowing the doubts and fears to fade into the still water, Devlyn imagined himself as a boat on a stormy sea, knowing that he had the power to calm the tumultuous waters surrounding him. He sat quietly, feeling the turbulent waters within begin to still as he admitted his fears to himself before letting them pass into nothingness.

The Child was right—they did not belong to him and neither did the darkness plaguing his heart. One by one, he allowed the rough waves to gentle as his fears first shrank to a manageable size, then dissolved. The waters within stilled at last, resembling the water in the cavern he stood in.

Knowing that what he intended to do next was going to hurt, he felt the wound in his back, mentally preparing for the onslaught of agony to come. The Child squeezed his hand, reminding him of her presence.

The reminder was consoling and gave Devlyn the courage he needed. Without a second thought, he plunged into his heart, and gasped at the piercing pain that followed, a pain so terrible that he expected to lose consciousness. He knew he screamed even as he probed further within, the pain intensifying as he pushed on. He hadn't realized that his eyes were closed until he noticed that he was squeezing them shut so tightly, they hurt. Reaching a point nearly beyond his tolerance, he prepared to withdraw when a faint reminder of that song within arose.

Encouraged, he pushed through the still-increasing torment, and was rewarded by a dim sound that reached his inner ear. It was not a true sound, like the wind upon the leaves of a tree, or someone speaking. It was a sound Devlyn recognized only on the inside. A sound that ears could not hear. A sound so intimate that it sung one's identity without anyone but those who knew it hearing it.

Recognizing the distant sound, he urged himself deeper within to that hidden place.

He found a quiet light in his heart, a light surrounded by a darkness, not the sinister sort which plagued him, but the infinite stillness within every soul, encompassing one's spirit. Whether from the pain or from touching that place after so long, a tear rolled down his cheek, the first of a torrent from both eyes.

The song he had known from infancy, the song his mother once sang to him, welled within, accompanied by the quiet light reverberating with strength and volume, expelling the darkness which had claimed his heart these past months.

The cavern transformed; his vision and hearing thrummed with light and song. The song of Saecrien and the River she held melded with his own song, and light poured into the cavern, not from the sun, but from Devlyn and Aliel joining their song with Saecrien, as a Phaedryn. Wings sprung from his shoulder blades as golden light exploded from his body.

No words came to Devlyn's mind. He dared not say I missed you, for how he felt was much deeper than those words could ever express. Even their unique form of communication, conveying that which came before words, before art or music, the very pillar of ideas, was inadequate.

Devlyn hovered over the water, quietly embracing his connection to Aliel, relishing in the presence he had so missed over the past six months, allowing the still embrace to communicate everything he wanted, and receiving the same from Aliel. Not even being locked in the box by Tenebrae ei'ana had been as awful as these past six months had been.

His despair became a distant memory, and the wound on his back faded so that there was not even a scar beneath the dried blood to show where it had been.

Devlyn's eyes shone his thanksgiving at the Child, and with that, he recognized her now as Saecrien herself, overflowing with love and admiration. He wanted to pull her into his arms and promise her anything she ever desired but knew that wasn't necessary as all she wanted was to see her brother once more.

"I'll find him, Saecrien; you'll see your brother again."

"I've never doubted it," she said, then dove into the water, surfacing just long enough to say, "This River from above will flow again. That which will bring it forth will not be joy and gladness, but grief and loss." Leaving Devlyn to puzzle over what she meant, she dove back into the water, swam for a bit and then disappeared entirely.

How long do you intend to linger? Aliel conveyed to Devlyn.

Smiling to himself, Devlyn batted his lighted wings, golden light exploding from his body. There was no room to flap his wings in the tunnel, but he started at such a great speed that there was no need, and he burst out of the tunnel and into the valley.

He pulled himself into the sky above the mountains, his body gleaming in the morning light of the rising sun. The golden eyes of a Phaedryn gazed upon Teraeniel's beauty, a beauty intensified by the wondrous light.

Returning to the ground below, he dared not separate from Aliel, not from fear of once again losing the connection, but because their bonding as a Phaedryn filled them both with such consolation that they could not bear separating just yet.

Once outside, Devlyn saw Rusyl returned to his dragon form, his sapphire scales shimmering once again as he lay basking in the sunlight. Wyn and Alethea waited with their griffins, who didn't seem to mind Rusyl at all, having met him before.

"Ah, I see Saecrien's waters saw to more than the verathn this day," Kyrendal said when Devlyn landed.

Devlyn grinned, ecstatic to feel his connection with Aliel returned.

"Are the seeds in place?"

"They are."

"Borephaen is only a week away." Kyrendal looked past Devlyn and into the tunnel that led to the lake.

Wyn joined them, carrying what looked like Devlyn's lierathnil over one arm. Devlyn withdrew from Aliel and gladly accepted the silky garments, blushing as he dressed in front of what he thought was an unnecessarily large crowd.

As soon as he pulled his tunic over his head, he felt the familiar weight of the lucilliae inside his hidden pocket. Knowing that it was safe and back in his protection was a relief. Prya had not given him the chance to return to his cave to properly dress before they'd gone to Tenethyl, and he'd worried about the lucilliae.

"It is time you returned to the world. Too much time has passed since you came to this forest." Kyrendal turned to Alethea. "I've greatly appreciated your company. Perhaps not all is lost."

Alethea pressed an open palm to her breast, then moved her fingers to tap her forehead and back to her heart, a farewell that Kyrendal returned. Wyn's eyelids shot wide open in apparent shock.

"What's wrong," Devlyn whispered.

"That's the highest form of respect, and they gave it equally to each other."

"And?"

"Kyrendal just acknowledged Alethea as his equal. He's the son of Kien and Kiara and was the first Chancellor of Gwilnor Academy."

Devlyn knew that Kyrendal was a highly regarded elf but, in his opinion, so was Alethea. It made perfect sense that they respected each other as equals. Wyn clearly thought differently though, so perhaps something unprecedented had just happened and Devlyn was utterly clueless as to what. Devlyn decided to offer the same farewell to Kyrendal, to which his ancestor simply nodded in return.

"You remind me very much of my father, Kien. He too was once a passionate young elf, placed in circumstances he never dreamed of, but with my mother, Kiara, the First Era ended and Teraeniel was gifted with wielding. Goodbye, Devlyn Lorenthien. I hope our paths cross again." Kyrendal turned away and headed to his cave.

22

LONGEST NIGHT

The sun had long since risen to its zenith and the canopy of the Illumined Wood once again blocked the sun's rays from reaching the forest floor. Devlyn, Wyn, Alethea, and Rusyl had flown as long as they dared each day before stopping to sleep. Rushing back to the Luminari and arriving exhausted would benefit no one.

As they approached the edge of the forest, they decided to walk out instead of fly. There was no telling who was now watching the Illumined Wood's borders. Devlyn didn't disagree with the decision but he also thought that if they flew high enough, they'd be safe from any supposed danger. Devlyn's impatience to return to Ellendren and the Luminari had grown significantly over the past day, leaving him exasperated that he now had to walk the last bit out of the forest. There was no telling how much further they would have to travel once they left the Illumined Wood. For all Devlyn knew, the Luminari could have made it all the way to the Shroud where they could do nothing but wait for him to catch up as they huddled together for warmth during the winter months.

He worried too, about how long they had been away. It was difficult to maintain a sense of time in the Illumined Wood, and not just the hours of the day but the days and even weeks themselves. When they'd first set out, he'd thought they might have been gone only a few weeks, but that thinking had been severely altered on the second day of their return trip.

How long have we been in the Illumined Wood? Devlyn asked Aliel.

Six weeks, Aliel conveyed.

Devlyn couldn't believe they had spent six weeks in the Illumined Wood. That meant the Luminari had also been traveling for six whole weeks.

Eager to get moving, Devlyn turned to Alethea to see if she was ready.

Don't forget what today is, Aliel relayed to Devlyn.

What day is it?

It's the fifteenth of Borenth—Borephaen. We should do something for Alethea and Wyn. The winter solstice is important for the Eldinari. Just as the spring equinox is important for the Luminari, Aliel conveyed.

Devlyn had never fully understood why those certain feast days were important to the elves. Cor'lera celebrated the spring equinox, most likely because of the Luminari elves' long influence over the small village. He remembered that either Ellendren or Kevn had mentioned the seasonal celebrations, along with their proper names, but couldn't remember their significance.

Wondering if it was somehow involved with the enthiel the month was named after, Boriel's face bloomed in Devlyn's mind. It was only a memory, but even that filled his heart with wonder.

Devlyn slowed his pace and approached Alethea. "Happy winter solstice." He had no idea if that was the proper greeting, but once he said it, he knew it wasn't. It sounded clumsy and lacked any sense of festivity.

"And a blessed Borephaen to you—may Boriel take your prayers and petitions to Anaweh, on this the longest of nights," Alethea said.

"Um, thanks, yours as well," Devlyn said, taken aback at the formality. He paused before going on. "I have a question for you."

"How unexpected." She smiled as Wyn and Rusyl shared a laugh.

"Did you know?"

"You'll have to be more specific if you don't want me to intentionally listen to your thoughts."

"About Kyrendal being the son of Kien and Kiara."

"Do you know why the Luminari raised the Lorenthiens as their Exalted Aryl? A title, which before being given to the Lorenthiens, had never existed." Alethea spoke as though she was discussing the obviousness of the cold weather beyond the Illumined Wood.

"But Kien and Kiara, they actually existed—they were Lorenthiens, and Kyrendal is their son! Aren is their great-great grandson through marriage!" said Devlyn, overwhelmed by the idea.

"Surely, you've learned more startling things since returning to this forest."

She has a point, Aliel chimed in Devlyn's mind, having already learned everything that Devlyn had done since they had been struck by the bolt of tenebrys.

It was of course true. During the time he'd spent first at the Monastery of Kyrendal and then in Tenethyl, he'd learned enough to fill five lifetimes, let alone a few weeks. Devlyn had not only been able to reconnect with Aliel but had been taught jienzu by a draelyn and discovered that he too was technically a draelyn of the Gold House. He had experienced the memories of his distant ancestor, Thien, and had seen the original Tenethyl fall to Ramiel. He was still adjusting to learning the origins of House Lorenthien and its connection to the draelyn. Learning that he also descended from a draelyn and the first wielders had left him rather stunned at the significance of it all. How could so much greatness belong to a single family?

As they walked, Devlyn's thoughts rumbled about, and he barely noticed that the temperature had dropped significantly. He didn't even mind that Alethea had yet to answer his question or explain her own question. Looking up from the path they'd been following, he saw that they had reached the edge of the Illumined Wood. Pulling his lieranthyl tight about him for extra warmth, Devlyn took his first step into the snow. The unnatural warmth inherent to the Illumined Wood never extended past its borders, and his feet sank into the frosty depths, the snow deepening with every step beyond the edge of the forest. His toes began to lose feeling the further into it he went.

Wyn and Alethea rode on their griffins, who didn't seem to mind the snow, which simply melted around Rusyl. Maybe he should walk behind Rusyl?

"Is anything out there?" Devlyn asked.

"I don't sense anyone—or rather, no one dangerous." Alethea patted Leithel and she leapt into the air, followed by Wyn on Eolwn and Rusyl.

Quieting his heart, Devlyn felt Aliel's presence and a joy that his heart was no longer tender from their forced separation. His vision flooded with golden light and the chill retreated from his bones. Strong wings of golden light pulled him into the sky, the bleak landscape transformed with the snow. The snowy landscape was beautiful, as though he was seeing it for the first time. Thick clouds hid the sun, preventing it from shimmering off its surface, which was a sort of blessing as it might have been difficult to see in the blinding clarity of it with his enhanced sight. But those grey clouds dominated the Borenth sky past the Illumined Wood, blocking any warmth the sun might offer, and were not a good sign.

Turning his attention north and west, Devlyn opened his mind and searched for Ellendren and the Luminari, who would be suffering in the cold, as unused to it as they were.

Devlyn felt them far to the north, passing through Sorenthil. It was jarring to sense such a large group trekking through the countryside. The number was far greater than those who had dwelt in Lucillia. The news of the migration of the Luminari back to Krysenthiel must have reached every village and town along the Illumined Wood. Cor'lera was only one village on the outskirts of that expansion, while there were dozens of villages and towns large enough to be called cities that had been closer to Lucillia.

The number of elves he could feel weighed him down; hundreds of thousands of elves were trusting him. They had chosen to leave the safety of the boughs of the Illumined Wood for uncertainty again.

He reached out to Ellendren, ready to put Alethea's training to the test.

Elle? He felt her presence but wasn't sure whether his thoughts managed to cross the distance separating them. Time passed as he soared through the sky, trying to catch up with the others, his lierathnil billowing in the wind as his wings took him ever swifter through the wintry sky.

Trying again, he felt his thoughts traverse the space between himself and Ellendren. Once again, he felt that distance, and every league weighed him down. He knew he could not always stand beside her, but he was tired of being away from her so frequently.

Several moments passed before he heard her thoughts in his mind, her clear and vivid voice echoing as though she sang to him. *Devlyn, are you coming to us—to me?*

Feeling the longing in their shared thoughts, Devlyn allowed his own emotions to bleed through. *Yes. I miss you.*

Devlyn felt her smile, making his own lips curve upward.

Alethea angled Leithel toward a village in the distance, lights in the homes flickering on as the sun started to set. Devlyn wished that they could reach the Luminari encampment tonight but knew that it would take a few more days. Instead of grumbling about the journey ahead, he followed Alethea's lead, all the while thinking about what they might do to celebrate Borephaen. He had never attended an Eldinari festival before, let alone their most cherished feast. Hopefully, the village had an inn that could function as an appropriate setting for a celebration. Whatever accommodations they had would certainly be better than burrowing in a snowbank for the night.

The village was too small and out of the way to have defensive walls. Once they were on solid ground again, Devlyn withdrew from Aliel and Rusyl transitioned. Even in his smaller form, the snow continued to melt around the dragon. Devlyn had thought finding clothing to withstand his own transformation had been difficult but he could always easily find a new outfit, even if it wasn't lierathnil. Rusyl would have better luck bartering with giants to find appropriately sized clothing. Wyn tossed Rusyl the robe he'd used at the monastery and he again wrapped it around his waist.

Wyn spotted the inn easily enough and they crossed the snowy cobbled streets, drawing attention from the villagers. Devlyn wondered who among their group looked most out of place, the elves, the griffins, the phoenix, or the dragon who looked like an oversized elf wearing only a piece of fabric around his waist in the winter? The days of staying disguised and unrecognized were over. Devlyn not only wanted Eklean to know that there were true elves and not just humans with elven blood, but that the legends of old had indeed endured, and that someone was fighting for them and wouldn't rest until Erynor was defeated. Ramiel would *not* claim Teraeniel as his own.

At every home they passed, villagers peered through their windows to see the curious group, wary of the strangers and staying in the apparent safety of their homes. When their little group reached the inn, Aliel's golden light lit up the stable beside the inn where a boy no older than Devlyn looked at the griffins, his mouth hanging open. "What am I to do with them?"

Wyn handed him a sack filled with the griffins' meal. "Give them a helping tonight and tomorrow morning. Eolwn and Leithel like company, so don't be afraid to pet them and say hello. They don't like staying indoors though, but they might decide to go into the stable because of the snow."

Turning away from the stable, Devlyn pushed open the door to the inn, Aliel hanging back. *Are you coming in?* Devlyn conveyed to Aliel.

I trust you are safe with them. I would very much like to stretch my wings and dance among the stars after being trapped for so long.

I understand, and I'm sorry I couldn't reverse it sooner.

I too felt the pain when you tried. You were not the only one who failed at over-coming it sooner.

Overcome with emotion, Devlyn thanked Aliel from the bottom of his heart.

The noise in the common room, which didn't seem to have many patrons given the quiet murmur coming from there, quickly fell when the folk saw the newcomers, Alethea and Wyn just in front of a half-naked Rusyl who towered over them, and again, Devlyn wondered who everyone was looking at, the elves or Rusyl.

The startled innkeeper looked at them and managed to ask, "Would you like rooms tonight?"

"Two would be fine, thank you," Alethea said, edging in front of Devlyn. "If you don't mind my asking, does this village not celebrate Borephaen? The winter solstice?"

"Can't say we've ever celebrated the shortest day before," the innkeeper said.

"Not even though the moon is full and the stars sparkle brightest? Well, we'll just have to fix that. Would you mind showing me to your kitchens? I'll show you how the Eldinari celebrate," Alethea said, taking charge of the situation.

Her reference to a celebration sent a few villagers out into the street to let others know, and word spread quickly, so that by the time the sun was a distant memory, more folk had come to the common room and spilled out into the hallway, curious about the strangers who had come to their village at dusk. Unusual and delightful smells from the kitchen greeted them as they walked in.

Devlyn and Wyn sat at a table near the fireplace, although Rusyl preferred to sit a bit further away given his own inner warmth. They'd been offered drinks and were soon chatting with the villagers who took turns sitting by them to talk about the events that were plaguing Eklean. They claimed to belong to the fallen kingdom of Gestoria. Devlyn remembered learning about Gestoria and how it had fallen to Erynor, after refusing to submit and support the expansion of his empire following his dominance over Krysenthiel. With no allies capable of helping them withstand the Erynien Empire, Gestoria had fallen within a year after Krysenthiel had fallen, its cities deserted, and its fields salted.

A small number of their descendants were scattered throughout the vast country, spread over the Plains of Orithil, harboring patriotism for their fallen kingdom.

"Truly, are you a Lorenthien?" asked an old man.

"Not just a Lorenthien," Wyn said as he clapped Devlyn on the back. "He's a Phaedryn and the future Exalted Aryl of Krysenthiel—once he gets married, that is." Devlyn was taken aback by Wyn's openness and wondered whether it had anything to do with the drinks in celebration of Borephaen.

With Wyn's words, Devlyn noticed a few girls near his own age suddenly start batting their eyelashes, and smiling coyly, making him uncomfortable. He had no intention of hiding his identity, but he didn't think Ellendren would be thrilled to hear of other girls vying for his attention.

The quiet inn their little group had walked into two hours before had transformed into a full-out party. Musicians had brought out their instruments and dancers had pushed the tables away from the center of the room. Shortly after Alethea had disappeared into the kitchen, full platters bearing a variety of food flowed into the common room, each more exotic than the last. Gestorian villagers tested the unfamiliar vegetable meals, eating their fill. Where Devlyn carefully avoided the bold young women, Rusyl was all too happy to oblige to a dance or ten, often lifting the much smaller women up in an unrecognizable dance and encouraging the Gestorians to attempt the same.

Alone in the corner of the common room, an elderly man sat, scowling into his cup, choosing not to participate in the festivities and hunching his shoulders up and head down into the thick woolen scarf wrapped about his neck.

"Who's the older gentleman in the corner?" Devlyn asked the girl who had sat next to him while he ate. He had already forgotten her name, trying not to speak to her too much lest she take it as encouragement.

"Old Man Dunnel," she said, throwing a quick glance over her shoulder at the grouchy old man before batting her eyelashes yet again at Devlyn. "They said he was mayor a long time ago, after spending a few years abroad as a soldier. I think he went to Daerinth as a town guard before coming back home."

Dunnel rose from his solitary seat and crossed the common room to sit across from Devlyn. He had either overheard the girl's words or he had noticed Devlyn staring at him.

"We trusted the elves once. Our loyalty was matched by none," Dunnel spat the words out. "Do you know how our loyalty was rewarded?"

Devlyn shook his head, somewhat frightened by the old man's fervor.

"Once Krysenthiel fell, we continued to fight in their name. We were the only human kingdom to not give up and cower behind our defensive walls. Our loyalty cost us our homes, our families, and our kingdom! We've nothing left to show for ourselves but a few scattered, unconnected villages, barely able to survive. All the elves ever did for us was bring destruction—if it wasn't for you elves, Gestoria would still stand!"

Outright fury replaced the uneasy fear in Devlyn's gut. "How dare you?"

The common room quieted, and the music stopped. Rusyl deserted the young woman he had been dancing with and crossed the room to stand behind Devlyn, an imposing presence despite wearing only a folded robe wrapped around his lower body.

"My ancestors sacrificed everything to share our Life immortal. If we had kept our immortality to ourselves, Krysenthiel would never have fallen, our people would not have died by sword and old age, nor would we have been forced into slavery. And you're telling me you would have preferred that we never existed!"

Wyn's hand fell onto Devlyn's shoulder, just as he realized how loud his voice had gotten in the near silent room.

Another flood of wondrous aromas flew from the kitchen as the door opened to the room full of shocked villagers.

"Speaking of potential fates," Alethea spoke calmly into the tense silence. "That which occurred in the past is written and ought to be honored. Forsaking the actions of those who no longer walk Teraeniel shames us. They followed their conscience and lived their lives as we do today."

No one spoke.

Devlyn and Dunnel exchanged an apologetic look, and although neither said it, the intent was there.

"Now, if you'll follow me outside, the cause for our celebration will soon begin," Alethea said.

Wyn's smile stretched his face as he made his way for the door.

Devlyn trailed the crowd outside and joined Wyn who looked to the stars above. But the stars were not visible, hidden by thick thunderous clouds roiling above.

Alethea stood gaping at them.

Considering the snow and clouds they'd experienced earlier that day, Devlyn didn't understand why she had expected the weather to cooperate with the feast day. If she had really wanted to see the stars on Borephaen, they should have stayed in the Illumined Wood another night.

Devlyn felt Alethea embrace the erendinth and begin to wield kiara. The threatening clouds stirred with her wielding, but not as Devlyn expected. They fought her interference, roiling ever faster.

Wyn looked troubled, as though fearful of what the clouds might be hiding.

Pressing into the erendinth himself, Devlyn tried to supplement

Alethea's wielding with his own.

"Do not," Alethea cried, her voice shrill.

Lessening his grasp over the erendinth, Devlyn watched in horror as Alethea was lifted into the air. What was happening?

She hovered for a moment then slowly rose as dense clouds reached down and swallowed her.

Ignoring her warning, Devlyn wielded aerys and animys at the cloud surrounding Alethea, searching the mysterious veil for her. Wyn added his own strength to Devlyn's.

Grateful for the support, Devlyn probed the cloud, but even as he did, it faded, leaving nothing behind.

Alethea was gone.

MISSING

A brilliant snow had fallen the night before, transforming Gwilnor Academy into a majestic sight, giving the castle an illusion of newness and purity. Flakes continued to fall through the morning, turning to ice by the late afternoon as the sun dipped behind one of the western mountains.

Snow now clung to the stone and windowpanes of the East Tower, covering the scorch marks left after the fire started by the rogue kien wielders. Under the fresh coat of snow, the castle looked as though nothing was wrong, a stark contrast to how Jaerol perceived the castle at present.

Inside, the castle corridors were colder than usual. Jaerol was accustomed to the castle always feeling comfortable, whether it was during the hottest days of summer—rare here in the Laudien Mountains—or the coldest nights of winter. Everyone, student and ei'ana alike, wore their winter cloaks as they made their way through the eerily quiet corridors. The only sounds were feet scraping on the stone floor, and even that was subdued. Friendly chatter was as rare as a Cyndinari looking forward to a snow storm; no one trusted themselves to speak outside the privacy of their rooms, terrified that they'd be punished.

Jaerol limped along with the quiet crowd, shuffling and bumping into others. His entire body ached and he wanted nothing more than to rest and regain his strength, but not even that was possible. The situation at Gwilnor had somehow worsened since Jaerol and Liam first started attending Fyreh and Myrah's middle-of-the-night secret lessons. Last month, Hannah had figured out that someone was secretly teaching students to wield, turning her insistence on finding the Seven Chairs of Septyl into paranoia. It was clear that she thought they were behind those secret lessons. She decided to quell the nocturnal lessons by implementing a cruel late-night schedule where bells rang randomly throughout the night. Everyone was expected to come out into the corridors for inspection and roll call before they could collapse back into fitful sleep until the bells called them out again.

And despite Hannah's cruelty, a cruelty shielded by her insincere smile, Jaerol and the other students still managed to meet Fyreh and Myrah for lessons. They were the only magisters in the castle at present, deposed or not, who were taking a risk to teach their students anything useful.

Jaerol had only mildly regretted that he had not fled the castle the night of the attack on Gwilnor, but after a month of interrupted sleep, he wanted nothing more than to be away from Gwilnor Academy and the Tenebrae ei'ana who now controlled it. Wherever the Seven Chairs had disappeared to that awful night, taking a small percentage of the castle's residents with them during the confusion, Jaerol hoped they were safe and far away from the Tenebrae.

Jaerol kept his head down as he melded into the line of mindless drones trudging through the castle without purpose. Despite the restrictions placed on the school, students were still permitted to walk the corridors at leisure, assuming they weren't required to be somewhere else or mingling with the opposite sex.

They had all come to Gwilnor with hopes of advancing themselves and the world they lived in. Most of the students had come to learn how to wield, but the knights and their pupils had also come to Gwilnor with hopes and dreams. However, the Tenebrae who now controlled Gwilnor did everything they could to extinguish any such spark.

Jaerol's thoughts wandered as he kept his eyes focused on the stonework beneath his feet. Suddenly, he felt a tug on his robe. He turned to see who it was but there was no one within several paces of him.

Great, now my sanity is even abandoning me. Jaerol rubbed his eyes, knowing that dunking his head in cold water would be a better way to make him more alert. But what he really needed was some uninterrupted sleep.

Dismissing whatever pulled his cloak as his imagination playing with him, Jaerol kept walking, eyes down. When the second tug came at his robe, it was strong enough to stop him in his tracks. That wasn't his imagination.

Daring a second look behind, he again found no one close enough to have pulled his robe, yet it was still sticking out from his body.

Then, another pull. He saw the fabric move with his own eyes.

He felt a trap springing into play. Wielding without supervision was forbidden. Whoever was pulling on his robes was clearly trying to get him into trouble. His swollen eye still had not healed from the last time he had wielded kien without permission in Yvonne's class and that was after his face hadn't fully healed following his duel with Razcul.

Yvonne had abandoned standard disciplinary measures and Razcul had been summoned to punish Jaerol. The shadow elf chose to plant a fist into the side of his face, worsening Jaerol's still swollen eye. Since the Crimsyns were no longer allowed to heal without express permission, something that was no longer extended to students, the bruise on his face now covered half of it.

A fourth pull came, and afraid that someone would notice the weird movement of his robe, Jaerol followed the tugs, making sure no one was paying attention to him. Although he had a mental tally of those he counted among the Tenebrae in the castle, he was sure that the number was much higher than his list.

The tugs led him into an empty corridor and he soon found himself descending a stair he had never come across before. From the moment Jaerol had enrolled at Gwilnor, he had made a point to learn as much of the castle's interior as possible. It was an enormous structure with seven towers and three main structures connected by bridges. He didn't think he would ever learn all its secrets by the time he concluded his studies and considering the current situation, even that was questionable.

He soon found himself two levels below in a narrow, dusty, and dark corridor where there were no torches to illuminate the cobwebs.

Perhaps foolishly trusting the tugs and expecting the worst, Jaerol turned at a corner into a corridor that he could not see. He expected that at any second, Razcul would appear to silence him forever. Jaerol could already hear Liam calling him an idiot for allowing himself to being led down here alone.

His body would remain lost far below the castle. Although he was sure that Liam would search persistently, this area seemed to be long forgotten. If anyone ever did find his remains, he'd be no more than a skeleton by then. Only the remnants of his school robes would identify him as a student, with no indication of his name or his origin. He'd be a forgotten skeleton and nothing more.

A hand grasped his shoulder, and his heart nearly exploded out of his chest at the touch. He turned in a flash, pressing into the erendinth to ward off the enemy coming from behind.

"Hello, Jaerol," said a familiar voice. Velaria!

The erendinth slid from his control and relief flooded into him, calming his heart rate.

Neither dared to wield a source of light.

"Follow me." Velaria wielded terys and the stone wall beside them parted and opened into an arched portal. She led him through it and sealed it behind them before wielding another archway on the opposite wall.

Light flooded into the small vestibule they stood in, revealing a bright large chamber beyond, more cavern than castle cellar. Dozens of faces, some relieved, some wary, watched Velaria come in with Jaerol on her heels.

Tables and chairs filled the room, and dozens of doors lined the walls. There was nothing nice about their hideout beneath Gwilnor, but it was the first time that Jaerol had felt safe in six months.

"Oh, good, you found him," said Mother Paurel, Chair of Vyoletryn. Jaerol was startled to see the elderly woman alive and unscathed, and even more surprised that she knew who he was. "Did you think those unsophisticated kien wielders could harm the Seven Chairs of Septyl?"

"Sorry, I didn't mean to gawk," he said.

"If that's all that filth has to throw at us, they're doomed," Paurel said with a confident grin.

"How are you all down here?" Jaerol asked, taking in the dozens of people filling the chamber. "How did you get away?"

"Well, if there hadn't been an explosion in the main courtyard, I and every other Vyoletryn would have died in the fire engulfing our tower," Paurel said.

"I'm happy it wasn't too late."

"That was you?" Paurel asked, disbelief mixed with joy in her voice.

"Yes. After Razcul attacked me in the Dragon Tower, I've been having trouble sleeping most nights, so, when I saw the flames, there was only one thing I knew to do."

"You blessed, wonderful, young man." Paurel pulled Jaerol into a warm hug, a show of emotion that he would never have expected.

"To answer your question, Velaria found this place, notified us and we fought our way down here," said Mother Selenya, Chair of Albien. "I believe only Melanie managed to find a route down here that didn't include a scuffle."

"I had to duck around a few groups patrolling the castle, but I managed to stay hidden." Mother Melanie, Chair of Arantiulyn, spoke up quickly, and Jaerol thought he caught a glimmer of something, he wasn't sure what, in her eyes. "We're happy you are alive and well, truly, Jaerol, but I don't see how bringing you down here will be of any benefit."

"We need someone we can trust above," Velaria said. "And seeing as none of us can safely leave this chamber without being recognized, we need someone already in place."

"What good will that do? All we'll do is jeopardize our position. Imagine what would happen if someone followed him," Melanie argued.

"A necessary risk. We are not hiding for the sake of staying hidden until the Tenebrae pack up and leave," Paurel said, ending the quarrel before it went further. "Please, Jaerol, join us."

Taking a seat next to Velaria with the other Chairs of Septyl at one of the long tables in the cavernous cellar, Jaerol felt a bit nervous. The only other time he had been in their presence before was when they had accepted him as a student wielder. He wished Liam could be here with him.

"I hope you can understand why we waited to bring you down here, since there's only so much we can do without drawing unwanted attention. Melanie's correct, we do take a substantial risk in bringing you here, but we need someone above to be our eyes and ears," Paurel said.

Jaerol shifted in his seat, noticing that with those words, every Chair was looking at his obvious injuries.

"Do we know who's in control? Have they tried to implant a new chancellor?" Melanie asked.

"Not that I know of. There's no way that Hannah doesn't belong to the Tenebrae though," Jaerol said.

A small smile found its way to Velaria's once concerned expression.

"Thanks to Velaria, she is awaiting trial and sits in a cell in the Temple of Ceur," Paurel said. "Has it become clear who else sides with the Tenebrae?"

"Pardon me? Hannah's not in a cell. I saw her last week. She's been turning the castle upside down trying to find you."

"I wonder how she managed to free herself," Velaria said. "Yelaris flew her to the temple with a note pinned on her unconscious body asking that she be tossed into the cells of justice."

"Should have saved us the trouble and burned her to a crisp when you had the chance," Melanie said.

"This doesn't bode well for us. The treachery isn't just in the castle." Father Phendien, Chair of Emradiel, shook his head with dismay, and rose to pace distractedly around the table.

"Those kien wielders had all originally come from the temple, so it's not surprising that they kept some of their ilk there." Melanie crossed her arms.

"Shouldn't the Chamber of Light have crushed them?" Loretta asked. The Chair of Crimsyn looked terrified. "Could something be wrong with the Temple of Ceur?"

"If the traitor was a temple knight on guard duty, helping Hannah escape would mean he only betrayed the temple after the fact." Selenya added pensively, seeming to consider other ways around the temple's workings.

"We should find a way to inform Ceurtriarch Aaron. He needs to know that there are snakes among his flock," said Mother Agnelle, Chair of Auburnis.

"Agreed, but I'm sure Aaron already knows that he can't trust everyone in the temple." Paurel stopped herself, clearly concerned about her younger relative. "Well, at least that woman is no longer chancellor and cannot access the office. She would have discovered our sanctuary long ago if she could have managed to get in."

Jaerol blinked, not understanding what accessing the chancellor's office had to do with locating people in the castle. He thought better than to ask the question, since he didn't think the Seven Chairs would share more of Gwilnor's secrets than they needed to.

"It's a good thing we took that precaution and rescinded her title," Loretta said. "Now, the others; who else can we know for certain are aligned with the Tenebrae?"

"A good place to start is those without any injuries," Jaerol said. "The Tenebrae have not been a patient group, and rarely delay in applying discipline."

Velaria looked at Paurel, lips pursed. Jaerol had never seen Velaria angry before. He imagined her storming the castle above, and exacting justice on anyone who wronged Septyl and abused Gwilnor's students.

"What of the Eldinari? Other than Father Phendien, none made it down here," Velaria said.

"I've only seen Fyreh and Myrah. They've been holding secret lessons for students who still want to learn how to wield. Hannah thinks you're behind the lessons. As for the other Eldinari, I think they've either barricaded themselves in their wing or they're prevented from leaving their quarters," Jaerol said.

"That certainly sounds like Fyreh; Myrah, less so." Phendien chuckled and took his seat at the table again. "He was known to cause all sorts of trouble for the Tenebrae the last time they came to Gwilnor. I'm sure the others have barricaded themselves in their quarters, awaiting our instructions."

"I think it's time we reached out to our known allies above," Paurel said.

"How can we know ally from foe? All we have is a vague indication that if they're injured, they might be an ally," Melanie grumbled.

"We have to do something. We can't leave our sister and brother ei'ana above to fend for themselves, thinking their Chairs have abandoned them, to say nothing of our poor students, entrusted into our protection," Paurel said.

Looking away from Melanie at Paurel's words, Jaerol saw that Paurel's eyes had turned entirely silver. He looked about, noticing more of the silver eyes, and then realized that all the Luminari hiding away down here, just as all the Luminari in the castle above, had lost the green that had once shown in their eyes. He hadn't felt comfortable asking anyone in the upper levels of the castle about it—asking questions was discouraged by the Tenebrae and it was impossible to tell who had betrayed Septyl and who was still loyal to Septyl.

"Forgive me for asking, but why have all the Luminari elves' eyes changed to silver? What happened to the green?"

Paurel smiled, her previously stern manner falling away. "Our pilgrimage has ended. I wish I could discover how the Luminari along the Illumined Wood are transitioning. We were never meant to live along the Illumined Wood forever. I cannot say what that means, but the hope has always been to return to Krysenthiel."

Kevn's eyes were aching as the last of a flickering candle lit a beautifully inscribed vellum page of the heavy tome that lay open before him on a writing desk in the Ceurtriarch's office. Other than Ceurtriarch Aaron Roendryn, no one was permitted to know what Kevn was studying, so Aaron had arranged for Kevn to stay in the Ceurtriarch's quarters and to study there.

Unable to remember the last time he had slept in his own bedchamber, Kevn raised his tired eyes from the tome and looked outside. The sun had set and by the looks of it, several hours ago. He stood and the chair creaked with the release of his weight after he'd been sitting in the same position for so long. He stretched his limbs for the first time in hours as his stomach rumbled. *Did I forget dinner again?*

"Find anything?" Aaron asked as he walked into the office, looking hopeful. Kevn had noticed the change in eye color as soon as it had begun and found it odd that some people still couldn't understand why the Luminari elves' eyes no longer held the emerald. Everyone knew that Lucillia had only been a temporary home for the Luminari and considering the prophecy involving Devlyn, it made perfect sense that their pilgrimage had ended. It was time for the Luminari to return to Krysenthiel.

"Nothing new." Kevn's eyes were beginning to adjust after staring at the intricately scrawled letters written in Aelish. Few bothered learning the ancient language, now accepted as dead and irrelevant, but Kevn adored it. He had never come across a language as wholesome as Aelish. The Common Tongue spoken in Eklean seemed empty after learning Aelish, and there were things he wanted to express to others, but since few would understand, he could never adequately explain himself.

"There has to be something on the Empyrean Sphere that we're missing." Aaron glanced down at the tome on the desk. Aaron was familiar enough with Aelish that he might be able to get the basic meaning of the passage, but he would miss the subtleties that Kevn's greater experience with the language would pick up, so he had enlisted Kevn's help.

"From what I've gathered, I think we're overcomplicating it. I've spoken with Clara and she keeps telling me that nothing is required but oneself. We don't have to bring a gift or anything of the sort. The only thing we need is to prove our worthiness before the six-winged anadel," Kevn said.

"That's what I'm afraid of." Aaron turned from the opened book and toward the balcony. "We're not the first to try. There've been reports over the past fourteen hundred years of ei'ceuril vanishing from the Chamber of Light; steward or not, even wise ones and archstewards weren't exempt."

"What if not everyone who entered the Empyrean Sphere vanished? What if they just never recorded what they had accomplished? After all, the ei'ceuril have not been trained to wield kien since before Krysenthiel fell. They very well might not have been aware that they could wield lumenys, especially since they were restricted from leaving the temple."

Aaron mulled over Kevn's words.

It made perfect sense to Kevn. It was like telling someone with a blindfold covering their eyes during their entire life that if they took the blindfold off, they would see. But, when sight was not even a possibility, how could they take the blindfold off?

"So, you're suggesting we just stroll in?" Aaron asked, disbelievingly.

"I have no idea how this six-winged anadel judges those who present themselves, but you're the Ceurtriarch and a descendant of Lucillia herself. If that's not qualification enough, I don't know what is. I, on the other hand, don't belong to any noble house, and my indecision will find me crippled."

"Still thinking about leaving?" Aaron asked as a friend and not as the Ceurtriarch, annoying Kevn who detested how talented his friend was at changing the subject. Aaron was a natural at guiding any conversation to matters of the heart.

"It's hard to describe," Kevn said, not ready to admit he did want to leave again.

"Try me."

Kevn fumbled with the trim on his ei'ceuril robe. "I like this life; it's just—something isn't right. Nothing's wrong, I'm not unhappy, but something is pulling me out—something deep in my heart that I can't explain."

"This isn't the first time you've felt this way, Kevn. You've been in and out of the ei'ceuril already, and I doubt I'll be able to convince Homas to permit your return again if you leave. Especially after the past year."

Kevn knew the truth behind Aaron's words. "I know," he said, after pausing and allowing silence to permeate the office. He felt Aaron staring behind him.

"You do know that you've become a phenomenal wielder, yes?"

That made Kevn smile. When he'd been told that he had to learn to wield the erendinth, he had done everything he could to avoid his lessons, but once he started, there was no stopping. Wielding had become second nature to him, like reading or writing. He could not imagine how he could stop wielding in the future. Granted, he could only wield while outside the temple and that only occurred during lessons that were held in the hidden valley nestled behind the city.

"If you leave, where will you go? It's not like you can go to Gwilnor in its current condition."

Returning to Gwilnor was out of the question. The castle had been spiraling out of control even before the Tenebrae had taken over. It simply wasn't safe there, especially for kien wielders. Perhaps he could find work at an inn and they'd be willing to give him room and board in exchange. A dozen different options flew though his head. What were his prospects once he left the Ei'ceuril for a second time?

"I might try to find Devlyn, to help him however I can. He wants to take down the Shroud. If he manages it, Septyl will be open to us again," Kevn said, his voice breathless as he spoke. He had always fantasized about going to Septyl but had never allowed himself to entertain the thought because of the Shroud. He dreamt of what it would be like to explore Septyl's library. The place had become almost mythical to him. "Imagine what would happen if it fell into enemy hands—the only reason we lost it in the first place, is because the betrayal was so inconceivable. No one imagined Erynor or his allies could betray us as they did. If we had known of an impending attack, Septyl would never have been lost."

"You speak as though you're already dedicated to Septyl," Aaron said.

"I suppose."

"Since you're decided, might I offer a suggestion?"

Kevn nodded, although he knew he wasn't going to like what Aaron was about to suggest.

"Enter the Empyrean Sphere with me."

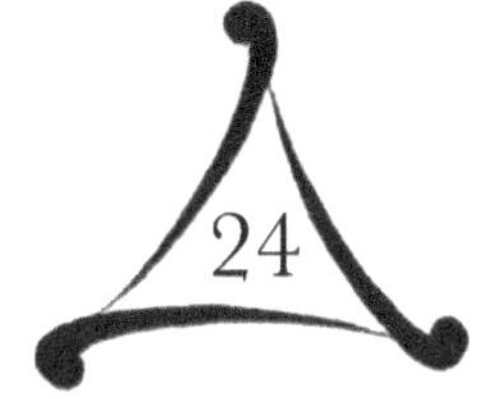

DELIBERATIONS

None of them slept well after Alethea's disappearance. They had spent the rest of the night and following days trying to figure out what had happened to her. Every attempt to reach out to her with their collective inner senses was met with silence. Alethea was gone and the only trace of her in the Gestorian village was her griffin, Leithel.

With heavy hearts, they had left the village and continued their journey to rejoin the Luminari. Inclement weather had set in, and it had taken two weeks to reach the encampment. It wasn't safe to fly during a blizzard but neither could they sit still, and it was best to press on. They didn't discuss what had happened, and instead kept their thoughts private as they journeyed onward. Talking about it made it more real.

The image of the cloud encompassing Alethea plagued Devlyn whenever his eyes closed. As terrible as he felt, he knew his feelings were minuscule compared to Wyn's. Alethea was related to them both, but she had been Wyn's mentor and guide for over a century, and they were close.

As they approached the makeshift encampment along the River Meyien, Devlyn noticed that the tents were arrayed neatly in ordered swooping swirls. The streets formed by the tents created whorls instead of a regularized grid. He had always assumed that the curved streets of Lucillia were a byproduct of the forest dictating the formal layout of the city. But the streets of Ceurenyl were similarly laid out, so apparently, elven urban planners despised straight lines. Devlyn wondered if there was any strategic reasoning behind it. Did it make places with a large population easier to defend? Or was it intended to bolster civic life?

They alit and Devlyn withdrew from Aliel. The world felt lesser without his golden lighted vision and his wings. Rusyl had decided to keep the dragons' ability to shapeshift a secret from the Luminari as there were doubtless servants of Shadow among the large Luminari population, so he waited next to the two griffins for Devlyn to take the lead.

In silence, they approached two guards near a marked entrance to the encampment. Devlyn tried to see whether the guards were concerned about the dragon, and immediately noticed their eye color—there was no hint of green left in them.

The guards standing at the edge of the tents looked at one another, unsure about what protocols might apply. Standing before them were Devlyn, Wyn, and the two griffins whom they'd seen before, but the phoenix and the blue dragon that accompanied them seemed to be confusing them. They had seen the group flying from the southeast and had noted Devlyn's illuminated winged form and the blue dragon. Their confused expressions wavered between awe and impossibility. Devlyn returning was one thing, but they seemed daunted by the dragon. Another guard strode confidently toward them from inside the encampment and she was obviously disappointed with the two guards. They stood at attention when they realized she had joined them.

"Lady Toryn," they said in unison.

"The next time you're unfamiliar with whoever is flying toward our severely under-protected camp filled with our entire population, be sure to alert us before you begin gawking and doing nothing! And I'm no noblewoman, thank you." Devlyn noticed that Toryn's eyes were also silver.

"Beg your pardon, but you are Lady of the Watch," the braver or dumber of the two said.

"Then why did this *Lady* of the Watch have to see flying figures zooming toward our camp with her own eyes and without so much as receiving a warning of potential trouble?" Toryn glared at the two guards, arms akimbo and hands clamped on her waist.

"Uh, sorry, my lady, but it was clearly the Phaedryn returning, ma'am."

"And did you know what a Phaedryn looks like before you took to gaping as though he was Anaweh incarnate?" Toryn winced at Devlyn, aware that she'd been perhaps a touch irreverent, and glanced at the phoenix before turning back on the two guards.

"No, ma'am," the two said together, crestfallen.

"Did you at least notice whether anyone flew in on the dragon?" Toryn cast a long look across the plains and then at Rusyl.

"He didn't have a rider," Devlyn answered for the embarrassed guards. "Would you mind leading us to Ei'lythel Ellendren?" He didn't need to witness their commander chastise them; he had other things to do. He had to find out what had happened since he had left.

Toryn led them into the camp. As they followed along the paths, Devlyn realized that he couldn't tell whether the tents had been pitched today or a week ago. He couldn't imagine why they would take such extensive care to plan out their encampment if it was to be broken down the following morning. Perhaps they intended to hold out here until the snows melted or the Shroud was removed? Aliel flew just above Devlyn, a sight that the elves of Lucillia hadn't ever seen, and people gawked as they walked by. If Aliel wasn't attraction enough, Rusyl certainly was. He stomped through the paths between the tents, his tail coming dangerously close to swatting the tents as it swung left and right.

Just before they reached a large yellow tent where Toryn stood beside Ellendren, Wyn veered off and led the two griffins away down another path. Rusyl turned his head back to watch him go, earning stares and whispers from the elves watching them. Devlyn couldn't help snorting when he heard someone suggest that the dragon likely wanted to gobble up those griffins for an afternoon snack.

Waiting outside her tent, Ellendren was either expecting them or simply going about the business of taking care of the Luminari. The aryls wouldn't allow her to sit around doing nothing all day if she expected to succeed her father. Ellendren might not be an aryl herself, but that didn't stop her from seeing to the wellbeing of the Luminari enroute to Krysenthiel. Devlyn simply couldn't envision Ellendren allowing the aryls to govern without her. While Lucillia was gone, they had mostly been rather reluctant to leave the Illumined Wood since many of those elves didn't dare believe that reclaiming Krysenthiel was even possible. Instead, they thought they had been bullied away from the protection offered by the Illumined Wood even without Lucillia and the other cities along the edge of the forest. The lost kingdom of Krysenthiel was nothing more than a fanciful dream, something to hope for when all the lights went out.

Ellendren moved toward them, relieved and happy that they had returned. As he lifted his arms to hug her, Devlyn saw that the brilliant emerald color had vanished from her eyes. "Your eyes too?"

"Oh, yes, all of us. If you weren't a Phaedryn, the same would have happened to your own eyes." Ellendren always seemed to understand what Devlyn was referring to. "Speaking of which, you've bonded with Aliel again! That's so wonderful," she said, too excited about Aliel to comment on Rusyl. "Do you know why you couldn't?"

"When I was struck by that bolt of tenebrys, a shadow or darkness covered my heart and blocked Aliel inside me." In spite of the pain he felt at the loss of Alethea, Ellendren's obvious welcome for both Aliel and himself made him feel a little lighter, especially when she wrapped her arms around him.

"Well, I'm happy you're back—both of you." Ellendren smiled at the phoenix, stepping back from her embrace. "And is this Rusyl? It's so great to see you well enough to fly again. You had us worried after Aren nearly killed you in Myrium."

Devlyn thought he saw the dragon snicker. Devlyn knew that Rusyl could do much more than just fly again. As a blue dragon, Rusyl had an intimate connection to aquaeys. The dragons didn't manipulate the erendinth in the same way as wielders did, but they had a mastery over the erendinth they were connected to that any wielder would be envious of. The draelyn were similar in that regard—they had of course learned to wield after Kien and Kiara, but they too had that same connection to whichever erendinth their dragon forefathers had been associated with.

Devlyn wondered what that meant for him. Since he belonged to the Gold House, theoretically, he should have no issue wielding lumenys, or at least interacting with it. That clearly was not the case though and he had yet to do more than clear a small opening in the Shroud during his first year at Gwilnor Academy. He again wondered how he had been able to do that. According to Clara, the only way to wield lumenys was by entering the Empyrean Sphere and beseeching the six-winged anadel. Perhaps him being a draelyn of the Gold House had something to do with it. Still, he didn't think being descended from a gold dragon would be enough to remove the Shroud and he bit the side of his cheek before saying what came next.

"I need to return to the Temple of Ceur." He tried to think of a more elaborate way to say it, including the reasoning behind it with a flowery explanation, but he had only the simple phrase.

"I was wondering when you were planning on that," Ellendren said softly.

"You expected it?"

"Of course. How else are we to destroy the Shroud without wielding lumenys?"

Devlyn was both pleased and worried to hear her say *we*.

"Don't give me that look—you and I both know that the more of us capable of wielding lumenys the better, not just for the sake of removing the Shroud, but for whatever Erynor throws at us, shadow elves, Aren, and the Deurghol included."

Standing with his mouth agape, Devlyn stared back at Ellendren, more impressed by her determination than anything.

"But…what about the dangers of entering the Empyrean Sphere?" he asked, finally capable of speaking.

"We'll be together—*we'll* be fine. Besides, I've been doing some research; the librarians have been kind enough to dig through the carts for the books I needed." Ellendren quickly changed topics. She seemed just as excited about this as she was to see Devlyn and Aliel bonded again. "It's about lumenys. I don't know if it will work, but I think our best chance at entering the Empyrean Sphere and to gain the ability to wield that transcendental erendinth will be during Aurephaen."

"The spring equinox? That's what, just over two months away?"

"Precisely and if my research has anything to say about it, even though Auriel has been terribly quiet since the Ceurendol War, he won't be able to ignore us on our high feast day. He is the enthiel that guides the Luminari after all."

Devlyn thought it over. It did make sense and they needed to start wielding lumenys soon. Removing the Shroud was all but impossible without it. "So, we just need to get to the Temple of Ceur by mid-Aurenth?"

"Yes. Arriving a few days early couldn't hurt either."

Ellendren looked past Devlyn's shoulder. "Are Wyn and Alethea tired? I saw Wyn walk off with both griffins, but I must have missed Alethea."

His heart plummeted into his stomach. Talking about wielding lumenys had filled him with hope but hearing his mentor's name made all that optimism vanish. He wanted to talk about anything except what had happened to Alethea, as though speaking about it would only confirm and solidify it. Looking at the ground and hugging himself, Devlyn felt his eyes begin to tear.

"Devlyn, what happened to Alethea?" Sensitive to his mood, she entwined her fingers in his.

"Elle, sh…she's gone." Tears flowed unhindered.

"What do you mean, gone?"

"It was the winter solstice—Borephaen—and she tried to banish the clouds, but they took her. One moment she was there, the next she and those clouds were gone."

"We'll find her."

"Elle, she's gone. We tried to find her—to sense her presence but she was no more. Every trace of her has disappeared."

"We'll try again."

Letting Ellendren comfort him, Devlyn hadn't noticed Wyn approach with the griffins.

"I've reached out to Dalenya; she's instructed me to make for Everin. Fendryl and a host of Eldinari star wardens are there, bolstering the city's defenses. I can give him and the other aryls there an account of what happened."

"I'm so sorry, Wyn." Ellendren rubbed his upper arm, her voice warm with compassion. "How long do you expect you will be?"

"It's difficult to say. There's no telling when I'll be able to present the events to the aryls or if they'll summon me back to Stellantis as well."

"Well, there's no reason for you to travel all the way alone," Ellendren said.

"It really isn't necessary to send someone with me."

"We'll have to talk about it somewhere privately. The aryls will want to be involved, of course. Now that you're back, Devlyn, I'll try to arrange a council meeting. You should both wash up and get something to eat before then. There's no saying how long the aryls will want to drag out those proceedings." Ellendren turned to go into her tent and before Devlyn could even consider his next move, a page rushed from her tent with a series of notes, presumably summons for the aryls.

Devlyn wondered what Ellendren wanted to talk to Wyn about that required him to stay here rather than go to Everin immediately. He looked exhausted and overwhelmed. But he needed to provide a full account of Alethea's disappearance to his people and as soon as possible, and eating was probably the furthest thing from his mind even though it would do him some good.

"I suppose we should take her advice, right?" Devlyn looked around for someone that could direct him to a bath.

A series of images flashed into his mind, Rusyl digging a hole in the ground then melting the snow and ice to turn it into a hot bath. As tempting as that was, Devlyn preferred the privacy of a tub inside a tent. Rusyl snorted in return, melting the snow immediately in front of him as he plopped down just outside Ellendren's tent. Wyn and the griffins did the same.

"I'll wait here; I'm not all that hungry and I can't think about taking a relaxing bath at the moment."

Devlyn had no intention of pressuring him and honestly felt much the same. How could Alethea be gone? She had been born on Eldinare, brought her people to Eklean, and survived the Ceurendol War only to vanish in a cloud. It was too much to consider and it shouldn't have been possible.

Rather than pondering Alethea's unexplainable disappearance, Devlyn strolled around the camp with Aliel hovering above him, hoping to find where he might get a bath and some food. Despite having stayed in Lucillia's palace, he had no idea where his place was in this camp. Did he have an attendant as he had at the palace? Did he even have a tent here? Perhaps there was a communal area for people who didn't have their own tents. Viren had likely hoped to have returned before Devlyn was once again amid a large population. He could already hear the Guardian knight commenting on a stray arrow or a concealed dagger on a servant of Shadow. His stomach rumbled, so perhaps he was hungry after all.

"Ei'ethil?" Lyren, the attendant who had assisted Devlyn in the Lucillian palace had approached without Devlyn noticing him.

"Hi, Lyren." Devlyn forced a smile. He was happy to see Lyren again but that didn't mean his mood was any improved.

"Princess…I mean Ei'lythel Ellendren asked me to show you to your tent. It would have been closer to the ei'lythel's but some of the aryls commented on the impropriety of having you and her sleeping so close to one another."

"More like they're still hoping to get Ellendren to marry one of their sons and me to marry one of their daughters," Devlyn quipped back, Trethien Narielle popping to mind. Were his parents still trying to reignite that broken betrothal?

Lyren smiled politely and led Devlyn to his tent. It was nowhere near as large as Ellendren's, but it wasn't a small tent either. From what Devlyn had gleaned from Ellendren about the aryls, they held more authority now that King Harnyl had passed with no one to immediately replace him. For his successor to become the next aryl, that person had to be married and seeing as Ellendren was the original next in line, her being unwed for the foreseeable future had emboldened the other aryls. And that didn't even touch on Devlyn's future role as heir to the Crystal Throne of Krysenthiel.

Devlyn walked into his tent to find a tub filled with steaming water in the middle of other simple furnishings. A bowl of fruit stood on a table beside the tub. Was he expected to eat and wash himself at the same time? That sounded terribly unsanitary.

"Is there anything I can get you, Ei'ethil?"

"No, thank you, Lyren. Did Ellendren say when this meeting with the aryls will take place?" He peeled off his lierathnil and stepped into the tub, not really caring that Lyren was in the room. Perhaps he was finally getting more comfortable in his own skin and allowing others to see him for who he was. As much as he hated to admit it, he had needed a bath. His skin was gritty and both he and his clothing stank. Perhaps that was why Ellendren had met them outside her tent and kept her hug brief.

"She was hoping to have them gathered within the hour. Would you like me have your lierathnil cleaned?"

"That would be great, thank you." It was the only set of lierathnil Devlyn had with him, the rest still in the wardrobe—presuming no one has taken them—in his room at Gwilnor.

Devlyn soaked for a few minutes until he felt himself relax, then quickly washed. Lyren had arranged an outfit for him while he bathed and had laid it out on the cot. The dark green pants were finely made and felt as though someone had measured him precisely since they fit snugly on his legs, tighter and more revealing than he preferred. Still, he liked how they looked. He pulled the cream-colored tunic over his head, loosely tying up the front. It had a nice gold-colored embroidery, but it was a light fabric and Devlyn was happy to see the deep blue cloak that Lyren had included. Devlyn would not have been able to stay warm otherwise. The only drawback of the outfit was that if he needed to bond with Aliel, he would either have to take the time to get undressed or accept that the entire ensemble would burn to a crisp. He hoped there wouldn't be any need to take on the Phaedryn form without notice. He ate some of the provided fruit, wishing that vaer could have been included.

He found Lyren waiting for him outside his tent, but instead of returning to Ellendren's tent, they walked in a different direction. The winding pathways between the tents disoriented Devlyn and since all the tents were short structures, it was impossible to gauge where Lyren was taking him. Even the surrounding landscape with the hills in the distance didn't provide any useful markers.

Shortly, they came to what looked like a temporary plaza where the Luminari had set up a large rectangular chamber tent at the far end. Devlyn recognized the aryls walking into the tent easily enough as they smiled at him and seemed pleased to see Aliel accompanying him.

"Will you need anything else? I won't be joining you inside," Lyren said.

"Any chance you can get me out of this meeting?"

"I don't think so. I'll head back to your tent and see to your lierathnil." Lyren tipped his head and left.

Devlyn took a deep breath and pushed the large flap of the entrance aside. Tables lined the tent's interior to form a large rectangle so everyone seated there could face each other. Of the sixteen seats around the table, over half were occupied. Ellendren had yet to arrive, but Devlyn assumed that the seats directly opposite the entrance were their places. They might not be married nor the Exalted Aryl of Krysenthiel yet but after the late King Harnyl Roendryn had given his parting speech to a decaying Lucillia, every Luminari knew who Devlyn was. As unlikely as the return of a Lorenthien was, it seemed just as unlikely as the Luminari returning to Krysenthiel. Devlyn took his seat and Aliel perched on the back, peering at the arriving aryls.

The remaining seats filled, Ellendren entering last and sitting beside Devlyn. While he had the stronger claim to the Crystal Throne of Krysenthiel, he could not assume that power until he became an aryl and as Ellendren was the heir to the Lucillian throne, she was trying to fill the power vacuum left by her deceased parents. Judging by some of the expressions around the tent, some of the other aryls had hoped to swipe that mantle away from her before she could secure her authority. They likely would still try.

Once the chatter settled, Ellendren stood again. "Thank you, revered aryls, for coming on such short notice. The purpose of this meeting is twofold."

"If a demonstration of the Phaedryn's abilities is not on the agenda, I would request that it be added," Silvia said. Even her pretentious tone sounded like her son's. A wave of agreement followed. Not even the aryls who had claimed they didn't need a demonstration when Devlyn had been with them in Lucillia dissented.

"Hundreds, if not thousands, of eyewitnesses saw him fly into our camp. Is it really necessary?" Ellendren asked, an apologetic look spared for Devlyn. There was no getting around it and Devlyn could already sense it.

"Our duties here keep us from watching the skies at every hour. Surely you weren't sitting outside watching the skies with nothing to do, were you, Ei'lythel?" Silvia asked, her voice laced with venom.

"You did agree to display your reestablished connection with the phoenix to us when able," Enoria said as Aliel puffed and fluttered his wings, brightening the tent even more with his golden light. That seemed to settle the aryls somewhat, but Devlyn knew that wouldn't be enough.

"I'd be happy to give a demonstration once my lierathnil is washed."

"We care little about your clothes matching," Ciraenth mocked.

"It's not that," Devlyn said, his cheeks blushing. "Only lierathnil can withstand the transformation. *Every* other garment disintegrates. Every other." He had no intention of letting so many people watch his clothing turn to ash, exposing himself. Especially around elves who also viewed the naked body in the same manner he still occasionally lapsed into. No one in this tent would find the transformation appropriate. Although the gathered aryls would see precious little while he was bonded to Aliel because the brilliant light made it difficult to see, the second he and Aliel separated was a different situation. The golden light would fade away leaving his nether regions exposed until he could find something to wrap around his waist.

Some of the aryls blushed in turn as the rest of them murmured. "We can certainly wait. We don't need two demonstrations in one day. Keeping one's modesty is important after all." Valerie's fierce blush clearly showed that she hadn't spent any time with Alethea. A sadness fell over Devlyn at the reminder.

"Afterwards, then. Let's pray nothing happens to this magical garment," Toral said.

"Right. As I was saying, we have two points to discuss. The first involves Evellion." Ellendren looked around the table to see if anyone objected to her continuing. "We received word from Ei'denai Fendryl Lierafen, Queen Lara of Evellion, and King Alexander Vaerin of Thellion."

Devlyn's mind blanked as he rounded on Ellendren. He only knew one Alex Vaerin. "Alex. You're talking about Alex, my cousin, Alex." Technically, they weren't cousins. Devlyn's father, Dolan, had been born to the Eldinari, but he was half Cyndinari, so he had been deprived of the Eldinari's Life immortal and had been adopted by the Telvin family, an adoption arranged by his Eldinari family. Dolan had lived his entire life thinking that Alex's mother was his sibling, as were Entiel and Lex. None of that mattered now. To Devlyn, he and Alex were family. Alex was the only family member he had grown up with in Cor'lera who accepted and loved him—pointed ears and all. "Are we talking about the same Alex?"

"His father, Clyde Vaerin, is the exiled heir to the Perrien throne," Ellendren said to both Devlyn and the other aryls.

"Truly?" Aegian chimed. "A Thellish king? I assumed the rumors filtering through the Cyrillean Pass to be just that—fictitious, without a shred of truth to them."

"Believe me, it's just as surprising to me. I got to know Alexander as a student at Gwilnor Academy," Ellendren said.

"That aside, what claim does a descendant of the deposed Dennion House have to reinstating the Kingdom of Thellion? Surely, if anyone wanted to reinstate Thellion, the Evellion monarchy have the stronger claim. They still use Thellion as the name of their house," Enithil said.

"The ei'ana of the Thellish court provided some remarkable details. I'd be happy to show you the letter I received, but formally recognizing Thellion and its king will have to be part of a later discussion. What we need to discuss now is that Evellion scouts have identified giants crossing the Vespien Mountains. Fendryl, Lara, and Alex want Devlyn's help in gaining an audience with the dwarven patriarchs and matriarchs. They're afraid, and I quite agree, that if the dwarves refuse to join the conflict, they'll have little chance of securing Everin."

"Haven't the Eldinari already pledged their support to Evellion?

Surely, one elven kin is more than enough. Besides, what more could the dwarves do?" Toral asked.

"That's beside the point; how do they anticipate getting an audience with the dwarven matriarchs and patriarchs? I can't even recall the last time a Roendryn aryl met with any of them," Kyiel said.

"We could reach out to Oma," Devlyn said.

"The stone seer we met at Gwilnor a couple years ago? Just because she's one of the few dwarves not currently underneath a mountain doesn't mean she can arrange a meeting with the dwarven matriarchs and patriarchs." Ellendren folded her hands, seeming to consider it.

"Do you know any other dwarves we can reach out to?" Devlyn asked.

"Only in Belin's Watch and seeing as the only way to get there is to fight our way through an occupied Evellion, I think your Oma is our only option." Aegian said.

"Is she still at Gwilnor?" Ellendren asked.

"I would imagine so. The last we saw her, she gave me the impression that she was secretly working with the Seven Chairs of Septyl," Devlyn said.

"Now that that's decided," Silvia cut in quickly, looking impatient and uninterested in dwarves and the northern kingdoms. "How long, pray tell, do you intend to keep us camped in this location? The Sorenth won't permit us staying here indefinitely."

"Queen Myranda Lariviere has issued an edict permitting our encampment here along the River Meyien," Ellendren said.

"After the Sorenth nearly declared war on us."

"Honestly, Silvia! A royal summons is quite different than an act of war. The young queen was nothing but courteous and understanding when Valerie and I attended her in Myrium," Naesiv chided.

"Fine, we have permission to camp in the wilderness like animals. Barred, mind you, from constructing more adequate dwellings. Now, how long do you intend for us to remain as refugees without roofs of stone or wood over our heads?" Silvia asked.

A murmur of agreement followed. While Devlyn didn't think that they had been in this location long enough to have grown so disgruntled, he could understand some of their frustration. Moving an entire population was no small feat and the rest between each campsite was likely a needed measure. After all, this wasn't an army marching west to their ancestral home. Families with children and elderly were moving their entire lives from cities and villages that no longer existed to those that might or might not still stand in the Shroud. Elderly elves required just as much help as the children did. The treasures from the Lucillian kingdom had been packaged and crated for the journey. It couldn't be easy to transport over a thousand years of history that had built the kingdom from the ground up since the birth of Roendryn and Feolyn.

"That's the other matter of business, Silvia." Ellendren didn't seem nervous, but Devlyn noted hints of hesitation. "Devlyn is our best chance at removing the Shroud. If he goes to Everin, we will be delayed in returning to Krysenthiel."

"How delayed?" Enoria asked.

"Ei'denai Fendryl, Queen Lara, and King Alexander didn't only ask for Devlyn to sway the dwarves into joining the battle against the giants and the now renegade Perrien military." Ellendren mustered her confidence and continued after a breath. "They want him to remain and help liberate the city. It has been under siege for four years and there is no doubt that there are shadow elves among Perrien's forces."

"Of course, I'll help. Alex and Fendryl are family and Queen Lara is one of the kindest people out there. Abandoning her to protect her city and kingdom from the giants and shadow elves alone would be cruel."

"That might all be true, but your life is not your own. If you hope to lead us into the future, you must demonstrate to us your leadership. And running headfirst into a losing battle is not the way to do it," Enithil said. He had been one of Devlyn's earliest supporters and had always been kind to him. Hearing him now question Devlyn's motives was like a punch to the gut.

"We can't abandon them either." Naesiv thoughtfully scratched his chin. "We've done that for too long as it is. We should have sent reinforcements the moment we heard Everin was under siege and Cyril had fallen."

"And what of our own? Do you see any walls surrounding our people? We'll be left defenseless if we send any help to Evellion," Ciraenth protested. It was followed by resounding agreements.

"And what do you imagine will happen when we have need of their help?" Therrin asked, his voice rising. "The Shroud is not our only enemy, lest you forget the reason Evellion is in the state it is. If we abandon them, our strongest ally will fall, and the north will be lost. We cannot fight this war on two fronts, nor can we afford to break alliances."

"We should have never left Lucillia." Silvia sneered as she sat primly.

"Lucillia no longer exists. It has gone back into the forest." Ellendren trembled as she said it. The reality of their vanished home weighed heavily on her.

"We could have avoided enacting that prophecy if that shield had never been put up," Silvia continued, her voice rising in confidence. She didn't have to say that Ellendren's parents had made a mistake, every aryl in the room knew what she meant. "I've yet to see a demonstration of what the Phaedryn is capable of, but the reports and eyewitness accounts are quite remarkable. Sending one of our strongest assets to Evellion, even though they are our allies, would be foolish. He's been gone long enough as it is—not that he was of much use before, given his prior condition."

"And what do you suggest, Ei'terel?" Ellendren mustered every fiber of her political training to keep her anger checked.

"It's clear that there is disagreement in this tent, so I recommend a vote. The aryls should decide what our position is regarding the north, especially as it will have immediate repercussions on our people here."

"Very well." Ellendren didn't move a muscle but Devlyn sensed her tension. "As the heir of the Roendryn aryl and the heir of the Lorenthien Exalted Aryl, Devlyn and I vote aye."

"My apologies, dear, but you misunderstood. I said the aryls. Seeing as neither of you have chosen a spouse, neither of you are an aryl, and hence neither of you have a vote." Silvia could barely keep her grin from spreading. "If you'll excuse us, this is a matter for the aryls."

Devlyn felt the air grow still as every elf present held their breath.

"How dare you speak to her that way!" No longer on the defense, Devlyn abruptly pushed his chair back to stand, turning to look every aryl in the eyes, following Ellendren's example. "The Roendryns not only served the Luminari elves for twelve hundred years, but Ellendren has proven herself time and again and will sit upon the Crystal Throne of Krysenthiel with me."

Lost within his own outburst, Devlyn did not notice Ellendren taking his hand in hers, nor did he realize that he had just publicly declared their intent to marry. Her hand was cold, but still managed to warm him. He felt disgusted with Silvia, and for the first time understood why Trethien was the way he was.

"I believe it's safe to say that this is an opportune time for a short recess. This chamber is adjourned," Ei'terel Lauriel said.

Every aryl stood and went out rather quickly, leaving Devlyn and Ellendren alone inside. There were no formalities as the tent emptied, only a swift escape into the cold air.

"I'm sorry for the outburst. I know it wasn't very proper of me and I know I shouldn't have declared you as my betrothed but…" Devlyn found himself unable to continue speaking as Ellendren planted her lips against his own. His heart fluttered, and he took her in his arms, never wanting to let go.

"What if we didn't wait any longer?" Devlyn asked, breathless, holding Ellendren against himself, his arms wrapped around her lower back. "These problems would dissolve the instant we marry."

Devlyn felt Ellendren smile against his chest.

"If we start to allow them to dictate our actions now, you will dread every day we sit upon the Crystal Throne. Our reign together will be forever shadowed by how we start it." She did not look up to his eyes as she spoke, the ferocity of her earlier speech now gentled and soft. "As much as I want to marry you, it's simply too early. I know we've known each other for almost four years now, but we're only sixteen."

"What's age when you have fate on your side?"

"And impracticality, it would seem," Ellendren said, holding Devlyn just as tightly. "Will every day be this eventful with you?"

"I might find a way to arrange that." Devlyn laughed through his words.

Devlyn and Ellendren left the chamber tent, hand in hand, the chill in her fingers all but forgotten.

PLOTS AND PLOYS

Devlyn had never seen Ellendren so angry. It was a bit of a shock, as just before they'd left the tent, they had seemed to be in perfect accord, and she had spoken softly and lovingly. The stark difference between their shared moment of intimacy just seconds ago and the facade she had put up the moment they were in public again shook Devlyn. She practically dragged him back to her own tent after they left the chamber tent, nearly popping his arm out of its socket as she jerked him along. Rusyl, Wyn, and the griffins still lolled outside her tent. Anyone who had walked past over the course of the day had kept a wide berth between them and the dragon. The only other dragon the Luminari from Lucillia had seen had been Rusyl's sister, Yelaris, when she had brought Devlyn to Lucillia three years ago after Erynor attacked Ceurenyl. Few of them had seen Yelaris close up, and she had not stayed in Lucillia long.

Wyn looked up as Ellendren strode into her tent, yanking Devlyn in after her, Aliel flying through the opening to perch on the back of a chair. Inside, Kaela sat at a folding table, drinking a cup of tea. She calmly watched Ellendren pace back and forth. Wyn came into the tent, pausing just inside the doorway when he saw Kaela sitting inside.

"I didn't realize you were here," Wyn said.

"I overheard what happened to Alethea—the tent's canvas is quite thin and doesn't keep the sound out," Kaela explained then took a sip of her tea. "I figured you wanted to be alone. I am terribly sorry about

Alethea. I have grown quite fond of her."

"I don't know what my people will do without her. She was a living vessel of our history. So few of the elves from before the Great Migration still dwell in Teraeniel—most have made the transition to Lumaeniel." Wyn looked from Kaela to her cup of tea.

"Would you like a cup?" Kaela smiled at Wyn's nod. She got another cup from a rectangular box on a nearby chest, returned to the table and tipped a cupful of tea from the ceramic teapot on the table.

Devlyn glanced at the two, aware of a tension between them and then spoke quietly to Ellendren. "Did I miss something?"

"Apparently I did too, especially after seeing the way she looked at Viren." Ellendren crossed the tent and took a seat opposite Kaela while Devlyn's mind swirled about that bit of information. He had only seen Kaela and the Guardian knight together briefly, and he had never picked up any hint of interest in each other. Viren certainly hadn't mentioned it. Was Kaela attracted to both the Guardian knight and Wyn?

Kaela passed the cup to Wyn. "You might have to warm it some, it's been sitting here for quite some time."

"Should I warm up your cup too?" he asked.

"I'm nearly done with mine but thank you." Kaela blushed as she saw Ellendren glaring at her across the folding table. "There's certainly no need for that. Now tell me, did our plan work?"

"Just as we expected."

Devlyn's jaw dropped. "What plan?" he asked, joining the others at the table.

Ellendren and Kaela giggled. "Our dear Ei'terel Silvia Narielle is as predictable as ever. She's doing everything she can to rein in as much power as she can. Truly, it's quite a concern but knowing her aims makes manipulating her all the easier." Kaela took another sip of her tea.

"How do you mean?" Devlyn asked.

"Well, it's quite simple, really," Ellendren said, her earlier pretense of frustration long gone. "All we had to do was make Silvia show her hand. None of the aryls want to see another aryl vie for power and reach beyond themselves. Silvia might have a few allies among the aryls, but her power grab today will not sit well with the others. Even the minor aryls will take note, and if Silvia isn't careful, one of them might wrest the aryldom of Winstyl from House Narielle."

"So, what exactly was the point of your plan then?" Devlyn asked, not following the sisters' logic.

"We need the aryls' support, especially since you two are neither married nor an aryl yet." Kaela smirked at Ellendren as though saying she and Devlyn should hurry up with their betrothal, unaware of the events in the chamber tent. "Our parents, and the Roendryn aryls before them, reigned in the manner of the Lorenthien aryls but could never be the Exalted Aryl. That title belonged only to the Lorenthiens. Honestly, the Roendryn aryls were more like a human monarchy than anything else."

"We also don't know what the Lorenthien rituals were to become the Exalted Aryl and whether or not those rites have to take place in Arenthyl," Ellendren said, providing another reason to prolong any nuptials.

"Well, let's start with a betrothal. That will stop some of Silvia's scheming."

Devlyn squirmed, inching away from the sisters. A wedding was the furthest thing from his mind just now. How could these two be thinking about a wedding when they were supposed to be figuring out how to provide help to Evellion, not to mention removing the Shroud and keeping the entirety of the Luminari protected from the Erynien Empire? Sure, he envisioned at some point that he and Ellendren would marry, but they were only sixteen years old. They were too young for that—even by mortal standards. Worse, he barely knew how to kiss Ellendren properly. What would happen when more was expected of him? Would Ellendren laugh at him if he was deficient in any way?

Wyn's left eyebrow rose in question at Devlyn, showing that he'd once again unintentionally heard Devlyn's very loud thoughts.

"Well, official or not, Devlyn did announce to the aryls that he intends to sit next to me on the Crystal Throne. Do you think there's any benefit in announcing an official betrothal while we're enroute to Krysenthiel?" Ellendren spared a glance at Devlyn.

He hadn't noticed he was holding his breath. Was he about to be formally betrothed? His silly thoughts of hurrying up the marital process had completely vanished after he had left the temporary privacy of the chamber tent and was in the public eye again.

"It is a shame that father didn't initiate that before his passing. He likely didn't want to put that sort of pressure on you a second time."

"It's rather difficult having only one parent to announce it, let alone from only one of the parties involved."

"That's fair." Kaela smiled at Devlyn, her captivating eyes looking through his insecurities. The way she looked at him made worry that she too could hear his thoughts. "I think it would be a mistake to hold off much longer though, especially if Devlyn is heading north soon. Unless you do enjoy Silvia's continued attempts to pair you with her son again."

"Certainly not. And it's not just Silvia either. Every notable family is trying to pawn their sons off on me. I'm surprised the same hasn't been happening to you."

"Oh, it has. I've even gone to several dinners to entertain them." Kaela batted her eyes at Wyn. Was she trying to get a reaction from him?

"And?" Ellendren pressed.

"It never went further than that. Honestly, it was an easy way to reintegrate back into Lucillian affairs after being away for so long. Besides, our lordly men are quite the boring lot. Half of them had never left Lucillia before they were forced to. At least Trethien has spent much of his time abroad."

"You're not considering Trethien now, are you?" Ellendren covered her mouth.

"I have yet to give any definitive rejections."

Devlyn shared a worried look with Wyn. Was this discussion making Wyn just as uncomfortable as he was? Before the sisters had the chance to pressure Devlyn into proposing, a low growl came from outside the tent. A series of horns began blaring almost simultaneously. Rusyl was trying to alert them to something outside and by the sound of the horns, an apparent threat was approaching the Luminari camp.

They all rushed out to see people running frantically about. Another series of horns blared from the east. Rusyl unfurled his wings, ready to leap into the air as a unit of archers hurried past. Wyn and Kaela took seats on Eolwn and Ellendren took a hesitant step toward Leithel. Wyn gave her a curt nod and nudged Eolwn into the sky, quickly followed by Ellendren. Without knowing the reason for the alarm, Devlyn hesitated about bonding with Aliel. Judging by the appearance of his outfit, it was likely expensive, and he didn't want to burn it to a crisp after only wearing it a short while.

Fly with Rusyl. We'll bond if we need to, Aliel conveyed, his long, illumined feathers trailing behind as he gained altitude.

Rusyl clawed at the dirt impatiently. Devlyn leapt onto the blue dragon and Rusyl immediately lifted himself off the ground and toward the commotion on the eastern side of the camp. It only took a clear view past the tents to understand the cause of the uproar. A great red dragon was flying directly toward the Luminari camp. Devlyn's concern dropped the moment he recognized Liara's large red form holding steady on the horizon. He had seen dozens of red dragons in Tenethyl, but he somehow knew this dragon was Liara. He wondered if Prya was with her. Surely the draelyn and the red dragon wouldn't be separated.

As Devlyn mentally reached out to the pair, a volley of arrows flew from the camp toward Liara and disintegrated when she roared fire at them, flapping her wings to back away, her body practically vertical now, exposing her vulnerable belly. Devlyn had no idea how Prya remained seated throughout that maneuver. Rusyl soared to the red dragon's defense, hovering between the archers and Liara.

"She's our friend," Devlyn yelled as the archers readied a second volley, but with Rusyl blocking Liara, and then Devlyn's yell, they paused.

Devlyn waved to Prya and Liara, and tendrils of smoke issued from Liara's nostrils in return. Understandably, the pair weren't thrilled with their reception.

Rusyl led Liara down in a wide swoop and the dragons thumped onto the ground, Liara's much larger size causing tremors that further terrified the nearby archers. Liara seemed to smirk at their fear. The griffins landed nearby without shaking the ground. While no more arrows came at them, the archers noticeably kept their bows nocked but aimed toward the ground.

Byron strode past the archers, an excited Toryn on his heels. Devlyn couldn't tell if her excitement was at seeing another dragon or that the archers had responded appropriately to the threat of a second dragon.

"Another ally?" Byron asked, looking from Devlyn to Prya, not realizing that Liara was just as much of a potential ally as Prya. Surely, he knew about the dragon flights and their involvement in the creation of Teraeniel, but he would have likely dismissed any stories regarding dragons having sentience. To most eyes, a dragon was a beast and nothing more.

Prya slid off Liara's back. "Not the best way to start off an alliance." Prya patted Liara's leg since she couldn't reach any higher than her knee from where she stood.

"Please accept our apologies. We still associate dragons with the Erynien Empire and forgive me for saying it, the Red Flight particularly. Until recently, we never hoped to dream that some had escaped his influence," Byron said. Devlyn saw he was noticeably trying not to stare at Prya's matching crimson hair and eyes. It wasn't the same shade of red typical to the Cyndinari but as far as Byron knew, they were the only elves with red hair.

"The Evil One's influence poisoned their minds and left them corrupted husks of what they once were, more beast than dragon now." Prya strode to Devlyn. "If you had waited a day or two, I would've been able to join you from Tenethyl. The Red Flight is not as eager to get involved in the affairs and wars beyond Tenethyl as is the Blue Flight. Still, I was able to get Mellory, Ealyn of the Ruby House's blessing and Liara was able to get Fyrinol, Primus of the Red Flight's blessing, to join you. I can't say that there will be an influx of dragons and draelyn to join this war, but make no mistake, you left an unshakable impression in Tenethyl."

Devlyn blushed, and nodded at the compliment, but uncertain whether there should be more of a response, he introduced the newcomers.

"Everyone, this is Prya, and this is Liara." Prya responded with a quick nod, and Liara blinked slowly.

"The draelyn?" Ellendren's eyebrows rose. "I've heard whispers of Tenethyl, but not enough to believe the city still existed."

"The original city is long destroyed. We draelyn and dragons gathered what little possessions we still had after our loss and the Great Blessing and sought a place to rebuild." Prya explained as Ellendren's eyes widened at the possibility of another ally.

"You called yourself a draelyn." Ellendren paused to reconfigure the words for her question. She took in Prya's appearance, her pointed ears and crimson eyes and hair. "Are you a type of elf? Or perhaps an older race?"

"Some of your legends might still remember us as dragon elves. I've already explained to Devlyn here that it's not a term we prefer to use."

"Truly?" Ellendren gasped. "Are there many of you?"

"Enough to fill a city. But as I already said, don't expect the entire lot to join your war, at least not the one against Erynor. Besides, there've been draelyn among the Luminari since you were identified as children of Luminare."

"I beg your pardon?" Ellendren asked.

"Oh, right," Devlyn quickly cut in, remembering how badly things had gone the last time he had unintentionally withheld information about himself from Ellendren. "It's the Lorenthiens; Thien was a draelyn, of the Gold House."

"Who's Thien Lorenthien?" Ellendren glared back at Devlyn, seeming to ask how long he had known this. She too had full recollection of Devlyn promising never to keep important details from her.

"His children joined his and his wife's name as their family name. Loren and Thien. Thien was a draelyn of Tenethyl and Loren was an elder one who had never left the Valley of Saeryndol. She became an elf after the Great Blessing and they both went to Luminare with the elves who adored the rising sun." Devlyn smiled, trying to defuse her anger for not telling her the moment he saw her. "I only just found out while in Tenethyl. I haven't had the chance to tell you about it yet."

Bored by the discussion that wasn't new or exciting to her, Prya looked past the gathered group and into the camp. "Well, are we expected to stand out in the cold all day? I might have ignys running through my being, but that doesn't mean my skin doesn't catch a chill. My flight from Tenethyl was quite long and that blizzard made it even longer."

"We'll have a tent assigned to you at once." Ellendren glanced over her shoulder to ensure that the archers had indeed lowered their bows and led the group through the entrance back into the camp. "In the meantime, you're more than welcome to come to my tent and warm up."

As the group made its way back through the camp, Byron looked worriedly at his youngest niece. While Rusyl had fit between the tents, Liara brushed against some of them, pulling ropes and canvas in the process, causing people to scramble out of the way, or scream and shout as the tents began wobbling around the people inside.

Before the group made it halfway back to Ellendren's tent, a messenger stopped them in their path. "Ei'ethil. Ei'lythel." He bowed before continuing. "The aryls request your presence."

"Thank you." Ellendren smiled as the messenger shifted nervously. "You'll have to excuse Devlyn and me. Kaela, would you mind showing Prya and Liara back to my tent?"

"I'd be happy to. Wyn, you'll join us, yes?"

Wyn nodded and went with Kaela and Prya, the dragons and griffins trotting along behind them as Devlyn and Ellendren followed the messenger to the chamber tent, Aliel flittering just above the tents.

Ellendren didn't talk during their walk back to the chamber tent, her mind moving at a dizzying speed. She was likely organizing several potential conversations, each dependent on what the aryls had decided. Had the Roendryn sisters' ploy worked? Devlyn's mind raced too as he considered the potential outcomes. Could they prevent him from helping Evellion? They wouldn't expect him to sit back and do nothing as his cousin fought to lift the siege, would they? After the earlier meeting, Devlyn feared they might take that course of action. The Luminari certainly needed him in his capacity as a Phaedryn but what about the rest of Eklean? He couldn't abandon Alex, Fendryl, and Lara to fight off the remainder of the renegade Perrien military still loyal to the Erynien Empire.

They reached the chamber tent sooner than Devlyn anticipated as his thoughts had distracted him. Ellendren moved toward it confidently. Devlyn attempted to imitate her confidence but that was no easy feat. Ellendren was the daughter of Vernal and Harnyl Roendryn, Aryl of Lucillia. Devlyn's parents might be just as respectable and accomplished, but he was too young to have learned any lessons from them before his father was murdered by Lex and his mother abducted and blamed for Dolan's murder.

Devlyn walked into the tent beside Ellendren where things seemed much the same as before. The Luminari aryls all sat where they had earlier—although they did appear noticeably more tired, and perhaps frustrated. The short recess seemed to have done little to rejuvenate the aryls. Devlyn and Ellendren retook their seats, front and center. The corner of Ellendren's lip curved ever so slightly. It only took a moment for Devlyn to realize that she had glanced at a very irritated Silvia Narielle.

"What is the aryls' decision?" Ellendren asked, her tone crisp.

Naesiv Aerquin stood to speak for the gathered aryls. "We would first like to apologize for comments made earlier. As the future Exalted Aryl of Krysenthiel, it was foolish of us to ask Devlyn to leave here and doubly foolish to ask the daughter and heir of our recently deceased Lucillian aryl to leave as well. We assure you that such folly will not be repeated." Naesiv glanced briefly at Silvia. "As to our decision, abandoning one of our oldest allies along with the newly reincarnated Kingdom of Thellion would prove disastrous. We cannot fight the Erynien Empire on two fronts, especially while we're wandering through the wilderness. If we want our allies to come to our aid, we must send them whatever assistance they seek in turn."

"Thank you, Naesiv." Ellendren surveyed the aryls. "So, it is decided then; Devlyn will first head to Ceurenyl to seek out the stone seer, Oma, and then assist Evellion and Thellion as needed. I would recommend traveling to Gneal before Everin—King Alexander has not yet moved his forces to march for the Cyrillean Pass."

TUCKED AWAY

Devlyn and Wyn had finally left the Luminari camp two weeks after the aryls had agreed to help Evellion. They'd been forced to prolong their stay due to another blizzard. Rusyl, Prya, and Liara had agreed to stay with the Luminari camp for added security. While Wyn flew on Eolwn with Leithel flying beside them, Devlyn bonded with Aliel, providing Silvia with the demonstration she had so eagerly wanted. He had no idea how she had reacted when she finally saw him as a Phaedryn but neither did he delay to find out.

Before leaving, Ellendren had made Devlyn promise that if he couldn't make it back to the Luminari encampment in two months, he would meet her at the Temple of Ceur on Aurephaen. The high feast day of the Luminari occurred in the middle of the month of Aurenth and while it was a full day of festivities, the main celebration took place at dawn. They were the elves of the rising sun, after all.

Worrisome rumors had drifted out of Gwilnor Academy and not one ei'ana in the Luminari encampment seemed to know the facts. Out of an abundance of caution, Devlyn and Wyn decided it would be best to sneak into the castle without anyone knowing they were coming. So instead of flying to the castle gates, they flew under the cover of night to the valley behind Ceurenyl. Devlyn found the cave with the tunnel connecting the valley to the Temple of Ceur easily enough. The last time he had walked through that tunnel, the apartment at the end had been his own.

Devlyn and Wyn wasted little time, leaving Aliel and the griffins in the valley and passing through the tunnel to his old apartment. A quick scan of the sitting room revealed that it was empty. Devlyn grabbed two white robes from the wardrobe in the bedchamber, giving one to Wyn, and put the other over his lierathnil. It was late and he didn't think anyone would recognize them but it was best to take precautions regardless. Few people would comment on seeing a white robe in Ceurenyl.

Pausing at an intersection of two corridors, he felt a pull toward the Chamber of Light. He still had no idea how to enter the Empyrean Sphere, but he had to discover a way to do so and soon. The entirety of the Luminari population were currently camped in Sorenthil, believing that he had the ability to see to the Shroud's removal. The longer it remained whole and intact, the longer they remained vulnerable.

Wyn tugged Devlyn's arm, pulling him away from the Chamber of Light and toward Therril's office with the window that was not a window, several levels below the main level of the temple. They followed the corridor into the lower levels of the Temple of Ceur. The Arenthylean bells chimed softly in the distance and it was difficult to tell the hour when they reached Therril's office.

Devlyn knocked once. He didn't know if the old elf stayed up late or was in bed with the falling sun. He was about to knock a second time just as the door cracked open to reveal a startled Therril.

"Oh-ho is it good to see you two," Therril said, his surprise shifting to relief. "Come in, come in."

With the door closed behind them, Devlyn surprised himself as he hugged the older elf. After Alethea's unexpected loss, Devlyn was overcome with emotion as he embraced the elf who happened to be another one of his ancestors. None of the Luminari knew that Therril had married Lucillia and fathered the twins, Roendryn and Feolyn. Nearly an entire year had passed since Devlyn had last seen the older elf, just before he had been kidnapped from his own bedchamber in the supposed safety of Gwilnor.

Therril must have seen his determination, for he did not dally in leading them to the secret passage into Gwilnor. "I assume you didn't come to see me to catch up." A large mischievous grin reached his eyes. "They'll think you mad for attempting to go to Gwilnor."

"What's happened there?" Wyn asked.

"A coup. The Seven Chairs have gone into hiding. Even here, we receive few details of what's actually happening in the castle. Aaron has forbidden all ei'ceuril from leaving the temple again, myself included. Not that there's anything for me to do at Gwilnor anymore—that awful chancellor disbanded my class altogether!" Therril said in a huff.

"That's awful," said Wyn.

"I think so too. I do hope the students kept their theoreticals books and have kept up with the syllabus."

"Do you know where I can find Velaria and Oma?" Devlyn asked. There wasn't time to talk about the classes at Gwilnor. He also felt somewhat guilty for he had no idea where his textbook was and hadn't read a single page of a theoreticals book since he had been abducted.

"Who's to say with the stone seer? She never remains in one place." Therril scratched his chin as though a beard should be there. "As I said, the Seven Chairs have gone into hiding. They're still in the castle though. They've managed to secret away a number of ei'ana and students somewhere in the deepest reaches of the castle. Septyl will not submit so easily, and the Tenebrae are beside themselves." Therril was definitely gleeful about that. "Now hurry, through the tunnel. Velaria and the others will find you before you get anywhere close to discovering their hideout. I'll reach out to Velaria telepathically as you head over."

Wyn was already through the false window and Devlyn glimpsed Therril's playful smile from over his shoulder as he followed Wyn into the tunnel. They walked in the darkness, one hand on a tunnel wall to avoid stumbling. They didn't dare wield any form of light once they passed the temple ward.

Cautiously emerging from the tunnel into the castle made Devlyn think nothing had changed in the floors above. The same cobwebs clung to the corners and thick dust coated the floors and surfaces, and the same scent of mildew affronted his nose.

As cautious as they had been inside the temple, they were even more so now, carefully listening as they crept through the castle corridors. When a hand suddenly gripped Devlyn's shoulder, his heart leapt and instinct drove him to reach for the erendinth but Wyn grabbed his elbow and they turned to see who was behind them.

An ei'ana he had never met before held a finger to her lips for silence. The little of her face that he could see beneath her cowl was rather stern and he couldn't tell whether she was an elf or a human. She briefly wielded a small globe of light to show herself and Devlyn caught a glimpse of a grey cloak inlaid with floral patterns of orange, marking her as an Arantiulyn. With a quick flick of her hand, she indicated that they should follow, and she turned away to lead them back down the corridor.

Gwilnor was a massive castle with three separate structures connected by bridges. The visible part of the castle soared above the mountain but the labyrinth beneath was at least as large. An entire underground maze layered several times over lay beneath the main structure. The Arantiulyn's extensive knowledge of these levels was impressive as she led them deeper into the foundations until she finally stopped in front of a solid stone wall. Devlyn felt her wield terys and a moment later, an archway opened in the wall. She led them through that archway into another space, repeated the wield, closing the opening behind her and opening another, revealing a large windowless chamber.

Despite the late hour, small groups of people sat and talked at long tables. They were mostly women, but there were a few men.

"Wait here," the Arantiulyn said, before disappearing through a set of doors.

Mere moments passed in silence. Devlyn looked at the groups, but didn't see his brother Liam, or any others he cared about. He prayed that Liam was well and tried not to worry about Jaerol, Andrew, Fyona, and Danielle. The list of names kept expanding as more faces flashed through his mind.

Velaria came into the chamber by the door the Arantiulyn had used. "Have you lost all your wits? Sneaking into Gwilnor! You're lucky Anna found you before a Tenebrae did!" As always, she wore the leafy dress with the flowers, some of them tangled in her fiery red hair. "It's a good thing that Therril thought to reach out to me so we knew to look for you."

With a shrug of his shoulders, Devlyn mustered an apologetic expression that he quickly lost when Velaria pulled him into a firm hug, relieved to see him alive and well.

But Velaria wasn't done with the scolding. Her silver eyes bore into Devlyn and Wyn, fury and delight warring on her face. "What was so important that you had to come here personally? There are other ways of communicating."

She was right. Devlyn felt foolish for not considering them in the first place, even if communication was not the sole reason for coming to Gwilnor. "We need Oma to get us an audience with the Schtamite." Devlyn tried to avoid fidgeting about the absurd proposal.

"Is that all?" Velaria planted her hands on her hips, one foot tapping. Devlyn felt the full weight of Velaria's disapproval. "You realize you ask the impossible."

"The giants have nearly reached Everin. Alex intends to join them with Thellion's banners and flags flying over his army. Fendryl, Lara, and Alex know they won't be enough to fight off the giants and the rest of the Perrien military still loyal to the Erynien Empire, and whoever else is hiding amidst their ranks."

"Hopefully Thellion's return hasn't come too late." Velaria mused as she thought to herself. She didn't seem the least bit surprised about the kingdom's revival.

"You knew?" Devlyn stared, eyes wide.

"I hoped. I did have my small part to play." Velaria's small smile appeared.

"How long have you been scheming this?" He couldn't keep the insult out of his voice. Alex had often said, from the first time they had met Velaria, that she wasn't telling them everything.

"Well before I came to Cor'lera. It was quite the brush of good luck that you and one of Thellion's heirs were so close. Septyl has long romanticized Thellion's return from her long sleep. Fortunately, the pieces needed to wake up that long-fallen kingdom have endured throughout the ages. Thellion is more integrated into Eklean than the elves are. Perrien and Parendior were always the heart of Thellion."

Devlyn thought back as clearly as he could to his first meetings with Velaria. He and Alex had assumed she was scheming and only telling them parts of the entire story. Just when Devlyn thought he now knew everything he needed to know about his life in Cor'lera, Velaria would say something that showed that there was more to the story. How many more strings were the ei'ana pulling? There wasn't time to allow for any distractions. Wyn had wasted too much time already because of the politicking among the Luminari and the vagaries of weather—he had to inform the Eldinari aryls of Alethea. Devlyn shook his head as though to clear his thoughts.

"We need more allies for Evellion and Thellion."

"And you think to get the dwarves involved?" Velaria raised an eyebrow. "*And* you want to get Oma to arrange a meeting with the Schtamite to do so."

"Well, I was hoping you could ask her."

"She'll do no such thing," a thunderous voice bellowed, and everyone in the chamber turned to look at Oma, striding through one of the doors at the far end of the chamber as though she owned the place.

"Oma," Devlyn said, stepping back at her angry tone. But Wyn wasn't bothered by it.

"Will you?" he asked. "The Eldinari have already pledged themselves to Evellion's defense."

Devlyn felt his breath catch, shocked at Wyn's blunt request although he had intended to ask the same thing. Though it would have been after a lengthier explanation with abundant details of the wellbeing of Eklean and all Teraeniel.

"It is forbidden—only dwarves are permitted into a schtam. Such has it always been, and such will it stubbornly remain," Oma said.

"If Everin falls, the schtams won't be far behind," Velaria said, a point Devlyn had heard her say before.

"So I've mentioned to my son, but he's as obstinate as his father." Oma's displeasure seemed to shift from Devlyn and Wyn to her son.

"Surely, Forvl would consider it differently if a Lorenthien presented it," Velaria said.

"He might think me a crazy old bat that only talks to rocks, but I'm still his mother."

"Were you a dwarven matriarch?" Wyn asked.

"Of course not," Oma said. "Unlike you elves, we dwarves don't base a monarch's right to rule on matrimony. My husband was patriarch and our son succeeded him when he returned to the stone and into Teraeniel—Mundi protect him and his thick stubborn head." Devlyn wracked his memories—had he ever learned Oma's exact status among the dwarves? "Besides, it's not my son you have to convince, but every matriarch and patriarch of the eight schtams. My son is only one of them."

"Would Forvl invite Devlyn and Alexander, as his guests, to sway the Schtamite?" Velaria asked.

"How did that boy get mixed into the equation?" Oma asked.

"You knew of his origins—his ancestry," Velaria said.

"So, Aewen made him a Thellish king, did she? I wondered how long she would hide in those ruins, tucked away in those wooded hills with only her winged beasts." Velaria did not press the question but

Devlyn was nearly on the verge of doing so himself when Oma went on. "You ask a lot, Ei'ana. Hmph, I'll think on it while the Phaedryn retrieves what he left behind."

Devlyn felt Velaria's eyes on him. He had only been with Velaria briefly for the first time in nearly a year and he had never been under so much scrutiny from her. Velaria was not the only one in the chamber to look at Devlyn though. The other ei'ana had been listening to the entire discussion and now also waited to hear why else he had returned to Gwilnor, if not to liberate them from the Tenebrae ei'ana.

Lowering his voice as best he could, he said, "Two of the lucilliae are hidden in my quarters, in the South Tower."

Hushed whispers rushed through the chamber. He knew he shouldn't have said it out loud. There was no place where it was safe to speak of them openly, not even the securest location.

An older woman shuffled up to them. "Is it true? Do you seek to return Ceurendol to us?"

Devlyn thought of ways he could have—should have—referred to the jewels without naming them for what they were.

Aliel, a common sight in Gwilnor after Devlyn had returned from his novitiate and well known to everyone here, appeared in a brilliant flash and hovered over his shoulder. A harmonious chorus erupted from the phoenix's core and filled the chamber with its warmth.

The jewel in the hidden pocket in his lieranthyl beneath the white robes of the ei'ceuril pressed against his chest. It gave off a blue hue even while veiled beneath the cloth. Aliel's presence stirred Devlyn to do something foolish. If Ellendren ever found out, she'd be angry enough to toss him from the top of the Dragon Tower before he had the chance to apologize. His hand disappeared into his lierathnil and his fingers wrapped around the warm and smooth surface.

As he pulled the lucilliae out for all to see, a tear rolled down the elderly woman's cheek. Already familiar with the sensation that the jewel of justice provided, Devlyn allowed the otherworldly experience to wash over him. As with the other jewels, the virtue imbued within this one was still a conundrum to him. He knew it as true but accepting it did not mean he understood it in the slightest.

An image of justice and mercy balanced in his mind and heart. While war with the Erynien Empire was certainly justified, those defending against them were willful participants in the slaughter and ending of lives, innocent or not. To say nothing of the thousands of displaced refugees and the homeless who had never been treated fairly in the eyes of the rich and comfortable, who could not be bothered by the suffering of others.

Velaria raised a hand to her mouth. "How do we reconcile this with our actions?" Her voice cracked with doubt. She seemed to understand the importance of this jewel's intent more than he did. "It'll have to wait—you need to get the other jewels before the Tenebrae discover you're in the castle." She ushered Devlyn toward the solid stone wall he'd come through.

"Will you help us?" Devlyn asked, turning to Oma.

"Hmph," she said, more of a grunt than speech but she nodded.

"All right, go with Wyn. I should be able to get to my old quarters, but I doubt I'll be able to make the trip back through the castle."

"Intent on jumping from your bedroom window, are you?" Wyn smirked.

Anna stood to lead Devlyn back out the hidden chamber but Velaria waved her to remain. "I'll go. I feel responsible for his safety here in the castle."

"Mother Velaria, surely you're not thinking of going above. If anyone sees you…" Anna said.

"I'll be fine, and our plans are already in place. They must go off without a hitch, and it now seems likely that it will be tonight." Velaria said. Her tone made Devlyn worry.

"What are you planning?" he asked.

"What we've always been planning here at Gwilnor—how to ensure the safety of our students."

An archway appeared in the wall and closed behind the four of them as soon as the second formed, leaving them without even a torch to light the way. Aliel disappeared again and Velaria led them through the twisting underbelly of the castle. Not surprisingly, she knew the castle's secret passages quite well. Soon, Wyn and Oma veered toward another corridor, and if it had been lit, Devlyn would have recognized it as the tunnel that led back to the temple.

A stream separated Gwilnor's southern wing from the rest of the structure. Before now, Devlyn had assumed that the only way to reach that south wing was by crossing the bridge connecting the White Tower and the Dragon Tower, home to the Albien and Azurelle Schools, respectively. But Velaria took him up a narrow winding stair that seemed to have no identifiable end. She stopped after they had passed several landings.

"I trust you'll recognize the tower above. Keep in mind, I have no idea what traps we might find there. Make sure Aliel is ready if necessary."

Devlyn nodded. Caressing his bond with Aliel, he readied himself.

They continued up the stair, taking one soft step at a time. They crossed dozens of landings before finally reaching the floor he had grown familiar with. A surge of emotions swept through him. The last time he had been in the castle, he had not left through this corridor nor had he been conscious at the time. He had been secreted away so that Queen Alesei of Tiel could present him as a betrothal gift to Erynor to gain his hand in marriage and become an empress. The attempt had thankfully failed, but Devlyn had come extremely close to never getting out of that box that had severed him from Aliel and the erendinth.

With a cautious glimpse, he looked past the landing and across the vacant corridor as they stepped into it. They passed each door, all in the same style with intricately carved details, until Devlyn recognized his own.

He turned the handle, wincing when the hinges groaned, metal scraping against itself, louder than he remembered. A swift scan revealed the room much as it had been, although as expected, someone had searched it. *Friends or foes?* he wondered. The lumaryl phoenix figurine that Ellendren had given him still sat on the fireplace mantle, shimmering in the dim light.

Devlyn passed through the salon and went to his bedchamber, pushing the door ajar. Someone had made his bed after he had been taken away. Crossing the bedchamber, he looked in the wardrobe and saw his other lierathnil still hanging on the pegs. He swooped them into his arms, seeing no reason to leave them behind. He was tired of wearing the same blue and grey outfit since Wyn had rescued him from Lankor.

The bedside table seemed undisturbed. Devlyn's heart raced. The two lucilliae had been left there for almost a year. Had those unidentified searchers tried to pry the drawer open? Devlyn's wield had ensured that the table was immovable as well as inoperable. Maybe whoever searched his room assumed that it was a false drawer—nothing more than ornamentation. Still, he had placed that wield there last spring. Did wields deteriorate over time?

He placed the lierathnil down on the bed and pressed into the elemental erendinth and embraced the transcendental erendinth, at least the two he could wield at the moment. Devlyn felt the subtle wield of the six erendinth he had left over the table. No one would have known it was there unless they looked for it. He pulled a thread and the wield evaporated into nothingness, the erendinth returning to their fluid state in the world. Devlyn crouched and opened the drawer to reveal the simple coin purse that lay just as he had placed it. His racing heart settled. He picked at the drawstrings and opened it, and violet and indigo lights shone out. Overcome with relief, Devlyn paid no attention to the two lumols nestled with the jewels. The warm light washed across his face as his mind was filled with wonder.

"You know," he heard behind him, "if you had hidden that pouch under your mattress, we would have never known you were trying to hide something—even if we suspected you were."

Devlyn's heart froze in his chest. Danyol. Devlyn had distrusted Danyol from the moment he had arrived in Yvonne's classroom as an assistant. Painful memories of those so-called lessons flashed across Devlyn's mind. He still didn't know which of the two, Yvonne's classes or being stuck in that box, severed from the erendinth, had been more detrimental to his training in wielding.

Devlyn's stomach roiled with panic as he turned around to see Danyol in the doorway. Where was Velaria? Devlyn knew that she could make herself invisible but why hadn't she warned him?

"What are you doing here?" Devlyn asked at last.

"Haven't figured it out yet? Not the brightest, are you? If the rumors of your lineage really are true and the Lorenthien line did manage to survive the Ceurendol War, I can't imagine how disappointed your dead ancestors would be to find out that you were their heir. They would either have to lower their standards, or more likely, you'll fit in perfectly and will fail as they did." Danyol sneered as he stepped closer.

A breath passed while Devlyn found that quiet place inside his heart, ready for what was to come. Light exploded around him as he bonded with Aliel, wings bursting from his back.

"Impressive," Danyol said, forced to shield his eyes. "But I did not come alone, and you will not be leaving either."

Dozens of footsteps rushed into the front room of his apartment. *Had they been waiting for me? Where was Velaria?*

Pressing into aerys, Devlyn sent a blast of wind at the Tenebrae ei'ana. He might as well call them servants of Shadow. There was no difference in his opinion. Ignys flared toward him, then bolts of that heinous lightning thundered into the bedchamber. He wielded the erendinth to deflect the dark, dangerous wields.

Into Light

Kevn stood beside Ceurtriarch Aaron Roendryn in the Chamber of Light. The hour was late, and the faint sound of glass-like chimes echoed through Ceurenyl, too quiet for those asleep at this hour, but for those still awake, they rang clearly.

The Chamber of Light was a curious place; Kevn did not believe for a moment that the phenomenon was wrought by mortal hands, nor by elves with Life immortal. Something about the light made him feel as though it did not belong in the World-Below, as though it was proper to a place wholly different from what Teraeniel was, yet despite its difference, it did belong here. Kevn felt that without it, Teraeniel would change, diminish to such a degree that it would no longer be Teraeniel; its connection with reality would dissipate.

He raised his hand to cover his eyes against the wondrous light surrounding him. It had greatly pained him to admit, yet again, that his heart did not belong to the ei'ceuril. It was with mixed feelings that he had confessed it to the Ceurtriarch. He was relieved that he had made his final choice, and he was prepared to once again leave the way of life that he loved so much but did not want. But the choice tore him to shreds, worse than the first time he'd left. His time with the ei'ceuril, the years of study and formation, had shaped him, and there was something about who he was that he liked, even admired, because of his experience. Even the time he had spent as a student at Gwilnor had been part of this journey. Today was different though, for this choice was irrevocable. He had no idea what would happen next, but he was confident that he did not belong here.

Kevn would return to the ei'ana, knowing it was the right thing to do even though he had no idea how much his detour with the ei'ceuril would cost. Even if it were possible to tell his younger self to make a different choice, he would not.

Aaron stood next to him, offering comfort as best he could, but his station overshadowed their friendship.

"Are you ready?"

Eyes lost in the luminosity around him, Kevn nodded, not sure that he could speak. He felt inadequate standing next to Aaron and felt unworthy to join him in what they were about to do. Aaron was not only born of the dignified lineage of Lucillia herself, but had been chosen and elevated to Ceurtriarch, High Archsteward and Arbiter of the Light—named by Ealyndol with his dying breath, no less.

"After you." Not only was it proper for the Ceurtriarch to enter the Empyrean Sphere first, but Kevn was terrified of meeting the six-winged anadel and it seemed easier to follow Aaron.

They were not the first ones to attempt to reach the Empyrean Sphere and gain the ability to wield lumenys over the past fourteen hundred years, but they hoped to be the first to return from the World-Beyond with full knowledge of what they were doing.

Kevn watched Aaron step forward into the light. He took a deep breath, and followed him in. He felt something change in him even as he no longer stood on the stone flooring but floated into the light. Something within himself was calling him beyond Teraeniel.

Velaria's voice echoed in Jaerol's mind and a sense of urgency stirred him from sleep. The hour was late and there was undoubtedly a patrol passing through the male dormitories. He should have asked permission to begin his novitiate when he had the chance. With the turmoil growing in Gwilnor, there was no telling when he would be permitted to advance in his studies and eventually become an ei'ana.

Rolling out of his bed, Jaerol went to Liam and nudged his shoulder.

"Not now," Liam mumbled, and pulled the covers higher.

"Devlyn's in the castle and he's in trouble."

Liam's eyelids popped open, and he jumped out of his bed and into his robes in a whirl.

"Velaria says it's too late to help. She's with Devlyn but she's afraid she won't make it out."

"What does she need?" Liam was ready to storm across the entirety of the castle to protect his brother.

"She wants us to know that this changes nothing. We have our orders."

"Did she say when?"

"Now," Jaerol said, his voice trembling from nerves.

"I thought we were going to wait until the spring. When it's warmer."

"She said we won't get a better opportunity than tonight." Jaerol pulled his own grey school robes over his head, quietly opened the door and peeked out. The corridor appeared empty, but it was always difficult to tell without wielding a source of light, which was out of the question just now.

Tiptoeing with Liam just behind him, Jaerol made his way through the North Tower. Pausing at an unlit stairwell, he listened carefully for any movement above, but no sound reached his ears.

Anticipating the crash of the tenebrys wield against him, Devlyn opened himself, allowing animys and umbrys to flow into him. The experience of touching those transcendental erendinth was both wondrous and terrifying. If it were any other time, Devlyn thought he would lose himself in contemplation over their presence in the World-Below. He knew they belonged, just as the elemental erendinth did, but these were invisible realities which made associating with them more difficult.

Wielding animys and umbrys together, while not an equal to tenebrys, could redirect the devastating wield but they could never overpower it, especially when the tenebrys wield came from an elf as powerful as Danyol. Through Devlyn's lighted golden vision, he saw a purple and black wave flow from his hands toward the tenebrys wield.

Unlike the menacing lightning racing toward him, haphazardly exploding and destroying everything it touched while simultaneously swallowing it in its void, Devlyn's wield of animys and umbrys flowed like an incredibly strong wave that rarely caused destruction. When the two wields met between Devlyn and Danyol, there was no loud crash or cataclysmic rupture. Devlyn's wield simply flowed over the other, weakening it and then pushing it away to explode out the window, shattering the glass.

Devlyn's only possible escape route was through the balcony off the salon. To reach it though, he would have to fight past Danyol and whoever else had forced their way into his apartment. He could always fly over them; the ceilings were twice as high as in most bedchambers in the castle. Still, how would Velaria get out of this mess? Was she still invisible?

The memory of being struck by tenebrys in Lankor lashed through him. He couldn't afford to have Aliel trapped away again. Fearing that Danyol might strike him with a bolt of tenebrys while he was in the air, Devlyn kept his feet planted and concentrated on keeping Danyol at bay.

"How could you betray your own people?" Devlyn asked. He had never liked Danyol even though he had come with the Eldinari from the Eldin Wood. Why would an Eldinari join the Erynien Empire?

"I did not betray my people. It was your like-minded ancestors who chose to forsake our superiority over the lesser races and offer them *our* immortality!" Danyol roared, throwing another wield of tenebrys at Devlyn's chest. Devlyn dodged so that it crashed against the stone wall behind him. "Besides, my cover was only a ruse to gain access to Gwilnor. My name isn't Danyol, a weak name chosen so that I might blend in, you fool. I am Razcul!"

Razcul's face shimmered and the wield that had concealed his true identity fell away. The smooth and clear features that had been present just a moment before melted, and a shadow elf stood before Devlyn, his corrupted scabbed skin clearly identifying him. Devlyn's stomach roiled at the thought of more disguised shadow elves lurking inside the castle.

He had sat in Yvonne's class for two months with Razcul. The hatred he held for Yvonne bubbled to the surface. Had the two of them been coordinating a strategic sabotage of future ei'ana and their ability to wield kien or kiara? How badly had things progressed at Gwilnor with the Seven Chairs of Septyl in hiding for who knew how long? Shuddering at the thought, Devlyn pressed into ignys and wielded it with the two transcendental erendinth he already held, launching a counterattack at Razcul.

The shadow elf sneered and tossed it to the side as though it was a child's doll, and it engulfed a wooden chair just as four ei'ana walked through the door behind him. Devlyn recognized only one of them but couldn't remember her name. It didn't matter—all of them had betrayed Septyl. Did they know they fought for the Erynien Empire? That, by association, they were helping those who sought to unleash Ramiel on the world again? Or did they genuinely believe they were reforming Septyl for the better?

It mattered little. With their infidelity, they had forsaken not only Septyl and all their sister and brother ei'ana, but all Eklean. Pressing into all four of the elemental erendinth and intermingling them in a specific way with the transcendental erendinth, Devlyn wielded an intensified beam causing an explosion that raised a terrific amount of dust to mingle with the smoke. It was the same wield Devlyn had used to put an end to the shadow elves who had attacked Myrium, and so he was shocked to hear Razcul cackle as the smoke faded and the dust settled.

How could an ordinary shadow elf be so strong? That wield should have easily overwhelmed and incapacitated Razcul while freeing the souls he had stolen, allowing them to pass to the World-Beyond after decades or even centuries of captivity. There was no telling how old this shadow elf was, but Devlyn somehow thought Razcul was no more than a decade older than him, not centuries.

Devlyn knew he couldn't withstand a shadow elf who was supported by the Tenebrae ei'ana. When he fought only Razcul, he could keep him at bay, but when they fought together, they easily cast Devlyn's wield aside. Devlyn prepared to take the risk of taking flight above them and flee the castle. There was no other way he was getting out of here. He just had to get to the balcony in the salon. *Where was Velaria?*

It was only when he heard one of the ei'ana scream that he reconsidered. Confusion ensued as the Tenebrae ei'ana divided again, some back into the salon, the other two staying to support Razcul. The shadow elf kept his attention on Devlyn, who was trying to see what was happening in the entry.

Sounds of fighting filled the room beyond; furniture and objects crashed against the walls amid sounds of breakage, screams, and yells. Apparently, Velaria had been waiting for the perfect moment to spring her trap on the intruders. What was she doing? She had to know the two of them couldn't fight all these attackers off. If she had stayed hidden, he might have been able to reach the salon and leap off the balcony.

Dodging another bolt of tenebrys, Devlyn lunged toward the bedside table where the two lucilliae still lay in the drawer. He scooped up the coin purse that held the precious jewels and lumols and stashed it away in the interior pocket of his lieranthyl with the other jewel. The room lost its indigo and violet glows, and he was mildly relieved that they were now safely stored. If he managed to figure a way out of here, he would have to find a better way to keep the lucilliae secure and not on his person. They were far more valuable than mere baubles or costly jewelry—without them the Luminari would never retrieve their Life immortal.

"Still under the impression that you're leaving, are you?" Razcul's lips curled into a sneer.

"Still think you can destroy Septyl?"

The commotion in the other room quieted and Devlyn held his breath, hoping for the best. His heart quickened when Razcul turned just enough to peer through the door while keeping his eyes on Devlyn.

"Destroy Septyl?" Hannah strode into the bedchamber holding a knife to the throat of a barely conscious Velaria being held by Yvonne.

Outrage, disgust, and a deep sense of betrayal swelled in his gut. This couldn't be the same kind, grandmotherly ei'ana he'd known before. He'd really enjoyed her classes in the art of wielding. He'd always thought that Yvonne was false but had never considered Hannah that way. But there was no denying it; the chancellor had betrayed Gwilnor Academy. How long had she been Erynor's puppet?

Yvonne looked exactly as he remembered her, still very much a devastating beauty with silky black hair falling over her shoulders, but now much scarier with Velaria's verathn—Velaria called it a wand— clutched in her right hand. Velaria was by no means a weak wielder but the verathn made her all the more powerful. How much deadlier could this woman possibly be with Velaria's wand?

"As always, you're quite mistaken. We're burning away the useless fat clinging to Septyl; when we're done, Septyl will be the Erynien Empire's strongest asset," Yvonne said.

Devlyn's eyes locked with Velaria's. She seemed to be telling him something, but he wasn't sure what.

Yvonne flicked the wand expertly in her hand. "It seems the Chair of Azurelle was of no use to you. Perhaps she should have remained hiding in her underground cellar; it's curious that they chose a location so like a dungeon." She drew a slender line along Velaria's cheekbone with the wand. "Tell me, did you really think you could sneak back into the castle without our knowing?"

Devlyn kept his face impassive, refusing to answer. Yvonne's flowery perfume reached his nostrils. Ever since his first class with her, he had despised the scent.

"I must give you my gratitude—I've been searching for the Chairs' hideout for the past eight months. Your service to me might even merit an award," Hannah snickered, gazing gleefully at Velaria. "Thought you were done with me, didn't you?"

Velaria managed to look composed despite her injuries. "Septyl will never bow to Ramiel's slaves and you will answer for your crimes against the living."

"Oh, my dear, young Velaria. You are just as naïve as when you first came to Gwilnor as a child." Hannah drew the knife threateningly across Velaria's skin, curling around one of the flower stems and slicing it off. The flower fell to the floor. "You ruined my chances at becoming the next Chair of Azurelle. Fara had all but guaranteed that I would succeed her after her death. But no, you and that dragon of yours had to destroy everything! Where is she now, Velaria? Is she going to save you?"

"You are a disgrace," Velaria managed. "As Chair of Azurelle, I rescind your place among us. You are no Azurelle."

"You still think you're in control?" Hannah slapped Velaria's face hard.

Devlyn's eyes met Velaria's and he caught a brief glimmer and her small smile. *She planned this! She planned on being caught. But why?*

To save Septyl—to save Gwilnor's students. They're getting out. Velaria's voice sounded in his mind. *We've stalled these ones long enough. Get away from here, Devlyn. They won't kill me, I'm too valuable alive. Now go.*

Clenching his hands, Devlyn struggled with Velaria's directive. He couldn't abandon her with these monsters, but he also knew that he could not overpower them.

"This can end a few different ways," Yvonne said, still restraining

Velaria. "We could kill you now; it's the obvious result if you don't cooperate. But that would only further complicate matters, since the phoenix would of course perish with you, and then be reborn and bond with another. Perhaps, it will be someone less foolish and more talented. We'll likely have ten to fifteen years before we're bothered by the nuisance again, but fortunately for you, Erynor has expressed his desire that that not happen."

Devlyn glared at her; it was clear to them both that he would not stand down. He was still fully bonded with Aliel as a Phaedryn, and possessed power beyond what Hannah, Yvonne, and Razcul were aware of, even if he had yet to tap his full potential. The stinging reminder that he was still incapable of wielding lumenys was a bitter reality. If only he had put more attention to it, he would have already managed it and Gwilnor would never have fallen to the Tenebrae in the first place. He had squandered several months in the Temple of Ceur with nothing to show for it. He should have spent every waking minute in the Chamber of Light, trying to figure out how to wield lumenys, even though he hadn't known what the Empyrean Sphere was at the time.

"Your friends, both here and in the chambers below the castle, will of course be punished," Hannah said. "There might be hope for them yet if they atone for their folly. Throwing away such potential would be irresponsible."

"Don't waste your time, Hannah." Razcul smirked as he lifted his arms to wield.

Devlyn did not recognize the wield he was forming, only that he wielded tenebrys. The sinister wield streaked through the air around Razcul as he confined it, leaving nothing but darkness in its trail.

Hannah and Yvonne made no move to interrupt the shadow elf. Even as Devlyn wondered who held seniority over the other here, he quieted his thoughts to respond but he felt a tug in his gut that told him he should run and run fast.

A blast of tenebrys exploded from Razcul. It had a dominating quality that would not dissipate when it struck its target.

Devlyn wrapped a shield of the erendinth around him. The little light in the apartment disappeared as the tenebrys wield closed around him, forming a cocoon of darkness. Devlyn had locked eyes with Velaria just before, and she had looked just as terrified as he felt. Only his wielded barrier kept the tenebrys at bay. The feeling was like being in the box he had been kept in, only this time it was not his ability to wield that had been blocked. Instead, this wield of pure darkness tried to suffocate him, and pull him into its darkness.

The tenebrys wield thrummed against his wielded bubble, squeezing and trying to pop Devlyn's shield. There was no possible way to punch a hole and launch a counterattack without first letting go of his shield. And the moment Devlyn stopped wielding more energy into it, the pressure would collapse the shield. He felt as though he was drowning—as though he was back in Lankor Bay and couldn't swim fast enough to the surface. Panicked, he reached out.

A piercing sound stung him—Razcul's wield was trying to collapse against him. His ears rang. Blind to what was happening outside the shield was one problem, but now he couldn't even hear anything as the ringing noise battered his ears.

Anxiety seethed as he held onto his protective wield. He explored its surface, prodding for any point of weakness, but blessedly found none. *How are we going to get out of this one?* Devlyn conveyed to Aliel. Within the shield, the golden light they gave off was in complete contrast to the tenebrys wield smothering them.

An image flashed across his mind. There was no place he knew better than the room materializing in his mind, even if he had been too young to take note of his surroundings the last time he had slept there. But there it was, his bedroom at the Cor Inn. The bedroom that he should have grown up in. In the home that he should have never been taken from.

As a child, he had dreamt of that bedroom. In every dream, he lay on a small bed, a bed he would have long ago outgrown. It was the only home he had known as a child, and he had only been able to go there while he slept. But he had always known it as his home. He had only been in that bedroom again on his thirteenth birthday.

The image was so clear in his mind, that without intending to, he desired to be there. It was a desire always within his heart, but never actualized.

With a final push of willpower, the darkness surrounding him blinked out.

Startled, he looked around and realized that the bubble of darkness hadn't blinked out at all. He no longer stood inside a shield of his own making in his apartment in Gwilnor's South Tower. There was no Razcul, no Hannah, and no Yvonne threatening to kill him.

A soft light began to glisten in the window.

The small bed of his dreams was gone and in its place was a normal sized bed for an adult. It was made of finely carved wood, and the mattress looked soft enough to make him want to drift off to sleep. Devlyn and Aliel withdrew from each other and he collapsed onto the bed. It felt safe here. They were safe here.

What just happened? Better yet, how did that happen? I thought seguians were restricted to the Time Key, Devlyn conveyed to Aliel. Ever since he had gone through time to visit the city of Lankor before it had sunk and learned of the lucilliae of justice's location, he had hoped that it was possible for him to create a seguian. If he could travel through time to a faraway city, there was no logical reason he couldn't also teleport without jumping through time.

It is in my nature—now our joint nature—to pass between time and space.

Are we in the same time? This place doesn't look anything as I remember it.

We've only traversed space just now, not time. It appears someone has restored your family's inn.

An unlit candle rested on a wooden dresser. Something about the candle spoke to Devlyn. He recognized it. Had it been there when he

was a toddler? What was so special about a candle and why did he recognize it?

You'll have to ask your uncle about it, Aliel conveyed to Devlyn.

As he took in his surroundings, he felt the pocket against his chest
and the lumpy coin purses inside it. What had just happened was impossible. He dug into the hidden pocket and put its contents on the bed,
then opened the purses. Violet, indigo, and blue lights shimmered across
the room. The three lucilliae were safe and away from Erynor's lackeys.
He picked up the lumols that had kept the first two jewels company in
the purse and saw his own impassive profile looking toward the edge of
the coin. The figure looked slightly older than he was now, but the resemblance had grown unmistakable, just as the profile on the other coin
depicted a slightly older Ellendren.

How did these two coins know that Devlyn and Ellendren were going to become the next Exalted Aryl of Krysenthiel? He still had doubts
about whether they could remove the Shroud and regain the lost kingdom. Devlyn flipped the coins to see the phoenix wing emblazoned on
the back. The first time he had seen the coins, he had assumed it was just
a wing, one that could belong to any bird. That thought had long died.
He now knew that wing could only ever be a phoenix's wing. Scooping
up the five heirlooms on the bed, he returned them all to one coin purse.

He squeezed his eyes shut as he bent forward to grip his knees. The
events at Gwilnor flashed across his inner eye. He could still see Hannah
holding a knife to Velaria's throat. He'd left Velaria with those monsters.
His heart ached. He didn't know what else he could have done, could
now do. He should have been able to save her.

She'll be fine, Aliel conveyed, attempting to soothe Devlyn's anxiety.

She was with me the first time I came back here, to where I was born.

I remember; I too was there.

And Lex…

Devlyn didn't want to see those dreadful memories any longer. Still
bent over, he opened his eyes and caught sight of a pile of colorful fabric

on the floor.

At his feet were his lierathnil garments. How had they managed to be transported with him? He had left them on the bed before Danyol—no, Razcul—had appeared. They must have been inside his shield without him realizing it. Still, he didn't think he had been touching them when he had transported here to Cor'lera. He picked up the three outfits and spread them out on the bed.

He couldn't stay in the bedroom much longer. He had to figure out what had happened here in Cor'lera since he had left nearly four years ago. There was no clear way of knowing what had happened to Wyn and Oma. Would they meet him in Gneal or Belin's Watch? Did they know that he had managed to escape? They had intended to travel together once they were away from the dangers of Gwilnor.

Devlyn opened the door to the corridor with the family portraits and left the room. Every portrait had been placed back in their original positions—all but the one that Lex had stolen. The innkeeper's quarters had been beautifully restored. It was a cozy space and Devlyn felt inclined to heat a pot of tea and spend the next hour lounging on the sofa with only his thoughts. Velaria came to his mind again as the guilt of leaving her weighed him down.

The extravagant door of stellendae wood leading to the kitchen had been restored—the shards had all been woven seamlessly back together. The door opened with an easy push to reveal a kitchen flooded with delicious smells. A familiar round face looked his way from the stove where she stood stirring a pot and another familiar bald-headed man sat at the table, mouth agape in surprise. Devlyn immediately recognized Natalie and Brother Bernard. Natalie had always been kind to him whenever he had to go into the village to pick up supplies for the abbey school. She looked much the same as always, but her eyes were silver now—the emerald entirely gone. Devlyn knew that if she walked in the sun, her light-brown hair would look as though someone had spun gold into her scalp.

Natalie rushed to Devlyn, swooping him into her bosom first, kissing him on the cheeks as fiercely as any aunt would. Even though Natalie was not related to Devlyn, he did not mind the embrace. He wondered what she was doing in the inn's kitchen. Brother Bernard was just as quick to abandon his seat and pull Devlyn into a warm hug. "Thank the Light you're okay."

"I don't understand; how are you both here?" Devlyn asked. Brother Bernard had been the only ei'ceuril at the abbey school of Cor'lera to show Devlyn any kindness.

"We could ask the same of you!" Brother Bernard laughed, jostling Devlyn by the shoulders, his merry blue eyes squinting nearly shut in joy at seeing Devlyn.

"It's a bit complicated and I don't entirely understand it myself," Devlyn said, looking at Aliel perched on the back of a chair.

"Well, to your question first, Arlyn asked me to come to the inn and get away from those stewards of Shadow—abominations that they are! There aren't any students at the abbey school any longer, so all I was leaving behind was the books." Brother Bernard sat down again and invited Devlyn to do the same. He looked disgusted as he admitted that stewards of Shadow existed and that they had been in Cor'lera all this time. "By the Light, look how much you've grown. Tell me everything— where did brother wind take you? Natalie, would you mind warming up a pot of tea?"

Devlyn smiled as Natalie hurried over to the stove, clearly also eager to hear of Devlyn's adventures.

DESERTION

Strong winds howled around the outside of Gwilnor and whistled through the window casings, the sound reaching Jaerol's sensitive ears. He was terrified that the sound might indicate something more treacherous than just the wind. The castle was already a cold place this time of year, a feeling only heightened by the Tenebrae ei'ana and their chilling presence. After Jaerol had been brought into the fold of the ei'ana in hiding, he had been tasked with learning the routine of the night patrol. Fortunately, he was already well versed with maneuvering around the Tenebrae and their middle-of-the-night patrols because he and Liam had to reach Fyreh's nightly lessons in the East Tower.

At first, the irregular routine of waking Gwilnor's residents appeared to have no rhythm or schedule. Each night, the Tenebrae ei'ana would wake the residents on either side of seemingly random corridors at their own whim, as though it was no more dependent on time than having to visit the lavatory in the middle of the night.

Once Jaerol gave it closer attention though, the less random the night patrol seemed. His first mistake had been assuming that because the patrols were different each day of the week, there was no underlying schedule. When he tried to find some semblance of a routine, he was disappointed since no Gwynthaen was the same as the one before, nor was any Thenaen the same, or any other day of the week.

One Lerenaen, he had noticed that the time of the roll call in his corridor had been the same as on a different day the week before. He had gotten into the habit of jotting down the exact time of the patrols, and when he lined up the previous Uraen with that Lerenaen, they were the same. There was in fact a precise, yet asymmetrical routine.

The weekly schedule shifted by two days. Gwynthaen's scheduled patrol became Uraen's patrol, and Uraen's patrol became Lerenaen's, and the same with every other day of the week.

The Seven Chairs of Septyl were ecstatic when he had broken the code. Since then, there had been some intricate planning, none of which involved him. Jaerol had thought they still had more time to devise their escape plan, but the message from Velaria had made it clear that it was time and that they would not get another opportunity as good as tonight. He hadn't received any further communication, only that he was to find his group in the North Tower and meet at the next checkpoint as planned. Jaerol went down the list of nine people assigned to him. Because he and Liam were both trusted by the Seven Chairs, they each had their own list and initially would carry out their own part of the plan. They had pored over each other's lists to ensure that there wasn't anyone suspicious on them.

Jaerol thought that the main pitfall of this plan was that the people on the list had not been told anything prior to the event. They had no idea that the Seven Chairs had been working toward escaping Gwilnor. The risk was too high. The more people who knew, the more likely the Tenebrae would find out.

The Seven Chairs' priority was to get the students out of the castle, with as many ei'ana and knights that they dared trust. However, because of the logistics involved, most of the knights and ei'ana would be left behind for the time being. With a few exceptions, it was all but impossible to determine which ei'ana had betrayed Septyl for the Tenebrae School. Once they were safe and away from the castle, it would be another question of how long those ei'ana had belonged to the Tenebrae School.

Few still inside the castle knew what was happening elsewhere just now. Soft feet padded across Gwilnor's stone floors as small bands snuck through the castle, each making their way to a different checkpoint. Only one person in each group knew where they were going, and that one person had the high confidence of the Seven Chairs. Jaerol had gathered his group of nine, Talen and Trethien among them, and only Trethien had protested at being woken up by Jaerol when he had collected him from his room without notice in the middle of the night.

The Chairs had not been idle during their concealment deep in the lower levels of the castle. They had spent their time investigating, considering, and finally deciding who could be trusted. Most likely at Velaria's insistence, the Chairs had chosen him to lead one of the groups. Everyone in the castle knew who he was. Other than Velaria, Jaerol was the only other known Cyndinari in Ceurenyl. Unlike Velaria though, Jaerol had been born far to the south in the heart of the Erynien Empire—the imperial capital of Broid. He had also been an Erynien emissary. Because of his antecedence, many in Gwilnor had chosen to keep their distance, fearing that he too belonged to the Tenebrae School. Even the small group he now led kept giving him sideways looks.

When he had approached them, he'd quickly explained that they were escaping the castle, and they could only bring what they wore on their backs once they'd dressed. Those who were full-fledged ei'ana were not pleased that they were expected to follow instructions from a Cyndinari. They could pretend they weren't prejudiced against him, but they were. And it wasn't just that they thought that the Cyndinari were a threat to Eklean, they also thought it was too soon to trust a kien wielder. The ei'ana were still fiercely divided over whether to instruct kien wielders. Jaerol thought it was a pointless debate now since the decision had already been made. The kien wielders once kept in the lower levels of the Temple of Ceur had been allowed to leave to learn to control their wielding. There were no more lay votaries at the temple.

Nonetheless, his small group followed him through the empty corridors under the darkness of night, preferring the possibility of escape to continuing to live at Gwilnor with the Tenebrae in charge. They didn't have much choice about following him, since only Jaerol had been told where to go. The Chairs had devised several safeguards to prevent their plot being discovered by any Tenebrae ei'ana or servant of Shadow.

They reached their first checkpoint at the base of the White Tower, where another group had already arrived. There were two more to come.

Jaerol looked over the other group, led by a knight, his arm in a sling due to what had been called an *accident.* Jaerol reread his own list to confirm that everyone who should be present was, and that anyone who should not, wasn't.

Jaerol was prepared to use the wields that Fyreh had taught his students and make his entire group invisible if a patrol came near them. Fortunately, they hadn't heard a patrol yet. Jaerol wondered what Velaria had done to preoccupy the Tenebrae ei'ana. He hoped that she and Devlyn were safe, but whatever they had done, it made sneaking through the castle all the easier.

Another group arrived, led by an ei'ana. She had scars across her face and likely more hidden beneath her clothing, but she walked as though she didn't feel any pain. *So that's how they chose us,* Jaerol thought. It was obvious. Who better to trust with the evacuation than those beaten by Gwilnor's current overseers? Jaerol knew the Chairs were intelligent, but he was still relieved that they had taken his recommendation on whom to trust. The Tenebrae had unknowingly marked those still loyal to Septyl.

The last group arrived, and immediately, Jaerol took count, realizing that there was an extra head. He looked quickly at the leader, one of the ei'ana wise ones, and judging by the colors she wore, a Vyoletryn. She stood proudly; her posture demanded authority and it looked as though she intended to pull it from beneath Jaerol's feet.

"Then we're the last," she said, with a hint of a question lingering in the air. By her tone, Jaerol didn't think this woman was uncertain about anything. What she said was law. Beside her stood the extra woman who wasn't on the list. She was an ei'ana, but unlike everyone else, looked as though she'd had plenty of notice to prepare. Her traveling cloak was thick and well-tailored, and the boots on her feet were the sturdy kind worn for trudging through the mountains. She even had a packed satchel.

She should not be here. Worse, neither she nor the wise one had any visible injury.

Jaerol knew he had only one opportunity. There was no time to think this through nor communicate it to the others. Quieting his mind and opening himself to the erendinth, he embraced umbrys. The shadowy power was often mistaken for malevolent intent. However, he knew that it was not umbrys that the shadow elves wielded, they wielded tenebrys, something that the rest of Eklean was learning all too late.

The wield he formed before he even allowed himself to breathe caused both the wise one and the extra ei'ana to crumple to the floor. The gathering was nearly forty people now, and they all gasped in shock.

"You attacked a wise one," a student said.

The ei'ana who led one of the other groups eyed Jaerol. "What do you know?" she demanded. Her voice was strained, but there was a hint of a threat there. Jaerol knew she held a wield, and she would use it on him if he answered wrongly.

"They're Tenebrae."

"Explain." She did not release her wield.

"We had strict instructions to keep to our lists. Any additions are suspect."

The ei'ana held Jaerol in her gaze for a long minute before asking, "What do you propose we do with them?" She looked down at the two women lying unconscious on the floor.

"We should take them before the Seven Chairs. As far as I know, they have not been able to interrogate any Tenebrae."

The ei'ana nodded, and rather than unleash her wield on Jaerol, she used it to lift the two unconscious women into the air. She nodded again, and Jaerol led the group anew. Everyone was shaken by what had just happened, but no one said anything, and they kept their thoughts private.

Jaerol had concerns about the size of the group, thinking it was risky to sneak this large a group through the castle. They had to reach the underbelly of the castle while staying away from any curious eyes. Luckily, the Tenebrae patrols had little need to make their way down here. The castle's upper levels were large enough to keep them busy throughout the night.

Then, the hair on the back of Jaerol's neck prickled. Pausing, he signaled everyone to stop.

They hadn't had to avoid any patrols yet and this felt too easy. Each of the group leaders had a designated route, and all had been warned not to veer from it. Still, something didn't feel right. Jaerol might have figured out the patrol schedule but there were simply too many Tenebrae in the castle that any one of them might decide to roam areas of the castle not on the schedule. He didn't think it was possible for the Tenebrae to find out about their route, but his gut told him that they'd been betrayed somehow. This escape mission had been under an incredible amount of secrecy and the exact timing for it had not been set. Jaerol had only known it was time when Velaria had signaled it earlier that evening.

Hushed murmurs from his group insisted that they needed to move forward. Everyone was scared and no one wanted to risk getting caught. Continuing to walk blindly simply wasn't going to work any longer. With hand signals, he urged everyone to stand flat against the corridor's wall and pressed into the erendinth. He wished he could tell whether someone was trailing them or waiting to spring a trap ahead.

He first ensured that no one following would notice him wielding and disguised his wield before pressing into terys to feel the stone in the corridor they crept through. He immediately felt his too-large group since most couldn't stay completely still and shuffled uneasily. His wield pulsed in both directions, ahead and behind.

Pressing into the stone, Jaerol's heart froze—five people were walking toward them. They had been followed! The followers had been going at the same pace as the group, and now that his group had stopped, these others were closing the gap.

His thoughts racing, Jaerol bit his cheek as he considered whether he'd be able to hide the entire group from five people at once. He'd only managed to make himself invisible to one other person before, so this was surely lunacy. Fighting the approaching patrol was of course an option, but he knew they'd wield tenebrys and would care little about loss of life. He had to try to hide his group first though. He didn't know what their chances would be if they fought them head on, but if this didn't work, they'd have to confront the approaching group anyway.

Jaerol hushed his group again and with a finger to his lips and an exaggerated posture of stillness in demonstration, he made them all stand still along the wall and wielded five separate wields over the approaching group. His heart raced as they drew nearer.

"How long do we trail them? It's not like we care where they're going," one of the Tenebrae said. It was too dark to see the person's face but Jaerol knew he'd heard the voice before. He didn't recognize her though.

"We'll stop them in the entry hall, but first, we want to make sure this group isn't merging with another. Our intelligence says the groups should be around forty each."

"We counted forty from the White Tower. We should've stopped them then and there."

"We had to wait for all the groups to merge. We couldn't alert any others before we captured them."

"Fine, but we've waited long enough."

Jaerol slowly let out the breath he hadn't realized he'd been holding once the five Tenebrae had passed. He kept his group in place until he was certain the Tenebrae had moved out of hearing range. Speaking still wasn't safe and Jaerol once again held a finger to his lips as he waved his group to follow him once he'd released his wield. Despite his previous instructions from Velaria, he led them away from their designated route and down a side stair instead, reaching the underbelly of the castle much sooner than had been intended by the planners. He was getting better at navigating this area of the castle since Fyreh's lessons had started and he and Liam had to figure out new ways to sneak through the castle undetected.

Once they were two levels beneath the main level, it looked like they would manage to disappear without further complications. Jaerol thought of Liam and hoped that he wouldn't face any trouble with his own group.

Jaerol had no idea where the Seven Chairs intended to take the entirety of those still loyal to Septyl once everyone was gathered. Gwilnor had been the home of the ei'ana since the actual city of Septyl had been lost, buried beneath the Shroud with the rest of Krysenthiel; anyone who breathed in that wretched mist would die in a matter of hours or days.

At last, they reached the designated tapestry with a faded seal of Septyl, seven different colored animals woven into the fabric. Jaerol knew this was where he was supposed to lead his group, but they were supposed to meet someone here who would take them to the next checkpoint. They were all beginning to feel anxious when the tapestry was pushed to the side from behind and Mother Selenya walked out of the archway in the wall.

"You're the first whole group to have made it." Selenya appraised them. The Albiens valued knowledge and wisdom more than any other School and as expected of the Chair of Albien, Mother Selenya was, without a doubt, the most intelligent woman in Septyl. Ambition and power had no place when the Albiens selected a new Chair. Their merit was purely academic, and Mother Selenya spent most of her day in the library among books and scrolls, her hair in a tight bun to keep it from spilling over her eyes.

She turned again to Jaerol cautiously. There was no doubt in her eyes about his allegiance; the question there was whether he had executed his duties exactly as he had been told. The ei'ana with the wield over the imposters came forward, the two still-unconscious women floating behind her. Selenya looked at their faces pensively, recalling them.

"Velaria was not wrong in having you pair with Deidre so soon," Selenya said as she walked around the two women. "A shame; this will leave Mother Paurel shaken, no doubt."

That was the closest to a compliment Jaerol would receive from the Chair of Albien. While Selenya was by no means a pessimist, neither was she known to give positive reinforcement.

"Come, we must continue," Selenya said. "We've been betrayed and must get as many to safety as we can. Jaerol, please cover the rear. I don't want any additions to the group. Be sure to seal the wall when you cross last." She looked into his eyes, speaking volumes without saying a thing.

Jaerol nodded in response, making the Chair smile, another unexpected acknowledgement. It was a thin smile, but few had ever received more from Selenya. Had he managed to impress the White Owl herself?

The tapestry was pulled aside again, revealing only the first several feet of the unlit passageway beyond. Selenya went in and a small globe quickly came to her palm, and when she held it aloft, Jaerol caught a glimpse of a downward sloping passage, carving its way through the mountains which Ceurenyl rested on. It was impossible to tell what direction or where it led to. With a lingering glance, he turned and made his way to the back of the crowd.

No one spoke, not even the younger students. The proud ei'ana's lips were still pursed, and glanced with what Jaerol perceived as disgust as they passed into the tunnel. He did not blame them. They had devoted their entire lives to Septyl, but the Seven Chairs had chosen to trust him, a student, a Cyndinari, and a kien wielder, over them. He had only lived among the Ei'ana of Septyl for a couple years.

The ei'ana holding the wield over the two imposters had passed them on to one of the other two, and she joined him at the rear of the group and stood beside him quietly. It wasn't out of shyness, but it was not the time to speak. They were so close to escaping the castle.

When the last of their group passed through the tapestry, the ei'ana performed a simple wield that returned the displaced dust in the corridor to cover their tracks. Then she and Jaerol followed the others into the secret passageway, returning the tapestry to its original position and wielding the stone wall whole once again.

Jaerol formed a glowing orb of his own, illuminating the way forward. It was a well-known fact to all who called Gwilnor their home that there were many hidden passageways crisscrossing the castle. Some made one's trek across the vast castle more direct, while others meandered more but allowed them to cross the castle undetected. It had never been documented how many hidden passages there were or if one person knew of them all. The only thing that was certain was that they existed and that some led out of the castle.

Realizing that he still had no idea of the ei'ana's name, Jaerol extended his hand in a formal greeting. "I'm Jaerol Solaris."

"Yes, the kien wielders, and you particularly, are quite the popular topic among us seasoned ei'ana. My name is Tabitha; I'm an Azurelle."

Tabitha's short black hair, dark eyes, and darker skin told Jaerol that she was likely born somewhere to the south, perhaps Sudern.

"You understand why I questioned you earlier, yes?"

"I do, and I would have done the same if I were in your shoes."

Tabitha smiled. It did not linger but he saw that she had a beautiful smile. "What are your responsibilities among the Azurelles?" he asked.

"Largely personal research. Most of my correspondents are in Dagger's Point, in the mountains and Sudern," Tabitha said, confirming her southern origin. "Duke Farneis' ability to remain opposed, if not publicly, to Erynor and his lackeys has always impressed me. If it weren't for the hostile environment of Sudern, I would be proud of it. But you know what it's like there, I'm sure."

Jaerol chuckled. It was true, Sudern was not a city for the faint of heart. "Do you still sleep with a knife?" Tabitha rolled up her left sleeve, revealing a long jeweled dagger strapped to her forearm. Her sleeve quickly hid the dagger and no one would be any wiser. "I've actually never been to Sudern," Jaerol said.

"The duke and merchants think they run the city, but in truth, the Goblin Guild does."

"Really?" Jaerol muttered. He knew of the guild; anyone with extra coin they wanted kept safe knew of it, and most were indebted to them as well. It was clever of the goblins who had never cared to compete with the other races in warfare. Instead, they contended across the world stage with their wealth and accounting. Their guild had ties to and in every major city and even saw to it that damaged roads were taken care of, to ensure trade. They never paid for the roads themselves, but rather gently but firmly coerced those responsible for maintaining the roads.

While the goblins never swore allegiance to Erynor, neither did they align themselves to anyone else. They cared little for the ruling parties of Eklean. It was no secret that the King of Torsil, and many other nobles and common folk, were deep in their debt. The goblins did not care what race a person was, so long as they borrowed the guild's money and later paid it back.

Before they realized it, Jaerol and Tabitha found themselves walking across a coarse threshold into a rough-cut tunnel. The lighting dimmed but Jaerol easily saw that it stretched on, his sight only limited when the tunnel turned.

It was still nighttime and would remain so for at least another four hours. Their numbers were much larger now, since others had arrived before them and had been waiting for Selenya to return. It was hard to tell with the lack of lighting how large their numbers had grown. They could have doubled, tripled, or even more. There was no way of knowing, and there was still no certainty as to where they were. The Seven Chairs had not revealed their destination. It did not look like the entirety of Gwilnor's residents opposed to Erynor had joined them though. Jaerol hoped they were escaping along a different trail as he craned his neck to see if Liam had made it here yet.

29

A Family Affair

The wood-paneled room lined with bookshelves brought back distant memories of a time before Devlyn had understood that he was different. As a ward of Cor'lera's abbey school, he had often been sent by Abbot Entiel to his sister Vine's home to spend the day with her family, which included Alex. Alex and he would run through the house, playing games and trying not to damage anything, especially the books. The Vaerins' library was extensive, and Alex's father was proud of his collection, claiming that many of the tomes had come from Gneal when his family relocated.

The books' origins had mattered little to Devlyn as a child, but now he saw the heroism involved when the deposed royal family had been exiled from their home. One book lay open on a low table, showing the royal lineage of House Vaerin, linking them to Perrien's first king, Dennion, after Thellion had fallen.

He was waiting for Alex's mother to appear. Somehow, she'd heard that he was at the Cor Inn and had invited him for tea. The maid who had answered the door had led him to the library, and while he waited, Devlyn scanned the old and faded pages, not daring to touch any of them, afraid the vellum would disintegrate at his touch. A musty smell filled his nostrils as he leaned over the open pages to better read the fluid script scrawled there. A long list of kings and queens, with their descendants and heirs filled most of the page. The last two who still held the monarchical titles were Harold and Kristine. Several lines below them was Alexander.

Alex's father was the eldest male of his family, a direct and unbroken lineage to Harold and Kristine, but Alex was the youngest of his siblings and unlike elven lineage dictates, humans placed the eldest before youngest. Yet Devlyn had seen the message himself; Alex was now the King of Thellion. Devlyn had hoped that Alex's mother and father knew about this already, since Devlyn did not have the energy to convince them that their son was now their king.

From what Devlyn had gathered, Perrien and Parendior were two separate provinces, just as they had been the last time a Thellish king wore the crown. Would Alex spearhead an effort to unite the human kingdoms of Eklean into one kingdom again? Devlyn didn't think his cousin would attempt that through force. Even if Alex tried to go about it through diplomatic means, what benefit would there be to a single human kingdom?

Devlyn's thoughts were interrupted when Alex's mother walked into the library and placed a platter on the table with the old book, but to one side of the table with plenty of space between it and the book. Vine might not care for her husband's collection, but she would never permit something in her house to become tarnished or dirty. Devlyn had learned that at a very young age.

The smell of hot tea filled the room, covering the otherwise musty scent, and immediately relaxed Devlyn.

"Good morning, Aunt Vine," he said, the relationship coming out of habit. "I'm sorry, we're not actually related, so perhaps I shouldn't call you aunt."

"I beg your pardon." A skeptical eyebrow rose.

"My father wasn't actually your brother. He wasn't even human— not even a little."

"So, Entiel was right all along? Not terribly surprising; Dolan looked nothing like the rest of us." Vine handed Devlyn a cup of tea.

"Afraid so. My father's mother was Eldinari and his father was Cyndinari."

"I thought those two elven factions didn't get along."

"They don't. He wasn't begotten in love."

"I see." She paused and seemed to be thinking about what Devlyn had just revealed. "So how did Dolan wind up in our family?"

"His grandparents, the Lierafen aryl, arranged it," Devlyn began to explain then stopped, noting that Vine did not follow the unfamiliar names. "Sorry, an aryl is the lord and lady of a prominent elven house. The Eldinari don't have kings or queens; the aryls reign as equals among their people."

"Fascinating," Vine said, popping one of Walei's candies into her mouth, the jar conveniently closer to her and not reachable by Devlyn unless she offered one.

Devlyn sipped his tea as an awkward silence gripped the room. He had never been particularly fond of Alex's parents, and it had always been evident that they never saw him favorably either. The quiet sounds of Vine chewing candy and him sipping tea made him wonder why he had come here in the first place. Sure, he had been invited but that did not mean he had to accept the invitation, even if they were Alex's parents, and in this case, especially because they were Alex's parents.

"The outfit fits you well, by the way. The purple is quite lovely," Vine said, breaking the silence.

"Thank you." It was the first time since Wyn had rescued him from Lankor that he had worn a different set of lierathnil. He had grown quite tired of what had been his favorite dark blue outfit after wearing it for so long. He now wore a purple robe over lavender trousers and a cream shirt. Intricate silver scrollwork lined the outer robe.

The thump of booted feet came from the corridor and before Devlyn had a chance to stand, Alex's father walked in. Clyde strode through the doorway, his powerful step making the tea set rattle on the table.

Teacup still in hand, Devlyn rose from the rose velvet sofa to greet

Clyde with a firm handshake.

"You've grown since we last saw you, nephew." Clyde grasped Devlyn by the shoulders, holding him at arm's length to take him in.

"Dolan was never my brother, Clyde." Vine lost no time in sharing that information.

"There isn't any need for that, Vine. Entiel and his ridiculous theories can stay locked up in that school as long as they want." Clyde's friendly tone turned impatient at what was clearly a long-standing argument between the couple.

"It's actually true," Devlyn interjected. "I found out a couple of years ago—after Alex and I got separated."

"Dolan was an elf, all along." Vine popped another candy in her mouth in the most self-righteous manner possible.

"Truly? Was he a Luminari as well?"

"Eldinari and Cyndinari," Vine said.

"Truly? I thought they didn't get on with one another." Devlyn smiled to himself at how similar Vine and Clyde were. He had never appreciated them as individuals or even as a couple before. "Fascinating. Now, Devlyn, is everything we've been hearing true? Are you actually what's called a Phaedryn and the future king of the elves? Has the Perrien Council been aligned with this Erynien Empire all along? Did Alex really manage to form an army and oust the council?"

The onslaught of questions caught Devlyn by surprise. How had all these details reached Cor'lera? The small village was so far removed from the rest of Eklean that surely the villagers weren't that well informed. And then Devlyn remembered that Alex would have stopped in Cor'lera. Though that didn't explain how Clyde knew about him being the heir to the Crystal Throne of Krysenthiel.

Without having to ask, Aliel appeared with a flash, making Vine shriek and both she and Clyde shield their eyes. Then Vine peeked out from behind one hand, patting down her skirts with the other in embarrassment at having been surprised.

"He's beautiful," Vine said after she had composed herself. "He, right?"

"It's a bit complicated. Phoenix are actually anadel, and anadel don't have genders." Devlyn couldn't really describe something he did not fully understand himself.

"So, because of your connection to this phoenix, you're in line to become the next elven king?" Clyde asked.

"Not exactly; my ancestors were Lorenthiens—an ancient elven line that was given the title of Exalted Aryl. The line was thought broken after Erynor came to power."

"Truly? All this time the Lorenthiens were holed up here in Cor'le-ra. Huh." Clyde paused to think about that before going on, seeming to know much more about elves than he had let on in the past. "Now about Perrien. We haven't had any news from across the River Arvil. Have you heard anything?"

"Well, the Perrien Council has been disbanded."

"So, they were aligned with the Erynien Empire."

"Yes, but that's not all." Clyde and Vine looked at Devlyn expectantly. "Alex is now the King of Thellion."

Alex's parents looked blankly at Devlyn. "Alex? Our Alex? He's not even our eldest son," said Vine. "How is that possible?"

"I suppose that doesn't make too much of a difference. Our family is only barely connected to House Dennion, and was never in line to the Thellish throne," Clyde said, shocking Devlyn at how knowledgeable he was of Thellion's history.

With an imploring look at her husband, Vine set her shoulders back and straightened her spine to make herself taller in her seat, looking as though she was pretending to sit on a throne.

"Yes, Vine? You're not hard to read, I hope you know that." Clyde responded to his wife's look before looking around the room filled with books. "Do you have any idea what it will require to move our family back to Gneal?"

"We're royalty—you've always been so but have never been able to claim your title. It's time we went home!"

"We can't just pack up and leave. Think of Sam; he and his new wife are expecting a child any time now. And what about our winery and our vineyards? Do you just want to abandon them as well?"

"I doubt Sam would ever leave Cor'lera. We couldn't drag him away if we tried. Besides, he's practically been begging for more responsibility at the vineyard. Just think, our little Alex now a Thellish king," Vine said, her hands still resting on her lap. "We have to go to him; he could need our help."

"He's all grown now; there's little help we could offer, and he'll be having to deal with your other brother soon enough," Clyde said.

"Well then, we'll just have to do something about that. Imagine what would happen if Lex turned his army away from Evellion to point swords at our son? I must be there. Families fighting one another just isn't right. Besides, you've always wanted to live in Gneal, the home of your ancestors and your inheritance."

Clyde quietly mulled over his options while Devlyn avoided inserting himself into the conversation. Gently setting his teacup down and standing to leave Alex's parents to deliberate on their own, he felt Vine's gaze pierce into him.

"And where are you off to?" she asked.

"I have to get to Gneal. I never intended to come to Cor'lera. It was sort of an accident, and there are things I need to do."

"How does one accidentally find oneself in Cor'lera?" Vine asked.

"The roads are horrendous this time of year," Clyde said, unconcerned by Devlyn's sudden departure. "They're much worse than any winter I can remember. How will you reach Gneal?"

"Well, I don't have much need for roads anymore. I could fly there but I think I'll try the same method that brought me here so suddenly."

"Which is?" Clyde and Vine asked simultaneously.

Caught between the two of them, Devlyn felt inclined to tell them the entire truth, even if he had never particularly cared for them as a child. They had been quite harsh and unforgiving toward him throughout his childhood. A memory of his last night in Cor'lera sprung to mind. Vine had insisted that he stay in the school's stable, cold and hungry, but had allowed Alex to go inside and retrieve food enough for them both.

A mental push from Aliel urged him to tell them; he must have seen something different in them, something that indicated they should know more.

"It's similar to a seguian used by time wardens." Vine and Clyde looked back at him blankly. "You know, the minums?" Devlyn could have said the sky was snowing pink grapes the size of oranges and their expressions could not have been more clueless. Again, he thought back to his childhood when he and the majority of Cor'lera had believed that all the elves were dead, and that he was a pointy-eared accident of nature.

"I'm sorry, I don't think there's time to explain it all; besides, the ei'ana can give a better explanation than I ever could. I guess I could show you, but I have to collect my belongings from the Cor Inn first."

"I suppose it won't kill me to step foot in that inn after all these years." Vine stood as though to announce that she was ready.

"Are you sure about that?" Clyde smiled wryly at his wife who responded with a humph and turned to leave the library, grabbing her large and suspiciously bulging purse. "We'd better follow her; she won't willingly agree to go to your family's inn a second time." Clyde shook his head at his wife's vagaries.

Devlyn and Clyde trailed after Vine, Devlyn wondering what she could possibly need from her large purse just to walk across the village. They left Vaerin Manor to walk the short distance to the Cor Inn.

It seemed that an unexpected effect of the Luminari pilgrimage coming to an end in Lucillia had affected every Luminari settlement since even the wooden wall surrounding Cor'lera's old town had returned to the Illumined Wood. Fortunately, the villagers had already started to construct a new stone wall around what had been the outer ring of the village. With the inner wooden wall gone, the distance to the inn was much shorter since they didn't have to first go through a gate where the wall had once divided the two portions of the village. They could take a more direct route through the streets that led to the inn.

The village itself had grown significantly, perhaps following the trend it had been on for the past few decades. The new stone wall wasn't the only significant new structure either. After the problems resulting from being held under siege by Lex, the villagers had apparently set about constructing a fortified castle on the outer rim of the village, soon after Alex had come and gone. Devlyn wondered about the impact Alex had had on Cor'lera, and indeed the whole of Parendior. For the first time, Devlyn didn't see Cor'lera as a divided village. Even the humans who had originally come from Perrien appeared fully integrated now and smiled at their elven neighbors. They even waved at Devlyn as he passed. Had they forgotten who he was—who his mother was and the crime she had been wrongfully accused of?

Vine stopped at the inn's door and stepped aside for Devlyn to go in first. Clyde offered her a supportive smile and nudge. With a crisp exhale, she followed Devlyn into the common room that was already crowded and noisy with cheerful patrons. A shocked silence fell when the patrons saw Vine, every pair of eyes focused on her. Vine had notably and vocally been against the re-opening of the inn, in part because it was bigger than her manor house. However, even the inn would soon be dwarfed by the castle now going up. And wherever a castle was built, a cathedral would follow. Devlyn sincerely hoped that Abbot Entiel would be ousted before that happened. His influence had done enough harm to Cor'lera.

Devlyn passed through the common room like he owned the place, which he actually did. He pushed open the door to the kitchen and was immediately struck by the wondrous smells. "Hello, Natalie. That smells amazing!”

“Why, hello there, Devlyn. I’m happy you think so!” She hadn’t turned around yet, busy with a pot on the fire. “Will you still be here for supper?”

“Sadly, no, I’ll be leaving in the next couple minutes.”

Natalie abandoned her pot and rounded on Devlyn, spoon still in hand. It was only then that she noticed the Vaerins standing in her kitchen. She gaped in shock, not sure whether to curtsey to the couple or offer them a bowl of stew. “Forgive me, I never expected to see you two step foot in my kitchen.”

“Times are certainly changing, aren’t they?” Clyde said, his arm around Vine’s waist.

“For the better!” Natalie grinned and pulled Devlyn into one of her motherly hugs. “Before you leave, you have to promise me something. Bring your mother home. I miss her dearly. This inn is not the same without her.”

A pang swelled inside Devlyn at the loss of the mother he could only faintly remember. The only time he had seen her face outside of a hazy dream was in the portrait of their family. Lex had stolen that portrait and had threated to burn it on Devlyn’s thirteenth birthday. “I will. I promise.”

“That’s good of you.” Natalie lingered until her stew started to bubble over the edges. “Oh dear!” She gasped and rushed back to her cooking.

“Where’s Brother Bernard?” Devlyn asked.

“Oh, he says he’s meditating in his room, but everyone here knows that he’s napping. He’s not fooling any of us with the sound of his snoring!”

“Will you tell him I said goodbye?”

“Certainly. You should know that he’s quite proud of how you’ve grown since you left Cor’lera—we all are. He wouldn’t stop talking about you the entire morning. I haven’t seen him in this good of a mood for a very long time; not since he had that library to fuss about."

"Thank you." Devlyn smiled and pushed open the door to the inn-keeper's quarters. Even though Natalie had assumed the role of innkeeper, she refused to move into those rooms. She had her own home near the inn and to her, the innkeeper's rooms were sacred.

Vine followed Devlyn into the sitting room, Clyde holding her hand as she started to cry. Emotion was one thing Devlyn had never expected from her. "Dolan didn't deserve what happened to him," she said at last, eyes taking in the cozy room. "He might not be my brother through blood, but he is family, just as you will always be my nephew."

"You do know that Lex killed him, right?" Devlyn asked, his voice low and almost ashamed to mention it.

"No, never!" she gasped, horrified. "Lex would never kill his brother!"

"He had a helmet covering his face when he forced his way in here. He was with a shadow elf. My da fought him off until Lex removed his helmet revealing who he was. Da couldn't fight his brother after that and Lex drove his sword through him. Liam was there and told me everything." Devlyn could see that his words weighed heavily on Vine, and then her face crumbled into shame.

"Oh Devlyn, we've been so unfair to you and your family. Could you ever forgive us—forgive me?"

"You believe me? Just like that?" Again, Devlyn thought back to his last night in Cor'lera four years ago and how his aunt had treated him then.

"If you had told me this a year ago, I would have never permitted you inside my home again." Vine spun around as though she wanted to leave. "Everything turned upside down when Alex passed through Cor'lera with those rebels. I couldn't understand why my own son would pit himself against Perrien and his own uncle. Naturally I blamed the elves and ei'ana for corrupting him, but after he left, our last conversation continuously played through my mind. And for the first time I thought, what if I was wrong?"

Clyde rubbed her back in support. Devlyn wondered if this was the first time that Clyde was hearing this story as well.

"I forgive you, Aunt Vine." Devlyn went to his aunt and hugged her as she turned back to face him. He had had years to cope with the truth of what had happened to his family in this very room and the terrible events that had continued to happen to them in Gneal's dungeons. This was the first Vine was learning of it.

Clyde looked like he too was about to cry, and as soon as Devlyn left Vine's side, Clyde took his wife into an embrace. "You have me falling in love with you all over again."

Vine dabbed her wet eyes. "I think that is enough sentiment for one day, yes?" She shook the jitters away and straightened her posture and squared her shoulders. "Now, let's see this magic you speak of. Enough impossible things have happened in one day, what's one more thing to add to the list?"

Devlyn took Vine and Clyde deeper into the innkeeper's quarters where he had left his lierathnil. Vine paused in the corridor lined with portraits. "I don't see Dolan here."

"Lex stole that portrait."

"If I ever see that brother of mine, he won't leave in one piece."

"This one is my mother as a toddler, and her family." Devlyn pointed to the newest portrait on the wall, a silver line connecting it to its predecessor and another silver line threading to an empty space, where his family portrait should have hung.

"You all look so alike." Vine's fingers hovered over the family. "Did any of her siblings survive Gneal's dungeons?"

Devlyn shook his head.

"Well, you have us. And your Uncle Arlyn is still alive. He's the one that brought life back to this inn, as well as to the entire village."

Devlyn smiled and turned to the opposite wall where there were many more portraits. His eyes stopped on the portrait that only had a single line stemming from it. Every other portrait showed a single parent gazing into their youngest child's eyes, artistically depicting what Devlyn had once thought was the line of Feolyn. The first portrait, the one he gazed at now, did not show Feolyn looking into the youngest child's eyes.

It was Gwendolyn Lorenthien.

Boy-King

Devlyn, Vine, and Clyde went into the small bedroom where he had left the three lierathnil outfits spread out on the bed. They were nowhere in sight, and the bed was freshly made. A quick search in the wardrobe revealed the garments hanging there. Natalie had apparently tidied up, perhaps hoping he'd stay in Cor'lera longer.

Devlyn had kept his invaluable coin purse on his person and only needed to collect his lierathnil. Clutching them over one arm, he indicated that he was ready.

"Aren't you going to fold and pack them?" Vine stared at him. "Hmph, you boys are all the same. Wait here." She left the room, and shortly after, Devlyn and Clyde could hear rummaging sounds and Vine and Natalie giggling somewhere in the innkeeper's quarters. Vine returned with a finely made leather bag.

"Natalie was kind enough to help find this. Now step aside so I can fold those."

Clyde pulled Devlyn back by the elbow. "Best not get in her way. Trust me." He smiled.

Vine only took a moment to expertly fold the silken garments, pack them away into the bag, and hand it to Devlyn. "Now, let's see this magic you mentioned."

Devlyn closed his eyes, sought the phoenix inside his heart and a burst of color and light filled the room, and the transformation took place.

Vine and Clyde seemed overwhelmed at the sight. Delyn had promised them something magical, but this was something else entirely. People didn't have wings springing out of their shoulder blades, and certainly not wings of golden light! Neither of the Vaerins said anything, staring in open mouthed wonder.

Devlyn scoured his memories over the past four years for an image of a place he was familiar with. He had only been to Perrien's capital once and there was nothing memorable about that visit. At the time, fretting over whether Liam was still alive, his attention had been completely devoted to rescuing his brother. He could barely remember what his brother had looked like then, other than Liam's emaciated body.

Going directly to the castle would be ideal. Unfortunately, Devlyn had never been inside it and could only visualize what it looked like from the outside, specifically, the view from the northern city gate. It stood near enough to the castle and would be as close to Alex as he could safely get.

A distant memory of the awe he'd felt standing beneath that north gate came to him. It had been the first time he had ever seen a city, and the great stone wall shielding Gneal had left an impression. He could still feel that tingling sense of wonder when he had walked beneath the great stone archway, the giant portcullis suspended above threatening to crash on unworthy visitors.

The image solidified in his mind and, trying to repeat what he had done before, he willed himself to the location, hundreds of leagues west. He focused on Gneal's north gate, scarcely aware of the touch on his arm. Eyes closed, he felt something inside him shift. A startled shriek beside him and yells before him came as did the clear sound of metal freed from scabbards. *It worked.*

Opening his eyes to view the chaos surrounding him, Devlyn raised his hands to calm the guards at the gate and let go of his bond with Aliel so that he didn't look quite so formidable.

"Identify yourself!" said a guard, his tone struggling to be demanding as he was clearly shaken by the appearance of the golden, winged figure.

"Ei'ethil Devlyn Lorenthien, heir to the Crystal Throne of Krysenthiel."

"And you?" the guard asked, looking to Devlyn's left.

Surprised, Devlyn looked to his side, only just then realizing that someone held his arm.

"Vine Vaerin, your king's mother." Her voice started with a tremor, then gained confidence when she identified herself as the King of Thellion's mother. Devlyn had no doubt that she would soon concoct her own title, something deserving of her station.

Falling to one knee, the guard bowed his head. "My apologies, Your Highness."

Vine's hand went to her lips.

"Forgive me, Lord Phaedryn, I'll escort you both to the castle, if you desire."

"That would be appreciated," Devlyn said, nonplussed by Vine's presence here in Gneal with him.

Vine kept her grip on his arm as they followed the guard, both taking in what little of the city they passed. The castle loomed above and appeared unchanged. There was no direct route to the castle's gate, so the guard led them south from the north gate, then made a sharp turn to the northwest. Gneal's old city had been expertly designed to make it as difficult as possible to reach the castle, in case an army breached the city gates.

Despite the lack of a direct route, the castle was visible to nearly the entire city and stood unobstructed once they were close enough. Compared to Gwilnor, the structure with its squat towers seemed small and insignificant, even if it was the seat of Perrien's rule.

A short walk up the hill that Gneal rested on brought Devlyn's attention to the ruined castle gate. Rubble had been pushed to the side, but the gate had not yet been replaced. Scaffolding lined the wall on either side of the opening, so Devlyn assumed a new gate would follow soon.

"What could do such a thing?" asked Vine.

"One of them shadow elves and her dragon crashed down on it, they did. Perrien's ancient granite didn't stand a chance against the weight of that beast," the guard replied, looking past the ruined gate.

The crossing of the castle bailey took no time, and the guard disappeared after he spoke with a knight standing before sturdy double door. Devlyn noticed a winged horse carved into the granite above the doors and recognized it immediately as the sigil of Thellion. The sight of the familiar grey courser upon a white field embroidered on the knight's tabard was reassuring. Despite the difficulties the Perrien army had caused, a small part of Devlyn was relieved to see the sigil again.

The knight did not speak to them but led them into the castle's entrance hall where draperies and tapestries hung from every wall and brought color to the stark granite. Passing through the entrance hall and into a wide corridor, Devlyn felt the eyes of past kings staring at him from the statues and portraits lining the walls.

Two more knights stood guard at another double door. Devlyn could hear raised voices coming from behind it. The knight leading Devlyn and Vine spoke their names to the knight on the right in a quick exchange that Devlyn barely heard and returned to his own post. At this knight's knock on the door, a muffled response from inside followed and both knights opened the doors to allow Devlyn and Vine entrance.

The knight who had knocked cleared his throat to announce the visitors, but Vine rushed past him and to her son before he could manage a word.

A startled Alex looked from over his mother's shoulder at Devlyn as he was buried in her embrace. *You brought my mother!* He glared as he mouthed the words.

"How could you not tell us you were going to become a king! We would have come with you. All you told us was that you were helping the ei'ana gather support for a rebel army—you said nothing about fighting yourself and claiming a crown. And why didn't you tell us about Devlyn's family? I felt the complete fool when I learned the truth today!"

"I didn't realize the ei'ana had schemed to place me on a throne until months later." He didn't bother answering any of her other questions.

The last time Devlyn had seen Alex with his mother four years ago when he was fourteen years-old, they had been near the same height. Now, Alex towered over her. Ecstatic to see him again, Devlyn had overlooked everyone else in the room, and while Alex dealt with his mother's surprise visit, he looked around. A young boy sat on a chair, his arms crossed and a book open on his lap. Sara and Reia stood to greet Devlyn and standing behind them was an elf he had never met before, yet somehow knew. Oliver and Karl nodded to Devlyn from the other side of the table among all those gathered in the room, including some others that Devlyn did not recognize.

"Good to see you are well and out of harm's way," Reia said, reaching out to shake his hand.

"Um, thanks. You, too," he responded, surprised at her gesture.

"Have you learned nothing of diplomacy and proper etiquette?" Reia asked, not so much a question, but an accusation, making him feel more ill at ease.

"Sorry." Devlyn was still focused on the elf in the white ei'ceuril robes, who smiled kindly at him. "Why do I know you?" The words felt awkward and out of place, but he couldn't think of anything more gracious.

"Your mother, Evellyn, is my sister."

"Arlyn?"

He nodded and smiled, drawing closer to his nephew to hold him at arm's length by the shoulders. "Would you look at how you've grown." The remark was kind and filled with pride. "You remind me so much of your mother—and father. Your eyes have changed, although I suppose every Luminari's has." With the comment, he turned his focus to Aliel.

"This is Aliel."

"I hoped it had worked all those years ago, but to finally see the proof…" Arlyn said, trailing off.

"I'm sorry, I don't understand?"

"I'll explain when we can speak privately."

"Right," said Devlyn, now even more puzzled. Aliel shared a sense of amusement through their connection.

Alex finally managed to free himself from his mother's grip, walked over to Devlyn and pulled him into a warm hug. He was still broader in the shoulders than Devlyn, but Devlyn was still taller and now possibly stronger due to the jienzu practice. The cousins' hug turned into a competitive squeeze.

"All right," said Alex, gasping. "I get it; I've missed you too." The two laughed. "By the Light, how long has it been?"

"Almost two years, I think. We were split up in Delenth, right?" Devlyn said, counting off the months in his head.

Pushing his hand through his sandy blond hair, Alex took a step back from Devlyn as the length of time washed over him. They had never been separated for so long before. "By the Light, has it been that long?"

"Alexander Vaerin!" Vine's tone carried a rebuke that was embarrassing in front of his council. Karl chuckled and Alex glared at him in return.

"Sorry, Mother." Alex turned back to Devlyn. "Right, well, I'm afraid a decent reunion filled with stories will have to wait. Are you familiar with the Daer Empire?"

"Yes, actually. They've been sailing along Tiel's coast."

"Have they begun to build settlements there?"

"Not that I've heard."

"Well, they have here, and they're forcing Perriens into slavery to do it. They're just off the Skrein coast on Perrien land."

"Their ships can sail through the Skrein Sea?" Devlyn asked, knowing that those waters were nearly always frozen. "Do we know anything about them, aside from their name?"

"Sanjin can tell you more when he returns. His people have fought for centuries to maintain their independence in the Daer Empire's shadow."

"Who?"

"Oh right, you've never met," Alex said. "He's a Charrenese prince who came to Alexandria to strike an alliance."

"Alexandria? Renaming cities after yourself already, are you?"

"Don't get me started. I had strongly discouraged setting up any foundations at Aewen Bridge, but I couldn't stop it once Aewen showed up. You know, the Aldinari elf that married Thellion—yes, the one and only, the first king of that old kingdom. Well, she's still alive and she showed the ei'ana how to wield buildings into existence, palaces and all!"

"Is that where your throne is?" Vine asked, her tone ecstatic. She had followed Alex further into the room and now stood close to his side, hanging on to his every word.

"At least for now, but it might move to Elothkar soon. That, or Elothkar will be a symbolic capital. Interpreting elves is impossible—no offense. Have you figured out a way to get the dwarves involved in defending Everin?" Alex switched the topic before his mother could start asking about his throne room.

"Do you remember Oma?"

"The batty old dwarf that talks to rocks?" Alex asked, his voice heightened.

"Her son is Patriarch Forvl VIII of Oern Schtam."

"And she never thought to mention it to us? Not that I would've believed her. That cave she called home looked fit for a vagabond, not a queen." Despite an uneasiness in his stomach at the remark, Devlyn smiled in agreement. "Is she coming here to Gneal or are we meeting her somewhere?"

"She's with Wyn, but we were split up before we agreed on where to meet. They'll likely go straight to Belin's Watch."

"Who's Wyn?"

"We do have a lot of catching up to do. Apparently, I have family in the Eldin Wood."

"Probably not as good looking or intelligent as I am." Alex smirked as the others in the room scoffed. Vine beamed in agreement with Alex's self-description. "I suppose we should start to make our way there then; especially if you've been to Cor'lera from Ceurenyl and then here. They'll be bored waiting for us to arrive."

"Not necessarily," said Devlyn, scratching his upper arm.

"Don't tell me you've learned some ancient elven secret magic," Alex said.

"More of a Phaedryn secret magic, really. It's similar to a seguian, but there isn't any portal, I just close my eyes and then, poof, I'm there. I didn't know I could bring others with me, but your mother grabbed my arm before I left Cor'lera, and well, here we are."

"So, we don't have to leave just yet." Alex smacked his head.

MEMORIES

The first of Marenth arrived and both Devlyn and Ellendren were celebrating their birthdays today. He mentally wished her a happy birthday and prayed that she was safe. The Erynien Empire was only one of the threats she was currently facing. Political infighting among the Luminari aryls was likely a more immediate matter.

Shortly after Devlyn had arrived in Gneal, Wyn had mentally reached out to Devlyn to inform him that he and Oma had indeed left Gwilnor and would reach Belin's Watch in about a month. That meant that Devlyn and Alex wouldn't have to leave Gneal for another two weeks. Unlike Devlyn's first visit to Gneal, the weather had yet to warm and instead of rain, it still snowed.

It was common for Perrien and Parendior to have snow well into the spring, so Devlyn wasn't necessarily upset about the cold weather continuing past the first day of spring, but he was tired of it. Even with the late snowfalls, this winter had felt colder than others, and he had spent most of it in southern Eklean, where it was warmer overall. Snow and ice still clung to the roofs of Gneal, including the castle's, despite the number of castle guards continuously shoveling the snow off.

Since arriving in Gneal, Devlyn had only ventured outside the castle twice to get some fresh air. Both times, the bitter cold had quickly forced him to return to the warm castle's interior. He thought of those who found themselves in that cold, because of work or because they had no home and was grateful that he was comfortable inside the castle while the cold weather gripped Gneal.

The castle was not what Devlyn had anticipated. He had only known its bland exterior before. After a few days in the castle, he was surprised at the luxuries inside the thick granite walls. Tapestries and carpets, rich golden chandeliers and heavy candelabras, and hearths with roaring fires brought an unexpected warmth to the castle's interior. Part of him felt guilty for enjoying his time here. The council that had once ruled from this castle was the source of Parendior's oppression. The council was part of the reason his family had been torn apart, the reason he had been raised by unfaithful ei'ceuril, and the reason Alex and his army had forcibly removed them from power. The dungeons where his family had been tortured and killed by shadow elves were deep in the castle. None of those killed there would find peace in Lumaeniel until the shadow elves who had stolen their souls were destroyed. Only Evellyn and Liam had escaped that fate. Now that the castle belonged to Alex as the Thellish king, Devlyn found it difficult to disassociate the council and the castle from their evil works.

At this early hour, the castle was quiet as Devlyn wandered through its vacant corridors, only the occasional guard or servant passing by in the dim light from the oil lamps that burned throughout the night. Arlyn had invited Devlyn to a morning meal to celebrate his birthday. His uncle had told him it was typical for Luminari to break their fast together on special occasions, a tradition that Devlyn had never learned as a child. The sun hadn't broken through the clouds since before he had arrived in Gneal, and he doubted that it would today. He struggled to recall the last time he had seen the sun, the last time he had felt its warmth upon his skin. Even for winter, it had been uncommonly cloudy over the past months.

Reaching Arlyn's quarters, Devlyn knocked softly on the door, not wanting to wake anyone else along this corridor. The door opened and Arlyn welcomed Devlyn inside with a smile. Seeing his uncle's face was like looking into a mirror and seeing himself thirty or forty years into the future, and Devlyn couldn't help smiling back. The only differences in their features were the shade of Devlyn's skin, the additional hues in his hair, and the golden color of his eyes.

"Happy seventeenth birthday, Devlyn," Arlyn said in a warm voice. "Please, come in."

"Thank you." Devlyn walked into the enormous apartment. "It looks like Alex has taken a liking to you."

"He has indeed, but that's not the reason I was offered this residence." Arlyn led Devlyn through the entryway and opened a nearby door. Beyond the door was a small, yet ornately decorated chapel that had a secondary door at the rear. "There was a time when the Perrien monarchy were faithful to Anaweh. They boarded a steward, often a wise one, to offer prayers and services for the royal household. I won't bog you down with the political weight that position once held, but it was just as coveted as the position of Gneal's archsteward."

Chairs circled the chapel, all facing inward with candles lining the round walls behind them. The center of the chapel had the customary round depression in the floor and directly above it, a small glass dome in the ceiling, currently covered with snow.

"Come, dawn is upon us," said Arlyn, closing the door to the chapel and shepherding Devlyn through the apartment to a seat at a table already loaded with a delicious meal of fruits and sugared pastries.

Not sure whether filling his plate entirely with a mixture of the assortments placed before him was proper etiquette, Devlyn watched Arlyn fill his own dish. Since Arlyn was serving himself generously from the offered food, Devlyn filled his own plate similarly then happily took his first bite of a luscious pear.

Neither spoke as they ate, enjoying the taste of the food. Arlyn finally sat back, apparently satisfied.

"The last time I saw my sister, you were not yet two, and your sister, Leilyn, was only six." Arlyn closed his eyes and tilted his head back. "Velaria and I had traveled to Cor'lera to inform your parents that the phoenix had hatched, and that we feared the imminent return of Erynor. Little did we know at the time that he had already reinserted himself in Broid. The Aryl of Lucillia, the Ceurtriarch, and the Seven Chairs had sent us on that mission to your parents. I had not returned to Cor'lera since it had been discovered that I had the ability to wield and I decided that I should go to the Temple of Ceur to become an ei'ceuril. It was only due to my reputation among the ei'ceuril that I was granted permission to go beyond the temple walls, despite my ability to wield."

Devlyn felt a pang of guilt at having left Velaria to deal with the situation at Gwilnor. He knew that she had planned the escape for the students and as many of the ei'ana and knights still loyal to Septyl as possible. She had sacrificed herself and was now Hannah's prisoner, just so that they could go free.

"After informing your parents of the danger they were in, and after they refused to leave Cor'lera, I offered a gift to their youngest children. I could not offer it to Liam, for the gift could only be bestowed on a descendant of Lucillia," Arlyn said.

"What kind of gift? I doubt Abbot Entiel would have permitted me to keep anything of value." Devlyn cast his eyes down, embarrassed because he knew that whatever Arlyn had given him had been confiscated by Entiel.

Arlyn chuckled. "Not even he could take what I gave you."

Raising an eyebrow, Devlyn looked at his uncle with curiosity. He didn't know of any gift his uncle could have given him. It must still be hidden away at the Cor Inn.

"I have the ability to show you. It is an old form of sharing memories, forgotten by most, but our family held dearly to this ability. Evellyn holds another memory, passed down from Feolyn and Gwendolyn. Would you allow me to take you into my memories?"

Devlyn felt comfortable with Arlyn, not just because he had a kind and honest look about him, but he did feel that his uncle was inherently trustworthy.

"Um, sure."

Rising, Arlyn moved his chair around the table and placed it close to Devlyn's, arms extended and his palms upward. "Move your chair so that you are close enough to grasp my forearms."

Devlyn followed Arlyn's directions, placing his hands above Arlyn's forearms. He expected Arlyn would start telling a story, or perhaps speak into his mind, but they sat together in the quiet. Nothing happened for a moment.

Then he blinked and saw that he now sat on a comfy couch in the sitting room of his family's home at the Cor Inn, his mother next to him and his father on her other side. Emotion swelled inside Devlyn at seeing his parents. A much younger Velaria sat on a different sofa that faced Devlyn's, her leafy garment and flowery hair noticeably absent.

"The Shadow is growing stronger," Arlyn said, speaking from Devlyn's mouth. It was only then that Devlyn remembered that he was experiencing Arlyn's memory. "The southern kingdoms have already abandoned the Light completely and revel in the forsaken Darkness. It is difficult to ascertain an exact date or even century to the Shadow's reemergence. It is even strong enough to dwell along the edge of the Illumined Wood. Worse yet, those corrupted by the Shadow no longer hide away in their corners as cowards afraid of the Light. They are taking up arms, slowly mind you, but a war will be upon us soon. The Aryl of Lucillia fear that it will be less than two decades from now until they will have no option but to enact the Protection of the Wood; it will keep everyone, friend or enemy alike, from entering or leaving Lucillia."

"I remember that tragic time when it began to move into Cor'le-ra," Dolan said. Devlyn could not remember ever hearing his father's voice, but the sound struck his heart. "A merchant from Gneal came through. He seemed pleasant enough; mind you, I was still very young when he arrived. None of the villagers expected that he would be the one to bring what we most feared. So much has changed in the past thirty years." He shook his head, as memories of the past and present rippled across Dolan's features.

"His family was affected more than most," Evellyn explained. "They were some of the first to give in to the growing Shadow. His brother Lex is head of the village guard. It was most likely he who granted you entrance."

"If not for my early love of you, the Shadow would have consumed me as well," Dolan said with a newfound courage. Devlyn's parents shared silent loving looks. "Sadly, that did not prevent me from leaving Cor'lera when I became a young man—I wanted to get away from my family."

"If you had not left, you would not have returned with the gift of your son, Liam," Evellyn said.

"Our sincerest sympathies. We feared its hastening spread but were unaware that it had touched you so dearly," said a young Velaria. "We have been sent by the Ceurtriarch, the Seven Chairs of Septyl, and the Aryl of Lucillia. The aryl had informed us that the royal line of Lucillia has a secondary branch, which Arlyn was already aware of. They also shared a prophecy spoken by Lucillia herself, many years ago, just before Erynor was banished and she gave birth to Roendryn and Feolyn. 'Two sons of Light I shall birth. Alone, one shall rule. When the Age of Shadow returns and the Darkness all but engulfs the Light, the last bird of Light shall hatch as a new sun rises. The lesser brother shall give his life and the glory of the Light shall shine from Arenthyl and reach every crevice darkened by the Shadow.'

"The wise ones believe that the one named must sacrifice his life for us to have hope for a peaceful future in the Light." Velaria paused for a moment, seeming to catch her breath. "They have two interpretations for the one named. He can either sacrifice his life in a very literal sense, or he can become an ei'ceuril. Their way of life is one of ultimate sacrifice. It has always been such. Lucillia would have known of the ei'ceuril; she could have meant nothing else when she referred to the lesser brother giving his life."

"Devlyn was not the only birth into our world two years ago," Arlyn said, looking tenderly at Evellyn. Queen Vernal Roendryn gave birth to a daughter on the same day. Twelve hundred years have passed since a child of both lines have shared the same birthday. Roendryn and Feolyn were the last ones chronicled by the wise ones. Just as those two were brought into the world together to champion the Light, it is believed that Ellendren and Devlyn share a similar fate."

"That doesn't explain the rest of the prophecy," Evellyn said. "Things are certainly bad, but you don't really believe the Age of Shadow is upon us. Do you?"

"The last phoenix egg protected by the Guardians has hatched. Two of the knights traveled from their citadel to Ceurenyl to inform the Ceurtriarch. Also, there have been rumored sightings of dragons."

"Not one dragon has been seen since the fall of the Erynien Empire. Surely none managed to survive by staying hidden all these years," Dolan said.

"As for that, I cannot say, but you know that there is always hidden truth in rumors," Arlyn said. "There's more. The few Arenthylean coins that we still possess have begun to show markings again. They're faint, mind you, but centuries have passed without so much as a smudge on them."

Dolan received the news with a worried look. "I don't care who sent you. But you won't be taking our son away. You have no right to decide the fate of a toddler. Not even a prophecy can dictate such." A longing stirred in Devlyn at hearing his father defend him.

"The prophecy says that the lesser child must give his life; it does not say how or when. Devlyn is more than free to grow with his family in his own village. We were sent to inform you and lend assistance in any way possible. And then, when the time is right, take him to the Temple of Ceur for his studies."

"If it was only that easy. You know the Shadow lives among us, and its servants are aware of where you hail from. They may not yet know your true nature, but don't expect to be welcomed among the people here," Evellyn said. Distraught, she added, "No assistance can be offered here, Arlyn. I'm sorry."

"Evellyn, if the situation is that dire, come back with us to Ceurenyl or to Lucillia. You'll be protected there," Arlyn said.

"The journey is long and the Shadow has his servants along the entire road. They would hunt us and it would end badly. This is no secret to you," Evellyn said. The sadness in his mother's voice made Devlyn want to cry. "We will keep a watch for the phoenix and tell Devlyn all that he must know. Even if we were to send him to Ceurenyl, he would have to wait several years before he could begin his studies. But think, if the phoenix were to return to Ceurenyl, how long would it remain free and unknown?"

"There remains one thing I can still offer. The nature of this assistance can only protect the children born from you, Evellyn of the line of Feolyn. And I doubt I'll have any strength remaining after I have given it to the two little ones."

"Arlyn, forgive me, but I know what you intend," Velaria cut in. "Such a feat is unheard of and the wise ones cautioned against it. Not only is it harmful to yourself, but the consequences of a kien wielder using the erendinth can be disastrous, even if you only intend to wield lumenys. I implore you, consider the temple's needs for your talents, especially in the coming years as the Shadow grows," Velaria said.

"Listen to your pupil, Arlyn. If the giving of this gift will be detrimental to yourself, please, reconsider. You must preserve your capacity to wield," Evellyn said, also understanding what Arlyn intended.

"The coming Shadow is far stronger than my strength in wielding alone. Withholding this effort would change little in the coming struggle. No greater protection could I offer them and no other use of my wielding could harm the Shadow more than how I wish to at present. I wish to whisper the Mystery of the Wood to Devlyn and Leilyn. Their guardian anadel, a lorendil, will come to them to guide and protect them. I can bestow this gift upon them with your consent.

"Whispering the Mystery of the Wood is no small task. A wielder must call forth the recipient's guardian anadel, mainly with lumenys, but all the seven aspects of the erendinth are wielded. The great influence needed to achieve such a goal comes at a price. Since the one conducting it is a wielder, the price is their ability to wield—my ability to wield. The strength required to accomplish such a task is beyond regular abilities, especially among kien wielders who are prohibited from wielding."

Evellyn and Dolan looked at each other, realizing the price that Arlyn was willing to pay to protect their children. He intended to extend his wielding to a degree that could forever diminish it. Devlyn observed the love they shared for each other in that gaze and was saddened that he had never seen it with his own eyes. And he had never imagined that he would have the opportunity to see it through another's eyes. That was a wondrous gift for his seventeenth birthday.

Dolan, still gazing lovingly at his wife, gave their consent to Arlyn.

Without delay, Arlyn made his way to the inn's sleeping quarters. He walked down the hall past the portraits of Feolyn's line and into Leilyn's room. She slept peacefully and Arlyn approached the bed quietly. Crouched beside the bed, he whispered in a language that Devlyn did not understand. Aelish?

A light began to shine softly from Leilyn's chest. As Arlyn whispered the Mystery of the Wood, shock coursed through Devlyn when he realized that his uncle first embraced lumenys and animys, followed by all the erendinth. Arlyn held an incredible strength and possession over them. Had he entered the Empyrean Sphere and learned how to wield lumenys? He must have.

The light coming from Leilyn's chest dimmed when he finished, and Devlyn felt Arlyn's grasp over the erendinth diminish, as though a mighty river suddenly lost much of its water.

Through Arlyn's memory, Devlyn also sensed that Arlyn also knew his ability to wield had weakened. Pleased with his success with Leilyn, Arlyn bent to kiss her forehead and left the room as quietly as he had entered. It seemed that he had only been in Leilyn's bedroom for a few moments, but Devlyn knew that well over an hour had passed.

Devlyn could also feel his uncle's fatigue due to overexerting himself. Arlyn leaned against the wall for support as he caught his breath.

While the process had appeared simple, it was clearly much more straining than Arlyn had anticipated.

Fortunately, Arlyn's capacity to wield was anything but common. The wise ones had warned him against wielding in general because of its effects on kien wielders, and the certainty that he would lose control.

The wise ones had wanted him to persuade the family to move to Ceurenyl, away from the Shadow's growing grasp over Cor'lera. Before Arlyn and Velaria had left Ceurenyl, he had been advised to offer any assistance he could, but at all costs refrain from whispering the mystery. What the wise ones had not anticipated, was the degree to which Arlyn intended to extend his strength. *It's a good thing I went to Leilyn first*, Devlyn heard Arlyn think, *I doubt I would have had the courage to whisper the mystery a second time after having done so with Devlyn. But how could I abandon Leilyn if it's avoidable? I could not live with myself if any harm came to her because of my lack of courage.*

Devlyn suddenly realized that Arlyn was the only reason that Leilyn had survived the night their father had been killed and their mother and brother taken as prisoners. He now understood what Leilyn had meant, when they had first met in the Illumined Wood, and she had told him that she had been guided to safety by her guardian anadel.

Arlyn moved to Devlyn's room at a slower pace than he usually moved mostly due to a growing weariness but also because he knew that his ability to wield was about to be even further reduced. Doubt flooded into him as he lingered at the door leading to Devlyn's room, appreciating the intricate carvings. His doubts increased the longer he followed the designs on the door. Finally, out of sheer willpower, he managed to open the door, fighting his natural instincts for self-preservation.

A lone candle flickered on the bedside table, illuminating young Devlyn's face with a soft yellow light. The small boy's chest rose and fell slightly as he slept deeply. Realization suddenly washed over Arlyn. Before him lay Devlyn, youngest son of his sister Evellyn, rightful heir to the line of Feolyn and hopefully the one prophecy spoke of as bound to a phoenix and who would lead the Luminari back to Arenthyl. Tears filled his eyes as his doubt was confronted by the truth that lay before him. *Poor child*, he thought, *if I could, I would take this burden from you and let you live in peace.*

The doubt which moments before had gripped Arlyn's mind now dissolved as he approached the side of Devlyn's bed and knelt beside him. He looked first at the child and then shifted his gaze upward to implore Anaweh for strength enough to see his task completed. After a few moments in prayer, he placed his right hand above the child's chest. Again, he whispered in his ear.

The process started as it had with Leilyn, and young Devlyn's chest began to glow under Arlyn's palm, but the light spasmed and flickered. Devlyn felt Arlyn's power diminish to a small droplet.

His physical strength withered with his wielding. Arlyn was thankful that he had been kneeling, otherwise he doubted he would have had strength enough to support himself. Fear gripped him as he realized that he would fail. In that fear, while still linked to the child, he also joined his entire being with the Light, pleading on the boy's behalf, near to collapsing.

Then the small flickering candle on the bedside table transformed. It shone brightly and steadily. The flame of the candle itself grew to such a size that the entire bedroom was lit bright as day. In his deteriorated condition, Arlyn could no longer whisper, but a whimsical sound emanated from the boy's chest, directly below Arlyn's palm, reflecting the whisper he had been sharing. Only, Arlyn's whispering of the mystery had been an imitation of what he now heard. It was like one's own reflection in a river; it was visible and recognizable, but it could never be mistaken for the real thing. Arlyn lost himself in the whimsical sound and light, time itself suspended. When the light began to fade and the tune dimmed, Arlyn felt its absence as an emptiness. The lighting in the room returned to the usual dimmer vibrancy of a small flickering flame, however, the candle was extinguished; the light now emanated from Devlyn's heart.

Astonished, Arlyn placed his head against the boy's heart and heard the whimsical song in Devlyn's heartbeat. Neither the ei'ceuril nor ei'ana wise ones had ever chronicled such a phenomenon. Searching his mind, he was unable to associate it with anything he had read or studied. He began to wonder what such a sign could mean, but in his weakened state, Arlyn was incapable of rationalizing soundly, so he placed the mystery at the back of his thoughts and hoped he would be capable of recalling the event at another time.

As Arlyn attempted to stand, he realized the extent of his fatigue. He had no idea how long the process had required. It could have lasted only a few moments but more likely, it had taken most of the night. Arlyn kissed the boy goodbye on his forehead and stood to leave.

The light emanating from the young Devlyn's chest dimmed and disappeared, casting the room in darkness. Not wanting his nephew to wake and take fright in the dark, Arlyn relit the candle by the bed and left.

# FEATHERS

Treacherous clouds refused to loosen their hold above Gneal and Devlyn could sense the growing anxiety spreading throughout the city. He shifted to a different jienzu form as he counted off his breaths, his body easing and tensing as he shifted. He was trying to get better about practicing the forms every morning as well as spend some of the morning in meditation. Often, he combined the forms and meditation together. There simply wasn't enough time to do both separately every morning, but it seemed to work since he could feel his body strengthening.

Spring had officially sprung and Devlyn had turned seventeen but the new season had yet to show any evidence of itself. The temperatures had yet to warm, and the skies stayed overcast. What was even more regrettable for Devlyn was that Alex had taken every opportunity since Devlyn's birthday to remind him that he and Ellendren were now of marrying age. Devlyn had nervously laughed the comment off the first time, but after what had to be the twentieth time, he had been frustrated enough to want to punch his cousin.

It also hadn't helped that Alex's mother was a staunch supporter of a wedding. Devlyn had no idea how she had learned about elven aryls nor how they had to be married to become an aryl, but she frequently reminded him that he would only become the aryl after he was married. Fortunately, Alex was eighteen and single and Vine had turned the full weight of her matrimonial interest on her youngest son. Devlyn had thoroughly enjoyed Alex's own frustration under his mother's tireless pestering. But Devlyn had yet to see Alex pay any one girl more interest beyond a fleeting glance.

He recognized that Alex and Vine had both made valid arguments. If Devlyn and Ellendren married soon, their troubles with the Luminari aryls would significantly diminish. He was convinced that there wouldn't be further need to plot and plan against Silvia's scheming if they wed. Still, he didn't think they would become the Exalted Aryl of Krysenthiel simply by marrying. Truly, Devlyn only had a faint idea of what their life would look like once they were an aryl. It's not as though he and Ellendren hadn't talked about their future together. In fact, Devlyn had all but declared their betrothal when he had said he couldn't imagine marrying anyone else or seeing any other woman sit by his side as high queen. Granted he had only said those words to soothe Ellendren last year after she had found out that he was a Lorenthien and his claim to the Crystal Throne of Krysenthiel had superseded her own. That all too brief moment they shared alone in the chamber tent came to him again. He still could not believe that he had declared his intentions to marry Ellendren in front of the aryls, telling them that she would also sit on the Crystal Throne. That wasn't an official betrothal announcement, but it was the next best thing.

He still thought they were too young. Destroying the Shroud and getting the Luminari back to Krysenthiel should be their priority. Granted, he was in the minority that thought an early wedding was a foolish move. He had considered confiding in Alex his worries about fulfilling his marital duties since he had no experience with any of that. He knew that he'd regret mentioning that fear to Alex and that his cousin would never let him forget it.

Devlyn tried to calm his thoughts again. Not only were they a distraction while meditating, but he knew that if he didn't learn to properly meditate, his loud thoughts would be heard by anyone who could listen.

After another hour of practicing the jienzu forms and making meager advances in quieting his mind, he went to bathe and get ready for the day.

To distract himself and avoid prying questions about his love life, Devlyn wandered through Gneal's castle, getting to know the place which had been a symbol of oppression for many Perriens and Parendians over the past century. He had discovered early on that Alex had not banished any of the councilors but had only restricted most of them to their quarters. In some cases, he'd moved the councilors to new quarters as their previous ones were better suited to Alex and his growing court. He understood that it was better to keep the deposed Perrien Council here in Gneal rather than allow them to crawl back to Erynor or bolster Lex's army in trying to conquer Evellion. Still, he couldn't decide if he wanted to see the councilors banished or force them into the dungeons they had tossed his family into.

"Hello there, Devlyn," Abbie greeted him from a side corridor.

"Hi, Abbie." He didn't stop and she joined him, keeping pace as he walked along.

"I haven't seen you in the Dream recently. Are you avoiding it again?"

"That place is getting more dangerous with every day. Are you still going there?"

"Don't bother lecturing me against it. And yes, it hasn't been this dangerous since the last time the Evil One was freed, yet the druids still go there. We must stop him from breaking free. If he claims the Dream, no one will be able to pass from this world to the next."

"His prison isn't in Somnaeniel, though."

"No. But as my brother and I have already told you, he'll begin by making the Dream his own domain. It won't be long until pockets of Darkness break through into this world."

Devlyn paused. "Is that what took Alethea?" He hadn't intended to ask the question.

"The Eldinari?" Abbie asked.

"Yes. Something happened to her when we traveled from the Illumined Wood back to the Luminari. It was nighttime and with all the clouds, it was difficult to see what was in the sky, but it looked like there was a tear in the sky with only darkness beyond. At first, I thought it looked like any other clouds. But thinking back, it reminds me more of those voids in Somnaeniel. The ones that Alethea warned were death."

"Then it's already begun." Abbie looked both terrified and thoughtful. "I have to speak to Eagan and the other druids. I don't know how we're going to fight this but avoiding the Dream won't be possible. If the Evil One takes the Dream, Life will die here."

Devlyn didn't know how to respond. Having to deal with Erynor was scary enough but being reminded again that Erynor was only part of Ramiel's plans was terrifying. The draelyn had shown Devlyn what the world was facing. They might have survived during the Elder Days but their home had been destroyed.

"Is there any way to stop him?" Devlyn asked, careful not to use the Evil One's name.

"None that we've figured out yet and until we can reach his prison to see the deterioration, there's little that we can do."

"You want to go to Verakryl—the Tree of Life?"

"I think we have to. We're blind until we can see the actual damage. The longer the Shroud remains, the more disadvantaged will we be."

A guard approached Devlyn and Abbie, bowing quickly. "You'll want to come at once, Lord Phaedryn."

"Is something the matter?" Devlyn asked as he instinctually reached out to Aliel flying somewhere above the castle.

"Nothing dangerous but His Majesty presumed you would like to see for yourself."

"See what?" Devlyn felt Aliel's excitement through their bond.

"I don't exactly know what to call them, my lord."

You should hurry, Aliel conveyed without spoiling the surprise.

"All right, lead the way. Are you coming, Abbie?"

"No. I must speak with the druids. We are running out of time and these wars are a distraction." She turned away.

Devlyn followed the guard to the bailey's outer wall where a small group gathered on a battlement where the wall bowed out in a semi-circle, leaving the bailey itself empty. The area where the group seemed to be waiting had been designed to accommodate archers as a defensive measure. But today, the gathering had the appearance of a reception committee.

Alex was in the center of the group, Vine right beside him. She was taking her role as the king's mother very seriously and ensured that she was always present, whether or not she was needed. The rest of Alex's court clustered about, many shivering in the cold weather as they waited. The clouds were making it difficult to see far in the distance.

"What are we waiting for?" Devlyn asked Alex. He could sense Aliel flying north of the castle, and through their bond, he also sensed that Aliel wasn't flying alone. Had the phoenix found Wyn and Oma on the griffins? That didn't make a whole lot of sense since they would have flown from the south, not the north.

Devlyn had seen maps of Perrien and Parendior, both as a child and more recently. He knew there were several cities and towns surrounding Gneal and some were to the north. But the further north one traveled, the less populated the country became. Except for people who had always lived along the Skrein Sea, no one else willingly relocated there. Even the people who had made a living fishing along the River Arvil refused to gamble their livelihoods on that frozen sea. Civilization had also stopped well before reaching the Wooded Hills of Thellion. That had of course changed since the founding of Alexandria. Alex had used the area surrounding Aewen's Bridge as a base of operations before bringing the fight to an under-protected Gneal.

"Sanjin is returning from the Skrein coast where the Daer have planted their new settlement. He and his hippogriff riders were the best candidates to send north. Not only can they fly but they've dealt with the Daer Empire before."

"Your secret new allies from the other side of the world?" Devlyn smirked. He'd yet to hear the full story of how that alliance had come about and so far, Alex had been too busy.

"I hope Lex hasn't heard of this alliance yet. Our element of surprise was ruined when we took Gneal, but I hope he won't be looking to the sky when we go to Everin." Devlyn locked his gaze north. He had only heard whispers about the Charrenese and their hippogriffs. "That's not right." Alex squinted northeast as figures broke through the clouds. "Would the winds have knocked them that far to the east?"

Having no idea what hippogriffs looked like, Devlyn kept his eyes focused on the approaching creatures. They were only indistinguishable blobs at first but then Devlyn could see their wings as they flew closer. Were hippogriffs supposed to look like ordinary horses with wings? Most of the creatures were grey while a few others were a dazzling white. Devlyn imagined that the grey ones would take on a silver sheen in the sun.

"That doesn't look like Sanjin and his hippogriffs," Karl said.

"It's Lady Aewen!" Aen yelped gleefully.

Aliel buzzed in Devlyn's mind. Those certainly were not hippogriffs. Now that they had come close enough, Devlyn could see that the grey ones were winged horses but the white ones also had a silvery horn protruding from their brows. Leilyn had told Devlyn that Aewen had a herd of alicorn in the Wooded Hills of Thellion but he would never have imagined that he would see that herd soaring through the air. Aliel had joined Aewen and her winged herd as they flew about the city. Gasps and cries of amazement echoed from below. It sounded like the entire city had heard of their coming and had rushed into the streets to see the spectacle.

The bailey was soon awash in a flurry of wind as the winged herd landed there. Devlyn followed Alex and the others down the nearest stair to join Aewen among the winged creatures. She had dismounted and walked to meet Alex and Devlyn. Her silvery gown didn't look like lierathnil but it was clearly woven of a fabric just as remarkable. Devlyn couldn't see a single seam and it rippled like water in the wind.

"Ei'ethil Devlyn Lorenthien." She inclined her head and continued to speak in Aelish or High Aelish, but Devlyn could only recognize his name and the names of some others, most notably his distant relatives that had been long dead.

"Ei'terel Aewen," Devlyn replied when she stopped speaking. He had no idea what she had said or how to address this remarkable woman, and hoped he guessed correctly.

"I was never an aryl and I have not been a queen since my eldest son took his father's throne." She smiled. "A difficult task awaits you, young Lorenthien. As the enemy strengthens, those dear to you have fallen. You know now what challenges to expect—the draelyn have shown you much." At her words, Aewen's eyes locked with his own and he felt as though they stood alone in the bailey.

"How can we sway the dwarves to join us?" Devlyn had no idea whether she was referring to Everin but that was the whole reason he had left the Luminari to come north.

"You must show them that this is not just a war between elves and humans."

"But how? I have no proof that the Evil One is involved."

"Their kind has dealt a loss to him before—you need only remind them."

Devlyn was about to ask her for more details when the world seemed to click. Something had changed in that moment and everyone was staring at him and Aewen as though they each had two heads or had spoken a different language.

"King Alexander Vaerin, I've brought you a gift." Aewen's gaze moved on from Devlyn to Alex as she gestured to the silver winged horses.

"They look like Perrien's grey coursers, but with wings." Alex stared in disbelief. "How are they here—how do they exist?"

"It's rather that the horses you know look like these. After Thellion fell, the herds diminished and their offspring forgot how to fly. If nurtured, the twenty I have brought here do not need to be the last of their kind. The alicorns will return with me—they wanted to bid farewell to their friends but they hope not for long. Elothkar awaits a Thellish king to return." Aewen turned to the alicorn she had flown in on.

"You're leaving already?" Aen had pushed forward and grinned toothily up at her. Aewen gave him an affectionate smile.

"This bailey is too small for Thellion's winged horses, the alicorns, and the hippogriffs." As she spoke, a horn sounded to announce another arrival, presumably the hippogriffs Aewen had mentioned. Her eyes locked with Devlyn's again, and he suddenly felt an overwhelming sense of loss and dread. Faces of loved ones sprang to the front of his mind—Alethea's most prominently. Devlyn blinked away tears at seeing his deceased mentor again. "Alethea might be gone but she is not lost." Aewen said gently.

"Where is she?" Devlyn pleaded. The absence that Alethea had left in his life was overwhelming. Devlyn had grown without either of his parents and had only found his siblings after they had been separated for a decade. Losing Alethea, someone who had helped him touch that interior part of his being, had crushed him. Besides Aliel, there was no one who knew him better than she did.

"You cannot pass through as she did, lest you will both be lost. But if you can find where she is, there might be hope to save her and many others." Aewen flung her leg over the alicorn, her gown swooping after her as though it was part of her.

The feathers that dotted the bailey were swept up again in the breeze created by Aewen and her herd of alicorns leaving Gneal. The winged horses that had been left behind looked expectantly at Alex, one of them neighing and drawing near to nuzzle his face. Devlyn couldn't decide if Alex looked irritated or embarrassed. Whichever sentiment he felt, he brought the creature's muzzle in and petted him, looking at Devlyn questioningly.

"And when were you going to mention that you've learned to speak another language? I know you weren't at Gwilnor long enough to master Aelish. I also remember how poorly you scored on those exams."

"Aelish? I wasn't speaking Aelish. I can barely understand it when it's written plainly in front of me," Devlyn said, confused by Alex's remarks.

"That's because you were speaking High Aelish." Arlyn stepped forward. "You had no idea?"

Devlyn shook his head in response. Other than Aewen's opening remarks to him, he had understood everything she had said as though she had spoken plainly in the Common Tongue. He certainly hadn't noticed himself speaking a different language.

"Great, more elf magic." Alex pushed his hands through his hair and turned toward the approaching hippogriffs. "Well, speaking of magic, it's time you met Sanjin. Don't forget, he's a foreign prince and his magic-person can do some crazy stuff too."

"I've told you many times, my friend, they're Mages of the Kilnae Del." A caramel-skinned young man approached, perfectly at ease wearing gold bands around his biceps and colorful silken garments. "And here is an elf I have yet to meet. I am Sanjin al'Sanhir, Crown Prince of Charren of the Royal House Irithru."

"Pleased to meet you. I'm Devlyn." He stuck his hand out in greeting, distracted when Alex slapped his own head.

"Even the elves use this hand gesture here?" Sanjin looked at Devlyn's hand as though it was covered in slime.

"Some do, but he isn't *just* Devlyn. He's Ei'ethil Devlyn Lorenthien, heir to the Crystal Throne and future Exalted Aryl of Krysenthiel, High King of Eklean, and Prefect of the Guardian Senate," Reia said, her irritated expression mirroring Alex's.

"Truly? We have never forgotten our position on the Guardian Senate. Perhaps my time here in Eklean will bear more fruit than a single alliance with King Alexander. Charren will be the richer indeed if the Guardian Senate returns to its former glory. Even more so now since the Daer Empire has found their way to Eklean's shores."

Alex groaned. "What did you learn from your trip there?"

"Exactly what we already knew. They will leave only if forced to and saying please won't get them off your land either. However, I suggest we turn our attention to Evellion before dealing with the Daer. They'll continue to dig themselves in in the meantime, but they'll be easier to deal with once you have defeated the enemy closer to home. The Daer respect power over everything else; returning from a major victory will place you in a better position of diplomacy with them."

"I doubt our expedition to Evellion will be quick. My uncle has had Everin under siege for almost four years now."

"Then I suggest we leave soon," Reia said.

BESEECHED

Under the ever-present threatening clouds, Devlyn and Aliel were a golden light in the blustery sky. They were part of the advance party flying westward to Belin's Watch, nestled in the Vespien Mountains. The rest of Alex's military force marched south for the Cyrillean Pass to engage the renegade Perrien forces there.

A select group had been chosen to fly the twenty, winged horses that Aewen had raised, and then gifted to Alex. They were the mythical creatures depicted on the ancient crest of Thellion, now Alex's crest. The group not only included Arlyn, Oliver, Karl, Sara, and Reia but fourteen riders that Alex had knighted. Devlyn had overheard Aen demand that Alex reserve one of the creatures for him the moment he was knighted.

Sanjin and his honor guard on their hippogriffs were part of the advance party, but Abbie Wintyr had reluctantly remained in Gneal. While she was certainly eager to join the fight, her main concern was Somnaeniel and the rising dangers there.

Since their entire advance party could fly to Belin's Watch, their travel was cut by a fortnight, and they need only make one overnight camp. They had left the comforts of Gneal's castle yesterday and had camped overnight in tents in the frigid cold. The deep snows across Perrien's hilly terrain would guarantee a slower pace for Alex's army. Devlyn glanced below at the white ground, relieved that he wouldn't have to trek through that snow.

Clouds continued to obscure the mountain range, but as they drew closer, they could finally see the rocky definitions. The peaks disappeared into the unsettling sky that seemed to fall ever closer to the land below. When they had planned their trip to Belin's Watch, Devlyn had explained that they would never find the entrance to the dwarven tunnels surrounding the city, especially from above, so they had decided to head to the part of the city above the mountain that was inhabited by humans.

The clouds made locating Belin's Watch near impossible, especially with the snow that blanketed the mountain. Devlyn at last noticed the wall that surrounded a group of buildings in a huddle, buried in snow drifts the size of houses. He likely wouldn't have recognized them as buildings without his heightened illumined vision. It appeared that a path had been shoveled out in front of the city gate, a task that had no foreseeable end.

Flying over the gates of Belin's Watch would have been an easy affair, but the group was aware of the Watch of Belin who guarded those gates. They had also discussed their approach so Devlyn landed nearest the gate, the warmth from his Phaedryn form melting the snow in a circle around him. The area in front of the gate barely accommodated the rest of the advance party, the sound of hooves, claws, and a bustling of wings following his own soft landing.

As expected, the Watch of Belin hurried out the gate in large numbers, each guard pointing a spear at the uninvited visitors. Archers lined the battlements above the gate, arrows nocked and ready to release. Devlyn and Aliel withdrew from each other and without Aliel's connection, the gloomy frigid weather pressed against him.

A dwarf approached, his visor drawn to conceal his features, but his axe remained poised, pointing at Devlyn. The spectacle of the flying mounts seemed to have had little effect on him. Dwarves cared little for anything that flew through the sky. They didn't even bother with messenger birds.

"So, you've returned. Your crimes have not been forgotten." There was something about the guttural sound of this dwarf that Devlyn recognized. The dwarf lifted his visor.

"I know you," Alex said, shivering in the cold. "You were at the tunnel gate the last time we were here."

"Aye, that I was. But you broke our laws and becoming a king will not protect you," Gorund said.

Devlyn could feel Sara and Reia glaring at him and Alex from behind. He liked the two—Velaria had trusted them enough to include them in their adventure two years ago—but they were ei'ana to the core and their silent judgement filled the hushed moments of astonishment from the others in their party.

"And what law did we break, precisely?" Alex was tired, and cold, and more interested in finding a warm hearth to sit by than answer accusations.

"Don't play daft with me," Gorund said.

"Is it customary in Eklean culture to treat monarchs in this fashion?" Sanjin asked, still on his hippogriff. While the cold seemed to have little effect on the Charrenese prince, his voice did carry clearly. He dismounted to approach Alex and Devlyn.

"I answer to my patriarch, not a boy-king."

"Has Oma returned yet? She would have arrived with an elf from the Eldin Wood," Devlyn asked, wishing they could all get out of the blustery cold.

"Don't think for a moment, elf, that your intentions are hidden from us," Gorund said.

"Good, so you're aware of the giants approaching Everin and are also aware of the consequences of what will happen if Everin falls into Erynor's hands." Reia crossed her arms, ready to breathe fire. Devlyn didn't think she knew about Oma taking Velaria, Alex, and him through the Great Dwarven Tunnel. Surely that was the reason Gorund was so upset with them. Only dwarves were permitted to enter the tunnel that connected every dwarven schtam in the Laudien and Vespien Mountains. Oma had been uneasy with breaking dwarven law but at the time, Velaria had won her over with the urgency of their journey. While they had managed to reach Everin before Lex had launched the Perrien military against Evellion, even that fortified city had not been safe enough for Velaria's liking, and they had quickly moved on to Ceurenyl through a seguian.

Gorund appeared unmoved by the ei'ana's words but he did step aside, allowing them access through the solid gate. "If I hadn't already been ordered to grant you entrance to Belin's Watch, I would drag the two of you to Patriarch Forvl himself!"

Devlyn led their motley group through the gate and tried to remember where Oma lived. The last time he had been here, they had come through the tunnels and Velaria had known precisely how to find the old stone seer. Devlyn, on the other hand, didn't even know how to reach the lower levels of the city. He had no idea how he was supposed to find Oma's cavern without a guide.

Other than a densely packed layer of snow, most of the snow had been cleared from the city streets. That frozen layer would require either a pickaxe or several sunny days to melt it away. Neither of those options appeared likely, so Devlyn walked carefully over the slick layer, slipping with every other step. When he heard a few muttered curses and some exclamations as some of the others slipped and slid, he wondered if he should have stayed bonded with Aliel to help melt the ice and snow where they walked. Rusyl would have melted the packed snow and ice with every footprint and he wondered how the Watch of Belin would react to the dragon walking through the street.

Few of the citizens of Belin's Watch were out and about, so the upper streets were deserted. Warm lights filtered through frozen windowpanes, putting Devlyn somewhat at ease. He had to remind himself that Evellion had been at war for nearly four years now. Cyril, one of their greatest cities, had fallen in a single day. That defeat had not only left the Cyrillean Pass vulnerable to the northern invaders but its citizens were still unaccounted for. No one here in Belin's Watch or any other Evellion city was foolish enough to believe that the now deposed Perrien Council had orchestrated those military maneuvers alone. The people of Eklean knew that Erynor had returned and had his eyes set on reconquering the continent. It was better to stay safe indoors.

A young dwarf appeared just a little way ahead of Devlyn. Like Gorund, he also looked familiar, yet Devlyn couldn't place him. The young dwarf stood to the side of the street, but kept his eyes on Devlyn, ignoring the other elves, humans, and winged creatures. When Devlyn was only a few paces away, rather than introduce himself, the dwarf turned and hurried down a nearby stair.

"You're not just going to let him walk away, are you?" Reia asked, only a few steps behind.

"Do you recognize him?" Alex asked, looking at Reia.

"Enough to know that he's wielded before."

Devlyn and Alex shared a look, both recalling the young kien wielder housed under Oma's care.

"Was that him?" Devlyn asked Alex. He didn't have to explain himself. Alex remembered the dwarf who should not have been allowed to wield just as well as he did.

"Not sure who else it could be."

They gingerly went down the broad stairs that resembled a ramp, hippogriffs and winged horses stepping carefully. Devlyn easily recognized the dwarven sector of the city that opened at the bottom of the stairs into a plaza. Snow and ice couldn't reach these lower quarters, and the dwarves easily walked through their streets as though the city hadn't frozen under the snow above them.

Here, more of Devlyn's memories surfaced. He didn't think that their entire party would fit in the tunnel that would lead to Oma's cavern, so only Alex, Arlyn, Reia, Sara, and Sanjin followed Devlyn down the tunnel, while the others stayed in the plaza with their flying mounts. The further Devlyn walked through this section, the more he remembered of his last visit.

Still, he was grateful to catch sight of the young dwarf, who seemed to be leading them. Velaria had directed them through dozens of turns before she had brought them to an unimposing door, the same door that the young dwarf now stood in front of. The dwarf was clearly waiting for them so they strode through the entryway after him and down the passage toward the cavern that Oma had once resided in.

The thick moisture in the tunnel brought back the distant memory of Oma explaining that it was not actually moisture, but the stones themselves, learning about who walked there. Oma had always made the stones seem alive, and the more Devlyn learned of the erendinth and how Teraeniel had been created, the more he thought that he would not be surprised to learn that the erendinth themselves were living beings. It was a silly thought but Devlyn no longer presumed much. That which he thought he knew or believed true had transformed, leaving what he thought he knew as fact in Cor'lera with the thirteen-year-old human boy that he had thought he was. At the bottom of the tunnel, Devlyn found Oma and Wyn standing at the center of a cavern. Eolwn and Leithel had made themselves comfortable nearby.

"Hmph, I thought you would never arrive," Oma said, striding toward them. "Do you have any idea of the trouble you caused? We almost didn't make it through the tunnel connecting Gwilnor and the temple before the stones screeched about what you had started."

"What I started? I was ambushed. They knew I was in Gwilnor."

"And you should have expected that. Did you bother to test the room for wields before you strode through? You're as blind as the day I met you!"

Alex grinned at the exchange, enjoying hearing Oma scold Devlyn.

"And you," said Oma, turning to face Alex.

"What have I done?" His smile disappeared.

"Hmph, what you haven't done is what concerns me, Alexander Vaerin, *King* of Thellion. How long have you been king, now? And you're just now requesting to appear before the dwarven matriarchs and patriarchs? Do you have any idea how insulted they will be at not being invited to the coronation ceremony, let alone a personal apology for your lapse in etiquette?"

"There wasn't any ceremony; one moment, I was a boy from Cor'lera, ignorant of his heritage, and the next, an elf claiming to be the widow of Thellion himself placed a crown on my head."

"That might be so," said a dwarf entering from a tunnel at the opposite end of the cavern, "but, you will have to learn the proper etiquette if you are to rise above the petty politics of humans."

The dwarf was dressed from head to toe in rich golds, heavy furs, and more jewels than Devlyn had ever seen on one person. Even Queen Alesei of Tiel hadn't worn that much gold—the sheer weight of it would have crushed her. Devlyn had no idea how this dwarf was standing. The excessive amount of wealth adorning the dwarf appeared gaudy, yet it somehow seemed appropriate.

"It's about time you arrived," Oma said.

"My apologies, Mother. Oern Schtam requires my constant attention, as do the other schtams furthest from Everin."

Reia and Sara curtsied and Arlyn raised a hand to his heart and bowed. At a poke from Reia followed by a hissing "Show some respect!" Devlyn raised his own hand to his heart and bowed in the elven fashion. With a quick look at each other, Alex and Sanjin made their own bows.

"Patriarch Forvl VIII of Oern Schtam," said the dwarf, inclining his head to the newcomers. "It's an honor to meet the descendants of so noble ancestry. I'm afraid we haven't the time for niceties. The schtams are meeting to decide our withdrawal from the peoples and wars beyond our mountain halls."

"You're going to bury yourselves away and let the rest of the world burn? The world you are a part of?" Alex said, his voice rising with every word.

"As I said, we have not the luxury for niceties. Now if you want to put an end to this foolishness, I advise you to hop back on those winged beasts outside and get to Everin in all haste," Forvl said.

"Why can't we just take the tunnel? The skies are treacherous enough without having to navigate through mountains," Alex said, and moaned when a rock struck his head a second later.

Forvl glared at his mother who was staring daggers at Alex.

"How much do they know?" Forvl asked.

"What does it matter? You're taking them into the Hall of the Schtams yourself," she said.

"We'll talk about this later, privately," Forvl said. "I'll not have the Great Dwarven Tunnel compromised further. I'm sorry, but you'll have to travel above the mountains. You came with a large group, and I will not permit gossip spreading of its existence more than necessity requires."

"Don't be absurd; our presence was required there a month ago, and this meeting is many more months overdue. Besides, no one outside our mountains believes that the Great Dwarven Tunnel is a myth," Oma said before turning to the young dwarf who had been standing quietly behind them. "Tell Sir Oliver to have the rest of their party meet us in Everin. They needn't wait for us. We'll get there a few days before them, so they won't have to worry about raising an alarm. And take these flying beasts with you."

The young dwarf ran out of the cavern and up the tunnel. Wyn placed a hand on Eolwn and Leithel and the griffins rose to follow the young dwarf up the tunnel.

"Hmph. Now, let's move," Oma said, walking toward the tunnel her son had come from.

Devlyn was relieved that this time, she did not require them to wait until the middle of night to secret them through the Great Dwarven Tunnel. A short walk brought them to the opening into a much larger underground artery, where the visitors paused to take in the wonder.

Thick veins of gold and silver ran through the walls of the tunnel, as water would flow in a stream. It was so spectacular that Devlyn found it hard to accept what his eyes were seeing even as light emanated in pulses along the different veins.

"There's a reason we do not permit other races into our schtams, and it's not because we're inhospitable," Forvl said. "We mine only a minuscule portion of the mountains' veins—a thimbleful that they do not miss."

"You speak as though they are alive," Devlyn said, staring at the thick veins.

"You do not listen. Have you heard nothing of what I've said since we first met?" Oma said.

Resting a hand on a golden vein, Forvl nodded his head. "They have sheltered us since before we can remember but we have never been granted haven within Verinien. There isn't a mountain that would not bow to her and that which she holds in her bosom. And there isn't a dwarf that won't acknowledge that the Luminari were granted that which we desired most. For that reason, my kin do bow to you."

Devlyn was left in silence at Forvl's regard for the Luminari and the mountain on which they had built Arenthyl. He had known that Mount Verinien was a special place, but to hear a dwarf speak so highly of it was a different matter entirely.

"Enough stories, time to go," Oma said.

Pebbles began to crawl up Alex's legs. "Oh, not again. Get ready," he warned the others who had not experienced the process before. The pebbles assembled quickly over his body, pulling Alex into a fetal position until he resembled a boulder. One after the other, the rest became covered in pebbles, too shocked to do more than gasp before they too looked like boulders. *You know, we don't have to roll through the tunnel like a ball*, Aliel conveyed. Pebbles began to climb over Devlyn's feet. He grinned to himself as he tapped that stillness within his heart.

"Hmpf. Think you can race us there, do you?" Oma said, the only other not yet in the form of a boulder. "Fine. Have it your way."

The pebbles on Devlyn's legs receded as Oma became a boulder and nudged everyone through the tunnel. Devlyn watched as they started slowly, picking up speed at a startling pace and disappearing from his sight, bending southward around the wondrous tunnel.

Closing his eyes, Devlyn brought to mind what he remembered of Everin. He needed a clear picture to go where he needed to be. It felt like shifting in Somnaeniel but there was nothing physical about the World-in-Between.

Trying to recall exactly where the others would arrive, he felt himself begin to shift as an image planted itself in his mind. Guilt and embarrassment clung to this memory, making it a much stronger image. A rounded room of light blue marble veined with a darker blue appeared around him. The comfortable sitting room sported a heavily pillowed couch and other furniture that begged one to lounge while sipping tea in pleasant company.

The rounded room dimmed as Devlyn separated from Aliel but the warmth and comfort stayed. He went toward the window, a window he knew looked over the entire city of Everin. Intent on looking out, he passed so closely to the solid desk of stellendae wood that his foot struck it. Gasping with pain, he tried not to yell as he berated himself for not being more careful. Worried that he had alerted the guards to his presence, he heard the door creak as it was pushed open.

Devlyn held his breath as Queen Lara walked into her private sitting room. He had no right to be where he was, uninvited, and readied his words of apology.

It was only when he stepped forward that Lara realized she was not alone.

"Devlyn," she gasped. "What are you doing here…how are you here?" Her voice was no longer that of the excited young woman he had met four years ago. A heaviness weighed her voice down, and her energetic youth seemed to have abandoned her.

"I'm sorry, Your Majesty, I didn't intend to come directly here, but my memories of this room were much stronger than any other place in Everin."

"Did a time warden create a seguian for you? They could have easily opened one in the designated areas."

"I don't know how to explain it, really, but I came here on my own; well, others are on their way, but I figured I might as well arrive sooner since I could."

Lara noticed the phoenix for the first time. A younger expression of elation and wonder showed over the lines of grief as she looked from Aliel to Devlyn. "It was all true, wasn't it? There's still hope." Her voice held a plea that it might be so.

Devlyn closed the distance between them, and aware of the trials she had gone through since he last saw her, took the queen in a comforting embrace.

When the queen cupped her hand over her stomach, Devlyn realized that it had swelled since he had last seen her. His eyes widened in disbelief as she smiled in acknowledgement.

"I'm happy you're here, Devlyn. You've already done so much for Evellion; the Eldinari have become great friends. Truly, their star wardens are the only reason the renegade Perrien forces haven't found a way into the city. But Fendryl has made it clear that the star wardens will not be enough to stop the giants and the Perrien forces together. We need the dwarves' help. I don't know how you managed to get the Eldinari to end their seclusion, but you must do the same with the dwarves."

Devlyn had done little to get the Eldinari to join the war. After Ellendren had called them cowards, Boriel, the enthiel who shepherded the Eldinari, had appeared to the gathered Eldinari aryls and all but commanded them join the fight. Was Devlyn supposed to summon Mundi to do the same for the dwarves?

In Her Own Right

Yellow canvas kept the frosty elements of snow and wind out of Ellendren's spacious tent, and a brazier in the center kept it cozy. It would have been her father's tent if he had survived the fading of Lucillia. She had never imagined that both of her parents would pass beyond the veil so soon. They had known the price required for the Protection of the Wood but it was too high a price. It was the one thing that Ellendren and Silvia agreed on—her parents should have never raised the shield. She didn't think anything would have changed and highly doubted that Lucillia's prophecy required both her parents dying before the Luminari could return to Krysenthiel. All they had gained was three years of inaction behind that shield, while their allies fought off the Erynien Empire.

Despite the dawning of spring, the frozen air refused to abdicate its hold on Eklean. It felt like winter remained in full force. Yet the full moon of Aurenth and the middle of spring were only a week away, with it the Luminari feast of Aurephaen. She would have to leave for the Temple of Ceur and meet Devlyn in the coming days. They had to learn how to wield lumenys and he wasn't doing it without her.

While the cold weather unsettled her and every other Luminari camped between the hills protecting Erithel and the Shroud, the lack of sunlight was dampening their spirits. Ellendren felt herself grow depressed with each passing day. The sun's disappearance behind the sickening clouds appeared more forced than nature allowed.

Many of the elves stayed inside their tents most of the day for warmth, something Ellendren couldn't understand. Even though her tent was one of the larger tents, she had to get outside several times a day to keep her sanity.

Fresh powdery coats of snow never lasted long, and even the sight of it had lost its beauty after the long winter. The puffy white snow had been packed firmly into the dirt, which melted during the day and froze anew at night, forming a muddy ice. All her finer silks remained packed away; not only were they not warm enough but the muddied ground would stain them beyond remedy.

Regardless of what she chose to wear, the golden Vyoletryn pendant showing two elves, each holding a staff with an eagle soaring above them, was always pinned on her tunic. She might not be an ei'ana yet, but she belonged to the Vyoletryn School.

A strong gust followed Kaela through the tent flap into the tent. Ellendren saw so much of their mother in her older sister. She feared that she would never amount to her older sister's strength, noting how her imprisonment at the Yanilean's Keep had barely affected her resolve.

The flap closed and the tent's temperature settled once more.

"Any news from Devlyn?"

"None." Ellendren was reading a report that listed the needs of their encampment. She received a similar report every day, and no matter how she responded, the report the following day would arrive as though nothing had been addressed or resolved the day before.

"There's been some interesting stories trickling down from Ceurenyl," Kaela said.

"How interesting?"

"The depressing sort. Claims that the Seven Chairs have betrayed Septyl, and that one of the Chairs is being held captive for her crimes."

"Have you heard which one?" Ellendren asked, then realized that it mattered little which Chair was a prisoner of the Tenebrae. Any of them being captured was detrimental to Septyl.

"I think she's one of the younger ones. But no one has been able to say with any certainty. After all, the number of travelers that manage to leave the city are limited. Our dear brother is doing everything he can to keep Ceurenyl under lock and key."

A low growl rumbled outside the tent. Rusyl was listening to their conversation and several images flashed across Ellendren's mind. The blue dragon was making it clear that he intended to join her when she left for Ceurenyl. His sister, Yelaris, had a special relationship with Velaria and if Velaria was in trouble, Yelaris would move mountains to save her. Rusyl would help Yelaris.

Putting the report on her desk, Ellendren pressed her thumb and forefinger to the arch of her nose. Something dreadful was happening in Ceurenyl. She had no idea if it was limited to Gwilnor or if the entire city had fallen to the Tenebrae's influence. Knowing that they had claimed Gwilnor as their own was troubling enough; the damage they were capable of was almost too much to consider.

Gwilnor had always been a place of inspiration and education for her students, most of whom were eager to learn to the best of their abilities. That's how she had always envisioned herself as a student, believing others shared similar sentiments. After all, gaining admittance to the most prestigious school on the continent was no simple task.

She wanted to hop onto Laureniel and soar over the city's walls in the quiet of night. She wanted to fight her way through Gwilnor and free the school of the evil that spewed from the mouths of the traitors she had once believed were ei'ana devoted to Septyl. Her own training and advancement among the ei'ana were delayed because of their presence and refusal to leave Gwilnor alone. If the Tenebrae remained in control, she might never profess the Ei'ana Counsels.

The last thought was too difficult to consider. Ever since she had been a child and had learned that the phoenix had not chosen her, all she had ever wanted was to become an ei'ana. She still remembered that exhilarating moment when she had stood before the Seven Chairs as a tiny eleven-year-old. Her mother had wanted to delay her from beginning her formal studies so young, but if anything, she was a determined girl. A trait that only intensified as she grew. Ellendren wondered how her life would have been different if she had not gone to Gwilnor at such a young age. She could have had a couple more years with her mother and father.

She wasn't one for dwelling in regret, so she pushed those thoughts aside. She would be going back to Ceurenyl soon enough though. Not to liberate Gwilnor or anything so foolish and risky, but to enter the Empyrean Sphere with Devlyn. Granted, from every account she had heard, that might be riskier than walking blindfolded into Broid.

"Have you lost yourself in your thoughts again, sister?" Kaela asked.

"Not completely."

"Well, that's a relief since I've been meaning to ask you something, and I need your full attention."

"And what might be so interesting as to require my complete attention?"

"As I'm sure you're aware, we are without an aryl. At present, the other aryls have more authority than the descendants of Lucillia do."

"What are you getting at?"

"Simply that we are currently lacking an aryl." Ever the skilled diplomat, Kaela sounded as though she wasn't trying to press anything.

"And…" Ellendren knew her sister had no intention of leaving it there.

"Are things as serious as everyone seems to believe between the Phaedryn and yourself? He did make a rather interesting declaration in front of the high aryls not so long ago. I know the Narielles are not particularly pleased, but I assure you that they do not share the popular sentiment."

Ellendren felt her cheeks flush at her sister's sensitive questions. "I am quite fond of him."

"And I'm quite fond of our brother as well." Kaela mocked Ellendren with a flip of her gold and silver hair over her shoulder. "I wasn't asking if you were merely fond of Devlyn."

"We've only just turned seventeen."

"Yes, you're both very young, but as I said, we are without an aryl and you have reached marrying age. The longer you remain unmarried, the more influence our family will lose."

"You can't seriously be recommending a wedding at our age," Ellendren said.

"I don't think you should rush into anything, but you know just as well as I do that the longer we are without an Exalted Aryl, the more comfortable will the other aryls become with the idea of not having one aryl above the others. And to put it less delicately, the sooner you marry, the sooner will my own position among our family be settled."

"How do you mean?"

"Sister, as long as you and Devlyn are unwed, you remain the heir to the Roendryn aryldom. If you're to be a Lorenthien, the Roendryn aryldom will pass to me, of course, and I cannot presume to assume that mantle until you belong to House Lorenthien."

"Don't you think it's proper for House Roendryn to fade with Lucillia?" Ellendren had thought extensively about her family and their future role in Krysenthiel.

"Our family has served the Luminari for twelve hundred years, I do not think it is proper for our house to fade and be swallowed by another. You are the only one of us to be joining House Lorenthien, sister. Father abdicated our house's monarchical role among the Luminari; he did not disband our house."

"I suppose I took it differently. I do not wish our house to fade either."

"Splendid. Now, hurry up and marry Devlyn." Kaela laughed as she teased Ellendren. "And just imagine what might happen if Devlyn meets someone else before you two are wed. She won't be as beautiful as you but he's a handsome boy from a powerful lineage. Don't expect that he won't draw the eyes of other girls vying to stand at his side. And don't expect them to play nice either. They'll want his affection and what comes with it. Devlyn might quite literally be a shining prince, but he has the same weaknesses as every other man."

Jealously and anger rushed through Ellendren at the thought of Devlyn allowing another young woman to ensnare him. As she bit her lip trying to come up with more rebuttals and convince herself that Devlyn would never allow someone to snatch his attention, relief rushed through Ellendren when Byron called for permission to enter.

The Lord Knight came in, dressed in his ever-present burnished steel and the tabard of Lucillia.

"Viren has returned with a full company of Guardian knights. They have requested the presence of a Lorenthien, but since Devlyn has not yet returned, they request your presence, Ei'lythel."

"Of course," Ellendren said. "Would you care to join us, Kaela?"

"I would be delighted." Her eyes seemed to light up at the mention of Viren.

Ellendren and Kaela followed their uncle across the extensive encampment to the fabled Guardian knights who waited at the outer edge of the tents. There weren't many elves out and about, but when they met someone walking along the path, Ellendren made eye contact and offered encouraging smiles.

As they approached, Ellendren quickly counted almost a hundred men and women, standing in a crescent formation a few rows deep. All of them were clad in semi-opaque armor made of woven golden metallic ribbons, the same armor Viren wore. It looked safer than what other knights wore and seemed to offer more flexibility as well.

Even among so many Guardians, Viren was easily identified, standing among others in the front line, but noticeably not in the center. A woman stepped out of the formation at their approach. She held a helmet beneath her arm and a crystalline sword hung from her waist.

With a hand to her heart, the woman bowed in the elven greeting and introduced herself. "Jeanne Darkel, leading officer of this band, and by extension, because we are all that is left of our order, First of the Guardians. We were charged under Ei'terel Ithendryl Lorenthien to protect the last remaining phoenix egg and to supply assistance to Eklean when called upon."

The Guardians were all Luminari with golden brown hair and silver eyes. Jeanne seemed to be a little older than Viren, although by elven standards, she might be a thousand years older, especially since these Guardians had survived from the time of Ithendryl. The absence of the Jewel of Life was only beginning to affect them since the phoenix had hatched seventeen years ago.

"Thank you for your service. I'm certain Ithendryl would be proud of your dedication and sacrifice," Ellendren said. "I am Ei'lythel Ellendren Roendryn, heir to what was the Lucillian throne."

"Viren informed me that a Lorenthien lives and has bonded with the phoenix," Jeanne said.

"Yes—his name is Devlyn. A previously unknown shoot of the Lorenthien line, as well as the Feolyn line, one of the twin sons of Lucillia, who freed our people from Erynor."

"You will have to tell me more of this Lucillia; Viren has spoken often of her. Ei'lythel, is it true that you and the Lorenthien are betrothed?"

Ellendren blushed. "We care for each other, but we are still young. This is only our seventeenth spring."

"But you were born on the same day?"

"We were." Ellendren didn't understand how that mattered.

"Only a Lorenthien aryl can sit on the Crystal Throne. Krysenthiel will need her Exalted Aryl," Jeanne said.

"Of course." Ellendren felt her sister smiling behind her and opted to change the subject. "Have you agreed to accept new members into your ranks?" All anyone seemed interested in talking to her about was her marrying Devlyn. Were they pressuring him just as much as they were her?

Jeanne raised an eyebrow. "Has Viren not mentioned how many years are required before one can be knighted?"

"Years we might not have." The fire roiling in her wanted to scream at this brusque woman. "Need I remind you of our delicate situation?"

"You remind me of someone I once knew." Jeanne crossed her arms and held Ellendren in her own silvery gaze with the slightest hint of a smile. "We can begin the enlistment process but know that it is doubtful that any additional Guardians will be knighted before our fates are sealed." Jeanne Darkel bowed again and turned to the knights standing behind her. With a swift motion of her hand, she dismissed them and the formation broke, the knights beginning to lay out their own tents in orderly fashion on the perimeter of the Luminari tents.

Ellendren turned to Byron. "Perhaps you could recommend candidates for the Guardians?"

"Of course, Ei'lythel. I should remind you, Krysenthiel had no knights of her own. Palace and city guards, sure, but Krysenthiel had no formal military."

"What do you suggest?"

"I think you know what I suggest."

"I believe I do. Is it possible?"

"We can start small, with a manageable number of our elite. As time passes, more can join the Guardians. Some of the aryls might not approve." Byron didn't have to mention which aryls he was thinking of.

Snow crunched beneath Toryn's finely made leather boots. She still hadn't grown accustomed to wearing anything of that quality but loved that her feet stayed dry and warm. She'd never be able to go back to wearing shoes that weren't custom made for her.

When she had marched with the Luminari from Lucillia, part of her had wanted to stay where her city once stood. She wouldn't have had to march through this snowy and frozen land, if she had stayed under the boughs of the Illumined Wood. She didn't necessarily care for the trees, but it had been home.

"And how is the Lady of the Watch today?" asked Jaek, sneaking up on her.

The title King Harnyl Roendryn had bestowed upon her still belonged to her by right, but there was no longer a city to watch over, only a large cluster of tents sitting on the frozen ground. Those tents had made her job even more difficult. Every pathway was an entrance to the Luminari encampment and their only defenses were what they had carried. In Toryn's opinion, the two dragons and that woman with the red eyes were much welcomed additions.

Smacking the back of his head, Toryn did her best not to smile at him. That was difficult, especially when he smiled at her and it seemed that he was always smiling at her.

"After all this time, my cheery grin still bothers you?"

"I said no such thing."

"Your eyes certainly did. You might enjoy it, if you let yourself."

"Have you just come to bother me and keep me from my duties?" Toryn asked, avoiding looking into Jaek's eyes. Looking into those eyes of his was dangerous. Once, she'd felt her knees waver from looking into his eyes.

Jaek continued to follow her as she strode toward her command tent. It was a modest accommodation, one that also served as her living quarters, even if the only evidence was a folded cot pushed to one side against the canvas. She hadn't brought any personal memorabilia from Lucillia like her father had. He was still living with and serving House Narielle, who had a few tents to accommodate their household. On top of the Narielle's possessions, he had to also see to his own. Toryn didn't know where he found the time.

As she was about to push back the tent flap, she heard a quiet shuffling sound inside the tent. Stopping to listen, she heard two people talking inside. She gripped the pommel of her sword and looked at Jaek, not surprised to see that he too appeared ready to confront the intruders.

"There's no need for that," came a voice from inside the tent.

Releasing the pommel, her sword fell back into its sheath as she pushed the flap open and walked through to see the Lord Knight and a woman she had never met before. Despite Byron's position and title, the woman sat at Toryn's desk, her hands folded on top. Her eyes bored into Toryn, delving into her very soul.

"Can I help you?" Toryn asked.

"That remains to be seen," the woman said, leaning over the desk. There was a frightening intensity about the woman, something that made Toryn want to stand back and disappear into the crowd. "I understand that you were the one who saw that the Protection of the Wood was fading." This woman's assured tone gave Toryn the feeling that she never misspoke.

"I did. It was only streaks of faint light and if anyone cared to look, they would've seen them as well."

"But they did not. You did and you were awarded the position of Lady of the Watch." Toryn nodded, not sure how she felt about this woman who had yet to introduce herself. "My name is Jeanne Darkel, First of the Guardians."

"And which order is that?" Toryn asked. Yet another knightly order!

"You might know them as Eklean knights or Guardian knights."

Whatever breath remained to Toryn vanished at the mention of the legendary name. "You jest."

"I will offer you one chance. Byron recommended you along with a handful of others that we can manage to train due to our current diminished numbers."

"To what purpose?" Toryn asked, looking at Byron rather than at

Jeanne.

"The young woman who will likely become the next Exalted Aryl with the Lorenthien heir has requested that we enlist elves here into our ranks." Jeanne turned to Byron. "It is irregular. Devlyn and Ellendren cannot become an aryl, the Lorenthien aryl, until they are wed, and even once they are wed, they cannot presume to lead as the Exalted Aryl until they are crowned as such in Arenthyl. When the Crystal Throne is unoccupied, the leadership returns to the aryls communally—there has never been a steward in that role of leadership. That aside, the Guardian knights answer only to the Guardian Senate, and seeing as the girl is not the prefect of the senate yet, she is stepping beyond her position. Much has been forgotten by the Luminari."

Caring little for political strife, Toryn simply looked at the First of the Guardians and waited.

"Naturally, you will have to relinquish your current position. The Guardians hold no ties to individual kingdoms, not even Krysenthiel, which most of our rank hails from."

"What will this entail?"

"You will be assigned to a Guardian as a squire."

"I thought only children were squires."

"Anyone who wishes to become a Guardian must first squire with one of our number; it is an integral aspect of our formation."

"Who will I be squiring for?"

"You will have to share the duties with Byron here," Jeanne said.

"You're going to be a squire too?" Toryn asked, incredulous. She was shocked that the Lord Knight of Lucillia had been reduced to a squire.

"I will not tolerate such outspokenness from my squire." Jeanne, her arms crossed, smirked.

Swallowing, Toryn felt the reality wash over her. Everything she had ever dreamed of was coming to pass. She had no interest in becoming a squire at her age, but if she swallowed her pride, she would become an Eklean knight—no, a *Guardian knight*.

35

INTRUDERS

The proportions of the meeting place for the patriarchs and matriarchs of the Schtamite made Devlyn uncomfortable, although
none of the dwarves seemed to be bothered by its size. Alex, Wyn, and
Sanjin seemed just as unsettled by the voluminous space but didn't dare
comment on it in front of the patriarchs and matriarchs. Even Lara and
Fendryl seemed out of their comfort zone down here in the Hall of the
Schtams. Significantly taller than it was wide, the room's height made it
feel smaller than it was. Devlyn's eyes followed the simple lines of one of
a forest of monolithic pillars that stretched up to the vaulted ceiling, a
ceiling that was barely distinguishable due to its staggering height.

A large, circular stone table sat in what might have been the center
of the hall, and around it, ten sizable thrones with a pillar behind each
throne had been placed. Eight of them were currently occupied, the schtam of each seated dwarf identified by stone crests that hung above the
thrones. The two vacant thrones of the southernmost tribes were there
as a reminder that they had been cut off from the Schtamite.

The bold, gold script of the crests was unfamiliar. It did not have
the languid flourishing of the scripts taught at Gwilnor, nor did it have
the multitude of letters of the languages he was accustomed to. There
were only two figures engraved on each crest, and Devlyn assumed the
sturdy lines depicted an entire word, rather than a single letter.

A multitude of dwarves stood behind the table and thrones,

grouped behind their respective leader. Devlyn recognized Uon of Glyol Schtam easily enough, as he stood closest to his matriarch.

With a longer look around the room, Devlyn was amazed at how different the dwarves were from each other. Before, he had clumped the entirety of the dwarven population into a single kingdom but he now realized that each schtam was a kingdom in its own right.

As for the matriarchs and patriarchs themselves, it seemed that the only trait tying them together was their disdain for fabric garments. If they did wear some type of cloth, it was hidden beneath layers of gold and precious jewels. The cut and colors of their clothing was as dissimilar as the clothing worn by the villagers in Cor'lera to those worn by the people of Yanil. Each schtam had its own rich culture.

Most intriguing about their garments were the quantities of gems—diamonds, rubies, sapphires, emeralds, and others—that had been embedded into the attire. Amid the jewels, larger rivulets of gold hung about their persons, but the gold was unlike any Devlyn had ever seen. It appeared fluid and seemed to flow whether the wearer was moving or not.

As lavishly as the matriarchs and patriarchs were dressed, their demeanor was anything but the calm regality usually presented by monarchs and nobles. Devlyn was aware that the presence of elves and humans in their mountain halls had infuriated them, something clearly demonstrated by fists banging against the stone table while they thundered in their own language. Schtach was not one of the languages spoken or taught by any of Gwilnor's magisters, so Devlyn could count on a single hand the number of times he had heard it before today.

Before walking into the chamber, Oma had instructed them that no one was to speak once inside. She'd seemed to hold Devlyn's attention for a moment longer, as though she really meant him. Surprisingly, Aliel had been provided with a golden perch made of the same material worn by the dwarves. The perch's magnificence was amplified by the phoenix's light.

Devlyn's attention waned as the dwarves continued to argue. The meeting had started at least two hours ago, and Delyn's legs grew tired. Prince Sanjin's patience was long gone and Alex's expression mirrored it. While Lara didn't seem impatient, she did seem tired. She was the only visitor offered a seat, and that was in recognition of her late pregnancy. Only Fendryl and Wyn displayed a heightened attentiveness, their eyes quizzical. It looked as though the Eldinari understood the discussion between the dwarves.

When a resounding bell tolled through the hall, the matriarchs and patriarchs stood, spoke what sounded like a pledge in unison and left, each in a different direction through the forest of pillars. The rest of the dwarves followed them, and Devlyn's group followed the Oern Schtam dwarves into their antechamber.

Patriarch Forvl VIII of Oern Schtam sat on his golden throne, which Devlyn could only assume was in fact solid gold. The throne was five times larger than necessary, but the patriarch sat in it as though it could still be bigger. He spoke privately to a dwarf twenty years his elder standing beside him.

Devlyn stood a few paces from the oversized throne with Forvl's heavy gaze looking down at him.

"The patriarchs and matriarchs were not pleased that I invited guests into our sacred chambers. Yet, it is my right to do so," Forvl said.

"Will they fight?" Alex asked, pointedly.

"It's undecided as yet."

"What were you talking about then?"

Forvl shared an impatient look with Alex. "After their anger abated, we discussed whether or not intruders should be invited to speak on behalf of their realms."

"Intruders? You invited us," Alex said.

"You will remember your place. You might be a king, but this is not your kingdom." Forvl frowned at Alex.

"And what happens if Everin falls? How long do you think you'll be able to keep Erynor from forcing his way into your tunnels and claiming your schtams for himself?" Alex thundered.

There were only a handful of times that Devlyn could remember seeing Alex this upset, yet for perhaps the first that he could recall, he shared in that anger toward the dwarves and their unwillingness to involve themselves in the struggle beyond their mountains.

It appeared that the patriarch was about to explode and expel Alex from the dwarven halls, probably indefinitely. Devlyn did notice that Lara seemed to look at Alex in a new light. Foreign monarchs rarely, if ever, fought passionately for another kingdom.

"Hmph. Stop this bickering and tell them what was decided before the bells toll again," Oma said. "Men. Doesn't matter what race you belong to; you'll see us all dead because of your thick-headed arrogance and pride."

Alex crossed his arms, while Forvl gripped the arms of his throne. Fendryl and Wyn smiled at each other and stayed quiet.

"I argued to allow the Thellish king and the Lorenthien heir to the Crystal Throne of Krysenthiel to speak."

Alex's face softened, but his arms remained crossed, as though he had spoken rightly.

"Was it agreed?" Devlyn asked.

"Only you are permitted to speak. We have maintained a great respect for the Guardian Senate, and since the Lorenthiens had overseen that revered council as prefects, the schtams have consented to permit one such as yourself to speak."

Devlyn was still trying to understand what his ancestors had created, both in Luminare, and in Eklean. Whatever relationship they had established with the dwarves all those years ago was a mystery to him. "When?"

"In three days, you will speak before us. I would recommend getting plenty of sleep between now and then. It will be taxing and you will have to be prepared to sway the patriarchs and matriarchs to join your cause," Forvl said.

Aurephaen was three days away. "I have to be in Ceurenyl at dawn on Aurephaen. Is there any way we can meet before?"

"The other matriarchs and patriarchs have left. The day cannot be changed," Forvl said.

"I have to leave before the sun rises on Aurephaen." Devlyn knew the dwarves were stubborn, but surely, they could make an exception.

"The matriarchs and patriarchs won't appreciate having a time and limit dictated to them."

"It's in regard to learning how to wield lumenys and removing the Shroud from Krysenthiel; to free Mount Verinien from that cloud of death." Devlyn tried to keep his frustration from his voice, but knew it simmered over. He hoped that mentioning that mountain would help sway the patriarch. There was a long pause, and then Forvl spoke.

"It shall be done. We too want that sickness covering Mount Verinien destroyed."

Still irritated with the stubborn dwarves and their inability to see the danger they were in, Alex imagined that having some alone time would brighten his spirit. He simply did not want to be around anybody for the rest of the day, especially not nobles and diplomats. Now that he was the King of Thellion, every word he said was scrutinized. *Better to hide away while angry than regret whatever I end up saying in public*, he thought. He didn't need another lecture from Reia on his propriety.

Alex headed to the suite Queen Lara had provided for him and threw himself on the bed in the cold room.

With the lengthy siege, the availability of many resources had diminished in the city. Fortunately, the dwarves had kept their trade routes open through the Great Dwarven Tunnel, which kept the city from being entirely crippled after the four-year siege. Still, wood could not be spared for all the castle's fireplaces and many rooms had a decided chill.

As he lay on top of the heavy blankets, he pondered his relationship with the Evellion queen and wondered what it would evolve into. Evellion had strict laws for its citizens, nobility, and royalty. Just as Devlyn couldn't become the next elven king—or whatever name they called it—so too was Evellion's monarch restricted to the male lineage. Only a son of the royal house could ascend to the Eagle Throne, although it was not required that he be married.

It was an old law, one that was still observed, in Evellion of all places. Most of Eklean's kingdoms had branched off from Thellion after its civil war had shattered it, but they had all developed their own rituals and customs rooted in Thellion. Evellion shared many similarities with Sorenthil and were close allies with each other, but Sorenthil had never based its monarchy on gender. The Sorenth seemed to have had more queens than kings in its history.

Lara and Amry did have two daughters and Lara was now pregnant with their third child. Alex did the math regarding Lara's pregnancy and realized that she had to be close to delivering, considering how much time had passed since Amry's assassination. The oldest daughter kept to herself, but the younger was often at her mother's side. She was still quite young and required the constant attention of her nurses. Alex had noted that she would be an incredible beauty, resembling her mother and father. If Lara didn't give birth to a boy, the monarchy would likely pass to a royal cousin. The next in line for the throne was the Duke of Cyril, if he still lived. He might have been among the first to be killed when Cyril had fallen four years ago.

Alex had only been in Everin for a day, but he had already discovered the varying levels of hierarchy and the plethora of titles shared by the residents. It seemed that every citizen of Evellion had some prestigious title or could trace their lineage back to one of Thellion's great houses. It was a relic of the kingdom he now led. He had no idea why it was improper to refer to everyone as lords and ladies. Instead, he had to learn their proper titles, and was expected to know their standing among the nobility.

Already, he had met four barons, three counts, and a duke. Due to the war, there was an increased number of nobles residing in Everin. Only the foolish nobles had remained in their country estates and as far as Alex knew, correspondence with them had completely halted. His uncle had likely already raided and ravaged Evellion's estates.

Not every noble had come to Everin though. The Dukes of Hanil, Overen, and Belin's Watch remained in their own cities, and it was unclear what had become of the Duke of Cyril since that city had fallen.

The matriarchs and patriarchs would not reconvene for three days, which was fine with Alex. He had little interest in venturing into the frigid city as he had the last time he'd been here. He remembered little from that occasion other than waking up with a headache some time later in Ceurenyl.

Although the bed was indeed comfortable, Alex didn't really want to spend the entire evening in his quarters. He rose and went into the corridor where two knights wearing blue tabards with a white eagle emblazoned on the left breast stood by the door. Since he couldn't bring his own men through the Great Dwarven Tunnel, he had been assigned two of Evellion's knights for the duration of his stay. He didn't have any reason to distrust the knights, but he did remember that it had been one of Evellion's knights who had assassinated King Amry.

"Do you know where I might find a sparring yard?" Alex needed to let off some of the frustration he was still feeling. The time he'd spent alone in his room had not provided the relief he needed, but he shouldn't have to worry about what sort of trouble his mouth could get him into in a sparring yard.

"Certainly. This way, if you please," said the knight on the left. He led the way through the castle to the sparring yard. Alex was delighted at how spacious it was. Even better, the yard was nearly empty. Only a young woman near his own age was there practicing archery. The girl had long blond hair pulled back in a thick braid with a blue ribbon loosely intertwined through. She stood a good deal shorter than he did, but was still tall, not as tall as Ellendren or other elven women, but definitely taller than most humans. Her clothing was finely made, but unlike the other women he had crossed paths with in Everin who tended to wear dresses, she wore loose blue trousers and a white blouse.

Her back to Alex, she pulled her right arm back to nock the arrow. It loosed with a speed that surprised him as it thwacked the target thirty paces in front of her.

"I reserved the yard for the afternoon," she said without turning to look at him, pulling another arrow from her quiver. "You'll have to return later."

"You don't prefer company?" Alex asked, now understanding that there was a reason for the empty yard.

"No."

"Would you mind if I join you? You're really impressive with a bow."

"I would mind. You'll have to return later." A second arrow struck the target.

Alex didn't want to leave. There was something about this young woman that was incredibly captivating to him. It might have been because most of the young women he had been around since leaving Cor'lera were studying to become ei'ana, capable of doing things that he was uncomfortable with. He might view their abilities differently if he could wield as well, but that was not a skill he desired to acquire.

"Would I offend you if I asked for your name?" Alex asked carefully, taking a step toward her. He tried to remember all his etiquette training and the rules around manners.

"What kind of a silly girl would become offended by someone asking for her name?" she said, turning to face Alex.

Alex felt his heart leap in his chest, and he suddenly wanted to stand closer to the young woman whose name was still a mystery. There were many beautiful young women at Gwilnor Academy, and he had even met a few who had tugged at his heart strings since he'd left, but none had had this effect on him.

A few strands of hair not caught up in her braid fell in front of her bright blue eyes. She had a perfect nose and the most beautiful lips he had ever seen, although there was no hint of a smile. If not for her alluring appearance, he would have thought her eyes icy.

"I'm Alex…uh, sorry, Alexander Vaerin." He bowed, but kept his eyes focused on her.

"Diana, Princess of Evellion." She did not offer a curtsey in return. Instead, she focused once more on the target in front of her, pulling another arrow from her quiver, aimed and the arrow struck the target again. He tried to ignore the chills that ran through his body as it dawned on him that he was talking with one of Evellion's two princesses, the eldest daughter of Lara and Amry. If she had been a boy, she would have already been crowned the next King of Evellion.

"You must share your secret. You're a talented archer."

"For a girl? You were going to say for a girl." Her head snapped round toward Alex, her eyes even icier than before. How was that even possible and why did that make her even more captivating to him?

"What? No, I…I meant nothing of the sort," he stammered.

"I'm sure. Well, if you're not going to leave, you might as well stop dawdling," Diana said.

Alex could only imagine what his mother would think of him bantering with Diana as he went to pick out a bow in the nearby weapons rack. His mother didn't think that anyone was good enough for her children, especially now that Alex was a king. He still had to marry though, more so now than before, and if his mother had anything to do with it, it would be soon. The reminder of his brief discussion with Vine regarding siring heirs still left him uncomfortable, even sick to his stomach. That was the last of that sort of conversation he ever wanted to have with his mother. She had even asked if there was a chance he might have sired any bastards. He winced as he honestly had no idea—no one had ever mentioned it.

"Here, try this one," Diana said, their hands brushing each other as they both went for the same bow. Diana immediately pulled her hand back. Alex blushed and tried to avoid considering what his mother would think of Diana. She was a princess, and that had to count for something, even if she wasn't a 'nice girl from Perrien.' His mother had never had anything kind to say about Evellion—few Perriens did.

The bow was finely made and felt like yew. Nocking an arrow and raising it to eye level as he'd seen archers do, he stood beside Diana—as close as he dared.

She no longer held her own bow but scrutinized Alex's stance instead. "Have you never held a bow before?"

"The Septyl knights at Gwilnor focused more on swords and shields than bows."

"So, they neglected to instruct their pupils in archery."

"It's not like I was there for an extended amount of time."

"Well, as a king, you should learn to use the bow. But don't expect that you'll be permitted near any battlefield. Especially with the current life expectancy of monarchs."

"I'm sorry," Alex said, remembering her father's assassination and feeling a little embarrassed. He dropped his arms, no longer straining to hold the bow and arrow ready.

"He knew the risks. The coward with the knife paid the same price. Now lift your elbow."

RUSHED

The Oern Schtam's antechamber felt colder than it had three days ago, yet an anxious sweat still clung to most of Devlyn. He knew what he had to say to the dwarven matriarchs and patriarchs but couldn't stop his nerves from getting the best of him. He still shied away from the memory of not being able to give the Luminari aryls a proper display of himself as a Phaedryn. Aliel was here with him now though, perched on the back of his chair. Keeping the phoenix out of the tunnels would have accomplished little. The dwarves knew what the phoenix were. They might have never bonded with them in the way that the Luminari had, but they knew the nature of the anadel among them. They recognized that Aliel was a lorendil. They seemed to know more about guardian anadel than they were letting on.

Oma sat quietly nearby with her eyes closed. Lara, Fendryl, Alex, Sanjin, Wyn, and the others were no longer welcome in the Hall of the Schtams, so they waited above the tunnels in the comfortable but still chilly castle. The matriarchs and patriarchs were deliberating privately in their hall before allowing Devlyn to speak to them. In all the dwarves' history, there was no precedent for this occasion. Considering the concession they were making, they had refused any other guests.

Stifling a yawn, Devlyn went over what he had prepared to say. He was exhausted. He had not slept well due to jitters, and then had had to wake up early. He was grateful that the dwarves had agreed to meet before dawn but meeting last night would have been preferable. They had outright refused an earlier meeting. As much as Devlyn didn't want to hurry their decision, he had little time to waste. Aurephaen would start at dawn and Devlyn had to meet Ellendren at the Temple of Ceur before then.

He had asked the elves who could wield lumenys whether there was any other way to learn to wield that transcendental erendinth, but they had all agreed that entering the Empyrean Sphere was the only way. The easiest way to do that without dying was to pass into the shaft of light in the Chamber of Light. Ellendren insisted that today was their best chance to successfully enter the Empyrean Sphere and not die. She was convinced that Auriel would protect them as the sun rose on his feast day. Ellendren was always thorough in her research and if this was the only way she believed they could reach the Empyrean Sphere safely, then Devlyn had to be there.

He had no idea how long it would take to remove the Shroud with lumenys but waiting until next year before he could even try was out of the question. The entire Luminari population was living in tents on the outskirts of Krysenthiel now, the Shroud looming in the distance. But before he could ensure the safety of his own people, he had to strike an alliance with the dwarves. If Everin fell to Lex's forces and the approaching giants, the entire kingdom of Evellion and the revived kingdom of Thellion would follow.

Devlyn wished Ellendren was here for these negotiations; she was always the better speaker, and she understood the finer points of diplomacy. Unlike Devlyn, she was less likely to offend the dwarven leadership by misspeaking. He was all too aware how the dwarves would close themselves off in their schtams if Devlyn unknowingly affronted them.

Even with the possibility of accidentally insulting the dwarves, Devlyn was more concerned that they would be scrutinizing his every word. The matriarchs and patriarchs would determine the Schtamite's role in this war based on Devlyn's plea. Their scrutiny would only intensify because of his inability to speak Schtach. He had noticed their varying dialects and how they differed significantly from the dialects spoken in the northern and southern reaches of the Vespien Mountains, and even more so from those of the western and eastern reaches of the Laudien Mountains. Yet another dialect was spoken in the Shadow Mountains, but those schtams had been struck from Schtamite. Confusing one dwarven dialect for another was just as unforgivable as claiming the Nuntol and Zorik schtams still belonged to the Schtamite. Devlyn knew not to make that mistake, even before Oma had drilled the point into him over the past three days of preparation.

A dwarf that Devlyn had never met walked into the antechamber. Devlyn thought she might be Forvl's daughter, since she appeared younger than the patriarch of Oern Schtam and wore just as many jewels.

"Are you ready?" Her voice was gruff but kind.

With a nod, he stood. Oma remained seated with her eyes closed. Devlyn had expected that she would have continued to instruct him in what to say and what not to say while they waited, but she had kept quiet the entire time. She didn't even open her eyes to see him walk off.

I'll be with you the entire time, Aliel conveyed to Devlyn.

If only I could communicate with the dwarves as we do, then I wouldn't have to worry about how what I say comes across.

Encouragement flooded through Devlyn, easing his anxiety. It felt as though he stood in front of a roaring fire in a cheery inn. He breathed in the warmth Aliel shared and walked through the antechamber into the room with the round stone table and the golden thrones.

A heavy silence pervaded the room. Devlyn felt everyone staring at him as he crossed to Forvl's side; as his guest, it was only proper. Once there, Devlyn wondered if he should greet Forvl. Was there a protocol he had forgotten? None of the dwarves spoke; they seemed to be waiting for him to begin.

Aliel's reassurance again washed through him, the warming light a comfort. With a silent gulp, Devlyn opened his mouth to speak, and realized that he didn't know the proper way to address the dwarven leaders. Again, he wished Ellendren was present—she would have never permitted such an oversight.

"Esteemed Matriarchs and Patriarchs," Devlyn began, finding it a safe avenue, "I wish to thank you for your generosity in allowing me to stand and speak before you at a time where it is easier to distrust strangers. I have come before you on behalf of all Eklean, and by extension, all Teraeniel and even Somnaeniel. The Erynien Empire has regained its vengeful strength and threatens to once again shadow the land with slavery and death. The southern kingdoms are already on Erynor's leash, and he pushes ever northward, hoping to crush all resistance to achieve ultimate dominion.

"Through some sinister magic, he weakens the Evil One's prison. His presence is visible in Somnaeniel. Pits of black ooze cover that place, and a turbulent sky has claimed it. That corruption is spreading to our world. Rifts have started to appear and swallow any who get too close. Truly, we've already lost a great elf. If we do not unite and overcome the Erynien Empire, every person of every race will know the fear and butchery Erynor wishes to force on us. The Evil One will not remain bound if Erynor steals the continent away from us." Pausing for a moment, Devlyn wondered what else he should say. How much more was needed to sway the dwarves to join? The dwarves had to already know the severity of the situation.

"Tell me, young Lorenthien," said a matriarch sitting across the table from Forvl. The crest hanging on the pillar behind her indicated she belonged to Glyol Schtam. As expected, Uon stood nearby. Her heavy jewels moved with her as she shifted, reflecting colorful light across the table. "We were once promised a gift—we understand that it was through no duplicity on your ancestors' part that that gift was not delivered to us, but should we help, we will expect that gift."

"And what gift do you speak of? What was promised to you?" Devlyn had not expected this. He didn't know anything about a gift. The matriarchs and patriarchs all shifted on their thrones, casting even more colorful rays around the room. They all knew what the Matriarch of Glyol Schtam meant.

"Access to the Lieben Stone."

The words sank into Devlyn. The Jewel of Life had many names—Ceurendol among the elves, and the Lieben Stone among the dwarves. "When you say access, what do you anticipate? It was always meant to be shared with everyone."

"We have no desire to remove it from its place in Arenthyl," said the Matriarch of Glyol Schtam. "Only that the Schtamite be granted privilege to enjoy the benefits of unending life, as was promised."

Before Devlyn could respond, a low rumble sounded and the room shook, sending dust from the ceiling onto the stone table.

The matriarchs and patriarchs looked at each other, then turned to the dwarves who had accompanied them, issuing instructions in Schtach, the differences of the various dialects evident as they all hurriedly spoke at the same time.

A second vibration and more rumbling followed.

Devlyn felt Aliel's concern flood through him. *Is it the giants?*

Yes.

Cold sweat returned to his brow. "Will you help us?" Devlyn asked, looking across the large table to the matriarchs and patriarchs. The sun would soon rise, and he had to be in Ceurenyl, enter the Empyrean Sphere, and return to Everin to help defend the city. He didn't have time for deliberations.

A third deep rumble echoed in the distance.

"We need your assurance that we will have access to the Lieben Stone," said the Patriarch of Jopht, brusque and determined. "We must be assured that it will not be used in a monetary manner. Our fear is that the Lieben Stone will be dangled in front us and only the wealthy will have access to it, draining the Schtamite of all our resources as we grasp for Life immortal."

"Ceurendol was created to remove the possibility of death from every race. My ancestors created it, knowing they too would become dependent on it for their own Life immortal to endure. It was never meant to be withheld from other people for the benefit of the Luminari. My ancestors sacrificed everything to create it—they gained nothing from its creation and ask nothing for access to it."

"We are agreed?" asked the Matriarch of Undol.

"We are agreed," Devlyn said. "Any dwarf of the Schtamite will be granted access to Ceurendol's fruit of life if they journey to Arenthyl. You have my word."

Each of the matriarchs and patriarchs stood, and in turn, struck their chest with their right fist, and spoke the name of their schtam. Eight times they repeated the action.

The dwarves that attended the matriarchs and patriarchs then left the room in a hurry, leaving Devlyn with the dwarven leadership. "Do you have an army prepared to protect Everin?" Devlyn asked, his fear rising with every rumble from above.

"Everin is lost," said the Matriarch of Undol.

The words pierced Devlyn in the chest.

"You just agreed to help us."

"And we are," said the Patriarch of Audun. "The mountains and walls encircling Everin can protect the city from almost any enemy. But they will not keep a giant from crossing. We are bringing the city's population into our halls. Not even a giant can force his way in if we do not wish it."

Struggling with the prospect of abandoning Everin to the giants was incomprehensible. Devlyn wracked his mind for a way to hold off the giants. Everin was one of Eklean's largest cities. Abandoning the city without a fight felt wrong. How many cities would they have to abandon because an army of giants joined in the coming battles? And no one had even mentioned the dragons at Erynor's disposal.

Devlyn had no idea what a fight with a giant entailed, or what the chances of success were. He felt for that quiet place within his heart. The room transformed as the familiar lighted vision greeted him, illuminating the dwarves and amplifying the magnificence of the gold they wore.

Time was limited and Devlyn was sure he couldn't reach the tunnel leading to the surface in a timely manner. Closing his eyes, he visualized a place just outside Queen Lara's sitting room. It still held the strongest sway over him in Everin, and it was high enough over the city to easily determine the giants' location.

Devlyn opened his eyes to frigid air. Wings aloft, he hovered above Everin, where confusion and panic consumed the city below as horns sounded in the predawn hours. Thousands of people ran out of their homes into the dark streets, following the instructions of the dwarves.

The people of Everin had spent the last four years under siege, in perpetual fear of Perrien's army breaching through their tunnels and claiming the proud kingdom. Four years of confidence that Perrien was being held at bay had been shattered; now every citizen, every soldier, and every noble rushed from their homes to seek shelter and protection among the dwarves who had remained indifferent to Evellion's plea for four years.

Turning from the chaotic exodus below, he looked toward the mountains surrounding the city. He couldn't see any sign of the giants, but the rumbling continued. The sound of earthquakes permeated the valley and surrounding mountains.

Angling upward, cold wind rushed past him as he headed toward the distant rumble. The mountain between the sound and himself was enormous and sheathed in snow and ice. Devlyn had no idea how the quakes weren't triggering an avalanche. Even if the dwarves tried to mount a defense of the city, nothing could be done until the giants reached Everin's walls.

He passed into the treacherous clouds wreathing the uppermost reaches of the mountain. He knew the mountains surrounding Everin had their own names, names that recalled great kings from Evellion's past. They might even honor great dwarves. Whoever they were named after, the mountain beneath and before him was one of the largest he had ever come across. Only Mount Saecrien and presumably Mount Verinien in Krysenthiel could be larger.

His connection with Aliel kept him warm as he flew high above the snow and ice below.

Then, rather than continue upward, he angled his wings to take him around the narrower peak of the mountain, to bring him toward the sound. Now, the thumping was no longer in the distance, but below. Clouds and mist obscured his view, but his lighted vision caught movement on the mountain slope. It looked as though large boulders were moving uphill. It was an unnatural sight that his eyes could not reconcile. Descending, Devlyn brought himself beneath the clouds and his heart sank.

Giants easily walked through the deep snow, leaving enormous footprints in their wake. They walked as easily as he would through a light, powdery snow. Devlyn understood why the matriarchs and patriarchs had decided to abandon Everin for their halls below the mountain. Even the safety of that stone hall now seemed questionable.

The mountains surrounding Everin provided some protection against the giants' advance, but the natural barrier would not halt them. As for Everin's defensive stone wall, the giants would find it a mere obstacle. If they did not push the walls over, they could easily climb over them.

Devlyn flew toward Everin, the wind now blowing strongly against him, and falling snow forcing him to shield his eyes. He made his way directly for the castle to find Lara and Alex. He didn't have the luxury to go into lengthy explanations about what had happened in the Hall of the Schtams. Devlyn had no idea how he was going to quickly share the dwarves' agreement to an alliance that also meant giving up on Everin either. He had to get to Ceurenyl!

Devlyn reached Everin's palace and rushed through the entry hall without separating from Aliel. "Where's the queen?" he demanded of the first knight he saw.

"In her throne room. The Thellish king and the elf lord are with her," the knight replied. He understood the gravity of the situation having felt the tremors just as everyone in the city had and had likely already received a message from the dwarves. They raced to the throne room.

The knights standing guard there opened the doors and Devlyn saw an exhausted Lara sitting on her throne, her advisors gathered on one side with Fendryl, and Alex, Arlyn, and the rest of the Thellish advance party on the other side of the throne. There were a number of nobles gathered there, although Devlyn couldn't understand why they weren't out in the city doing something more useful given the approaching giants.

"What have the dwarves decided?" Lara asked.

"They want us to abandon Everin."

"We cannot. Surely they know their schtams will fall if Everin does." Lara looked at her advisors. "Is there any way to force the dwarves' hand in helping us mount a defense of the city?"

Devlyn looked anxiously about and caught Arlyn's eye.

"You cannot wait another moment," Arlyn said, reminding the others that Devlyn had important reasons for leaving now. They had all understood and accepted it but that was before the giants had made their presence known. Before, Everin only had to concern itself with Lex's forces. But now, the long-standing threat of the giants was a reality—they were here.

"Can't this wait until after we are safe? Surely you too won't abandon us?" one of Evellion's nobles said.

"If he stays here, much more will be lost." Arlyn moved to Devlyn. "They are still a long way off—they won't reach the city until the afternoon. We'll hold them off as long we can if they reach us before you return."

"The Eldinari star wardens will mount the defense until we devise a better plan," Fendryl said.

"But what about the dwarves? The most they're willing to do is open their halls for us to escape," Lara said.

"I think I have an idea that might force the dwarves into action," Alex said.

Devlyn didn't have time to hear Alex's plan. The longer he waited here, the longer it would take for him to return. With a final apologetic look around the room, Devlyn vanished.

HOPE

Howling winds lashed across Devlyn's face when he appeared on the highest balcony of Gwilnor's tallest tower. The Dragon Tower was both memorable to him and one of the few places he felt safe shifting to. He didn't think he'd run into Razcul or any of the Tenebrae ei'ana up here. He had considered going directly into the Chamber of Light but had no idea what might happen if something went wrong. There were too many unknowns with that shaft of light and his newfound ability to shift.

Taking a cautious look around the balcony that ran along the tower's outer rim, Devlyn wondered again what the state of the castle was. He hadn't heard any news about what had happened after he was here last. No one in Thellion or Evellion had heard about the recent events at Gwilnor; in fact, they only knew that Gwilnor was in peril because he had told them. He was sure that Velaria was captive somewhere in the castle below, assuming she was still alive—a thought too difficult to consider. He hoped the students had been able to escape following her sacrifice. The lack of communication coming out of the largest settlement of wielders in all Eklean, possibly all Teraeniel, was terribly troubling.

Devlyn feared the Tenebrae ei'ana and shadow elves had expanded their control past the castle and had seized control over the entire city. He dreaded what was happening in the city streets if shadow elves were walking openly. Risking a look toward the city gate and the grey defensive walls, he was relieved to see them intact with turrets strategically spaced. A long bridge crossed the river beyond it, connecting the mountain road over the watery ravine to the city. Devlyn could not say why but seeing the gate whole and secure brought a sense of relief.

The city appeared just as he always remembered it. Few people moved about the streets, but the marble fountains in the main plazas splashed water as they always did, even at this early hour. From his vantage point, he noticed the lightening sky and first flicker of sunlight in the distance and leapt from the Dragon Tower's balcony. The entire castle came into view as he flew toward the temple, looking over his shoulder only once to take in the entirety of it. The seven towers pierced the sky above the courtyards formed by the castle's long halls and chambers connecting the towers. Those seven-sided towers were taller than any stone structure should be capable of. Even in its burnt condition, the East Tower looked as imposing as ever.

Pushing Gwilnor from his thoughts, Devlyn focused his view on the Temple of Ceur. White opulent stone, almost transparent, formed the seamless dome at the top the structure, with half and quarter domes spilling out below it to buttress the great central dome. The temple stood above the entire city that flowed down from the mountain it clung to.

Devyn reached the temple and flew across the arched bridge over the narrow stream flowing from the mountain. As he did, the Arenthylean bells began to toll. The robust sound of the first bell of the morning rung through the city, a single bong resonating and signaling the start of Aurephaen. That bell was followed by a symphony of all the other bells, twenty-four total and each different, welcoming Aurephaen in a wondrous tune.

Devlyn alit in front of the public entrance. Despite how much he enjoyed flying, there was always a reassuring feeling whenever his feet touched the ground. Twelve temple knights stood guard, the large doors behind the knights towering over them. Devlyn had never seen such a large guard at the temple entrance before.

"My Lord Phaedryn," said the knight standing in the center. "Princess Ellendren is waiting for you in the Ceurtriarch's quarters. She told us to expect you."

"Thank you," Devlyn said as he pushed the doors open, not caring that the knight didn't use Ellendren's proper title. Stepping into the dark corridor while bonded to Aliel as a Phaedryn offered a new perspective of the mysterious entrance. His illumined vision did not brighten the darkened length—it seemed only the Chamber of Light was capable of that—but the ominous feeling he typically felt in his stomach was absent. Familiar columns on either side lined the length, representing all the peoples of Teraeniel.

Reaching the far end, Devlyn met the seven ceremonial temple knights. "Who wishes to enter the Light?" they asked in unison. Hearing them speak took Devlyn back to the first time he walked through this space when he was only thirteen.

"Ei'ethil Devlyn Lorenthien. I am not worthy to enter into such splendor, but by the will of Anaweh, the Creating Light."

The doors parted and opened, transforming the vast corridor behind him. Incredible light poured into the space. He wondered about the symbolism of this ritual. What was the point of entering the temple only to walk through a darkened corridor before reaching the explosive light? Devlyn had never considered the architecture and function of the temple as symbolic before. The more he thought on it as he stood looking into the deepest reaches of the Chamber of Light, the more he thought that it must tell a story or represent a historical event.

One step into the Chamber of Light, he felt the same warmth he felt when bonded with Aliel spread from within his heart and wash over his entire body. Never having experienced this odd, yet somehow proper feeling, Devlyn found himself incapable of moving his feet further. When he considered the feeling, he realized that he was rather unwilling to move.

As he stood still, Devlyn thought he heard someone call out to him.

It sounded far off and otherworldly. Could it be the six-winged anadel calling him into the Empyrean Sphere? Devlyn perked his ears to listen more attentively, perhaps even devotedly. Entering the Empyrean Sphere was the whole reason he had come here.

"Devlyn—oh, don't be ridiculous, Dev, you're not in euphoria," said a familiar and welcoming voice.

Refocusing his eyes that he had yet to close, Devlyn spun around to see Kevn. Devlyn smiled and went to his friend who he had not seen in what seemed eons.

"You're still here?" Devlyn asked as he withdrew from Aliel. Oddly enough, nothing about the Chamber of Light changed. Typically, when he parted from Aliel, everything dimmed.

"Not for much longer," Kevn said. His studious and blank expression made it seem as though he had just been pulled from a book or tome written in Aelish.

"You sound cheerier than when I last saw you."

"I suppose so."

"You've made your decision then, I take it."

"Once my business here is done, I will make my way to Septyl."

"The palace-city of the Ei'ana? What about the Shroud?" Devlyn stared back. Had Kevn figured out a way past the Shroud? Dozens of questions were half formed before Kevn could reply.

"I hope you'll have that taken care of before I get there. If not, I'll wait as close as I dare." Kevn had them walking again. "Now, come on, Ellendren's waiting for you. She's with Aaron. She seemed agitated and rushed, likely because you weren't here yet. So, I left her and her brother alone to catch up."

Kevn led him around the perimeter of the Chamber of Light, lest they start floating to the domed ceiling. When they reached the large, beautiful, and intricately carved doors that led to the Ceurtriarch's quarters, Kevn easily pushed them open. Only two knights stood guard, and they stood by as Kevn moved into the antechamber. As Devlyn started to follow Kevn, his eye was caught in the beautiful molding above the doorway into the antechamber. Devlyn followed the lines and features upward, where they culminated in a single, inset jewel. The jewel was a beautiful emerald color, reminding him of the color his and all the Luminari eyes had been, until they had all returned to silver when their pilgrimage along the Illumined Wood had ended.

It was not the first time that Devlyn had noticed the jewel above the Ceurtriarch's door, but it was the first time that it caught him within itself. Transfixed in its depths, he heard Kevn ask him something, but the words didn't register.

Purpose and resolve filled his interior mixed with feelings of unwavering possibility and promise. He saw every dream he had ever dreamt in the jewel—every fear squashed by the sheer strength of his longings. The feelings started in his mind and flowed through him, warming every part, before resting with his already weightless heart.

Ellendren and Aaron had seen the two of them through the opened doors and came out to greet them, curious about why Devlyn and Kevn lingered.

"You made it!" Ellendren hugged Devlyn and Aaron smiled warmly.

"I almost didn't. We had just reached an agreement with the dwarves right before the giants reached Everin. They haven't attacked yet, they still had another mountain to scale but they were already making the city quake as they marched," Devlyn said from over her shoulder as he hugged her in return.

"You make it sound like that just happened within the hour," Kevn said.

"Less than, actually."

"How is that possible? Did a minum open a seguian for you?" Kevn asked. "I thought they were all in hiding."

"Not exactly." Devlyn scratched his head. "Because of my bond with Aliel, I can shift between time and space at will. It was how I accidentally escaped a shadow elf and the Tenebrae ei'ana at Gwilnor a couple of months ago," he said.

"Sounds useful," Kevn said as Devlyn looked back up toward the jewel above the door.

"Devlyn, is that…" Ellendren breathed, also looking up and getting caught up in the green jewel.

"It is."

"Are you going to stand in the doorway all night?" Kevn asked.

"Through the *portal*, is hope endured," Devlyn recited, remembering what Aaron had said were some of the last words spoken by the previous Ceurtriarch as he died.

"Who would have thought Ealyndol had spoken so literally," Aaron said. "Don't just stare at it, take it. You'll need that if we're to get Ceurendol back whole."

Devlyn bonded again with Aliel and floated upward to reach for the lucilliae above the Ceurtriarch's door. The green shimmering light filled his vision with a wondrous hope, dimming when his fingers grasped the warm jewel of hope. Suddenly, everything seemed possible and within reach.

Returning from the height to the others surrounding him, Devlyn held the lucilliae for them all to gaze upon. Each took it in their own hands to allow the hope of their shared ancestors pour into them and fill their being. Aaron gave it back to Devlyn and he in turn placed it with the other three lucilliae inside the coin purse he'd pulled out of the secret pocket against his chest. The mix of violet, indigo, blue, and now green lights flurried across his vision before he closed the pouch and returned it to the pocket. It was now noticeably bulging against his chest. He didn't know how much longer he would be able to carry them on his person, especially now that others were aware of what he carried.

"Shall we go inside? Ellendren has already told me why you both came." Aaron led them into his apartment.

The sitting room appeared just as Devlyn had last seen it. Ellendren sat nearest her brother on the only couch, while Devlyn and Kevn took the chairs. Ellendren looked concerned about something and Devlyn didn't think it was related to their current task.

"What's happened?"

"I received a letter from Hannah. She expressed her extreme displeasure at my lack of cooperation with Gwilnor Academy and its ei'ana and students," Aaron said.

"Is that all?" Devlyn tried not to laugh at the absurdity of the Ceurtriarch supporting the Tenebrae seizing control of Gwilnor.

"She's all but demanding my support to encourage the missing ei'ana and students to return to Gwilnor. Apparently, the Seven Chairs arranged a coordinated escape from the castle and quite a few have disappeared. However, a number of those who were meant to be part of the escape didn't make it out." Aaron paused, letting the gravity of the situation sink in. "Velaria and Liam are among that number."

Even though Devlyn had known that Velaria had been captured, hearing it again didn't make it any easier. And the news that Liam too was a prisoner, again, made it worse. Hadn't he suffered enough? Instinctively, he knew that Jaerol was already planning a rescue mission to save Liam. He'd try to rescue as many as he could, but Devlyn knew that he would go back for Liam, just as Ellendren had come after Devlyn and his abductors last year.

Devlyn weighed his options. The only reason he had come to the Temple of Ceur was to learn to wield lumenys. Ellendren had been certain that they would be able to enter the Empyrean Sphere today. The sun was rising as they spoke, and as the elves of the dawning sun, they had to try it now. As much as Devlyn wanted to help save Velaria and his brother, he had to get back to Everin first. People were likely already thinking that he had abandoned them, the dwarves would break their shaky alliance, and the giants would scale unhindered over Everin's defensive walls soon enough.

"Well, let's stop wasting the hour and get you two into the Empyrean Sphere and back. I'd rather not think of the repercussions of you not getting back to Everin as soon possible," Kevn said, speaking what Devlyn thought.

"What about Gwilnor?" Devlyn asked, still torn between who needed him more.

"Let us worry about Gwilnor," Aaron said with a look at Kevn.

"Right, well, I'm sorry to tell you both this, but there's little Aaron or I could tell you about the Empyrean Sphere. It's a wholly different reality. None of my research was helpful or even close to the actual experience. Not even the temple's oldest scrolls offered any insight," Kevn said.

"So, what, we just stroll through the center of the Chamber of Light and wait there to float away into another realm?" Devlyn asked.

"Is there any way to prepare?" Ellendren asked.

"Enter with an open heart. It can be quite scary actually, but that feeling fades," Aaron said, holding his sister's hand comfortingly. "A seraph, a six-winged anadel, is there. The key to returning from the Empyrean Sphere and not moving on to Lumaeniel for good is to have the express desire to learn to wield lumenys for the sake Teraeniel—all of it, people, animals, land, trees, water…you get the point."

"You didn't find it in a book, did you?" Devlyn asked.

"If there's any mention in a book or scroll, I haven't found it, and it's not from lack of trying either," Kevn said, his eyes shifting to the corner where a messy stack of old leather-bound books sat.

"If not from books…" Devlyn trailed off as realization struck. "You didn't? You knew the consequences!"

"We did—to both. The risk was necessary," Aaron said. "If it wasn't for Kevn, we likely never would have returned."

Standing, her brother still grasping her hand, Ellendren turned to Devlyn. "We can't linger here. There's no telling how much time will pass once we cross over, and we're both needed elsewhere. You need to get back to Everin."

Devlyn caught the look between Ellendren and Aaron; the gaze shared between them spoke volumes of their relationship. Devlyn knew Ellendren loved her brother, and the look he saw between them reminded him of how much he missed Leilyn and Liam.

THE SERAPH

Devlyn walked with Ellendren into the Chamber of Light, Aliel hovering at his side, the intensity of the light increasing with every step he took. He held Ellendren's hand in his own, unwilling to lose sight of her in the blinding brightness.

The Chamber of Light was massive; walking directly across took nowhere near as long as walking along the edges, however it still took longer than one might expect. Step after step, Devlyn and Ellendren moved forward until the luminous light ceased shifting, and Devlyn could no longer identify their direction. The walls of the ill-defined space clouded, reminding him of a dream.

Devlyn felt Aliel's presence and encouragement to bond again. They did, and just like in the larger chamber his vision didn't change in the shaft of light. Wings folded against his back, Devlyn felt a familiar weightlessness, no longer feeling the pressure of his body weighing him down. Still grasping Ellendren's hand, they floated and seemed to be moving upward. There was nothing to gauge direction in the blinding light.

Heart already opened due to his and Aliel's bond, and Ellendren holding his hand, Devlyn felt something shift—the light no longer brightened his vision, but a terrifying and all-encompassing darkness claimed his mind. The experience reminded him of the first time he had bonded with Aliel, and how that quiet light within his heart triumphed, but this was not an internal darkness. Devlyn felt every fear and doubt press against him. He could not see it physically, nor even imagine it, but the solitude of this darkness consumed him. His entire past stretched behind—every choice he had ever made weighed as though on a scale.

Holding Ellendren's hand helped. She kept him grounded and the terror at bay. As firmly as he held onto her, she held on just as hard to him. He couldn't imagine coming to this realm without her. He didn't think he could survive this darkness on his own without her.

Blinking didn't help alleviate his disorientation here; his eyes might as well be closed for all that he could see. Not even the light given off from his bonded form with Aliel pervaded into this space. So complete was this darkness, that he couldn't even see his illumined body.

A presence more powerful than anything he had ever encountered thrummed through his consciousness, permeating his entire being. Whatever it was, it was everywhere. Devlyn felt it from every side—above and below. He tried to stay strong and confident for Ellendren, knowing she was doing the same for him.

Terrifying flames exploded around them; Devlyn felt his eyes burning from the intensity and even his skin felt as though it peeled away from his body. The fires roared through his being, delving into the most interior place within his heart, tapping and engulfing it.

Soaring around him and Ellendren, the fires brushed against them, repeatedly swooping inward and then out to return to the sphere they floated in. Devlyn wondered if this was the place they sought, or if it was something entirely different. It certainly was not what he had expected when he'd first heard of the Empyrean Sphere, imagining it as a place of wondrous light in the World-Beyond. Was this folly—had they made a mistake coming here?

Somehow seeming to know his doubts, Ellendren squeezed his hand tighter.

The unrelenting flames continued to roar but gaps in the inferno began to show. Six distinct swashes became visible as they loosened their hold around Devlyn and Ellendren. As the flames unfolded, Devlyn saw they all originated from a singular point, a fiery figure, brighter than those blinding flames.

A face of light looked at them from a figure that resembled a person, its legs and arms difficult to register, but it remained recognizable.

ONLY ONCE BEFORE HAS A WEDDED PAIR STOOD BEFORE ME, thundered the voice. Devlyn knew the creature was speaking to them, not vocally, but in their minds.

"We have not married," Ellendren squeaked, her voice weaker than Devlyn was accustomed to hearing.

YOU STAND BEFORE THE SERAPH, HEARTS AND HANDS JOINED—IT IS DONE— YOU ARE ONE.

Devlyn dared a glance at Ellendren, her eyes wide with wonder, and in that moment, he recognized her as more than the young woman he loved, the woman he hoped to one day marry. He saw his wife. He saw Ei'terel Ellendren Lorenthien, just as he knew she saw Ei'denai Devlyn Lorenthien. And together, they were the Lorenthien aryl.

Lost in her gaze, Devlyn felt his heart ablaze and without any clear intent to do so, he kissed his wife.

WHAT DO YOU SEEK? the seraph thundered in their minds.

"To wield lumenys, to help bring Balance to Teraeniel," Devlyn replied. This felt like an impossible dream.

Two of the seraph's wings moved and the flame from one wing reached into Devlyn, just as the other reached into Ellendren. His entire being exploded in a burning desire, stronger than anything he had ever felt. Bonded with Aliel, and now with Ellendren in a connection just as intimate, Devlyn felt yet another's presence.

Ellendren no longer appeared as he remembered her, but her clothing disintegrated, and her entire body was alit in the light he was accustomed to only seeing about himself but had never seen cast upon another. Golden wings of her own flowed from her back, her silver eyes became golden, and her entire body glowed a vivid golden light. Instinctively, he knew she was bonded with Tariel.

Left in shock and awe, Devlyn looked from her to the seraph. "How is that possible?"

Forget not where the phoenix come from.

The fiery seraph began to fade, and it was only then that Devlyn noticed his surroundings diminish with the seraph. It was like the Chamber of Light, but more. The Empyrean Sphere had a brightness and subtlety that nothing in the World-Below could emulate, and not even the World-in-Between could mirror. Hundreds, perhaps thousands, of anadel floated around them. There was no identifiable horizon, it simply continued, everything continued outward and beyond.

Fog seemed to roll over his eyes, his surroundings dimmed and faded. Looking around, Devlyn saw that he and Ellendren were simply back in the Chamber of Light. The dimming was their withdrawal from the Empyrean Sphere.

Weight pressed back down on Ellendren's legs as gravity returned. She stumbled and felt a piece of fabric slide over her shoulders. Aliel and Tariel filled the Chamber of Light with their harmony as they flew through the domed space. Her heart felt light at the sight of the two phoenix before realizing that the fabric placed over her shoulders was all that was covering her. Devlyn blushed as he tried to avert his eyes.

She recognized Devlyn's outer lierathnil garment and pulled it more closely about her body. She knew that he had seen her and that he still found it difficult to look away from her. To her surprise though, she didn't feel as anxious as she had expected with Devlyn seeing her naked for the first time. Instead, something burned inside her chest. That desire bloomed inside her as she remembered him naked in the past. She had always felt comfortable with him and his moments of unintended nudity had never bothered her before. But now, she didn't just love Devlyn and feel comfortable around him, they were married—they were the Lorenthien aryl.

Overwhelmed with everything that had occurred in the Empyrean Sphere, she stepped out of the shaft of Light with Devlyn. Aaron and Kevn waited for them, their expressions stunned.

"Thank the Light you're okay!" Aaron rushed over, only just realizing that the gown she had worn was gone. He looked at Devlyn accusingly, as though Devlyn was the reason for his sister being disrobed. "What happened?"

Ellendren looked at Devlyn, both unblinking as they gazed into each other's eyes. "Something wondrous," she said; Tariel called out and Aliel answered her.

"You're a Phaedryn—how?" Kevn asked, noticing there were two phoenix flying about the space.

"That's not all." Devlyn squeezed her hand without fully answering Kevn.

"Were you able to learn how to wield lumenys?" Aaron asked.

"Yes—I can sense it now and it feels like I can wield lumenys even here inside the temple." Ellendren paused. They had anticipated returning with the ability to wield lumenys, but they had also both returned as full Phaedryns and wed. It still seemed an impossible reality, but Ellendren could not help but smile every moment she remembered that Devlyn was now her husband, and she, his wife. Together, they were the Lorenthien aryl, and would become the Exalted Aryl of Krysenthiel. She wondered if the Luminari aryls would accept that she had been married without a formal ceremony and by extension she and Devlyn could take their place as the Exalted Aryl of Krysenthiel. She wondered what was involved to become the Exalted Aryl. She imagined a coronation would take place in Arenthyl. Did they need proof that they were married? Ellendren had no idea how she could obtain evidence of being married by the seraph. If anything, Aaron could vouch for them—he was the Ceurtriarch after all.

But first, she had to tell Aaron what had happened. She had always been the reserved and cautious one of her siblings. How was she supposed to tell her brother that she was married? She still couldn't believe it. There had been no public ceremony. There had been no declaration of intent, no betrothal period, no exchanging of gifts, no banquets or parties—neither of them had even said yes. Months were required to properly prepare for a wedding; not only for the banquet and ceremony, but to ensure that neither person was making a mistake. She knew that she hadn't made a mistake in marrying Devlyn, but she didn't know if their marriage had any precedent. Had the seraph ever declared two people married before? Every convention she thought she had known about getting married had been voided by the seraph's words. There weren't even any witnesses. Ellendren abhorred the idea of eloping. She could never understand why anyone would want to get married in secret, especially someone who was a public figure. But that was exactly what she had just done, even if she had never intended it to happen.

"Has something else happened?" Aaron asked.

"Devlyn and I are married." She said it simply and plainly, tugging Devlyn's lierathnil about her. Goosebumps flashed across her skin as she said it. An inner joy bubbled to the surface as she smiled.

"Because of how we entered the Empyrean Sphere, hearts and hands joined, the seraph declared that we were one. So, we're married." Devlyn answered the questioning looks from Aaron and Kevn.

"Truly?" Aaron said, then his shock turned to an exuberant joy and he laughed in elation. He hugged and kissed Ellendren before doing the same to Devlyn—they were family now. Kevn added his own congratulations and best wishes.

"Thank you. If you wouldn't mind, I would like to get something more appropriate on." An outer robe was hardly appropriate in the Chamber of Light.

"Of course! There's actually a lierathnil outfit in my apartment. I think it will fit you perfectly. A past Ceurtriarch must have intended to give it as a gift," Aaron said then turned back toward his apartment. He disappeared once they were all in his sitting room. He returned shortly after with a beautiful set of yellow and silver lierathnil.

Ellendren accepted the garments and left to get dressed in a private room, then returned to the sitting room with Devlyn's outer garment draped over her arm. He looked at her as though he had fallen in love with her all over again.

"Back to Everin with you." She handed the lierathnil back to him.

Devlyn hugged her and whispered, "I love you," into her ear.

She whispered it back and kissed him before they parted and he turned to leave, saying farewell to Aaron and Kevn as well. Even as Devlyn left the temple and soon after shifted to Everin, Ellendren could feel him in her heart. She knew exactly where he was. A tug pulled her toward him in Everin far to the west of Ceurenyl. She'd never heard of a married couple experiencing that before. Was it a secret that no one mentioned? Ellendren wondered if it was a side effect of being married in the Empyrean Sphere, declared so by the seraph, or if it was because they were both Phaedryn now. That connection with Devlyn was still fresh and she wondered how else it might be useful.

Brushing her hand along her yellow and silver garment, Ellendren looked from its sheen to her brother. "Thank you for the lierathnil; it fits just right."

"Consider it a wedding gift, even if it's too small of a gift for you."

"I'd hardly consider lierathnil insignificant, Aaron. It's really lovely." Ellendren remembered what Viren had said about lierathnil and how expensive the garments were.

"I'm sorry Devlyn had to leave so soon. I wish I could have hosted a banquet for you. You are both deserving of a celebration grander than this city has ever seen," Aaron said.

"Festivities will have to wait," Ellendren said, her expression calm and loving. "Besides, Ceurenyl is not the proper place. It should take place in Arenthyl."

Aaron nodded in agreement. "The ei'ceuril are no longer bound to the Temple of Ceur, sister—or should I say Ei'terel? I will expect an invitation."

"And you better be there. Same goes for you, Kevn."

The sheers over the door to the balcony rustled and two heavy thumps announced two arrivals. Only Ellendren did not stir at the tremor. The curtains parted and two very tall, very large, and very naked people walked in—their sapphire eyes sparkling. Ellendren, Aaron, and Kevn averted their eyes from the blue-haired man and woman.

"Hello Rusyl, I see you are reunited with your sister, Yelaris," Ellendren said, prudently averting her eyes even as she nodded in greeting to the two blue dragons.

"Forgive our appearances, it's been ages since we last allowed others to see our smaller forms," Yelaris said.

"Yelaris?" Aaron asked.

"The dragon?" Kevn squeaked.

"Yes, child. We expect great things from you." Yelaris towered over Kevn, but her smile was warm.

"I did not know this was possible—I assumed but had no proof. None of my research came anywhere near to explicitly stating that dragons could change forms. The closest I came was a series of dialogues that could only have occurred as we're speaking now."

"And how did you think the draelyn came to be if we could not change forms? We are not barbaric beasts who mount unsuspecting and unwilling mates—the males who chose to mate with the elder ones would have just as quickly squished those ancient women before the act was done. Not that I or any other female dragon ever understood why our males wanted to mate in their lesser forms," Yelaris said.

"The dragon elves! They exist? Is Tenethyl real too? I thought it had been destroyed," Kevn said, unable to restrain his excitement.

"You'll find a more satisfactory library soon enough. Heed her call," Yelaris said as she turned to Aaron. "Do you have robes large enough for my brother and me?"

"There's plenty of fabric but you'll have to knot it around your-selves. We don't have anything specifically tailored to your size." Aaron snapped his fingers and an aide appeared and disappeared quickly to follow his instructions.

"We'll manage."

Ellendren smiled when she saw Tariel swoop across Aaron's sitting room. Ellendren couldn't believe that she and Tariel had bonded. Ellendren had fantasized about the stories of the Phaedryn ever since she was a girl. She had once hoped that the news of the last phoenix egg hatching on her birth had meant that the phoenix would choose her. It had never been upsetting to know that Aliel had chosen Devlyn, but she had dreamt her entire life of becoming a Phaedryn.

Weren't you curious why you never met your lorendil in the Illumined Wood? Tariel asked. It had taken Devlyn over a year to learn how to communicate with Aliel, but because Ellendren had already learned how to communicate with Aliel in their time together, she had been able to speak with Tariel immediately.

I had assumed my guardian anadel preferred to stay hidden, Ellendren conveyed.

No anadel prefers to stay hidden and invisible. We wish to interact with others just as much as anacordel do. Too many anacordel are blinded to such as us though—you are not blinded, Tariel conveyed as she landed on the golden perch that Aaron had set for Aliel that morning.

39

BATTLE OF EVERIN

Sleet battered the city, coating the knights standing on Everin's battle-ments in ice. The frozen casing weighed down their already heavy steel helms and breastplates. Devlyn wished he could do something to lighten their burden, especially since he didn't have the same problem—the ice melted before it even came near his illuminated body when bonded with Aliel. They'd stayed bonded since he'd shifted back to Everin, letting the people know that he had returned. He had not yet become the Exalted Aryl of Krysenthiel nor yet the High King of Eklean, but he would not let people here think that he had abandoned them. The citizens and defenders had no way of knowing that because of the seraph, he was Ellendren's husband and by extension the Lorenthien aryl. Only Wyn had discovered what had happened in the Empyrean Sphere by unintentionally gleaning it from Devlyn's thoughts. There was little time for congratulations and even less time to tell others. Alex was organizing the defense of the city and had more pressing concerns at the moment—he didn't need any distractions. Devlyn had barely greeted Alex before receiving his orders that he was needed on the battlements and that Wyn would fill him in on the rest. So here he was, on the battlements with Wyn and ice-encased knights, waiting for the giants to approach while pondering his so very recent change of status.

He was still befuddled by the seraph's declaration. How could those simple words see him and Ellendren married? Neither of them had

had the chance to even agree to it. The seraph simply declared that they were one, and so they were wed. He wondered how much his life would change now. If all went well, he and Ellendren would soon become the Exalted Aryl. This war was far from over and his relationship with Ellendren and his title mattered little if they lost. If anything, his identity would only bring about more suffering if Erynor won the war and Ramiel was freed.

Too much about the future was uncertain and Devlyn knew he could do little to solve those problems from the top of Everin's defensive walls. Before he could worry about what the future might hold for himself and Ellendren, Everin had to be secured.

Even if the dwarves stubbornly refused to defend the city, Alex and Lara had agreed that the dwarves' offer of refuge was not enough and they refused to let Everin fall. The repercussions of the razing of Evellion's capital would be felt across the entire continent. The dwarves might think their schtams were unreachable but they would crumble just as quickly as Everin if Erynor gained access to their tunnels.

While Lara had planned to send another delegation to the dwarves, Alex had devised the wild plan that they were currently executing. The combined forces of Evellion, Thellion, the Eldinari, and the small Charrenese contingent would defend the city as they had always planned to once the giants arrived. That plan depended on baiting the dwarves into helping them. No one thought they could defeat the giants without the dwarves. If the dwarves did not send help, they would seal their fate in their tunnels as they abandoned their allies.

Devlyn worried about the gamble Alex was taking. It was an insane idea that depended on the dwarves' sense of honor. Their time was running out though and Alex didn't want Devlyn or any other defender leaving the battlements until the dwarves committed themselves to the battle.

During the few hours of Devlyn's absence, the available flying mounts had surveyed the area surrounding the city. Wyn had told Devlyn that Lex's army was still intact and bringing siege engines into the tunnel to Everin's main gate. Fortunately, the aerial units had also brought news that the larger Thellish force marching from Gneal had traversed the Cyrillean Pass and were near the crossing at the Eindol River. If they hurried, the army could hammer Lex's forces against the mountainside before they could break through the sealed mountain tunnels. In addition to the winged horses, Prince Sanjin's company of hippogriff riders supplemented the Eldinari star wardens and their griffins. Devlyn had no idea what sort of advantage the sky would give them but it was one that the giants did not have. Everin's defenders needed every possible advantage.

The mountainous terrain might have slowed the giants but it did little to halt them. Steep peaks and craggy ravines forced them along a particular path toward Everin though, allowing the city to best prepare for a defense. The same mountains that gave Everin its elongated shape also meant that only three stretches of unconnected defensive walls were required. The natural geological defenses were the reason King Evellion, eldest son and heir to the last Thellish king, had relocated here when fleeing Thellion's civil war. The summer palace had once served as a hunting lodge, the only structure in what was now Everin and a favorite spot for the Thellish court before civil war divided the kingdom. The Thellish refugees didn't have the luxury to build walls around an entirely new city for protection and at this location, they had not had to.

The smallest segment was the south-facing wall, where Devlyn and most of the defenders readied themselves for the approaching giants. There were only three turrets looking over the valley created by the two mountains on either side. A steep slope flowed between the two mountains, forming a small creek at the center where the slopes met, removing rainwater and sewage from Everin. The longest segment of Everin's walls faced east and looked down toward the valley between the Laudien and Vespien Mountains with the Cyrillean Pass in the far distance. There were no reports of giants circling the southeast mountain, but neither did the defenders want to risk an undefended wall, especially when giants were concerned. Another segment of wall faced north where the geography made the chance of an attack from the north highly unlikely, and only a small number of defenders guarded the four turrets there.

Despite Everin's tall and sturdy walls, they had not been designed as a defense against giants. If the giants did breach the walls, they would easily obliterate the southern portion of the city, but the densely built structures would also slow their destructive rampage through the city. Their bodies were too large to pass through the smaller streets and alleys and they'd only be able to proceed along the main arteries of the city. Devlyn shuddered at the sight of the giants drawing closer. Seeing them while he had been safely flying high over them before he'd gone to Ceurenyl was one thing but seeing them marching toward him through the valley was quite different. He had counted nearly a hundred of them that morning, an appalling number, considering the damage a single giant was capable of in a human city.

"It'll be all right," Wyn said, aware of Devlyn's thoughts, fears, and doubts.

"Their legs are the size of tree trunks," Devlyn shot back defensively. Hundreds of armored knights surrounded him but he suddenly felt the noticeable absence of Viren and his crystalline sword.

The small earthquakes caused by the giants' plodding steps settled and Devlyn held his breath and squinted to see through the icy sleet. The giants had stopped their march toward the city walls but still moved about in the area where they'd stopped. Despite his amplified eyesight, Devlyn couldn't see what the giants were doing clearly through the falling sleet. Then a hazy form solidified in the sky, growing larger and clearer as it approached at a frightening speed. He almost missed grabbing the boulder, pressing into terys to catch the projectile the instant he understood what was coming at them. His heart plummeted when he saw dozens more solidify in the sleet all flying toward Everin's wall. Dodging boulders was not an option. They had to be stopped before they struck the defensive walls.

Pressing into terys, Devlyn shattered the boulder nearest him. Rock shards showered down, luckily not near Everin's wall or her defenders. Other wielders replicated his wield, but some of the ei'ana opted to redirect the boulders back on the giants. Since the Ei'ana Counsels restricted them from using the erendinth to injure others unless under threat, they took advantage of the perceived threat to launch the boulders back at the giants.

Capable of launching the massive boulders with a single arm, the giants would perceive the retuning projectiles as though someone had thrown a rock at them. However, a well shot stone could still incapacitate them.

Bound to no such counsels, Devlyn began redirecting every boulder back at the giants. The ei'ana who had launched the first back into enemy lines were not just the ei'ana who had lived their entire lives at Gwilnor. Many of them were Eldinari elves who were born in a different age, before Erynor waged his war against the living. These same Eldinari wielders carried bows on their back, waiting for the giants to come into range to launch arrows at them.

After redirecting a number of boulders, it struck Devlyn that he was capable of much more than simply throwing rocks back at the giants. Already pressed into terys, he wove aquaeys into the sleet the boulders flew through, crystalizing the outer surface into a hardened globe of ice.

He sent the first ice-covered boulder whizzing through the air, its speed increasing until it hit the giant who had originally launched it. The boulder struck true and the giant stumbled backward before crashing down. A strong tremor shook the ground so that Devlyn and the defenders on the wall had to brace themselves. A heart wrenching scream to his left made everyone turn and Devlyn gasped when he saw an unprepared knight slip and fall off the wall to the ground and lie there, his armor crumpled. It happened so quickly that Devlyn couldn't have saved him by flying after the knight.

But the boulders stopped coming at them. As dimwitted as the giants were rumored to be, they had realized that throwing boulders was only a detriment to themselves. The steady rumble of their approach started up again as the giants continued their march toward Everin. It couldn't strictly be called a march, since the giants moved independently, and there didn't seem to be any noticeable leader, unlike normal military formations. Still, the giants acted together—there had to be a leader or chief among them. Perhaps those rumors about the giants' intelligence had little foundation to them. Their large, heavy legs made them incapable of sprinting. Yet given their size, they could still cover more distance in a few steps than the fastest of sprinters. No matter how thick and tall Everin's walls were, they stood little chance against the slowly approaching giants.

"Would they hurry and get here already! I've been posted here all day," the knight beside Devlyn complained.

"Be happy they're not running at us," Devlyn said.

"Why's that?"

"Creatures as big those beasts?" another knight responded. "They'd likely start an earthquake. Those vibrations could shake down every building in Everin, this wall included. Anyone not yet in the dwarven tunnels would be buried alive. And even those tunnels might not withstand the vibrations from a hundred giants sprinting."

"Aye, it's a miracle the giants haven't triggered an avalanche yet," another knight said.

"Wielders are ensuring that they don't." Wyn looked at the snowy mountains surrounding Everin on every side.

At their approach, orders were shouted along the battlements and arrows flew into the air. The arrows had been modified over the past weeks with the giants in mind, but they seemed to make little difference other than to annoy the giants, although many did manage to pierce their skin. "Our arrows aren't doing a thing," someone yelled.

"Keep at it! Aim for their heads," someone else hollered nearby as one of the smaller giants reached the defensive wall and began pounding on it, his fists like heavy hammers. Without any boulders available on top of the wall, the ei'ana had nothing to launch at him and everyone had to take care not to be shaken off the wall.

With each punch, Devlyn thought the wall would crumble, relieved that it remained standing following every explosive thump. A second giant reached the wall, adding his own weight behind each strike. The two were on opposite sides of the center turret. "Good thing they're not pounding on the same area." Devlyn braced himself as a shockwave went through the wall.

"This is worse," Wyn said, terrified. "They're trying to destabilize that turret. They're not pounding at random."

Pausing, Devlyn focused on the two giants and noted that the strikes on the wall were indeed synchronized. The vibrations went back and forth between the two giants and through the turret.

Devlyn felt the ei'ana wield terys into the two southern mountains and the wall, trying to stabilize and strengthen the stone. More giants reached the wall, prioritizing their attack on the turret. The giants struck the wall in unison on either side of the turret. The pounding sounded like two steady drumbeats, answering each other. The shockwaves grew stronger with each beat and Devlyn watched in horror as tremors went through the turret.

Petrified that the turret would collapse, Devlyn pressed into ignys and poured fire down on the nearest giants. They growled at the flames but continued to beat against the wall. There had to be a way to stop them! Devlyn looked around, hoping to see the dwarves, but they weren't anywhere to be found.

The archers were hard-pressed to be effective. Staying on their feet and not toppling over the wall was difficult enough, aiming was all but impossible. They still managed to strike their targets and the giants nearest the wall looked like pincushions, although they ignored the arrows as though they were nothing more than a bee sting. One of the giants howled up at the wall when a well-aimed arrow struck his eye. That only infuriated him more and his punches turned wild. Devlyn had to steady himself against the increased pounding. The shockwave intensified and whole stones fell from the corbeling at the turret's upper level. The upper room was wider than the lower shaft and its exterior walls were only supported by those corbels. Its structural integrity failed and its wall and pointed roof toppled on either side of the defensive wall. Screams came from the men and women who had been inside the turret. The weight of the roof smashing down damaged the turret even more, bringing more stones crashing down. The turret's foundations had to be solid stonework to not have crumbled under the collapse.

With their focus now on battering the wall and bringing the rest of the turret down, the giants neglected to keep a watch on the valley behind them. The defenders cheered when a legion of heavily armed dwarves swarmed out of a tunnel in the mountainside behind the giants' lines, a tunnel that only dwarven eyes could see. Devlyn caught sight of the tunnel only after the dwarves had appeared and it wasn't the tunnel's opening that he had seen, but rather, where the line of dwarves had appeared.

Devlyn thanked Anaweh for what was clearly a miracle. For the first time since he'd seen the giants that morning, he believed they might have a chance to win this battle. Each dwarf carried an axe, its head larger than their own. The Eldinari wouldn't permit those axes within a league of their forest. Devlyn watched as the impressively armed force slipped unnoticed behind the giants who were too absorbed on bringing Everin's wall down. Luckily, the defenders' cheering hadn't alerted the giants to the dwarves.

In an orchestrated attack, four dwarves per giant, the dwarves swung their axes into the giants' ankles. Their axes were incapable of disabling the larger giants entirely but were quite effective in slowing them down and distracting them from their attack on the wall. Devlyn couldn't believe that the giants were still standing. "How is that possible? Those axes should have chopped their feet off cleanly!"

"Their hide practically turns to stone as they mature. The dwarves will have better luck with the smaller ones," Wyn said, sweat and sleet beading down his face.

Unfortunately, the dwarves' concerted attack quickly fell into chaos when the giants turned their wrath on them, each dwarf half as tall as the giants' shins. Swifter than the giants, the dwarves managed to maneuver around their stomping feet and fists slamming into the ground. Speed was essential to this battle, and Devlyn had to wait to contribute his own. Despite Alex's inexperience, Lara and Fendryl had conceded to the Thellish king's plan. His ruse had worked and the dwarves had come to their defense.

With the dwarves scattered among the giants, the first of Evellion's army descended through the undamaged turrets to engage the giants as well. They wouldn't be half as efficient as the dwarves' surprise attack had been but they couldn't let the dwarves entirely fight their battle either. From Devlyn's perspective, it looked like shiny lines of silver moved across the valley. Several bands of Evellion soldiers marched toward the giants, each band focusing on one.

In a normal battle, Alex and Lara would have sent out their cavalry, however horses were utterly useless on the steep slopes. Instead, the human defenders would have to strike against the giants on their own feet. The humans might stand taller than the dwarves, but they also had narrower shoulders and leaner muscle all around. They would never be able to swing an axe as strongly as a dwarf could. Alex had planned on the dwarves joining the fray and with their engagement, the first two phases of Alex's plan had ended. It was now time to take advantage of the skies. Devlyn worried about ice coating the wings of the griffins, hippogriffs, and winged horses, as the weather had yet to improve.

As Devlyn watched the battle unfold below, a horn echoed across the city. That wasn't the right signal for him and the others who could fly to enter the field. This was something else—something that Everin had managed to avoid for four years. Turning away from the battle below to search the city, he saw a thin line of smoke rising near the northeast gate. There was a collapsed tunnel beyond that gate that emptied out onto the valley between the Laudien and Vespien Mountains. Since Evellion's inception, that tunnel had served as the main entrance to Everin. But it had been caved in years earlier to prevent Perrien's army from breaching the city, and at this point in a siege that had lasted four years, the tunnel's outer gate in the Cyrillean Pass was likely beyond repair. Wyn also saw the smoke plumes and shared a nervous look with Devlyn.

More plumes of smoke twirled into the cold sky as the first column thickened, turning hazy as it mixed with the sleet. The defenders standing near Devlyn looked anxiously toward the smoke. An entire city separated them, there was nothing they could do and Devlyn knew it.

"I'll get to you as fast as I can," Wyn said as he gestured for the nearest knights to accompany him on a sprint across the city.

Spreading his wings, Devlyn leapt from the wall, not toward the giants as originally planned, but to the curious smoke rising inside Everin's northeast wall. The southern part of the city he flew over was quiet, the streets empty as this part of the city had been safely evacuated to the dwarven tunnels. Devlyn could just make out a reserve column of knights on horseback racing out from the castle. They disappeared behind a stretch of buildings as Devlyn continued toward the northeast gate. That low, desperate horn continued, now joined by high-pitched sounds and when Devlyn drew closer, he heard people screaming, shouting, and wailing.

An inferno had engulfed the buildings closest to the gate, spreading from one limestone building to the next. Amid the resulting chaos were shadowy figures wielding ignys laced with tenebrys to set everything nearby ablaze. The city was too large to have been entirely evacuated before the giants arrived, so this part still had people preparing to escape since it was further away from the south wall and the giants' approach.

Pressing into ignys, Devlyn wielded the flames away from the buildings and threw them back at the shadow elves who had called them forth. The vile creatures cackled as the fire swirled around their bodies, seeming to take pleasure in the flames as though they were enjoying a hot bath. It was impossible to tell how many had breached the city gates. If they had managed to finally break through the tunnel, then the renegade Perrien army would be close behind them.

Quieting his mind, Devlyn searched for Alex. He was far from considering himself an expert with his interior sense and communicating in this way, but he had to let Alex and the generals in charge with the protection of Everin know what was happening. *Your uncle is here.*

It was a simple message, all that he could manage, but he hoped it was sufficient to alert Alex. Devlyn wanted to say more but could not afford dividing his attention further since a bolt of tenebrys barreled toward him.

Looking away from the tower window and straightening from a slouch, Alex looked over his shoulder. "Did you say something?" The palace war room was packed; only Lara had left since the battle had begun. Alex had spent nearly every waking hour in this room, up high in the palace's tallest tower where it provided an incredible vantage point. Alex could see the entire city and surrounding valleys from the windows up here.

The advisors and strategists had been bent over to study the maps of the city and the surrounding mountains and looked up at Alex's question.

"Everything all right, Your Majesty?" one of them asked.

"I'm probably just tired. I thought I heard Devlyn, but that's not possible," he said, rubbing his eyes.

The giants had thrown the first boulder at the city walls just over an hour ago, and while things could be going better, the only damage to the city had been a defensive turret until smoke began to rise near the northeast gate. Evellion knights had been quickly dispatched to the scene to report the cause of the fires, but shortly after they'd left, he'd thought he heard Devlyn in his mind.

"What did you hear?" Arlyn asked. While his presence was not necessary in a war council and he contributed little to the overall strategy, Alex liked having the ei'ceuril's soothing presence around. Praying would not save the city, but they would take any advantage they could get.

"Pardon me?"

"What did Devlyn say?"

"I thought I heard him say my uncle was here," Alex said, embarrassed to admit that he was hearing things in front of his advisors and even more so in front of Diana. He told himself that he was exhausted and nothing more.

"It would be wise to send more reinforcements to the northeast gate, as well as any ei'ana we can spare." Arlyn joined Alex by the tower window that offered a view over the entire city. "I'm afraid Lex and his army have managed to excavate the tunnel. And by the looks of it, they're likely accompanied by shadow elves."

Diana walked over to him and placed a hand on the hand that Alex still pressed against the windowsill, just a quick touch, then she stepped back. He had met Diana only three days ago, but thoughts of her constantly occupied his mind, keeping him from sleeping and distracting him from planning Everin's defense.

Turning away from the window, Alex nodded to Sanjin.

Sanjin left the room and Alex waited for the winged horses, griffins, and hippogriffs to take to the sky. They had been waiting for orders in the palace plaza, where vibrant flowers should have sprouted weeks ago.

A few quiet moments passed and then the flying mounts soared above the city toward the northeast gate. They were supposed to be joining the fight against the giants soon, and he hoped that what was happening at the northeast gate wouldn't take too long to resolve. Alex wanted to join them, but it had been agreed that he had to remain in the palace to orchestrate the city's defense. He thought it wasteful; he could have joined them. He could be doing something. Instead, he watched as others fought. Thankfully, the dwarves had joined the fight. Alex didn't admit how nervous he had been that his plan would fail and the dwarves would truly abandon Everin as they had promised.

Breached

Devlyn was too easy a target for the shadow elves. From above, he was able to redirect the multitude of tenebrys wields launched at him, but because of the dozen or so shadow elves below, he could do little more than keep them from striking him. Overcoming any of them would be impossible with his current plan of attack. Now that he could wield lumenys, he considered how he could put it to use. The insecurity he'd felt at not being able to wield it lingered. Without having had the chance to practice wielding this transcendental erendinth, he didn't know any wields to accompany it. He had no idea what to do with this new power.

With his feet now planted firmly on the ground of a cobbled alley, he sensed the area around him, quickly discovering that people were still huddled inside their homes. It might be a better alternative than being out in the streets and having their souls stolen by a shadow elf, but all it would take was one of those uncontrolled wields of ignys and tenebrys to set their homes ablaze. The only way to protect the civilians was to confine and eliminate the shadow elves somehow or at least push them back through the tunnel and out of the city.

Dashing from the confined alley into a broad avenue, Devlyn ran toward the gate where the shadow elves were still concentrated, causing as much destruction as possible. New fires blossomed from the surrounding buildings, and the desperate screams of the citizens were continuous.

Devlyn worried about the inferno spreading. It wouldn't take much for the wind to spread those flames—not even the freezing rain quelled the spread since the shadow elves continued to fuel the flames with ignys and tenebrys.

Ear-splitting screeches accompanied their attack, the shadow elves cackling with glee at the people trapped in their homes. It was the same atrocious sound that Devlyn had first heard when Erynor and his shadow elves had attacked Ceurenyl. Their elation at killing civilians disgusted Devlyn. How could they get so much pleasure at causing so much pain?

Reaching the plaza in front of the northeast gate, he saw that a dozen shadow elves had fanned out, launching tenebrys bolts recklessly in every direction and to Devlyn's horror, they had bound together, multiplying their strength. It was impossible to see any of their faces, as shadowy tendrils covered their bodies, making them barely distinguishable as separate entities. Devlyn could only see blobs in the shadowy cloud surrounding them. That cloud, Devlyn noticed, looked a lot like the one that had swallowed Alethea. Ramiel was involved in that forbidden power. Devlyn didn't know if the forsaken anadel was the source of tenebrys or if there was something else involved. But now wasn't the time to think of Alethea or tenebrys' metaphysical nature. He couldn't afford distractions right now.

"No one told us the lofty Phaedryn had run away to Everin," said one of the shadow elves.

"It would be a shame to take him prisoner, just for him to escape again," said another.

"A pity the Tieli queen couldn't keep her pet canary caged."

"Let's kill the Phaedryn!" said the first. "But who would get his shiny gold soul?"

They bickered among themselves until a different voice seemed to quell them. "The prize is mine." Devlyn didn't think he'd ever heard that voice before, but it sent chills down his spine all the same. "Come closer, little one. The pain will only last as long as you want it to."

"Who are you?" Devlyn asked, all too happy to stretch out this conversation since it had paused the shadow elves' destructive wielding.

"We have met before. But I was prohibited from taking any souls for myself that day. Oh, but I lusted for your family. We didn't know then that the golden blood of the Lorenthiens had managed to survive and was hiding in that insignificant village but I knew something was special about the family we had been sent after. I could taste it." Despite the noise of the fires, the falling ice-rain, and Devlyn's thumping heart, he heard the shadow elf audibly lick his lips as he stepped forward out of the shadowy cloud encasing the shadow elves. Murky tendrils still wrapped about his body, clinging to his limbs and torso.

"What do you want?" Devlyn still had no idea who this shadow elf was, only that he seemed to have been involved with the horror of his family's abduction all those years ago on that night that left him an orphan.

"You, of course. I wasn't even permitted to steal your father's wretched soul. Lex's blow saw him dead before he hit the floor—his soul gone to the World-Beyond. The closest I got was a piece of your sister. I only did so to get your willful mother to stand down." It clicked. This shadow elf wasn't just involved with his family's abduction but he had been in the room of the inn when Devlyn's world shattered. Liam had told him about that night, about the shadow elf that had been there with Lex. "But I was given a more deserving reward before I left Gneal. I'm not sure of the relationship to you but I know now that I had my first Lorenthien that night. And she was delectable."

"Stop wasting our time, Ilynor," one of the shadow elves hissed. Devlyn felt his blood boiling. He didn't know who the other shadow elves were but Ilynor had consumed one of his relative's souls, to say nothing of what he had done to Leilyn.

"You younger ones are ever so impatient. What have they been teaching you at the Imperium? A shame Ianthol never returned; he'd ensure you'd be better trained."

"We're not that young," spat a different shadow elf. "He disappeared after all of us graduated."

"Clearly his lessons were wasted on the likes of you," Ilynor returned calmly. The shadow elves began their screeching again when a bolt of tenebrys exploded from Ilynor, as though the process of wielding that forbidden power had caused them pain.

Already pressed into the elemental erendinth, Devlyn stilled his spirit and embraced umbrys and animys. Forming his wield, Devlyn met the tenebrys wield in a clash as he struggled against it. He considered embracing lumenys as well, but he had no idea what he could do with it or how it would alter the wield he already knew worked just fine when it came to fighting shadow elves. Other than when he'd fought Razcul at Gwilnor, that wield had always worked well against shadow elves. Still, there were twelve of them bound together now, and Ilynor seemed anything but weak. With a final push, Devlyn's wield overpowered the other and he redirected it skyward, away from himself and the city. The shadow elves' maniacal laughter continued.

There was only one way to prevent the shadow elves from wreaking havoc on Everin. Devlyn had stopped them before, killing them and freeing the spirits trapped inside, but never twelve at once. Six shadow elves wielding together would be unstoppable, but twelve of them together had god-like powers and strength that Devlyn had only encountered in Aren or in a Deurghol. Devlyn thanked Anaweh that neither of them was here.

Forming another wield of the six erendinth he already had influence over, Devlyn became aware of the plethora of souls in each of the shadow elves. More than one of those souls was a family member that had been stolen away when he was a toddler. Devlyn had been born into a large and loving family—parents, aunts, uncles, grandparents, cousins, and siblings, all torn away from him and each other. Nightmarish memories of his childhood returned as he remembered Abbot Entiel and the abbey school. Only Alex and Brother Bernard had shown him any kindness there.

Pushing those despairing thoughts aside, Devlyn focused on the threat in front of him. If these shadow elves feasted on Everin's inhabitants, not only would they prolong their cursed life, they would also become more powerful in the process. Devlyn had momentarily stopped them from spreading their cursed flames from building to building, but only because he currently held their attention. How long could that possibly last? Overcoming them all was simply impossible. He knew the cavalry from the castle would arrive soon, but what good could they do against shadow elves? Wyn and some of the knights from the wall were sprinting across the city to reach him, but only Wyn would be able to help Devlyn in this matter. He knew it was only a matter of time before Lex's renegade militia poured through the breached gate, and he hoped more defenders would come to meet them. Devlyn couldn't engage Lex's forces and the shadow elves simultaneously.

The immensity of his wield electrified the air as he fought against the twelve shadow elves. The erendinth were invisible to the naked eye, yet to any wielder, their touch and presence thrummed through the air in a colorful array. The shadow elves saw what he was doing—what he was trying to achieve—and laughed as he poured more of his strength into the wield to undo them.

He could barely identify or distinguish one shadow elf from the next but he could focus on Ilynor. There was no doubt that he was the one who directed their diabolical wields of poisonous flames impervious to water against the sides of buildings.

Holding the wield, he felt the tenebrys wield across the plaza, deteriorating and corrupting the erendinth it molested. The two wields thrummed and battered against each other, each trying to suffocate the other.

Ilynor exerted his dominance over his wield, thrusting his will and strength into it. The incredible resistance reminded Devlyn of Aren and the Deurghol, and how they'd inflicted the wound on his back and caged

Aliel deep in his heart, unreachable. Refusing to submit and let go of his wield, Devlyn pushed himself harder. He was reaching his limit; something that was supposedly non-existent for a Phaedryn and an elya.

Despite his concentration and connection to the wield, he heard the clip-clop of horses on the cobbles, and men shouting. It sounded like they were coming from behind the shadow elves. He could not break his wield and soar into the sky to see who created the added commotion—he barely had strength to stand. He hoped the reinforcements from the castle had arrived, with Wyn and the others shortly behind. His heart sank when Lex and his renegade Perrien army pushed past the gate, swords held aloft and many of the soldiers riding grey coursers. Whatever Everin defenders had been stationed at the gate were certainly dead. The soldiers who had laid siege to the city over the past four years were now in Everin.

Devlyn stood alone.

There could be no help from the people in the surrounding homes who had bolted and barricaded their doors and windows. These were city folk. Some of them might be veterans, but most would have never lifted a sword or bow. Neither would they have tools lying about their homes that could be used as weapons. They certainly wouldn't have farm equipment that could do just as much damage as a traditional weapon.

Glancing at the renegade soldiers, Devlyn tried to think of how he could stop them and the shadow elves on his own. It was too late to transfer his wield to redirect the tenebrys lightning at Lex and his army; he was already committed, and if he loosened his hold even in the slightest, the tenebrys wield would easily overpower his own wield and strike him. Devlyn couldn't afford to be severed from Aliel again. He had to keep that wield as far away from himself as possible, even as the tenebrys lightning splintered—indiscriminately searching for living beings to consume. Devlyn tried to contain those haphazard lightning forks to the larger tenebrys wield.

Sweat dampened his brow; there was no telling whether the invaders had even noticed him fighting the shadow elves. All Devlyn could do was maintain his wield, pressing more of himself into it. He was the only one preventing the streaks of death from lashing out from the shadow elves' wield and into someone's home. If given the freedom, tenebrys tendrils would latch on anything they touched—even the invaders.

Then he saw something from the corner of his eye that eased him a little. Flying mounts swarmed over his head as night fell over the city. He had hoped that Alex had heard his message to send help, that he would have understood the desperate situation at the gate, but for all he knew Alex could have disregarded the warning as foolishness. Alex would be unfamiliar with someone speaking inside his mind.

Metal clashed against metal, the sound ringing in Alex's ears, the vibrations unsteadying his hand as he led a cavalry charge on Dennion, his winged horse, toward the northeast gate. Devlyn was somewhere amid the fighting ahead. His brilliant body gave off a light that should have allowed Alex to easily locate him. That shadowy cloud up ahead worried Alex though—was that why he couldn't see Devlyn? Knowing that Devlyn could take care of himself, Alex gripped his sword tightly in his right hand, a shield bearing the crest of Thellion in his left.

He had watched Sanjin lead the other flying mounts toward the battle, but the urge to be a part of it, part of the soldiers now fighting in his name, had intensified. He had refused to remain stuck in a tower to watch people fight and die from afar any longer. His advisors had tried to convince him to stay in the war room, but Diana had handed him his sword and shield. She kissed him on the cheek before he dashed out of the room, and as he rushed to his own flying mount, he cherished the touch of her lips.

His plans for the battle had changed once the northeast gate had been breached. Alex now assumed that the invaders could have broken through months ago but had waited for the giants to arrive. He couldn't believe that he had miscalculated the defenses at the tunnel gate. The southern wall and the giants had been given priority. Cursing to himself, he realized that he should have expected the renegade militia would breach the city during the battle. Because of his miscalculation, the city's defenses were spread too thin and wide. The entire city stood between the breached gate and the southern wall. The only forces that had been able to come to the gate were the ones that had not yet engaged the giants. Fortunately, that number was largely made up of flying mounts but Alex knew they couldn't take on an entire militia. He hoped his own army would reach the city soon. The last he had heard was that they were near the Eindol River. With the gate breached and Lex's renegade militia pouring into Everin, the Thellish army was the only chance for the city's survival. Even if the dwarves managed to defeat the giants, Lex's army would devastate the city if it wasn't stopped.

Alex prayed that his larger army would arrive as he swung his sword at the soldiers he fought, soldiers who technically owed their loyalty to him. They rode atop grey coursers, they wore Perrien's colors, and even had the same features and characteristics of the soldiers who were fighting with him. Sandy blond hair stuck to their sweaty foreheads and angry blue eyes glared back into his own. There were others among Lex's forces who were clearly not from Perrien. They had dark brown hair, and no armor to speak of. Alex had only seen them once before and that was when he had first heard of giants marching toward Dwota's Gap.

Alex knew that none of these Dwonians belonged to the same tribe as Tye who had come to warn the leaders of the Lucillian Alliance that giants were heading for Dwota's Gap. They were fierce fighters and Alex was glad that he'd only crossed one of the Dwonian warriors so far and he was especially thankful for the advantage of being on Dennion who had taken Alex up into the air above the Dwonian's vicious sword, enabling Alex to strike back with a killing blow.

Alex was doing his best to avoid striking mortal blows against the renegade militia. He wanted to bring them back into Thellion's fold.

That courtesy didn't extend to the Dwonian warriors who had belonged to Erynor since the Ceurendol War. Thellion needed a large and strong army in the days to come, not just in the battle against Erynor and his empire, but to defend Thellion from the Daer who were enslaving his own people and forcing them to build a Daer colony in Perrien.

The thought of his beleaguered and enslaved people added strength and resolve as he searched for his uncle, determined to put an end to Lex's mutiny.

Another sword swung at him. "Do you not recognize the crest of Thellion?" he yelled at the renegade Perrien soldier. "It's engraved into the walls of Gneal!" Frustrated, Alex swung his sword downward, driving the other one away and then pressed Dennion forward.

The process repeated several times before Alex finally saw a lone figure on a grey courser watching the battle from the battered gateway. Lex carried himself as though he was a lofty lord.

Alex wondered if his uncle would recognize his own nephew. The last time Lex had seen him was four years ago when he had been only fourteen and skinny as a twig. Alex had a fleeting hope that his uncle would put a stop to his renegade militia, but Alex remembered what Velaria had said all those years ago and knew it to be true. Lex would never listen to Alex; that they were family meant nothing to Lex, especially in the face of his callous ambition. The realization hurt, but Lex belonged to Erynor; he was accompanied by and allied with shadow elves. Nothing Alex could do or say could reconcile that.

There were too many soldiers between himself and Lex; fighting through them all would only diminish the number of soldiers he hoped would bolster his own ranks. Nudging Dennion with his feet and pulling the reins, his shield latched to his arm, Alex rose above the battle, Dennion's grey feathered wings filling Alex's peripheral vision.

Dennion knew where Alex wanted to go—a bond already existed between them that Alex could not understand. Somehow the creature understood him. Other horses had all understood his body language and the longer he rode a specific horse, the more accustomed it grew to his movements, but his connection to Dennion was different. The winged horse seemed to understand what Alex wanted before he could even nudge the horse forward, as though he already knew Alex's intentions.

The approaching broad wingspan caught Lex's attention, and to Alex's delight, his uncle looked up. Flying over the hundreds of men separating them, Alex landed in front of Lex, their eyes boring into each other.

"So, the rumors of a child declaring himself a Thellish king were true." Lex looked exactly as Alex remembered him, although there was a fresh scar lining his right cheek. "Had I known my own nephew was foolish enough to stake himself against the Erynien Empire, well, let's just say I would have been more discerning in Cor'lera."

"Happy to see you as well, Uncle."

"There's no need to lie. You forget how well I know you—we do share a name after all. Don't forget the origin of yours."

"And that's where the similarity stops."

"How unfortunate. Imagine what you could have done as a Thellish king with stronger allies. Erynor would have given you all the lands it once held."

"Is that so? The last time I was in Binton, their king tried to have me killed."

"So that's why Erynor was so peeved with Lawrence. He'll be lucky if he's permitted to wash his emperor's feet in the future." Still holding his sword, Alex's fingers tightened around the hilt and Lex noted it. "Don't be ridiculous—attacking your own uncle? How do you thi…"

Alex's jaw dropped at the sight of the feathered tail of an arrow, the shaft buried in his uncle's chest.

Still staring at Alex, Lex managed to cough out, "Coward."

Alex looked over the plaza, where swords still clashed against each other and if the clouds had not continued to blanket the sky, the moon and stars would have lit the blood-stained city below. No one on the ground level paid any attention to Alex and Lex—they were too focused on fighting to stay alive. Turning his gaze away from the soldiers, Alex looked about to find out where the arrow had come from. On a distant roof, standing with her bow still drawn was a young woman, her blond hair tightly braided. Alex could just make out the blue ribbon flowing in the chilled wind. He had no idea how Diana had managed to scale the side of that building amidst the battle and flames. As though the fighting didn't make the situation difficult enough, every building that wasn't ablaze was layered in snow and ice. He couldn't imagine how she had made it to the roof. It was incredible.

Eyes still focused upward Alex caught sight of winged creatures heading toward the battle. They were not the winged creatures of Thellion and Charren, no, these numbered well into the hundreds.

Their wings were invisible in the rainy night sky; only someone looking carefully would see the creatures descending on the city.

Alex launched himself and Dennion back into the fighting, yelling at the renegade Perrien militia to surrender and that he was their rightful king. Some dropped their swords but many more kept fighting.

Falling to his knees, Devlyn held onto his wield, straining to maintain the immense yet nearly unbearable power flowing through him. He knew he was vulnerable and shook his head to dispel the whispering in his mind. It wasn't Aliel—he recognized the phoenix's communication better than his own voice at times, but whatever words flew through his mind just now did not originate from Aliel.

Dismissing the thoughts for exhaustion, he pressed more fiercely into his wield. He thought he might be screaming, but it was overwhelmed by the high-pitched cackles and screams from the shadow elves in front of him.

They knew Devlyn was not strong enough to subdue them together, and they mocked him for it. How could a boy of seventeen think he could free the spirits from twelve different shadow elves, all of them older than himself, some by hundreds of years, their longevity empowered by their victims' spirits.

Knees aching from the cold of the cobbled street, Devlyn shook his head again as the voices returned. They sounded odd and foreign, speaking in a language Devlyn recognized but could not understand. It was far too beautiful to belong to the wretches confronting him. Rather, it sang in his mind, fluid and musical, calling out to him. A fleeting thought told him he was close to death, and anadel were ushering him from Teraeniel and into Anaweh's Light in Lumaeniel, the World-Beyond.

He dismissed that thought. It was too soon to die; he was needed here below. Eklean needed him, the Luminari elves needed him, but most urgently, Ellendren needed him and he needed her. Straining his exhausted mind, he heard the voices sing, no longer in Aelish, but in words that Devlyn understood.

This burden is yours alone no longer, came an intelligible voice. Devlyn recognized that voice. Wyn and Fendryl were standing beside him—each lending their own strength to Devlyn. A swell of vigor returned to his fatigued body and mind, for it wasn't just Wyn and Fendryl bonding with him. Dozens of Eldinari wielders, all of them star wardens, had joined him.

Renewed, Devlyn intensified his wield, sending it pulsing, each surge stronger than the one before. The wield blossomed to a proportion difficult to quantify as it heaved against the shadow elves in a formidable wave, drowning their tenebrys lightning. He didn't have to focus only on Ilynor now; with the combined strength from the other wielders, he could feel every shadow elf. He felt the souls inside each of them and delved into those wretched husks of corrupted and blistering flesh.

One shadow elf cracked with a loud scream, his body erupting in a cacophony as tiny lights escaped the shadowy form, melodious songs flowing into the night sky from the spirits leaving their prison to end their prolonged pilgrimage.

The tenebrys wield, weakened after that first shadow elf collapsed and turned to ash, still tried to reach Devlyn. He could feel the rest of the shadow elves trembling and trying to withdraw from their connection but collapsing instead. More spheres of light rushed toward the sky, their hosts turning to ash, bereft of their stolen vitality. Devlyn's wield only became stronger as five more shadow elves fell.

Another five fell in a swift burst until only Ilynor remained. The shadowy cloud about them had all but dissipated since he couldn't divert any of his remaining strength in maintaining its presence. His scabbed and decaying skin was deteriorating at a quickening pace and Devlyn could see hundreds of lights swimming inside his husk, begging for release. Finally, Ilynor exploded with a shriek and the shadow elf was no more.

Ilynor's screaming died as the spirits he had incarcerated were liberated, their incredible lights flowing with music as they scattered into the cold sleet above before fading from the World-Below.

An incredible exhaustion fell over Devlyn, his connection with Aliel the only thing preventing him from collapsing. He could hear swords clashing and soldiers and knights fighting but had no idea how the battle was going. Griffins encircled Devlyn, protecting him since he was too exhausted to stand let alone defend himself.

The arrival of the griffins seemed to have daunted the attackers. The renegade Perrien soldiers nearest the Eldinari star wardens dropped their swords to surrender, uninterested in fighting elf and griffin alike.

The fighting did not entirely stop, but it was slowing. Swords clashed against swords across the plaza.

Fendryl lowered his hand on Devlyn's shoulder. "You have done enough for tonight."

Devlyn withdrew from Aliel, too spent to continue fighting. Someone—he thought it was Fendryl—pulled him up and onto the back of a griffin. His consciousness slipped away.

PROMISES

Devlyn woke slowly. He lay on his side, on a soft feather mattress, and as he became more conscious, he realized that he could hear festive shouts and songs, the volume increasing the more awake he became. The merriment sounded like it was taking place not only throughout the city but just outside his door. He rolled over under the covers, his body aching. It seemed that someone had undressed him and washed most of the dirt and sweat from him.

Part of him wanted to get up, but a much stronger part wanted to drift back to sleep, something that was proving impossible with the noise of the celebrations taking place everywhere. He determinedly kept his eyes shut, knowing that if he opened them, he would never fall back to sleep.

The last images of the battle swam into his mind. He could still hear the shadow elves laughing at him. He shivered as ice ran through his veins. *No, the shadow elves are dead,* he reminded himself.

And the spirits of the stolen are free, Aliel conveyed.

Devlyn smiled at that, still too cozy to move. Then, realizing that he preferred to join in the festivities rather than dwell on his memories, he rolled over and sat up, nearly tumbling to the floor. He sat for a moment longer, giving his body time to adjust as he scanned the room for his clothing. All four sets of his lierathnil hung in the opened wardrobe. The one he had worn in the battle had already been laundered. *How long have I been asleep?* He looked out the window and saw that it was night again and wondered if he'd slept an entire day.

He grabbed his blue and grey lierathnil—the colors felt appropriate given Everin's victory. The entire palace would be wearing blue tonight in celebration. Dressed, he slowly made his way through the salon of the dim guest quarters to the door that led to the corridor. Aliel's light was more than he needed to avoid walking into furniture, but when he pulled the door open, he had to squint against the vibrant lights outside his darkened room.

There seemed to be dozens of people celebrating in the corridor, which accounted for some of the noise. Someone caught sight of Devlyn and clapped him on the back and another jostled his shoulders. Everyone seemed to know who he was and had been waiting for him to come out.

The people looked like castle servants, some still wearing their uniforms. Devlyn recognized a few of them, although they seemed far more relaxed than he had ever seen them. That they were singing and dancing in the corridors was unlike their usual professional manner. He smiled at the striking difference. Other than the bubbly Queen Lara, most people in Everin were stuffy and proper.

"What's going on?" Devlyn asked a young man who skipped past. It was a silly question.

"The whole city is celebrating! Not only have we won the battle, but we have a new king! Her Majesty gave birth to a healthy baby boy during the attack! The elves are launching wondrous colored lights into the night sky. The dwarves have joined the celebration too. I've never seen someone dance like a dwarf before. I've rarely seen them leave their halls for the surface above," the young man said before his friends swept him away.

Closing the door behind him, Devlyn followed the crowd, but at a much slower pace. The further he walked through the palace, the louder the celebration became. There were lighted candles and dancing couples everywhere, old and young singing at the top of their lungs. None of the words were intelligible since no one sang the same song.

He finally found his way to the palace's exquisite ballroom. He admired the frescoed dome devoted to a beautiful depiction that included Evellion's western journey from Thellion's civil war, Belin the dwarf in the Vespien Mountains, and the summer palace looking over the valley.

The excitement he'd seen in the corridors was also displayed by Evellion's nobility who were dancing and laughing, having abandoned their usual staid decorum. Devlyn swore he saw an elderly baroness dancing with one of the much younger servants, the difference in their stations not clear since none of the nobles had dressed for the occasion. No one sat at the high table on the dais, but cups, plates, and empty platters rested there.

Two dwarves brushed past in a quick swirl of thick, colorful fabrics, the woman holding her skirts up to avoid tripping and the man's eyes gazing at her lovingly. They were so wrapped up in their dance that they nearly toppled into Devlyn before dancing on without a care in the world.

The elves had joined in the festivities as well, although not to the degree of the long-stressed Evellions released from the siege.

Looking across the sea of faces, Devlyn searched for anyone he might know. Before he had scanned half the ballroom, he was tugged from behind and twirled into a dance with Alex hugging and squeezing him. Devlyn had never seen him so happy before. His tactical plan had worked and the dwarves had joined the battle as he'd gambled, but that had not been a guarantee that they would win the battle.

Alex grinned broadly, bursting into laughter every now and then while pulling Devlyn deeper into the ballroom. He said something, but there was so much noise that Devlyn only saw his lips move.

"What was that?" Devlyn tried not to yell over the dancers.

"I'M BETROTHED!"

Devlyn's eyes popped open. He had no idea his cousin had been courting anyone. "Really? Who?"

"DIANA!" Alex hollered.

"Princess Diana?"

Alex's wide smile managed to broaden as he pulled Devlyn into a tight hug, trying to squeeze the air from his lungs, still twirling them about the dance floor. Devlyn had never seen Alex's smile like this before, all his teeth visible.

"You should see what she can do with a bow. She planted an arrow in Lex's chest right in front of me—said I had no right to kill the man who had had her father assassinated and tortured her people for four years. I nearly asked her to marry me then and there!"

"What's to become of Evellion?" Devlyn couldn't help himself. After spending so much time with Ellendren, his mind couldn't avoid thinking of the potential ramifications of Evellion's eldest princess marrying the King of Thellion. Not to mention that the kingdom of Evellion was still in shambles, entire villages had been abandoned, and the state of Cyril and its citizens was still unknown.

"What? Oh, stop worrying yourself over politics for an evening! By Anaweh's Light, enjoy yourself!" Alex beamed, then pulled a rolled up piece of parchment from his pocket and handed it to Devlyn. "By the way, I found this among Lex's possessions. We cleaned out his camp after the renegade army surrendered."

Devlyn unrolled the parchment, expecting to find a letter revealing Lex's official affairs and allegiance. His knees buckled when he saw the loving family in the picture Lex had taken from him on his thirteenth birthday. Three smiling faces looked at him, but two faced each other. A beautiful woman with silver and gold hair looked at the toddler, the artist clearly rendering the child's golden brown hair with hues of black, silver, and copper.

Seeing his family again tore at his heart. Devlyn had to hold onto Alex's shoulder for support as he took in the picture. His father was gone from the World-Below, at the hands of the one who had stolen this portrait.

"Sorry, I should have waited," Alex said, his temperament completely changed as he rubbed Devlyn's back in support.

"No, you shouldn't have. Thank you, Alex. You don't know what this means to me."

"It means I have to finally accept the story you told me when you visited the Cor Inn that first time. Even the part about Velaria turning invisible right in front of Lex's very own eyes!" Alex winked.

"I still have to figure out how that trick works." Devlyn laughed.

"That would've been the first thing I learned."

Devlyn hugged Alex again. "Thank you, cousin." They might not share familiar relations by blood, but Alex was the first family that Devlyn had really known.

"But we're not…"

"Yes, we are."

"Are you two getting sentimental about the announcement?" Devlyn didn't see who spoke behind him. Alex loosened his hold over Devlyn and pulled Diana toward him.

"Diana, have you met my cousin yet?" Alex asked with a sheepish grin as he bowed and extended his arm out. "Devlyn Lorenthien, heir to the Crystal Throne of Krysenthiel, future High King of Eklean, soon to be Prefect of the Guardian Senate, and Phaedryn extraordinaire!"

"Impressive. Did you get a tutor so you could remember all that?" Devlyn smirked, uncomfortable with the introduction.

"I'll have you know that I paid some attention to Kai and Ethyl during their classes."

Diana laughed as she inclined her head and curtsied, her braid woven with a blue ribbon dangling over her shoulder. "I can't thank you enough for ridding Evellion of those monsters."

"Having twelve fewer shadow elves in the world benefits us all," Devlyn said, bowing with one hand on his heart in the elven way. "I'm told you denied Alex a confrontation with his uncle."

"He's the one who tried to deny me. The nerve! And then getting all upset over it because he thought it was his right as king. It's not too late to cut this engagement short if that's going to be your attitude going forward either," Diana said, her eyes playful.

"Only if you intend to marry me sooner." Alex's eyes danced as he looked at Diana and for a moment, Devlyn thought they very well might shorten the betrothal.

"And how long do you think it takes to actually plan a wedding? Between a princess and king nonetheless!" Diana laughed.

"We say a couple words, Arlyn says a few more, we kiss, we dance, leave all the nosy bystanders behind as we…" Alex's eyebrows leapt up and he grinned wolfishly.

"Oh, you are delusional."

"Perhaps not as delusional as he seems," Devlyn said as Ellendren floated to the front of his mind.

Alex understood Devlyn's meaning for he rounded on Devlyn. "Have you been holding out on me?"

"Not intentionally."

"Oh really? We've been together for an entire month and you were only gone this morning. Are you telling me that in that short time, you and Ellendren became betrothed?"

"Look at him! I think it's more than a betrothal!" Diana said. "How is that possible? You and Ellendren? Forgive me, but that was quick—rushed even."

Devlyn blushed. "We didn't even announce our intent to each other. It's just that when we entered the Empyrean Sphere together to learn to wield lumenys, the six-winged anadel declared us wed."

"Truly? Surely, you'll still have a ceremony and a formal coronation though, yes? Eklean will demand nothing less," Diana said.

"I think so. We didn't exactly have the time to talk about it. I did have to rush back here, after all." Devlyn scratched the back of his head, growing uncomfortable with talk of his new status in life as a married elf.

He still didn't know why that six-winged anadel had declared them one; he and Ellendren were too young to be married. Their marriage meant much more than sharing their love with each other—they were now the Lorenthien aryl and would become the Exalted Aryl of Krysenthiel when they took back Arenthyl.

From the corner of Devlyn's eye, he saw Ei'denai Fendryl dancing with Queen Lara. Fendryl towered above the no longer pregnant queen. They danced slower than everyone else. Devlyn couldn't believe she had recovered so quickly after giving birth. Perhaps the ei'ana had helped and quickened the healing. Excusing himself, Devlyn left Alex and Diana, and made his way across the ballroom. Fendryl and Lara paused their slow and fluid steps, and welcomed Devlyn, Fendryl with a nod and Lara with a hug.

"I'm relieved to see you were able to make it tonight," Fendryl said. "You were asleep before I even had you on my griffin."

"Thank you for that. I take it the giants and renegade army were defeated?" Devlyn asked. He still had no idea how the battle had ended, aside from them being victorious.

"The giants are not the most intelligent among anacordel, but smart enough to know when they are beaten. I can't say if it's the last we'll see of them, but they won't be quick in returning to Everin. As for the renegade Perrien militia led by the former general and Thellish king's uncle, Lex Telvin, their forces folded once the Thellish army arrived, shortly after you defeated the shadow elves. They surrendered their weapons and went peacefully. I'm under the impression that Karl, a son of Gneal, is leading the interrogations," Fendryl said with a kind smile.

"I trust you know how grateful all Evellion is to you." Lara's voice was relaxed, but Devlyn picked up a note of relief.

"Your daughter made it quite clear," Devlyn said. "And congratulations. How is the baby doing?"

"Thank you. I don't know if my Amry expected his death to come so early, but he was insistent on bringing another child into this war-torn world. He'll scold me from beyond the grave, but I've named our child after him. He'll be King Amryian II."

His thoughts drifted from the next king to the future of Evellion. Devlyn looked warily at Lara. He knew that Ellendren would lecture him if he didn't ask about the forthcoming roles of Evellion and Thellion. "If you don't mind my asking, Your Majesty, what will happen to Evellion with Thellion reborn?"

"It has been discussed," Lara said. "There has been much debate among the nobles here in Everin, particularly among the dukes. We have been a sovereign kingdom for thousands of years directly descended from Thellion, yet our independence could not prevent our near destruction. If it were not for the intervention of others, nothing would remain of us."

"Has anything been decided?"

"Alexander and I are meeting later this week, perhaps on Saraen, with hopes that Saraquel, or Sariel as you know him, will guide us. It is appropriate for the anadel who watches us humans to be honored on the day of the week named for him. It has already been determined that Perrien and Parendior are retaining all their individual rights, with Thellion maintaining suzerainty over them. The same would likely remain true for Evellion. Our kingdom and line of kings would continue as a province of Thellion. But do not mistake me; while I'm overly delighted that the young king and my daughter seem to have quite the agreeable relationship, their marriage is very much part of Evellion joining Thellion once more. Our relations could have been quite strained if they had seen each other differently."

"We all wish them a happy union," Devlyn said.

"Will you remain until Saraen? Your presence will be greatly appreciated as Evellion decides her fate," said Lara, returning to their earlier topic.

"I'll have to discuss it with Ellendren first. I believe she'd skin me alive if I remain here another day without her consent," said Devlyn, running his hand through his hair, counting how many weeks—months—had passed since he had left the Luminari encampment. He could only imagine how far his reputation had plummeted among the aryls with his extended absence.

With the hope of what was to come, Devlyn's thoughts turned sour as the loss of Alethea sprung into his mind.

"A number of the Eldinari aryls are in Stellantis because of her loss," Fendryl said before Devlyn could voice his thoughts. Startled yet again by the evidence of the Eldinari elves' awareness of thoughts, Devlyn did his best to disguise his surprise.

Fendryl smiled. "Wyn's report about Alethea's disappearance has stirred great unrest among the Eldinari. Our defenses at home must be strengthened if Ramiel is tearing a veil in our world."

"Aewen mentioned this to me, but I don't understand. What do you mean by tearing a veil?" Devlyn asked.

"Anaweh created three realms. Lumaeniel, which has always been, Somnaeniel, which is the bridge, and Teraeniel, the physical realm. Ramiel envisions only two realms—the realms that have always existed: Lumaeniel and the Void. He wants to rival Anaweh in Lumaeniel from his own realm, the Void. It has ever been his intent. If he succeeds in tearing the veil away between the Void and Teraeniel and Somnaeniel, his realm will destroy Teraeniel and Somnaeniel as we know it. You've seen the pits of darkness and the holes in the sky. If left unchecked, they will grow and become more common. The sky will tear and children will fall into the nothingness until there is only the Void."

"Is that where Alethea is? Aewen led me to believe that we could save her," Devlyn said, focusing on what he was able to understand.

"She is lost to us, Devlyn."

"Do you think she was called by Anaweh?"

"The Great Transition does not occur as such," Fendryl replied. "We will mourn and celebrate Alethea in time, but that is not what tonight is for."

Devlyn wanted to ask more questions; there had to be more to Alethea's disappearance. She couldn't simply be gone. He did not want to give up on Alethea but his mind returned to something else that he could do. The whole reason he had needed to learn to wield lumenys was to remove the Shroud.

"I'm not sure if you heard, but Lucillia is no more. All that remains is a statue of the woman the city was named after. I managed to persuade the Luminari to journey for the Shroud—I intend to reclaim Krysenthiel."

"Truly?" Lara asked, her hand raised to cover her mouth. "The Shroud has stood for over fourteen hundred years."

"You're aware that Erynor will do everything in his power to prevent that?" Fendryl asked. "What Everin has faced will be considered child's play."

"Can we trust on your support?"

"We did not leave the Eldin Wood to remain along her borders."

"Thank you, Ei'denai," Devlyn said, his palm raised to his heart, his head bowing slightly.

"Ramiel's prison is weakening. We must reach Verakryl and reseal the prison beneath the tree's roots before it is too late, Ei'denai," Fendryl said in return.

Epilogue

Dark clouds hung over Broid again that night. They'd grown darker over the past months and rarely did the sun make an appearance. Confined to the imperial palace, Evellyn had forgotten what it was like to feel the sun on her skin. Its absence left her melancholic. Broid had been built on the coast of what became known as the Erynien Bay, and one of the joys for her citizens was to watch the ever-present sun sparkling on the water. She could only imagine how devastating the lack of sun was to those accustomed to it. The Cyndinari drank in the sunrays as though it sustained them.

The lack of sun also brought a chill that Evellyn was sure the Cyndinari never had to cope with before. She wished she could wear something more appropriate for the weather, instead of the thin silks falling loosely about her body, but her wardrobe was dictated by another. Every morning a servant came into her cell, presenting her with clothing for the day, preselected by a Cyndinari who had not lost all their senses to the Darkness. The sight of Cyndinari with vibrant red hair and bronzed skin sparked a sliver of hope in her. Perhaps they weren't completely lost—perhaps they were just as much Erynor's—no, Ramiel's—slaves as much as she was.

Evellyn was not the only one forced to constantly stand in the imperial throne room. At any one time, there were at least fifteen others, most of them Cyndinari elves, approved by Erynor to serve him personally.

They were banned from the abominable practice of claiming another's spirit for their own to elongate their life. If they had, their bodies would decay and the natural beauty Erynor enjoyed so much would fade. Their clothing left as little to the imagination as her own garments. Other than the servants cleaning the palace and cooking in the kitchens, none of Erynor's servants were old. Their role in the Erynien court depended on their youthful appearance and they were easily replaced, sent to a less visible role the moment Erynor grew tired of them. Besides herself, the oldest among his personal servants had not yet seen thirty springs.

The imperial throne room was quiet for the moment and other than herself and the other servants, blessedly empty.

Evellyn knew Erynor would return soon. The longest he had been away from his throne before was eight days. Today marked the tenth day of his absence and an anxiety filled the palace. Every servant was uneasy, expecting him to return in a rare fury. Evellyn shared their fear.

While the palace was always more enjoyable when Erynor was away, Evellyn feared that his current absence was partly due to her Devlyn. The image of Erynor flying from Broid on that beast of a dragon petrified her and she had not slept soundly since he had disappeared ten days ago. He had attacked Ceurenyl the last time he had been gone for an extended period, and directly confronted Devlyn, who had miraculously escaped unscathed.

Distracted by her worried thoughts, Evellyn was looking out the window when the grand doors banged open, both doors exploding outward to smack against the wall. Erynor fumed through the room, scowling, fists clenched. His eyes bore into Evellyn as he walked directly to her.

Unwavering, Evellyn returned his gaze, careful not to show any emotion or depth; she buried her heartbreak and the secret she held deeply inside in self-preservation. No longer able to receive consolation from Dolan, her only solace was thinking of her children.

Reaching her faster than he should have been able to, Erynor grabbed her by the throat and lifted her from the ground. His grip burned against her skin as though fire issued from his fingertips. Her initial shock quickened to panic. She tried to pry his scalding fingers from her throat, while also trying to support herself.

Tightening his grip, Erynor spoke. Evellyn saw his lips move and heard words but could not make any sense of them.

"Father!" one of the Deurghol called out. There was never any way of knowing which of the Deathless was Erynor's eldest son. They all looked and acted the same, but she knew one of them was his supposed heir. Evellyn could barely see him, too overwhelmed with the unbearable pain. But as she squinted, the shadow lessened a bit around that Deurghol and she saw his tender eyes through the encasing darkness looking directly at her. A silver light shone through. It was brief and dimmed before she could believe her sight was true. She blamed it on the lack of circulation as Erynor throttled her.

His grip on her throat lessened when he flung her away. She collided shoulder first with a pillar, and pain exploded across her body.

The other servants watched hesitantly, none daring to make direct eye contact with Erynor or Evellyn.

"Never interrupt me again; is that clear?"

"Yes, Father."

Hands moving slowly to her throat, Evellyn massaged her assaulted and tender skin and breathed deeply. Erynor's screaming finally began to register just as his attention returned to her.

"Your son lost me the north! Twelve of my shadow elves are gone thanks to him and those cowards from the Eldin Wood!"

Evellyn knew he was expecting her to look up at him, but she could not easily move her injured neck.

"Look at me," he roared.

Lifting her chin, her eyes eventually met his. There was no shame or apology on behalf of Devlyn in her expression. She dared to let her pride and resolve stare back at the Erynien Emperor.

"You dare mock me," Erynor said just above a whisper.

His tone terrified her. She expected that after keeping her prisoner for fifteen years, today was the day he would finally kill her or steal her soul for one of his wretched shadow elves.

"I should have had him killed while he wept on that weak craven you married." Turning away from Evellyn, Erynor motioned to the Deurghol and to Aren that they were to approach.

"The Luminari camp outside my Shroud," Erynor said, taking a seat on his throne. "I want you to discourage them. I want them to know that there is no life for them anywhere! Not Lucillia! Not Krysenthiel! Not Luminare! Not anywhere!"

The Deurghol and Aren nodded.

"Take as many legions north as you require. Do not fail me a second time."

"And should they destroy the Shroud?" one of the Deurghol asked.

"Should she die, burn them all."

She? Evellyn mused.

Here ends the Fourth Part of

The Jewel of Life:

Burning Desire

Look for the Fifth Part of

The Jewel of Life:

Spires of Arenthyl

Appendix A
Glossary of Terms

Abbey School

The preferred system of education for children throughout Eklean. Those deemed capable are sent to higher studies, preferably at Gwilnor Academy.

Aelish

Native language of the elves. Largely forgotten, only used in academic circles.

Aerys

An elemental erendinth. The essence of air.

Albien

One of the seven Schools of Septyl. Albiens focus on truth and care for many of Eklean's libraries. Motto: Truth is discoverable. Emblem: A naked male and female elf holding unraveled scrolls with an owl perched behind, cast in gold on a white field. The chair of Albien is known as the Seeker.

Aldarch

Deific rulers of Aldinare who reigned from their sanctums.

Aldinare

Western Skyland of the Aldinari, one of the four elven kindreds. Lost to the Darkness. Only a hundred Aldinari escaped the Skyland with their lives.

Alicorn

A legendary beast native to the Skyland of Aldinare. A winged unicorn.

Anadel

Spiritual creatures that predate Teraeniel and Somnaeniel. Their native home is Lumaeniel. There are four known classifications of anadel: irythil, enthiel, lorendil, and naril.

Anacordel

Creatures of body, soul, and spirit.

Anaweh

The Creating Light.

Animys

A transcendental erendinth. The essence of spirit.

Aquaeys

An elemental erendinth. The essence of water.

Arantiulyn

One of the seven Schools of Septyl. Arantiulyns focus on strength and protection and oversee the Knights of Septyl. Motto: With fortitude, we will protect. Emblem: A naked male and female elf in a fighting stance with swords in hand with a lion prowling cast in gold on an orange field. The Chair of Arantiulyn is known as the General.

Arcane Gems

Sources of magic used by the Mages of the Kilnae Del.

Archsteward

Part of the Ei'ceuril hierarchy, they are elevated wise ones. Before kien wielders were restricted to the Temple of Ceur, archstewards lived in every major city of Eklean tending to those faithful to Anaweh, the Creating Light.

Arenthylean Bells

Twenty-four bells composed of four materials that ring every hour.

Aryl

The united head of an elven house composed of a king and queen or lord and lady.

Auburnis

One of the seven Schools of Septyl. Auburnises focus on inner peace. Motto: To love is our gift. Emblem: A naked male and female elf offering a garland with larks flying above, cast in gold on a brown field. The Chair of Auburnis is known as the Pilgrim.

Aurephaen

Feast day of the Luminari, commemorating Auriel and the dawning sun. Celebrated on the 15th of Aurenth, the spring equinox.

Azurelle

One of the seven Schools of Septyl. Azurelles focus on the advancement and training of the erendinth. Motto: The zealous soul must be temperate. Emblem: A naked male and female elf wielding the powers with a dragon behind, cast in gold on a blue field. The Chair of Azurelle is known as the Blue Dragon.

Belin's Watch

An Evellion city in the Vespien Mountains comprised of humans and dwarves. Named for Belin, the dwarf who sheltered Thellion refugees in their greatest hour of need.

Borephaen

Feast day of the Eldinari, commemorating Boriel and the sleeping sun. Celebrated on the 15th of Borenth, the winter solstice.

Bowl of Theniel

Sea set apart by the merpeople as sacred. The place where Theniel brought the waters to Teraeniel.

Centaur

Anacordel dedicated to protecting the forests of Eklean, particularly the Illumined Wood. The upper body is like an elf's but broader and more rugged while the lower body looks much like a four-legged horse.

Ceurendol

The Jewel of Life. Created by the Luminari by placing their life essence within seven jewels of incredible brilliance which allowed them to share their immortality with every race in 1.3a (7085.3E). Also known as the Light Diamond, the Lieben Stone, and the Heart of Hearts.

Ceurendol War, the

A cataclysmic war instigated by the Erynien Empire which began over a philosophical difference over the Jewel of Life and whether immortal life was proper for the 'lesser races.' The war divided Eklean in two factions, those faithful to the Luminari and those subjugated by the Erynien Empire. As the fate of the war grew clear, emissaries and merchants from other continents withdrew from Eklean, fearing the Erynien Empire. 322-500.3a (7407-7585.3E).

Ceurenyl

City founded by the ei'ceuril. Home of the Temple of Ceur and Gwilnor Academy. The only city not to fall into Erynor's control when Krysenthiel was lost to the Shroud.

Ceurtriarch

Leader of the ei'ceuril, known as High Archsteward and Arbiter of the Light.

Chancellor

The head of Gwilnor Academy under the authority of and appointed by the Seven Chairs.

Children

When capitalized, refers to the proto-race.

Citadel, the

Seat of the Sha'ghol on Cyndinare.

Cor'lera

A small village in eastern Parendior and in disputed territory claimed by both Lucillia and Perrien. The vineyards of Cor'lera produce the coveted ice wine, the Cor'leran Blue.

Crimsyn

One of the seven Schools of Septyl. Crimsyns focus on healing and run many hospitals and infirmaries throughout Eklean. Motto: Through healing, hope is given. Emblem: A naked male and female elf dancing with a dog, cast in gold on a red field. The chair of Crimsyn is known as the Physician.

Cyndinare

Southern Skyland of the Cyndinari, one of the four elven kindreds. Lost to the Darkness.

Cynethol

Home of the Cyndinari, situated among the Kinzdol Islands.

Daereneth

Continent south of Ogren and west of Ja'Horan. Tropical continent.

Deurghol

The Cyndinari directly responsible for the Shroud. They are neither living nor dead. Also known as the Deathless.

Draelyn

A mixed race anacordel of dragon and elven origins.

Draelish

Native language of the draelyn.

Dragon

Legendary creatures bound to the erendinth.

Druids of Kweil Aitch, the

Secluded faction of humans who learned to walk Somaeniel, the World-in-Between early on.

Dwarf

Anacordel who sought the deep roots of the mountains.

Ealyn

Leaders of the draelyn of Tenethyl.

Ei'ana

An organized group of wielders. Since the Balance was lost during the Ceurendol War, there are only kiara wielders among the ei'ana. There has not been a kien wielder among the ei'ana for over a thousand years.

Ei'ana Counsels

A series of norms ei'ana are to follow in regards to wielding. The counsels prohibit men from becoming ei'ana due to their inability to wield safely after the Balance was lost. The counsels also require ei'ana to bring kien wielders to the Temple of Ceur for their own protection and the protection of their communities.

Ei'ceuril

A religious order, currently a majority of men, focused on serving Anaweh, the Creating Light. Because a kien wielder is not capable of wielding with control, every male ei'ceuril capable of wielding is confined to the Temple of Ceur.

Ei'denai

Elven lord serving as aryl with his spouse. Head of House.

Ei'ethil

Elven lord.

Ei'lythel

Elven lady.

Ei'terel

Elven lady serving as aryl with her spouse. Head of House.

Eklean

Continent where the anacordel first stirred as Children.

Elder Ones

Anacordel that evolved from the Children before the Great Blessing, at which time the different races were solidified.

Eldin Wood, the

Home of the Eldinari.

Eldinare

Northern Skyland of the Eldinari, one of the four elven kindreds. Lost to the Darkness. The Eldinari were the first to evacuate their Skyland for the lands below.

Elemental Erendinth, the

Forces wielded to influence the elements. *See Erendinth.*

ELF

Anacordel who changed little when the different races were created. Because they wished to retain their original form, their immortality remained, and they were gifted the Skylands. There are four elven kindreds, the Luminari, Cyndinari, Aldinari, and Eldinari.

ELYA

Powerful wielders born of any race who learn to wield instinctively and are not limited to the restrictions common to normal kien and kiara wielders.

EMRADIEL

One of the seven Schools of Septyl. Emradiels focus on beauty and life. Motto: Only the prudent thrive. Emblem: A naked male and female elf gesturing with open palms toward the beauty around them with a stag behind, cast in gold on a green field. The chair of Emradiel is known as the Tender.

ENTHIEL

Anadel dedicated to one of the seven irythil. The enthiel are very involved with the anacordel. A single enthiel guides an entire people.

ERENDINTH, THE

The erendinth are the wielded powers believed to have created Teraeniel. Tradition says that there are seven powers, three transcendental: lumenys, animys, and umbrys; and four elemental: aquaeys, aerys, terys, and ignys. Much is forgotten or unknown about the full extent of the erendinth which are dependent on inner spiritual and emotional workings.

ERENDINTH GAMES, THE

A game of wielding created at Gwilnor Academy, involving the wielding of all seven erendinth.

FAUN

Short nocturnal anacordel with the hind legs of a goat from the navel down. Some fauns have horns.

GIANT

Anacordel that were drawn to the frozen north. During the Great Blessing, their physical features became capable of withstanding the harsh tundra of Glacien.

GLACIEN

Northern frozen continent spanning the northern pole. Connects Eklean and Ogren.

Goblin

Anacordel native to the Kinzdol Islands. Known for their monetary shrewdness.

Goblin Guild

Infamous bank and guild of Eklean. Regulates the majority of Eklean's currency. The Goblin Guild is based in the Kinzdol Islands with branches in every city and most villages.

Great Blessing, the

Event recorded in the Theseryn where Anaweh blessed the growing differences among the anacordel and solidified their choices by making each their own distinct race.

Guardian Knights

Order of knights once based in Krysenthiel that served and protected all the land from injustice. The Guardian Knights were largely composed of Luminari and were defeated during the Ceurendol War.

Guardian Senate, the

An international body, crossing countries and continents to ensure the wellbeing of Teraeniel. Disbanded toward the end of the Ceurendol War.

Gwilnor Academy

The foremost school dedicated to the education of wielders, located in Ceurenyl.

Holy Tomes

Volumes recorded by various ei'ceuril, some being prophets, and from which the ei'ceuril base their beliefs and practices.

Human

Anacordel that differ among themselves more than any other race. They traveled the furthest from the Valley of Saeryndol, migrating across the entirety of Teraeniel.

Ignys

An elemental erendinth. The essence of fire.

Illumined Wood, the

A vast forest with mysterious qualities and inhabitants.

Imperium

Selective school for Cyndinari youth. Its violent academic style educates the next generation of shadow elves.

IRYTHIL

The seven anadel who, under Anaweh's guidance, introduced the erendinth, thereby creating Teraeniel.

JA'HORAN

Continent south of Eklean. Inhabited largely by nomadic peoples.

JAHRO ISLANDS

Island chain in the Unarian Sea. Believed to be the home of pirates.

JIENZU

Heart, mind, and body practice of meditation, breathing, and body positions called forms, used by the draelyn and ancient elves to achieve balance. Largely forgotten.

JUDGES OF YANIL

An order that once ruled beside the Yanilean. The judges are now a secret organization that strives to uphold law and order with limited influence.

KEEPER

Head of the time wardens and possessor of the time key.

KIARA WIELDER

A female wielder. Kiara wielders learn to control the erendinth easily but require a kien wielder to reach their potential strength. Because the Balance was lost, kiara wielders are not able to reach their potential strength.

KIEN WIELDER

A male wielder. Kien wielders reach their potential strength easily but require a kiara wielder to learn control of the erendinth. Because the Balance was lost, kien wielders are not able to wield safely, and if any male begins to show an aptitude to wield, he is sent to the Temple of Ceur where wielding is impossible.

KILNAE DEL

Order of mages native to Charren, headquartered in the Charrenese capital, Karithel.

KINZDOL ISLANDS

An archipelago in southern Eklean, homeland to the goblins and Cyndinari.

KWEIL AITCH

Island east of the Illumined Wood. The place where the veil is thin between Teraeniel and Somnaeniel.

Lay Votary

A non-clerical class of ei'ceuril.

Lethien

A mixed race anacordel of elven and human origins. Largely extinguished by Erynor during and after the Ceurendol War.

Lorendil

Anadel that guard and protect individual anacordel. Some anacordel are known to communicate with their lorendil.

Lucillian Alliance, the

An alliance of the Eklean kingdoms established to return peace and order to Eklean following Emperor Erynor's disappearance.

Lumaeniel

The World-Beyond. Dwelling of Anaweh, the anadel, and those anacordel who have passed beyond.

Lumenys

A transcendental erendinth. The essence of light.

Luminare

Eastern Skyland of the Luminari, one of the four elven kindreds. Lost to the Darkness. The Luminari evacuated their Skyland for the lands below where they established Krysenthiel.

Mar'anathyl

City on the Skyland of Luminare. Governed by the Lorenthien aryls.

Masters, the (Seven Masters, the)

Vigyl Vyoletryn, Cyrelle Azurelle, Lanielle Emradiel, Lyon Arantiulyn, Mainor Auburnis, Caelyn Crimsyn, and Saeyrn Albien are the founders of the Seven Schools of Septyl and Gwilnor Academy.

Meridean Conclave

Governing council of the merpeople.

Meridephaen

Feast day of the Cyndinari, commemorating Meridiel and the noon sun. Celebrated on the 15th of Meridenth, the summer solstice.

Merpeople

Anacordel who longed for the depths of Teraeniel's oceans.

MIERVAE

Anacordel who longed to nurture Teraeniel's forests. Miervae are also referred to as Great Trees and begin their life as Settlings.

MINUM

The least of Eklean's anacordel. A short mixed race anacordel of goblin and human origins. Before the elves migrated to Eklean, they were enslaved, sold by goblins to humans.

NARIL

Anadel reminiscent of the seven erendinth. There are seven types of narils and they are commonly known as nymphs.

NYMPHS

See Naril.

OBSERVANT

Non-wielders who have dedicated themselves to one of the Seven Schools of Septyl.

OGRE

Brutish anacordel covering the vast majority of Ogren. Mixed race anacordel of giant and human origins.

OGREN

Continent east of Eklean and west of Qien. Mountainous land with a mixture of forests and deserts. Inhabited by giants, humans, and ogres.

PHAEDRYN

Those bound with a phoenix.

PURGED DESERT OF DWONIA, THE

A vast wasteland in western Eklean that was rumored to have at one point been fertile. Home of the Twelve Tribes of Dwonia.

RETURN

The final stage of formation of an ei'ceuril toward becoming a steward. Often occurring in the Illumined Wood.

SANCTUM

Expansive complexes housing the aldarchs and their courts on Aldinare.

SCHTACH

Language of the dwarves.

Schtam

(1) A dwarven people. (2) The dwellings of the dwarves.

Schtamite

The eight dwarven schtams.

Seguian

A portal created to traverse space and time. Traversing time is restricted and only the keeper can use the time key to traverse time.

Septyl

(1) The order of Ei'ana composing the Seven Schools of Septyl. (2) The city of the ei'ana in Krysenthiel and now lost in the Shroud.

Septyl Knights

Order of knights dedicated to Septyl. The knights receive their training at Gwilnor Academy and vow to serve one of the Seven Schools of Septyl.

Seraph

Six winged anadel in Lumaeniel.

Servants of Shadow

Secret organization carrying out the orders of shadow elves and, in some instances, the orders of the Deurghol.

Settling

Tree-like creatures that wander about in their youth until finding an appropriate place to settle their roots and grow into a Miervae, also known as a Great Tree. Settlings have unique vitality qualities.

Seven Chairs of Septyl, the

The leaders of the Ei'ana. Each of the Seven Schools elects its own Chair who leads his or her particular School and participates in the leadership of Septyl. Responsible for admitting student wielders into Gwilnor Academy and selecting a chancellor.

Seven Schools of Septyl, the

The order of Ei'ana, composed of Albien, Arantiulyn, Auburnis, Azurelle, Crimsyn, Emradiel, and Vyoletryn Schools.

Shadow Elves

Cyndinari who consume the spirit of others to prolong their own life.

Sha'ghol

Past rulers of the Cyndinari. First to communicate with Ramiel after her was imprisoned and wield tenebrys.

Shifting

(1) The ability to teleport in Somnaeniel. (2) The Phaedryn ability to teleport physically in Teraeniel.

Shroud, the

A diseased-looking fog placed by the Cyndinari over the entirety of Krysenthiel. It severed the Luminari from the Jewel of Life, cutting them off from their life essence and making them mortal, as well as any others who had benefited from it. An unanticipated result was that the Cyndinari also lost their immortality with that placement of the Shroud over the Jewel of Life. The Shroud's mysterious origin is one reason no one has been able to remove it.

Skylands, the

Four island countries, Aldinare, Cyndinare, Eldinare, and Luminare, floating in the clouds thousands of feet above the ground. The dwelling places of the elves before they were forced to evacuate to the land below.

Sojourners

The exiled of Dwonia who sought reentrance after forming an allegiance with the Erynien Empire.

Somnaeniel

The World-in-Between. A realm visited by dreamers. Gateway between Lumaeniel and Teraeniel.

Star Warden

An elven military unit, typically ensuring the protection of their lands.

Steward

A clerical class of ei'ceuril with the ability to wield.

Stewards of Shadow

Ei'ceuril stewards who forsook Anaweh to support Ramiel.

Temple of Ceur, the

Home to the ei'ceuril and pilgrimage site for the faithful. It is impossible to wield within the temple walls. All kien wielders are confined to the Temple of Ceur.

Temple Knights

Order of knights dedicated to protecting the Temple of Ceur and the city of Ceurenyl. Some of the temple knights are men who were brought to the temple when it was discovered that they could wield. These temple knights are prohibited from leaving the temple.

TENEBRAE

An unrecognized School of Septyl intended to replace the other seven Schools. Its adherents focus on power and dominance. Motto: Might conquers. Emblem: A naked male and female elf standing triumphantly on seven broken emblems, cast in gold on a black field. The chair of Tenebrae is known as the Conqueror.

TENEBRYS

A corrupted form of the erendinth, unrecognized by the Ei'ana of Septyl as one of the erendinth and absolutely forbidden to wield. The essence of Darkness.

TENETHYL

(1) Jeweled city of the draelyn hidden in the Illumined Wood. (2) City destroyed by Ramiel's forces before the Great Blessing.

TERAENIEL

The World-Below. Composed of the continents Daereneth, Eklean, Glacien, Ja'Horan, Ogren, and Qien.

TERYS

An elemental erendinth. The essence of stone.

THESERYN

Holy tome recording the creation of Teraeniel and the anacordel, written by the first Ceurtriarch of the Ei'ceuril. The Theseryn states that seven irythil, under Anaweh's guidance, introduced the erendinth thereby creating Teraeniel.

TIME KEY

An artifact created by the Luminari to restrict the ability to traverse space and time. It was entrusted to the minums, the least of Eklean's races.

TIME WARDENS

A select group of minums entrusted by the Luminari with the ability to create seguians, allowing them to travel to any place and any time.

TRANSCENDENTAL ERENDINTH, THE

Wielded forces to influence the ethereal realities of lumenys, animys, and umbrys. The ability to wield the transcendental erendinth is forgotten.

TREE SPIRITS

Narils who agreed to bond with the trees under Sariel's guidance.

UMBRYS

A transcendental erendinth. The essence of shadow.

VAER

Fruit native to the Illumined Wood.

VALLEY OF SAERYNDOL

Birthplace of the Children, the first anacordel.

VERAKRYL

A crystalline tree within Mount Verinien which brought life to the world and is connected to Anaweh. Also known as the Tree of Life.

VERATHEL

Sprouts of Verakryl, the Tree of Life.

VERATHN

Weapons of power.

VESPEPHAEN

Feast day of the Aldinari, commemorating Vespiel and the setting sun. Celebrated on the 15th of Vespenth, the autumn equinox.

VOID, THE

A realm that existed before Teraeniel and Somnaeniel. Realm of Ramiel and the fallen anadel.

VYOLETRYN

One of the Seven Schools of Septyl. Vyoletryns focus on justice and diplomacy. Motto: With justice, peace. Emblem: A naked male and female elf holding a staff with an eagle soaring above, cast in gold on a violet field. The chair of Vyoletryn is known as the Watcher.

WIELDERS

Anacordel capable of wielding the erendinth.

WINGED HORSES OF THELLION

Ancestors of the grey coursers of Perrien.

WISE ONES

(1) Part of the Ei'ceuril hierarchy. There is no certainty how many are among the ei'ceuril. (2) Part of the Ei'ana hierarchy. There are seven wise ones for every School of Septyl.

YANILEAN, THE

The undisputed monarch of Yanil, always male. Used both as the monarch's title and as his name during his reign.

Days of the Week

(Based on the seven anadel involved in the creation of Teraeniel)

Gwynthaen–Thenaen–Uraen–Ramaen–Lerenaen–Saraen–Karaen

Months/Moons

(Based on the anadel attached to the elves)

Spring – Marenth, Aurenth, Delenth

Summer – Dynenth, Meridenth, Reventh

Autumn – Kyrénth, Vespenth, Orenth

Winter – Estlenth, Borenth, Lierenth

Currency

Goblin Guild currency – 16 iron angots for a copper lewt. 9 copper lewts for a silver jent. 13 silver jents for a gold crown. 3 golden crowns for a lumol.

Luminari currency – 8 kenols for a narol. 4 narols for a lumol.

APPENDIX B

DRAMATIS PERSONAE

AARON ROENDRYN

Luminari. Ceurtriarch. Prince of Lucillia, brother of Ellendren. Ei'ceuril.

ABBIE WINTYR

Human with emerald eyes. Student at Gwilnor Academy. Druid of Kweil Aitch.

AEN FINAMARC

Lethien from Cor'lera, squire to Alex Vaerin.

AGNELLE PHANSTIENNE

Luminari. Ei'ana and Chair of Auburnis.

ALESEI

Queen of Tiel. Of the Royal House Ziera.

ALETHEA LENWYN

Eldinari. Emradiel ei'ana and former Lenwyn aryl.

ALEXANDER (ALEX) VAERIN

Human from Perrien, whose family migrated to Cor'lera. King of Thellion.

ALIEL

The first phoenix born since the fall of Krysenthiel, bound to Devlyn.

AMRY THELLION

Former king of Evellion. Married to Queen Lara. *Deceased.*

ANDREA FARNEIS

Human from Sudern. Septyl knight. Nephew to Duke Farneis. Known as Andrew.

ANGENNIA (ANGE) SORICCI

Human from Yanil. Judge of Yanil.

ARBOL

A faun searching for settlings.

AREN LORENTHIEN

Luminari. Led a rescue party to Aldinare and did not return. Now a Dark Phaedryn in service to Erynor.

ARLYN

Ei'ceuril steward from Cor'lera. Devlyn's uncle on his mother's side.

BASTIEN

Human from Sorenthil. Temple knight.

BERNARD

Human from Perrien. Ei'ceuril, librarian, and magister at the abbey school of Cor'lera.

BYRON ROENDRYN

Luminari. Lord knight. Brother to Vernal.

CAIRN

Human. Chief of Tribe Laith. Son of Suin.

CATALINA TURLAN

Human from Yanil. Supreme Judge of Yanil.

CECILLE FARNEIS

Human from Sudern. Daughter to Duke Farneis.

CIAREN

Draelyn of the Gold House.

CLARA

Aldinari. Ei'ceuril, steward and abbess of the Monastery of the Poor Ladies in the Ashton Wood.

CLOVIS

Cyndinari. Attendant to Yloran. Known in Lankor as Bieto.

DANIELLE AERQUIN

Luminari of House Aerquin. Student wielder at Gwilnor Academy.

DAPHNE ASHTON

Human from Mindale. Lady of Ashton Wood. Emradiel ei'ana.

DAPHNEL

Human from Ceurenyl. Temple knight.

DEVLYN LORENTHIEN

Ward of Cor'lera's abbey school. Physical features indicate Lucillian ancestry.

DIANA THELLION

Princess of Evellion. Eldest daughter of Amry and Lara.

DOLAN LORENTHIEN

Father of Devlyn, Leilyn, and Liam. Husband of Evellyn. Son of Eldinari Lei-enya Lierafen and an unknown Cyndinari, although this is undisclosed. Raised in the human Telvin family of Cor'lera. *Deceased.*

Eagan Wintyr

Human. Druid of Kweil Aitch, and Abbie's brother.

Ealyndol Roendryn

Luminari. Former Ceurtriarch. *Deceased.*

Elayne Thenrel

Luminari. Guardian knight.

Ellendren Roendryn

Luminari. Princess of Lucillia. Student wielder at Gwilnor Academy.

Emdian

Human from Sudern. Ei'ceuril steward.

Enrico Desillio

Human from Yanil. Noble in the Yanilean's court.

Entiel Telvin

Human from Perrien. Ei'ceuril, steward, and abbot of the abbey school of Cor'lera. Devlyn's uncle on his father's side.

Erynel Meriden

Cyndinari. Former Sha'ghol and Erynor's mother. *Deceased.*

Erynor Meriden

Emperor of the Erynien Empire. Disappeared after Lucillia gave birth to the twins, Roendryn and Feolyn in 7857.3E. First Cyndinari born on Eklean.

Etienne Jiethel

Human from Briel. Grand chamberlain to His Majesty, King Irvienne Haert of Briel.

Evellyn Lorenthien

Luminari from Cor'lera. Mother of Leilyn and Devlyn. Widow of Dolan. Captive of Erynor.

Ferinn

Merperson. Currently resides in Myrium. Consort and widower of the late Queen Karina Larviere.

Forvl VIII

Dwarf and patriarch of Oern Schtam. Son of Oma and Forvl VII.

Fyona Orendi

Luminari. Student wielder at Gwilnor Academy.

FYREH GLAEDA

Eldinari. Azurelle ei'ana and magister at Gwilnor. Twin brother to Myrah, husband to Suella, and father to many children.

GALITHINOL

Dragon of the Gold Flight. Father to Weilyn and grandfather to Thien, Vivien, and Theseryn.

GENEVIE DALIETH

Human from Briel. Brieli knight and lieutenant.

GORDON CARVIL

King of Torsil. Of the Royal House Carvil. Supporter of Erynor.

HANNAH TORIN

Human from Mindale. Azurelle ei'ana and chancellor of Gwilnor Academy.

HARNYL ROENDRYN

Luminari. Aryl of Lucillia. Married to Queen Vernal. Father of Aaron, Kaela, and Ellendren.

IANTHOL

Cyndinari. Shadow elf. *Deceased*.

ILYNOR

Cyndinari. Shadow elf.

INDRYL

Luminari. Tenebrae ei'ana, once believed to be a Vyoletryn ei'ana.

IRVIENNE HAERT

Human from Briel. King of Briel.

JAEROL SOLARIS

Cyndinari. Former Erynien emissary. Student wielder at Gwilnor Academy.

JAEK

Luminari. Lucillian sentry.

JARIS ILN DESARIS

Cyndinari. One of the Sha'ghol.

JAX

Minum and time warden.

JEANNE DARKEL

Luminari. First of the Guardians.

KAELA ROENDRYN

Luminari. Princess of Lucillia, sister to Ellendren and Aaron.

KAELIEN

Elder One. Queen of Tenethyl. Aunt to Gael. *Deceased.*

KAEYTH ILLIERO

Luminari. Ei'ceuril novice.

KAI

Human with physical features that suggest an origin other than Eklean. Azurelle ei'ana and magister of politics at Gwilnor Academy.

KARINA LARIVIERE

Former Queen of Sorenthil. Widow of the late King Dorian. Wife to Ferinn. Mother of Myranda. *Deceased.*

KARL OLNEY

Human from Perrien. Observant of Vyoletryn.

KEVN WEYVIEN

Luminari. Has studied to become either an ei'ceuril or an ei'ana.

KIARA

A mythical woman believed to be the first female wielder.

KIEN

A mythical man believed to be the first male wielder.

KYRENDAL LORENTHIEN

Luminari. First chancellor of Gwilnor Academy. Crafter of the verathn. Monk at the Monastery of Kyrendal. Son to Kien and Kiara.

LACUS

Human from Torsil. Ei'ceuril steward.

LARA THELLION

Queen of Evellion. Widow of the late King Amry. Azurelle ei'ana.

LARIEL

Phoenix.

LAWRENCE MAROVEN

King of Mindale. Of the Royal House Maroven. Supporter of Erynor.

LEILYN LORENTHIEN

Sister of Devlyn, living in the Illumined Wood. Daughter of Evellyn and Dolan.

LENORA HANARYLD

Human from Ceurenyl. Ei'ana and Chair of Arantiulyn. *Deceased.*

LEX TELVIN

General from Perrien. Leader of the renegade Perrien Militia. Brother to Entiel, Vine, and Dolan, who was adopted. Uncle to Alex.

LIAM LIERAFEN

Son of Dolan. Half-brother to Devlyn and Leilyn. Student wielder at Gwilnor Academy.

LIARA

Dragon of the Red Flight bonded to Prya.

LILLIANNA

Human from Mindale. Ei'ceuril and formerly an Emradiel ei'ana.

LORAL VICALEN.

Luminari. Attendant in the Narielle household. Father to Toryn.

LORETTA JAVIE

Human of Sorenthil. Ei'ana and Chair of Crimsyn.

LUCILLIA

The woman who gave birth to the twins, Roendryn and Feolyn.

LYREN FENTHYR

Luminari. Attendant in the Roendryn household.

MARA

Elder One that lived in Tenethyl.

MELANIE BIRKWELL

Human from Mindale. Ei'ana and Chair of Arantiulyn.

MYRAH GLAEDA

Eldinari. Albien ei'ana and magister at Gwilnor Academy; twin sister to Fyreh.

MYRANDA LARIVIERE

Queen of Sorenthil. Student wielder at Gwilnor Academy.

MYRASHA

Dragon of the Purple Flight.

NAITHOS

Dragon of the Blue Flight.

NATALIE

Luminari living in Cor'lera.

ODUIN DUR SETHARA

Cyndinari. One of the Sha'ghol.

OLIVER PENAULT

Human from Perrien. Septyl knight of Vyoletryn.

OMA

Dwarf of the Oern Schtam. Stone seer.

ORANNA

Luminari. Azurelle ei'ana and former chancellor of Gwilnor Academy. *Deceased.*

ORENIEL

Centaur of the Illumined Wood.

PAOLO FARNEIS

Human from Sudern. Duke of Sudern.

PAUREL ROENDRYN

Luminari. Ei'ana and Chair of Azurelle.

PHENDIEN SHENDIELLE

Eldinari. Ei'ana and true Chair of Emradiel.

PRYA

Draelyn of the Red House. Bonded with Laira.

RAELINTH

Cyndinari. Attendant to Yloran. Known in Lankor as Pico.

RALENIEL

Elder One that lived in Tenethyl. Married to Weilyn.

RAMIRA BIR GINTHOL

Human from Yanil. Supreme Judge of Yanil at the time of Nauto's Wrath.

RAZCUL MIETHEN

Cyndinari. Shadow elf disguised as an Eldinari assistant magister at Gwilnor. Known as Danyol.

REIA

Luminari. Arantiulyn ei'ana.

RENAUD LARIVIERE

Human from Sorenthil. Temple knight. Royal cousin to Queen Myranda Lariviere.

RUSYL

Dragon of the Blue Flight.

SAECRIEN

One of the Children who watches over the Waters of Anaweh.

SAENDRE LIORITH

Luminari. Student wielder at Gwilnor Academy. Assistant magister to Kai.

SANJIN AL'SANHIR

Human from Charren. Crowned Prince of Charren of the Royal House Irithru.

SARA

Human from Briel. Auburnis ei'ana.

SELENYA WAEYN

Luminari. Ei'ana and Chair of Albien.

SKIMP

Minum and time warden.

STEPHEN

Human from Evellion. Temple knight.

SUIN

Former chief of Tribe Laith. Father of Cairn. *Deceased.*

TABITHA

Human from Sudern. Azurelle ei'ana.

TAEN TAERINIOR

Luminari. Ei'ceuril novice.

TERAN

Cyndinari. Uncle of Jaerol.

THERRIL

Ei'ceuril magister of theoreticals at Gwilnor Academy.

THIEN

Draelyn of the Gold House. Married to Loren. Son to Weilyn and Raleniel. Grandson to Galithinol the Gold. *Deceased.*

TIERA WELDON

Luminari. Ei'ana and Chair of Emradiel.

TINDOL

Human from Dwonia. Member of the Sojourners.

TORYN VICALEN

Luminari. Lady of the Watch.

TRETHIEN NARIELLE

Luminari of House Narielle. Student knight at Gwilnor Academy.

TYE

Human from Dwonia. Member of Tribe Fendur.

VELARIA TREYVEN

Cyndinari born in Lucillia. Ei'ana and Chair of Azurelle.

VERNAL ROENDRYN

Luminari. Aryl of Lucillia. Married to King Harnyl. Mother of Aaron, Kaela, and Ellendren. Direct descendant of Lucillia. *Deceased.*

VINE VAERIN

Human from Perrien. Mother of Alex. Devlyn's aunt on his father's side.

VIREN DEKENUREL

Luminari. Guardian knight.

VIVIEN

Draelyn and ealyn of the Gold House. Granddaughter of Galithinol the Gold, and daughter of Weilyn.

WALEISIUS

Merchant in Cor'lera, more commonly known as Walei.

WEILYN

Draelyn of the Gold House. Married to Raleniel. Son to Galithinol. *Deceased.*

WYN LIERAFEN

Eldinari. Grandson of Dalenya and Fendryl. Star Warden. Emradiel ei'ana.

XANTH

Cyndinari. Shadow elf.

YELARIS

Dragon of the Blue Flight. Bonded to Velaria.

YLORAN ETH GNASHAR

Cyndinari. One of the Sha'ghol. Known in Lankor as Enna.

YTHINOR THE BLACK

Dragon of the Dark Flight. Bonded to his half-brother, Erynor.

YVONNE KARDOL

Human from Yanil. Crimsyn ei'ana and Magister of the art of wielding at Gwilnor Academy.

The Seven Irythil and their Associated Enthiel

URIEL – Lord of the Stars, whose name means Anaweh is my Light. Irythil who brought Anaweh's Light to Teraeniel.

> **AURIEL** – The Dawn Star. Guardian of the elves of Luminare.

> **MERIDIEL** – The Noon Star. Guardian of the elves of Cyndinare.

> **VESPIEL** – The Evening Star. Guardian of the elves of Aldinare.

> **BORIEL** – The Night Star. Guardian of the elves of Eldinare.

GWYNTHIEL – Lady of the Lorendil, whose name means Strength of Anaweh. Irythil who brought Anaweh's spirit to Teraeniel.

RAMIEL – Lord of Death, whose name means Arrogant toward Anaweh. Betrayed Anaweh and all creation. Irythil who brought shadow to Teraeniel.

THENIEL – Lady of the Seas, whose name means Anaweh Heals. Irythil who brought water to Teraeniel.

> **NAUTO** – Guardian of all humans living along the coasts.

> **AQUAE** – Guardian of the merpeople.

SARIEL – Lord of the Land, whose name means Command of Anaweh. Irythil who brought substance to Teraeniel.

> **TERA** – Patroness of harvest and nourishment. Often referred to as Mother Tera.

> **MUNDI** – Guardian of the dwarves.

LERENIEL – Lady of the Winds, whose name means Friend of Anaweh. Irythil who brought air to Teraeniel.

KARIEL – Lord of Peace, whose name means Who is Like Anaweh. Irythil who brought fire to Teraeniel.

Seven Chairs of Septyl

Chair of Albien — Selenya Waeyn. Luminari. The White Owl.

Chair of Arantiulyn — Melanie Birkwell. Human from Mindale. The Orange Lion.

Chair of Auburnis — Agnelle Phanstienne. Luminari. The Brown Lark.

Chair of Azurelle — Velaria Treyven. Cyndinari born in Lucillia. The Blue Dragon.

Chair of Crimsyn — Loretta Javie. Human from Sorenthil. The Red Dog.

Chair of Emradiel — Phendien Shendielle. Eldinari. The Green Stag.

Chair of Vyoletryn — Paurel Roendryn. Luminari. The Purple Eagle.

High Luminari Houses and Aryls

Aryl of Arenthyl and Exalted Aryl of Krysenthiel — House Lorenthien

Aryl of Lucillia — Vernal (deceased) and Harnyl of House Roendryn

Aryl of Reinyl— Therrin and Zara of House Reyndien

Aryl of Ostyl — Naesiv and Valerie of House Aerquin

Aryl of Winstsyl — Toral and Silvia of House Narielle

Aryl of Tenyl — Iridil and Enoria of House Taerinior

Aryl of Delmira Wood — Ciraenth and Aegian of House Ginielle

Aryl of Eandyl — Enithil and Binoral of House Clarion

Aryl of Verenthyl — Kyiel and Fyona of House Lauriel

High Eldinari Houses and Aryls

Aryl of Lierthyl — Fendryl and Dalenya of House Lierafen

Aryl of Virathyl — Naerelle and Eohire of House Shendielle

Aryl of Drethyl — Vanoreh and Elialen of House Illia

Aryl of Ladrithyl — Indryn and Diera of House Allandis

Aldarchs of Aldinare

Gael of Quel'anir – The Reverend Mother, also known as the Nurturer. Her followers dedicate themselves to nature and caring for the ilithae trees, native to Aldinare.

Orien of Eln'dinai – The Just Father, also known as the Judge. His followers focus on upholding law in Aldinare.

Nialth of Dur'linos – The Philosopher, also known as the Learned One. Her followers dedicate their life to study.

Theseryn of Thas'thallas – The Faithful Servant. His followers devoted their lives to worshipping Anaweh, the Creating Light. Theseryn left his sanctum of Thas'thallas to establish the Ei'ceuril order and became the first Ceurtriarch.

Lerathel of Val'quin – The Artisan. Sister to Nialth. Her followers are practitioners of the arts and designed the great cities and sanctums of Aldinare.

Endruil of Kir'enon – The Shepherd. His followers are caretakers of the alicorns native to Aldinare.

Aeryth of Ai'lyr – The Rogue. Her followers prefer to hide in the shadows and wield the fabled Aldinari bows.

Irithel of Mel'inor – The Smith. His followers develop advanced weapons and tools, often forged from aldaryl.

Ealyn of Tenethyl

Vivien — Ealyn of the Gold House. Granddaughter of Galithinol of the Gold Flight.

Daela — Ealyn of the Amethyst House. Granddaughter of Myrasha of the Purple Flight.

Torik — Ealyn of the Onyx House. Grandson of Jiertha of the Grey Flight.

Mellory — Ealyn of the Ruby House. Granddaughter of Vulgath of the Red Flight.

Niron — Ealyn of the Sapphire House. Grandson of Naithos of the Blue Flight.

Allister — Ealyn of the Opal House. Grandson of Ithinol of the White Flight.

Helen — Ealyn of the Jade House. Granddaughter of Fenoral of the Green Flight.

Dragon Primus

Lyvenol — Primus of the Gold Flight. Warden of lumenys.

Eilynol — Primus of the Purple Flight. Warden of animys.

Orythnol — Primus of the Grey Flight. Warden of umbrys.

Aerinol — Primus of the White Flight. Warden of aerys.

Caephenol — Primus of the Blue Flight. Warden of aquaeys.

Thereinol — Primus of the Green Flight. Warden of terys.

Fyrinol — Primus of the Red Flight. Warden of ignys.

Tolvenol — Primus of the Dark Flight. Warden of tenebrys.

Appendix C

Civilizations of Teraeniel

Aldinare

Remnant of Aldinari rescued from the Skyland Aldinare by Aren and accompanying Phaedryn. They are considered part of Krysenthiel.

Race: Elf

House/Aryl: Avign, Eraen, Kenoril, Threilen

Audun

One of the eight schtams composing the Schtamite. Situated at the westernmost edge of the Laudien Mountains.

Head of State: Patriarch Dridn IV, son of Dridn III

Race: Dwarf

Briel

River valley kingdom situated between two rivers forming the River Reifen and the slopes of the Dead Wood.

Capital: Briel

Head of State: King Irvienne of the Royal House Haert

Motto: Seek the message

Sigil: Black raven on a yellow field

Race: Human

Brunst

One of the eight schtams composing the Schtamite. Situated within the Vespien Mountains. Close friends with the Eldinari.

Head of State: Patriarch Thraen, son of Anuun

Race: Dwarf

Charren

A kingdom spanning across two continents, Ogren and Daereneth.

Capital: Karithel

Head of State: King Sanhir of the Royal House Irithru

Race: Human

Daer Empire

Oldest continuous human empire in Teraeniel and advocate of slavery and colonialism. Situated on the continent of Daereneth.

Capital: Daer

Head of State: Body of the Daer Senate

Race: Human

DWONIA

Desert country once controlled by the Twelve Tribes of Dwonia. Only two tribes refused to ally with Erynor and remained in the desert.

Heads of State: Chief Kodin of Tribe Fendur and Chief Genin of Tribe Vadir

Capital: Nynev

Sigil: Red lion on a yellow field

Race: Human

ELDINARE

Eldinari society secreted away in the Eldin Wood.

Head of State: Aryl Fendryl and Dalenya of House Lierafen

Capital: Stellantis

Sigil: White tree on a green field

Race: Elf

ERYNIEN EMPIRE

Cyndinari empire founded by Erynor Meriden, its sole emperor. Responsible for the Ceurendol War and enslavement of the Luminari.

Capital: Broid

Head of State: Emperor Erynor Meriden

Sigil: Bronze sun on a red field

Race: Elf

EVELLION

The mountain kingdom where the Laudien and Vespien mountain ranges meet. Original inhabitants were the refugees of Thellion.

Capital: Everin

Head of State: King Amry and Queen Lara of the Royal House Thellion

Motto: The pure will soar

Sigil: White eagle on a blue field

Race: Human

FRIETON

The free city-state of Frieton. Given to the minums on their release from slavery.

Capital: Frieton

Head of State: The Keeper (identity unknown)

Race: Minum

Gestoria

Fallen kingdom situated on the Plains of Orithil. Once great allies to Thellion and Krysenthiel. Obliterated during the Ceurendol War.

Capital: Quellion

Motto: Will triumphs pride

Sigil: White gold winged lion on a blue field

Race: Human

Glyol

One of the eight schtams composing the Schtamite. Easternmost and only schtam in the Illumined Wood.

Head of State: Matriarch Vylma, daughter of Toreldn

Race: Dwarf

Harol

One of the eight schtams composing the Schtamite. Situated in the Laudien Mountains.

Head of State: Matriarch Loewn, daughter of Brenola

Race: Dwarf

Ja'horan, Tribes of

Nomadic civilization on the continent of Ja'horan.

Race: Human

Ja'nalihn

Short lived kingdom covering all of Ja'horan.

Race: Human

Jopht

One of the eight schtams composing the Schtamite. Southernmost schtam in the Vespien Mountains and staunch defenders against the Shadow schtams from northern infiltration.

Head of State: Patriarch Oerth III, son of Oerth II

Race: Dwarf

Krysenthiel

The kingdom of the Luminari. Currently lost within the Shroud. Translates to land of the golden flowers, named by a human trying to speak Aelish, the language of the elves, to describe the countryside.

Capital: Arenthyl

Head of State: Exalted Lorenthien Aryl

Sigil: Seven golden kryseniels blossoming from a larger central kryseniel on a white field.

Race: Elf

LUCILLIA

Kingdom of the Luminari after gaining their freedom from the Erynien Empire. Named after Lucillia, the woman who gave birth to the twins, Roendryn and Feolyn.

Capital: Lucillia

Head of State: Aryl Vernal and Harnyl of House Roendryn

Race: Elf

MINDALE

A kingdom east of the southern Vespien Mountains.

Capital: Binton

Head of State: King Lawrence of the Royal House Maroven

Motto: Mind over body

Sigil: Brown ox on a green field

Race: Human

NUNSTOL

Shadow schtam that was cast off by the Schtamite for their actions in Mount Cyngol.

Head of State: Patriarch Uriden, son of Urodrn

Race: Dwarf

OERN

One of the eight schtams composing the Schtamite. Belin belonged to Oern schtam and sheltered Evellion and his people as they fled Elothkar.

Head of State: Patriarch Forvl VIII, son of Forvl VII

Race: Dwarf

PARENDIOR

A hilly country north of the Laudien Mountains and west of the Illumined Wood. Most Parendians are farming folk, and when Perrien invaded, they had no means of defending their land.

Motto: Protect the harmony

Sigil: Purple doe on a beige field

Race: Human

PERRIEN

A kingdom north of the Laudien Mountains where the citizens overthrew their monarchy and replaced it with a council and doubled their territory by invading Parendior.

Capital: Gneal

Motto: Swift to action

Sigil: Grey rider and horse on a white field

Race: Human

QIEN EMPIRE, THE

Empire of the Hundred Kingdoms on the continent of Qien, west of Eklean.

Capital: Zhongshi

Auxiliary Capitals: Beishi, Dongshi, Nanshi, and Xishi

Head of State: Empress Qien Wei

Race: Human

SORENTHIL

A kingdom along the River Meyien.

Capital: Myrium

Head of State: Queen Karina of the Royal House Lariviere

Motto: Flow with the waters

Sigil: Blue dolphin on a light blue field

Race: Human

SUDERN

A city state on the Dagger's Point peninsula. After a bloody civil war with Josque, the inhabitants declared themselves independent.

Capital: Sudern

Motto: Hidden daggers

Sigil: Red ship and dagger on a white field

Race: Human

THELLION

The fallen Eklean kingdom covering all the lands east of the Vespien Mountains. Met its downfall through a civil war relating to succession.

Capital: Elothkar

Head of State: King Alexander of House Vaerin

Motto: Eternal wisdom

Sigil: Silver winged horse on a white field

TIEL

A southern kingdom bordering the Erynien Bay and the Unarian Sea.

Capital: Josque

Head of State: Queen Alesei of the Royal House Ziera

Motto: Eternal wisdom

Sigil: Orange serpent on a blue field

Race: Human

TORSIL

A weak kingdom with little influence on its neighbors.

Capital: Trest

Head of State: King Gordon of the Royal House Carvil

Motto: Stronger together

Sigil: Grey wolf on a red field

Race: Human

UNDOL

One of the eight schtams composing the Schtamite. Deeply religious and situated in the Laudien Mountains surrounding Lake Saeryndol. They have strong ties to the Luminari.

Head of State: Matriarch Miurel IV, daughter of Miurel III

Race: Dwarf

VORN

One of the eight schtams composing the Schtamite. Situated at the northernmost edge of the Vespien Mountains.

Head of State: Matriarch Tiltha, daughter of Tilma

Race: Dwarf

YANIL

Southern kingdom along the Erynien Bay. Yanil was once jointly ruled by the Yanilean and the Judges of Yanil.

Capital: Lankor

Head of State: The Yanilean

Motto: Deep as justice

Sigil: Black castle on a blue field

Race: Human

ZORIK

Shadow schtam that was cast off by the Schtamite for their actions in Mount

Cyngol.

Head of State: Matriarch Jiora, daughter of Jiorza

Race: Dwarf

Cyngol.

Head of State: Matriarch Jiora, daughter of Jiorza

Race: Dwarf

About the Author

Ryan D Gebhart first started writing the Jewel of Life series in 2012 in Philadelphia, PA, shortly after concluding his undergraduate studies in philosophy. This unexpected passion evolved over the years and has remained a constant companion through his career changes, from a Franciscan friar, to a claims processor, receiving a graduate degree in Architecture, and now working at an architecture firm and teaching at the Catholic University of America in Washington, DC. Ryan D Gebhart is originally from Wilmington, DE.

Keep up with Ryan D Gebhart at www.RyanDGebhart.com